VOLATILE
WATERS

TAINTED WATER SERIES

INTERCONNECTED STANDALONE

VOLATILE
WATERS

TAINTED WATER SERIES
INTERCONNECTED STANDALONE

INDIA R. ADAMS

Editing: Kendra Gaither, Kendra's Editing and Book Services

Proofreading: Megen Watkins

Cover: Jay Aheer, Simply Defined Art

Formatting: TRC Designs

Link's Water Sign: Dezeray Adams

AUTHOR WARNING

Volatile: liable to change rapidly and unpredictably, especially for the worse.

It is very important that you know what you are about to read. If you are looking for a smooth ride, you should not continue with this novel. The main character is the most unpredictable character I have ever written, and may ever write.

Volatile Waters is in the Dark Genre, and this warning should *not* be taken lightly. If you are a Young Adult reader and read *Blue Waters* and *Black Waters*, the next book for you to read will be *Ashen Waters*. Though the subjects discussed in *Ashen Waters* will be on the dark spectrum, due to Whitney's journey, they are not described in such detail as found in this novel and *Red Waters*.

AUTHOR'S NOTE

I, India, am an advocate against human trafficking, sex trafficking, and violators of human rights. I am also an advocate for not masking over one problem with another. I firmly believe getting to the root of the problem is the best way to succeed. Sexual slavery is a violence that is beyond horrendous. If reading *Volatile Waters* twists your stomach, I ask you to imagine what it makes the victims feel like, especially the children. Yes, my story, *Volatile Waters*, is fiction, but the basis of the violence is now an epidemic all around the world. This is *not* a third-world issue, as once believed. For those individuals who wish to see or participate in some of the situations I describe, I implore you to reconsider and search your heart for an ounce of humanity. For those of you who are disgusted by these atrocious scenarios, maybe, after reading *Volatile Waters*, you will communicate with your government and share that we will no longer be quiet. We will demand stricter laws and more funds to intervene, save, and rescue the taken. We will do whatever is needed to prevent such vulgar crimes.

Change must be. Change for all involved.

This is Yury's story.

Volatile Waters is an interconnected stand-alone in the *Tainted Water* series. If you would like to experience this series as a whole, it is recommended that you start with the first novella, *Blue Waters*, which is available for free when signing up for India's newsletter.

Order of Tainted Water novellas

Blue Waters
Black Waters
Red Waters
Volatile Waters
Ashen Waters

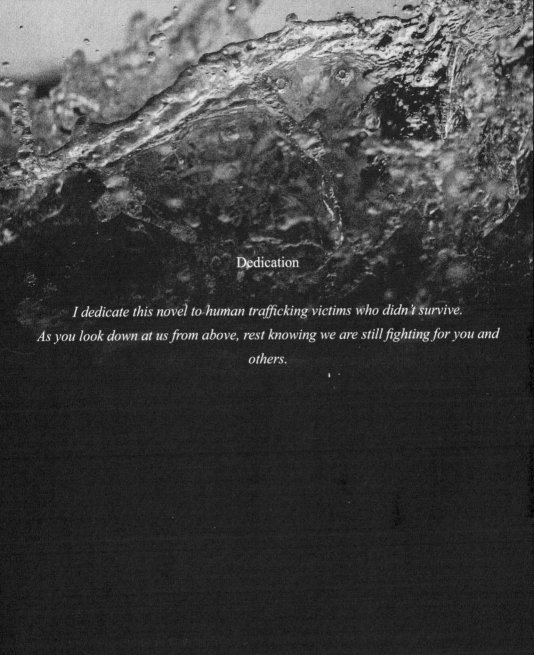

Dedication

I dedicate this novel to human trafficking victims who didn't survive. As you look down at us from above, rest knowing we are still fighting for you and others.

CHAPTER ONE

A Dare

There was beauty in her living… But her death could've meant I would have avoided the grip of the new emotions I despised. Her death would've prevented my world from being tossed into a blender—razor-sharp blades dissecting everything I thought I knew.

Whitney dared me to keep my eyes closed.

She dared me to continue to live with the ignorance that had been my closest companion. One cannot diverge from perverted sick ways of living unless they have experienced an alternative. I hadn't. The twisted way I was raised and the brutality I witnessed every day was my everything, and it was all I ever thought it would be. But there was to be more… And a redheaded wench that would help change my very existence.

Yes, there was beauty in her living… but first, we had to suffer in damnation, together.

CHAPTER TWO

Stolen Control

One does not choose the environment they are born into, so can you truly blame what they become? Can you fault the cruel ones for being monsters when inhumane behavior is all they know? A baby is birthed with a pure soul, but if compassion and empathy are never present from that day forward, the child will eventually lose his natural kindness.

I would know.

And, if tears from victims are treated as victories, is it really a surprise that the same child soon yearns for more wins?

Hiding at the top of the vast staircase, in my father and uncle's mansion home, I stared down at the devils in disguise—Father and Uncle Семён, which is Russian for Semyon.

Father's name was Макар, pronounced Makar in English. We all had the same eyes that I would later learn to be considered haunted blue. Our dark hair only intensified the allure.

They stood in our rich foyer, discussing the 'package' about to be delivered. Back then, when I was seven, I didn't see the mockery of the décor—everything being white when my family represented only darkness.

That darkness even hid in the shadows. In those shadows stood more male family members who were trained to watch Father and Uncle's backs, and other acquisitions I would learn about as I aged. One member, in particular, was a cousin of mine, Кирилл—pronounced Kirill in English. Another I would someday know well was Adrian.

Father suggestively grabbed at his crotch under his fancy suit pants while speaking in our native Russian tongue. *"The pictures he sent promise a beauty."*

VOLATILE WATERS

The men in the shadows hungrily readjusted their stances.

As usual, Mother wasn't home this night. She was incredibly young and far more interested in spending Father's money than showing me affection or being present. Yet, I longed for her. Children can be so full of hope.

The dimmed chandelier glowed above while Uncle paced, staring at the closed front doors as if craving them to open and deliver a meal he could devour. "If she is half of what I have imagined, I do *not* want to sell this one."

"*Personal pet?*" Father's lifted brow danced suggestively.

"*To train as we wish, finally.*"

It would be only hours before I would understand that Father and Uncle's employer, a human trafficker deep in the trade, did not appreciate them secretly building their own channels in the same line of business. Father and Uncle were going rogue.

Father wiped at his mouth. "*Train as we wish.*" He spoke as if he'd desired such an opportunity. Being young, I was unaware of what my father could hunger so much for. But now, as a man, I know he was craving the freedom to be in control.

When the doors opened, a beautiful woman walked through, holding the hand of an older cousin of mine, Uffe. He was casually dressed, but nothing was casual about the evil grin he possessed. The petite woman with huge brown eyes and an enchanting face smiled innocently, unaware of the silent discussion building around her. She even waved to my father and spoke in Romanian. "*Hello, I am Marina.*"

Father dipped his chin. "Shall we speak English, a language we all know?"

Shyly, Marina nodded, "Of course," oblivious to the security guards slowly creeping closer.

Uncle told his son, Uffe, "Such a rare sight you are soon to marry."

Shutting the doors behind him, my cousin chuckled in a disturbing manner. "Marry. Yes." In Russian, he asked, "*Have my money? It better be worth*

15

the risk I took getting her here. Marina was marked for 'him.'"

Father and Uncle were sending their boss a message by stealing his property, this chosen victim who had many hours of deceit invested in her.

Father swallowed as if trying not to drool while replying in Russian, *"First, we have a taste."* He stared at Marina while reverting to English. "Then we *pay* for her."

The silence was deafening as Marina nuzzled closer to her pretend fiancé, finally sensing the looming danger.

To her horror, my cousin pried her fingers from his arm then shoved her forward. "Make it quick." He smiled at his victim. "I have a wife waiting for me." From his front pocket, he retrieved a wedding band and slipped it on the proper finger. In Russian, he growled, *"A wife I don't want to be killed over this betrayal."*

Marina began to tremble. As she stood alone, her shoulders caved in fear. "W-Wife? What is going on, my love?"

Uffe waltzed forward. "Going on?" Grasping the back of Marina's neck, he pulled her to him, slamming his lips to hers. I could see her body wanting to melt into his, but the reservation couldn't be denied. Maybe this kiss was different, and on a deep level, she could sense the deception.

Ending the kiss, he licked at her swollen lips. "I wanted to taste you one more time before you are tainted by others."

Marina pulled from his hold and ran for the door…

Kirill moved with much speed, wrapping his arms around her from behind, and hoisted her into the air. Little tan legs kicked out from under a sundress, but Kirill only laughed. Tears dripped down her perfectly high cheekbones as my father stalked forward. "I could've made much money with this body." All family members circled their prey as Father caressed her wiggling hips. "But all my hard work to build my own empire deserves compensation." He grabbed her chin with force and lowered his voice. "That will be you."

Uffe laughed as he walked out the front door, Marina crying out for

him. So many hands groped at her body, too many to fight off at once. The way my family members all craved her, following as she was forced into the newly modified basement, crying and screaming for the man she believed loved her, unbuckling their trousers, had me wondering about what they claimed to deserve. Bearing not one ounce of regret on their faces, they had me thinking they were doing nothing wrong.

My mind was being trained, my thoughts shaped before I was in training myself.

Marina's cries could no longer be heard when the basement door closed. The house went eerily quiet. Alone, I went to my room and crawled under the blankets.

When I heard the doorbell so early in the morning that it was still dark outside, there wasn't another sound in the house. Once the doorbell chimed again, I crept down the extensive staircase. On the bottom floor, my bare feet tiptoed across the white marble tiling. After hearing tires spin down our long private driveway, I gathered the nerve to open the door.

Until that dark morning, I had been innocent of what torture looked like.

The naked body, lying on the bricked entrance, had dried blood from every orifice that they had used, but it was her chest that grabbed the attention of my young mind. Her breast had been violently removed. Yet, her eyes were closed in a relaxed fashion, as if not having felt the pain.

That is when I knew my mother was dead.

No one came running as I screamed in Russian.

No one came to the rescue of a terrified little boy who vomited next to his mother's corpse. So, I ran to the last place I had seen the male figures in my life enter. Banging on the locked basement door, I cried hysterically, snot and tears dripping all over my pajamas.

The door swung open, and half-dressed men raced past me and to the wide-open front door, guns in hand. Collapsed on the floor, I watched as they examined my mother in a heartless fashion. Father was more upset about the

poem stapled to her bare stomach. He ripped it off, her dead flesh taking the brunt of his anger.

In Russian, he read,

> *My business is my business. Yours is now yours.*
> *Get in my way again, and I will steal your whores.*

Standing over my dead mother, as if she were merely a chess piece in their vicious game, Uncle slapped Father on the back. "At least, now, her endless spending will cease."

Father nodded, appearing perplexed. "This could have been worse."

To try and comfort myself, I pulled my knees to my chest, shaking.

Uncle checked his cellphone. "No news of other retaliations."

"An eye for an eye. Now, it is done." Father held up the piece of paper. "This poem tactic, it is good, no?"

Barely interested, Uncle shrugged his shoulders. "Effective, I suppose."

"I will remember this way of delivering a message." Gesturing to my mother's corpse, Father told other family members, "Get this cleaned up. At least, I got a son out of her." His eyes searched his surroundings to find me by the basement door, still on the cold tile, drying vomit on my chin. His expression showed disappointment. "I see he has some growing up to do."

I don't know exactly when Marina was brought up from the basement, but one day she was in the main house, the first of the live-in sex slaves we would come to refer to as the Elites. The Elites were high-dollar sex slaves that had been trained for buyers who favored BDSM. Our slaves were literally handpicked and specialized in the fields of Bondage and Discipline, Dominance and Submission, Sadism and Masochism, and Slave and Master—a client favorite.

Exiting my bedroom on the second floor, I heard unusual noises—grunts and moans—from my father's bedroom. None the wiser, I opened the door to see something my innocent mind could not comprehend. In the center of his huge room was Marina, bent over and tied to a moving table, one Father willed

toward the front of his naked hips, repeatedly. Father's head was leaned back, his mouth gaping, eyes closed, and he was panting in rhythm to the fast-moving contraption.

Marina's legs were tied apart, and her face was very red. Veins were raised from her neck. My heart pounded as I realized she was trying to scream but couldn't, due to the ball strapped inside her mouth that was secured around her head. As the table kept moving, her eyes slammed shut, tears falling.

To avoid being noticed, I slowly retreated back into the hallway, only to run into my Uncle's chest. He whispered in my ear, "You like what you see?"

Horrified, I shook my head, staring at my father maneuvering the table with large handles I had seen on an exercise machine.

Uncle whispered again. "You will when you learn that they like it."

I slid past him and pressed my back against the hallway wall. "But, but, she is crying, Uncle."

I didn't understand why he laughed at my statement. "'Crying uncle.' This is truer than you know." He gently tugged on my shoulders. "Yury, the time will come when you will understand this is a game. There are winners, and there are losers." He pulled me back to the doorway, forcing me to see Marina, now unconscious, but the act still taking place. Father's arms were sweating as he worked the long handles. Uncle asked, "Does he look like the loser?" At that moment, my father roared his release.

I tried to escape, but Uncle held tighter. I stuttered, "B-But, what about her?"

"Who is more important, your father or some stranger? The one who provides for you or some шлюха?" The slur meant slut in Russian.

Natural Instinct: the act of survival.

In my case, it came at all costs.

The one who had kept me alive thus far was the man, now spent and bent over the unconscious woman while he struggled to catch his breath. His sweat dripped onto her naked back and shoulders. Opening his eyes toward his

bedroom door, he saw us… and smiled. "The шлюха slept during the end of my upper body workout."

My innocent head tilted. "She is only sleeping?"

He stood, giving a swat to Marina's ass. "She has had a long day of training." After putting on trousers, he leaned to the side of the table, made a clanking noise, and then one long handle was maneuvered to lean in the opposite direction. He repeated the steps. The other handle now matched. "But her day is not over yet." He grabbed an item from his dresser then walked toward the front of Marina. He ripped open the small paper packet, the size of a quarter, before holding it under her nose.

She suddenly jolted awake, frantically peering around. As soon as she recognized who was standing in front of her, she started to sob, almost choking on the ball in her mouth.

Father grabbed her chin. "We have company, so best behavior," he shrugged, "or I will teach you a lesson." Terror crossed her face before she did her best to gain composure, nodding her silent promise to obey. "Good little pet." Father unbuckled the leather at the back of her head then slowly pulled the ball from her mouth. Marina moved her jaw back and forth, trying to work out strained muscles. Father chuckled. "Yes. Prepare your mouth."

She froze.

He gestured to us in the doorway. "My brother is your next… *tutor*, Pet."

Uncle left my side while unbuckling his slacks. "My nephew is worried you do not like your training." Marina looked to the burgundy carpet his shoes were crossing, then to him as he stood right in front of her face, stroking his flaccid penis. "I told him he is wrong."

As his erection grew, her eyes closed before she whispered, "I enjoy my training, Master," then obediently opened her mouth.

The days began to blur together after that misguided lesson. It became a common occurrence to see 'delivered packages,' watch them cry, and then witness their disappearance into the basement, only to return weeks

later completely different. They emerged broken and obedient. Some were trained for whatever fetish had been paid for, then taken away and delivered to the purchaser. Some slaves became entertainment for family members and employees. Never were there any outsiders in our home. The slaves for entertainment and employee benefits were always mostly naked and stayed crouched on their knees, waiting to be told what to do next. The instructions ranged from "eat" to "suck this." Slaves were allowed to make no decisions for themselves.

It is disturbing to learn what one can become accustomed to.

A year had passed, lessons were learned, and Father and Uncle eventually lost interest in Marina as they found pleasure in new pets. Pets would go hungry unless someone else fed them, which always came at a price. As slaves, they had to earn everything, including baths. Oral sex for clean water was an everyday event that did not seem absurd at the time. And, there were plenty of guards to volunteer for the daily chore. In fact, it was surprising to have the house completely quiet, with no slave being trained in my presence. That's why, when alone in our kitchen nook, reading a History book for my homeschooling, I was startled to hear a stomach growl.

Marina was mostly naked, sitting in the corner, with her bent legs tucked underneath as trained. A gold collar was around her neck with a gold chain leash hanging between her bare breasts. A matching chain was wrapped around her thin waist and through her legs to represent underwear, which left nothing to the imagination. Her tan skin made the gold shine, catching my attention. Gold was for special events, or, at least, that is what I saw slaves dressed like before being sent off to a human auction or being delivered.

From the table, I asked, "Marina, are you hungry?" Her eyes quickly looked around to see if any other male was in the room. No slaves were permitted to talk to me without a family member present. I explained, "Uncle and Father are at a business dinner, and Kirill is in the basement." Her eyes met mine, so I asked again, "Are you hungry?"

Ever so quietly, she replied, "Yes... Master."

Surprisingly, my chest boomed with pride. I had never been the one in charge. I had never had the opportunity to have a say over someone else. And, for some unknown reason, I liked it.

I collected a block of cheese from the refrigerator, cut a chunk into pieces, and grabbed a loaf of bread from the counter. I was too young to cook, nor had I ever been taught, but I was not going to let the one soul who gave me control over her go hungry. I would take good care of my... pet.

Back in my seat, I mimicked the men in my life. "Come."

On her hands and knees, she scurried forward then sat at my feet, her legs properly tucked underneath her, her hands in her lap. I pulled a piece of bread from the loaf and held it out. As trained, she did nothing until instructed.

"Open your mouth."

The woman took the order from my eight-year-old self, possibly too hungry not to.

I was shocked at the sight of her tongue. Until then, I had seen everything from a slight distance. With no one around, I felt daring and touched her tongue as I placed the bread there.

Not closing her mouth or chewing until given permission, she watched as I studied her. The bread started to soak in her salivating mouth, but I held back from allowing her to chew. Instead, I touched around the food she was dying to swallow, enjoying my first glimpse of control over my own life, while stealing someone else's.

No one asked me if I wanted to live like this, with naked women in my home for the amusement of warped family members. No one asked me if I wanted my mother to be murdered, if I wanted to find her mutilated body. So, my finger explored Marina's mouth because it was finally my choice to do so.

Some opportunities should be denied.

As if witnessing me cross the line of innocence, and slipping into the same delusion as the men who raped nightly, my pet's eyes filled with a sadness I

wouldn't understand or care about for years to come.

My legs were too short for my feet to even touch the ground, yet I felt I had the right to order about this human who was starving and neglected.

I slipped my finger from her mouth. "Chew." We never lost eye contact as her jaw slowly started to move. When she swallowed, I asked, "Want more?"

"Yes, Master."

While I did my homework, I had a sex slave rest her head in my lap. I fed her one little bit of food at a time. I even offered her water from my own glass.

The sensation of her head getting heavier, her body sated from her first meal in days, was most empowering. It was an act I would come to crave like my father's approval. I wasn't going to let Marina move until he saw me following in his footsteps.

"What do we have here?"

Marina and I were sleeping by the time Father arrived. Her head still in my lap, I lifted mine from the book it rested on and smiled proudly. "I fed her."

Uncle was very amused. Smoking a cigar, he boasted, "The prodigal son is showing promise!"

Affectionately, my fingers ran through her hair. "I am her Master now."

Father chuckled as he moseyed over to me. "Think you are ready for such a title?"

"Yes. Can she sleep in my room now?"

Father was still smiling when he fisted her hair and yanked her from my lap. "First lesson, little Master in training: Never get attached." He started dragging Marina away from me. She was wincing but not putting up a fight; the punishment for such disobedience wasn't worth it.

I chased. "Hey! That is mine!"

Uncle held his bouncing belly through all his laughter. "Fight for what is yours!"

Father spun around to face me, carelessly dragging Marina with him. "Do I not play with another now?" Crossing my arms, I locked my jaw. He was

already stealing my one ounce of control. "Have I not taught you not to play with fire?" I stared at my pet, wanting her back. She was jostled in front of me while Father demanded, "This flame will burn. She has been trained for seduction. Now, it is time for her to seduce." He yanked her face to his and stared at her until she nodded, comprehending his silent demand.

Again, I chased as Marina was roughly guided down a hallway and into the foyer. Father didn't stop until standing in front of a tall man with dark hair and blue eyes. I hid in the hallway, shocked at the sight of a stranger. He had to be someone very important to be allowed in our home, or someone who could bring Father and Uncle a lot of money.

The stranger swallowed, instantly hungry for my pet, then forced himself to look away as he spoke in English. "Makar, I already told you I sell drugs, not women." His accent was American.

Father and Uncle were looking to expand their reach into another country. And they were looking to do it with the man who had been selling us drugs for our slaves that were manageably addicted. Future owners found the expense of drugs to be a small price to pay to keep their slaves orderly.

Father grinned as if knowing a best-kept secret. "It is called broadening your horizons, Harold Thompson." He placed his hand on Marina's shoulder. "Kneel."

She did.

"Show him what you want to share."

As if transforming into a magical siren, Marina leaned back with lust in her eyes. Her hand rested on the cold tile behind her as she slowly spread her bent legs apart. I couldn't see the gift offered, but it must have been tempting. Harold Thompson's jaw hung in midair as he stared at the juncture between her thighs.

Father instructed, "Touch what you want to give him." One of Marina's hands slipped between her legs. Within seconds, Harold stumbled back two steps. Father kept smiling. "See? Broaden your horizons. Have a taste. If we can come

to an arrangement in the U.S., maybe she can go with you."

Harold's eyes snapped to Father's. "My wife is at the hotel with my son. How the hell am I supposed to explain—" His eyes found Marina's offering again. He ran his palm over his gaping mouth.

"Hand him your leash, Pet."

Oozing sex appeal, Marina rose to her knees and reached for the gold leash hanging between her breasts. One of her hands touched Mr. Thompson's thigh as the other held up the chain of control.

Harold's fingers twitched.

Big brown eyes gaped up at him.

He took the leash.

"Wonderful!" cheered Father. "Marina, take him to your table in the guest quarters and give him what I'm quite certain his wife will not."

Marina's hips swayed in an alluring fashion as she crawled up the stairs, a drooling American following her. The house was spookily quiet until they disappeared down another long hallway, then the clicking of a door shutting echoed.

In Russian, Father asked Uncle, "*Birth control?*"

Uncle was an OBGYN full time before switching professions. "*None for months. Only her mouth has been fucked. This visit was perfectly planned. She is ripe. Stupid American is as good as ours.*"

In a knowing manner, Father turned to see me in the hallway, not surprised I'd witnessed the whole betrayal. He dipped his chin. "*Yury, never forget. The way to quench desire is to give her to another. Soiled in sperm not your own, you will no longer crave her.*"

Father and Uncle hadn't become bored with Marina; they simply put out a fire she was causing in their souls. A definite hazard in their profession.

By morning, another blaze had erupted. Harold Thompson had become bewitched by the sexually trained beauty and had agreed to start selling women in America. He took Marina back to the hotel to convince his wife that Marina

was strictly a business deal in the U.S., unaware he had just sold his soul to a deceptive Russian family. He had also sealed the horrid fate of Harold Thompson, Junior.

A.K.A.… Crash.

CHAPTER THREE

The Curse

As my lessons became more powerful, the hint of the monster in me developed. The more I craved control over my own life, the less I was given. Part of my training was to be demoralized and rebuilt to certain specifications. Ironic, seeing how that is exactly what we did to sex slaves.

My life was a never-ending boot camp that became more gruesome as time passed. By age twelve, puberty was in full swing, and I was growing into a young man. Most children were in school, oblivious and naïve to the nearby dangers of the world. I was still home tutored—for my protection against retaliation from competing organizations—and being trained for Father and Uncle's booming business of ruling over abducted victims and profiting from their loss of human rights. For the past four years, their torture being our gain was ingrained into all my thoughts. Human decency was against the belief system being shoved down my throat. In fact, I was raised to not view these humans as anything other than the means of success.

Uncle's son, Uffe, had ceased engaging in the profession he was once a part of. He was to take over the family's growing empire, but his wife threatened to leave him. I overheard that she was not "fond" of him having sex with young women to lure them back to Russia. So, instead, Father and Uncle put different talents of his to use. He was a wizard with false documents. It would be years until I was to see him again, but paper deliveries arrived, often, for Elite transports.

It was believed that Kirill would be next in line to rule, but his perversion had stooped to the point of no return. He was not able to put out the flame Father had warned me about years ago, so Uncle kept Kirill's appetite sated

Once the decision for me to take over someday had been made, Kirill began to carry ill feelings toward me. I had no time to fear his jealousy. I was soon to learn what I would be in charge of.

Going into the basement for the first time took some guts and a sturdy shove from Father. It was nowhere as luxurious as the mansion above, but that is not what I found terrifying. It was the crying. The way the sadness clung to the grey block walls. I had a hard time believing these slaves wanted this treatment like Uncle claimed. Upstairs, slaves had their emotions in check. Downstairs, they were taught to ignore their fight for survival and accept the fact that they were now completely owned. Their wants, or needs, were no longer a concern. What *we* wanted, against their will, was to be their only goal.

The basement consisted of two cold concrete hallways with many doors. Behind each door were ridiculously poor excuses for bedrooms. Behind other heavily bolted doors were training rooms that resembled deviant torture chambers. Chains hanging from the ceiling, with leather cuffs dangling from the ends, were to both restrain a slave and serve as suspension bondage. Whips and canes of many different fabrics—wood, plastic, and other semi-flexible material—hung from hooks on the walls. Cabinets were full of items ranging from butt plugs to heinous strap-on dildos and sex toys that resembled, to most, torture devices.

The only positive thing in this scenario was that Father refused to train children here. Young men were now on the menu, as supply to a demand, but Father and Uncle were not enticed by little girls or boys. This is not to say they didn't sell them. It is only to say that Father nor Uncle would fuck them; therefore, they were trained at different facilities.

Keeping children from our home was also a safety factor, for little girls were Kirill's weakness. He became bored with raping women and men, much to the disappointment of Uncle. But, for the love of making money, Father and Uncle used this perversion to their advantage. Kirill was willing to do anything

when it came with the promise of little girls' bodies. If Father and Uncle needed someone taken out, Kirill would go and kill. He became a dangerous weapon for our enterprise.

The game of survival continued, and I eventually became accustomed to the cries in the basement. The sounds finally blended into my life like a family who had a dog who barked too often. At times, it was a nuisance, but I learned to shut it out, just like my emotions. If we were low on supply, and there were no cries, it would catch my attention more than the pleas for help.

I no longer shuddered when walking past a room and getting a glimpse of Kirill having his way with the youngest male or female slave he could find in our collection, or Uncle teaching a slave how to torture the male genitalia; some men enjoyed their slaves trained to cause pain. The more I witnessed and experienced, the more desensitized I became, hence the exposure and Father and Uncle's overall goal. In fact, down the hall from my bedroom, when I heard a woman wailing one day, begging for mercy, I could find no sympathy in my heart. In my already twisted young mind, I could only be curious. I wanted to know what could bring someone such agony. I wanted to understand why her cries made me yearn for more.

Father and Uncle were cursing and shouting their frustrations as I entered a guest bedroom. The pregnant woman, screaming from the mattress, "*Something is wrong!*" was not only holding my interest due to her suffering but because she was the one who'd had me first.

Months earlier, Uncle and Father had felt it was time for me to step into manhood, with a woman to lead the way. They were not referring to a son in the kitchen with his mother baking a cake. No. It was between a woman's thighs where they felt I would learn most. My lesson took place on the very mattress from which the same woman was now screaming.

They had watched when I was forced to lose my virginity. The leaders of my family drank cocktails while Uncle smoked his cigar, and they laughed as I fumbled my way through my first sexual experience, which happened to be with

a sex slave. It was against her will, of course, as she had recently been introduced into the trade of human trafficking. The red-headed Russian was merely an exchange for a debt. Her husband's gambling addiction became her demise in every thinkable way.

Memories of her arrival are forever burned into my soul.

I met her late one evening while in one of our family's makeshift warehouses. We never spent much money on these establishments because it was a bad investment. Relocating often was a must for us in the human trafficking industry. So, using a fake name to protect our personal living space-slash-headquarters, we purchased abandoned warehouses in poor parts of town. We used them until some crusader would get wind of our presence and attempt to shut down our production.

During this time, Father was still building his number of staff, employees beyond family members who could be trusted on the streets. We had 'recruiters' and 'handlers.' Recruiters did just that; they recruited soon-to-be slaves. Handlers helped with transport, containing slaves, and all-around protection; they were guards. At first, these employees were only reached by burner cellphones and never invited to our home. Therefore, our main headquarter location could not be located if they were arrested or tortured for details by competitors. But, once they were involved with us for a certain amount of time, in deep and no longer abiding by laws, their status would change.

Not being able to find a doctor who was willing to join our party of madness, Uncle was still the doctor to examine bottom-level entries—freshly abducted victims. This particular night, the 'shipment' consisted of four young girls who were ushered in from the dark night by handlers, all with tears wetting their scared faces. Each child, purposely dressed in easy-access old T-shirts, appeared to be of a different nationality and clearly did not understand our Russian language. That didn't stop the recognition in their eyes when they caught sight of another child in the room. Me. Hope lit their faces as bright as a full moon. They assumed I would call for help.

30

They were wrong.

I had already been corrupted. I had already found pleasure in the control we possessed over the slaves at my home. I was the true product of an environment created by greed.

These unlucky girls needed to be internally inspected for the ultimate money maker: their virginity.

A handler released the little oriental girl to Kirill. Kirill didn't miss a beat, or grope, as he laid her on top of an old examination table. The terrified little girl shook as he strapped each leg into a stirrup. As if examining a herd of cattle, Uncle reached between trembling thighs for his inspection. As the other three girls huddled together, knowing they were next, the first child cried out for help. She was ignored.

Standing next to me, Father questioned over her wails, his demanding voice booming, "The verdict?"

Uncle held up dry fingers and beamed. "деньги!" Money.

Without Elite training needed, the oriental child would soon be handed over to a client who only wanted to rob her of her innocence. If she survived the act, and once her owner lost interest, her future was unknown. She could be resold (for a lesser price, of course), kept for guest entertainment, handed down to employees, or killed.

Kirill, appearing disappointed, unstrapped the child and gave her back to her handler. The handler's next job was to deliver the 'product' to the one who had already paid a hefty deposit for such innocence.

Uncle motioned the handler for the next child to be brought to Kirill, so she, too, could be examined. I couldn't help but notice the nervousness of this particular handler as he handed over the Hispanic child with ivory skin. Kirill also appeared suspicious as he strapped down the child, eyeing the handler.

As soon as Uncle stepped between her thighs, he cursed. "Blood. Fresh." She was too young to have started her menstrual cycle. There was only one other option.

31

Kirill's stare raced to the nervous handler as he pulled a gun from the back of his pants. Within seconds, a gunshot rang through the air. I jolted then watched the guilty handler collapse to the ground. Besides one slave, who died from a mishandled breath play training session, this was the first dead person I had seen since my mother. Momentarily, I was in too much shock to hear the children screaming, struggling in the remaining handler's grips, all staring at the body.

I would like to say Kirill killed due to being disgusted by the child rapist, but that would be a lie. Father, Uncle, the other handlers, and I all knew the kill was out of pure jealousy.

I would like to say Father kicked the dead man on the ground out of disgust, but he was hollering about the loss of his деньги.

A free, and alive, handler retrieved the hysterical and damaged girl from Kirill and waited for instructions.

Father, exasperated from kicking the dead handler, growled, "She is to go to the factories."

Factories. That is what we called the lower end of human trafficking.

Lowest bidders, a.k.a. Scrappers, collect all the leftover scraps they can cheaply get their hands on, drug them, then line the bodies up in spaces as degrading as fields of tall grass to condemned apartment buildings. Men know where to find these lowlifes, hand over an inexcusably cheap rate, and have sex with whatever half-conscious girl or woman is available. Hence *Factory*. These girls entertain approximately twenty to thirty-five men a day.

My family somehow thought we were much better than Scrappers by taking pride in our assets, believing we cared highly for our slaves. In truth, we gave them medical care, trained them to react accordingly, and dressed them in gold before selling them to the richest of clients.

With the next crying child strapped down, Uncle continued to search for 'Money.' As a grumble escaped him, we all knew what it meant. This child had already been stripped of her worth. My father groaned slut, "шлюха," in Russian.

32

The brunette couldn't have been older than twelve, hardly the age of already acquiring many lovers. It was most likely the case of incest, a perverted family member, or an adult in regular contact with the child. This, in turn, made her an easier target for us to begin with. An abused child is already confused and in need of affection and love. Trained abductors pretend to care, to be different from the rest, through texts, messaging, or other means of communications, truly exploiting a need and luring in victims.

Social media, chat rooms, and technology have made all children reachable. *All*. Teenage girls sneak out of their bedroom windows or skip school, believing they are soon to meet the young man who 'understands' them, ignorant of the fact that the man or woman who has been talking to them for weeks is a predator. Naïve teenagers slip into a car, expecting Prince Charming, but are greeted by a trafficker, and are never seen again by family and friends. They are drugged and taken to what most consider 'underground.' But they are truly just under our noses.

In every respectable profession, there are predators. Our clients ranged from Law Enforcers to men with more money than they knew what to do with. We practically owned the police department due to clients and money.

Kirill wiped his drooling mouth, knowing he was soon to reap the rewards of the child with no hymen. Reluctantly, Father nodded to my perverted cousin, who was already unbuckling her legs. "Yes. Have her, but leave no marks. I need to recoup some cash from the whore."

Brown hair whipped through the air as she was hoisted over the Kirill's shoulder with no more care than a butcher carrying his piece of meat. Kirill casually remarked, "You can start filming me." Uncle and Father both recoiled. Kirill shrugged, his shoulders lifting the girl. "Keep most of my face off-camera to not get caught. Film live or make the video viewable. With the proper software to hide an IP address, we can enter the Dark Web and make money."

"Is this true?" asked my now intrigued father.

Kirill patted the crying child on the ass. "You think one of these once in

Grunts of pleasure from Kirill almost applauded Father's decision. Soon, the little blonde girl would experience terror, just like the one presently underneath Kirill.

A ruckus at the entrance to the warehouse had us all turning our heads and handler guns being pulled from holsters. A handler was being challenged by a red-headed woman fighting back, unlike the scared children. When she heard the cries due to Kirill having his way, she began to struggle more fiercely, screaming in Russian, "You filthy pigs. May you and my husband rot in Hell!"

Father chuckled as he put away his piece, moseying over to the enraged woman. "So, the debt has been paid by you." He avoided her snapping jaws while trying to run his fingers through her red hair. "Do you have fire," he reached for her core, "everywhere?"

She spit in his face.

He smiled.

Wiping his cheek with a silk handkerchief, he toyed with her. "It will be a pleasure to… break you. Then sell you."

Not heeding his own advice, she became Father's favorite pleasure after that night. He nicknamed her Seafoam due to the enchanting color of her eyes. Her fair skin glowed from under her wild red hair.

Maybe it was brotherly competition, but Uncle fell for her, too. One night, I saw him sneaking her into his chambers down the hall. He was kissing the back of her neck, not the way he usually treated slaves. She smiled at him.

She never smiled for Father.

Seafoam's determination to not cave to his every demand made Father hungrier to mete out punishment than I had ever seen before. Bruises and wounds covered most of her body. I knew this because my training included learning how to handle a non-submissive slave. Uncle always looked away or left during these times. But, no matter what whip or stick Father used, or how often he raped her, no matter how many times he forced orgasms from her exhausted body, Father simply could not figure out how to break her spirit.

Not until he realized her secret.

She was pregnant.

This made him see red.

Seafoam was tainted.

Did Seafoam's husband know she was with child when he offered her as payment for his gambling habit? I would learn that answer some years later when I killed him, deciding that was the way to *truly* enter manhood. His murder was the only revenge I could offer the poor woman, who finally broke when forced to have sexual intercourse with a twelve-year-old boy.

Father was smart. After learning Seafoam's condition, he exploited it, violently. Uncle couldn't persuade him to do otherwise. As punishment for a circumstance out of her control, being tainted, Father used her love for her unborn child against her. With bloodied knuckles, he refilled his glass of vodka, angrily laughing about how he was getting two birds with one stone. "What did I tell you, Yury?" He didn't wait for my reply because he knew there wouldn't be one. "The way to quench desire is to give her to another. Soiled in sperm not your own, you will no longer crave her."

Seafoam and I both sobbed as I knelt between her legs. But we had no choice. I was the one taking every brutal hit until she complied. My father punched me in the face until she stopped refusing me. She gasped when more of my blood sprayed her, after Father smacked the back of my head, demanding I proceed. I had fallen to my hands, trying not to land on her naked body, my blood flinging onto her pale skin.

From the mattress, she peered up, giving me the first glimpse of motherly affection I had ever received. Under such vile circumstances, I'm surprised I had the sense to recognize compassion, but it was present. And it reached past all the walls I had built to protect myself. Seafoam's eyes were full of sorrow and regret she would never recover from, when she whispered, "Shh, you will be okay, Yury."

Crying like the terrified child I had reverted to—not the soon-to-be

Master of our godforsaken family business—I tried to wipe under my nose, only to see more of my blood smear across my hand. It's an image I remember vividly, to this day. And I changed. Right then and there. It was the only way to overcome unavoidable tragic events that were already a part of my future. The evidence was written in blood, glaring at me from my own skin.

Seafoam kept saying, "Shh," as she held my busted lip together with one hand and reached between our bodies with the other, in efforts to get me erect. "Close your eyes, Yury."

Petrified, I did as she asked and begged my body to cooperate, so this night from hell could end.

She wiped my tears, my blood, and helped me slip inside her.

Eventually, my body properly performed for my father and uncle, and I was allowed to go to my room. Lying in my bed, I denied myself more tears and demanded my heart grow cold. Exactly what my elders wanted. What fed my freeze of emotions was something I wouldn't recognize, not for years. Hatred.

Seafoam chose a different route. She didn't let ice soothe her aching soul. She simply let her soul flee, her spirit as well. Father tried to spur a fight with her, but none was left. He grew bored. That meant it was time to find another use for her. The rest of her pregnancy was spent with strangers who had a fetish to be with a woman in her condition. I hadn't seen her in months because she was no longer permitted at our luxurious home. Uncle, sounding disappointed, had said she was transferred from motel to motel. Father laughed about the men who craved her full womb.

Now, here she was, in the guest bedroom, hemorrhaging. Uncle's actions between her legs, working frantically to stop the bleeding, told me his "fire" had never been put out. He was fighting for this slave's life. He barked orders. "I need more towels!"

The American—the bastard who stole my pet—was present and in a pure panic. He yelled at Father, "This is barbaric! How could you have let so many men be with a pregnant woman? She's full term!"

37

Father spit on the floor. "This bitch deserved every bit of it. And she's making me thousands online."

Don't be fooled to believe men won't pay to see a pregnant woman raped, repeatedly.

Father glared at Harold Thompson. "The same goes for any who betray me."

All blood drained from Harold's face. At the time, I had no idea what Harold had done, nor the repercussions that had been set in motion, but Harold paid a heavy price, indeed. A hit had been placed on his eldest son.

Seafoam kept yelling to Uncle, "*Something is wrong!!!*" But one glance at me, and her yells of fear morphed into a complete breakdown. I don't know what she saw in my expression, but she suddenly cried to God and the devil, asking why I was now ruined, her daughter soon to follow the same fate.

My jaw locked at her accusations. I didn't view myself as ruined, and her stubbornness against being silenced was infuriating. She was recapturing control of her life in her final minutes, and I hated it. To the only woman who ever showed me an ounce of kindness, I said, "*Shut up, you whore,*" while she lay on her death bed.

As Seafoam struggled to push a baby from her womb, she placed a curse on my father. "*With the blood from my body as a sacrifice, I pledge for you to find agony in your death. Let it be by the hands of one of your own. Let your spawn be your downfall and your demise. And I pray that my daughter witnesses it all.*"

Resembling a madman possessed from within, Father stood next to the bed soaked in her blood, suddenly with a knife in his hands, raised it above his head, then slammed it into her chest.

"Nooooooo!" bellowed Uncle in a pain I was not accustomed to.

"Shit!" screamed the American.

Leaving the knife where it stood, Father stumbled backward, staring at the woman he'd just murdered as if she might rise at any moment and damn him deeper into hell. I think he already knew it was too late; we all had been damned

for some time.

Do we reap what we sow?

I was to learn the answer one day. So was he.

A cry that shook my very spine bellowed against the walls of the room. The voice was tiny but promised revenge. I could hear it, and so could my father. "Kill it!" he screamed to my uncle who was wrapping the infant in a towel.

Uncle, whose mannerisms mirrored a destroyed man, pale skin splattered with blood, solemnly held the bundle out to his brother. Wanting far from the curse, Father's back slammed against a wall as if desiring to disappear. "Do not touch me with that filth."

In a tranced state, Uncle said, "I will not murder this child. If you want it done, grab the knife from her mother's chest and seal your curse."

Father's eyes raced to Seafoam, then to Uncle, then to the American. He growled to Harold, "Take it. And I want her in the trade by two."

"Sex trade?" asked an exasperated Harold, eyes full of horror.

Father glared at the infant. "My rage for her mother is hers to inherit. Men pay high dollar to fuck such young bodies."

Harold screamed, "You've gone mad! No way!"

Father flew from the wall and went face to face with Harold. "Don't forget, Marina has never been paid for. I still own her and will do as I please with her." Harold grabbed his chest, where the flame for his slave burned bright. Father pounced on the weakness. "Take the heathen, have her trained, and I will let 'Harry's' heart continue to beat. Do not think the American *Junior* title fooled me. As does Marina, your youngest son belongs to me, too."

Harold's betrayal was now revealed, and he knew it. His eyes filled with tears that lingered, refusing to fall. I could see the water vibrating as his whole body shook in parental fear. "Please. He's only three."

Father snarled his upper lip. "Ripe age for DarkNet."

Harold winced as his skin grayed, then he surrendered. "I will take the girl."

"At least, one of your sons will be saved."

A broken voice croaked from Harold's mouth. "And my eldest?"

Father trembled with anger and... the curse. "Already gone."

As his tears finally tumbled, a sob broke from the American because he was well aware my father made no false threats. While Harold was caught up in the horrendous acts happening at my home, a caring older brother had left the hotel room, for only minutes, to retrieve a hot cup of cocoa for his toddler sibling. It was the window needed. The young man never had a chance and was gunned down on the sidewalk by the waiting handler, as Harold Junior watched from above.

With a bag full of needed baby supplies and a fake birth certificate, which would one day be a threat strong enough to bring her back into our lies, Harold Thompson Senior headed to the parked car where his wife had been waiting, unaware of the tragedies and crimes her husband just witnessed. Sliding behind the driver and into the backseat, he handed his wife a crying infant, hoping it could replace the son his wife didn't even know had just been lost, and he prayed she would someday forgive him.

CHAPTER FOUR

The Unveiling

Ten years later…

Cold and calculated, that is what I became. I allowed myself no wants, no attachments. If I had a sexual desire, I simply had it met. The only emotion I allowed myself to feel was the sick power of control.

After a morning stretch, I sat up in bed with an erection begging for release. In the corner of my bedroom floor, I knew she would be there: my newest pet, with the lightest green eyes I could find. I had yet to understand the need for such a rare color and believed oral sex was the answer. "Did I give you permission to use that blanket?"

Pet, huddled on the dog pillow provided, slowly shed the blanket I tricked her with, exposing all her bare skin. I knew that, by leaving the blanket next to her sleeping quarters, she would assume it was permitted. I'd set her up to fail so I could punish her. In punishment, I found pleasure. "Come." I pointed to the carpet at my feet, between my legs.

As her eyes watered, I became even more aroused. Due to what I did to her last night, she knew I was still nude. My heart thundered as she forced herself to crawl to me, knowing I would soon be inside her mouth. Kneeling between my thighs, my pet slowly peered up to me.

In the rush of excitement—having complete power over her—I moaned. She shook.

I whispered, "Yes, feed my dark soul," as tears dripped down her lovely face, tan from working in the fields in America. As my uncle had demanded of Marina, forcing me to watch, I repeated his demand and the cycle he and my

father had paved. "Open your mouth."

After, as I slipped into slacks, there was a knock on my door. I stepped around Pet, who was attempting to hide her vomit by pushing it under my bed. I smiled while opening my door, knowing another punishment was coming, and lifted my chin to my cousin in the doorway while buttoning my pants. "What?"

Cousin's eyes raced to Pet. He smirked. "Your father wants to speak with you, but I see you are busy."

Heartlessly, I spoke to be overheard, "She needs more practice swallowing what is *given* to her." Glancing over my shoulder, I chuckled. "And keeping it down." I patted his shoulder as I exited my room. "See to it."

"Master, please!" begged Pet, with an accent gained from being born and raised in Oklahoma.

Fire raced up my spine as I faced her in a hurry. In the doorway, I glared at her. "Did you just speak to me without permission?"

Terror crossed her expression as she realized her morning was quickly becoming a nightmare. Silently, she pleaded, begging for mercy I was incapable of giving. I told my cousin, "Take her to your room. Don't give her back until she learns to stomach ejaculations."

As I descended the stairs, hearing her cries fade down the hallway, I thought of all the mothers and wives in my family and how they lived in fancy homes, not asking where the money came from, and how their sons and husbands earned their immense wealth. Only Uffe's wife dared to question our line of work.

The guilt not only belongs to the ones committing the crimes; it also belongs to the ones willing to turn a blind eye and reap the rewards.

Entering Father's office, I saw him sitting behind his desk watching a TV monitor. The live feed was coming from one of the rooms in the basement where cameras had been set up to make us more money. Kirill had been correct. Many are willing to pay high dollar to watch all kinds of abuse.

What was being filmed at this time was a young woman being whipped across the back. Her throaty screams announced the damage being done to her skin. The punisher wore a full, black ski mask over his head, to not be identified when law enforcement watched the video. They could always find us and other criminals online; they just weren't able to locate the establishment where the crime was taking place. Callously, we would laugh at their frustrations, knowing they wanted to rescue the person being raped, while they watched.

Staring at the screen, I commented, "That whip is leaving permanent marks."

Father turned off the screen. "Yes. We have a client who likes to lick scars. She is to be delivered in two months."

"Trained?"

"And with anal scars."

I took a seat while voicing our motto, "They pay. We deliver."

He shuffled paperwork. "Yes, and others are willing to pay while we prep her for delivery. Hence the live feed."

"You should triple the fee for the anal scarring. That's a rare one."

He placed a file in a desk drawer. "Already done. Very pleased with the profit." He leaned back in his chair and ran a palm over his face. "What a bloody mess that was."

From the leather chair in front of his desk, I sarcastically said, "Sorry to have missed it."

"All in the name of money. Speaking of, Uffe's wife has gone into hiding."

"Why?"

"Because I want to kill her."

Uffe had been murdered six months earlier. My uncle refused to go to the funeral. I always wondered if that meant we were responsible for the death.

Intrigued, I smirked. "Do tell."

"The bitch threatened me, claiming she has copies of a false birth

certificate for a Russian infant." He lifted a brow, asking if I was following. I wasn't. He rolled his eyes and said, "So, I need you to go to the U.S."

I snarled. "What the fuck for?"

"My curse."

My stomach soured. Seafoam's child. "She's still alive?"

"The American says no, but he also says Marina is dead."

"And?"

"He didn't sound sad." Now, this conversation was making more sense. He was beyond infatuated with her. "Not to mention, she is the mother of his only living child. It does not feel right. If that child is alive, we are to be profiting off of her. Same goes for Marina. Money or their deaths. Take Kirill in case you need someone to disappear permanently."

My jaw locked. "I am capable of murder."

He waved his hand through the air. "That wasn't murder. That was a misfortune of events."

"But she is dead, no?"

Father rolled his eyes. "Yury, you were too inexperienced to know she was choking on vomit behind her gag." He laughed. He actually laughed. "You thought she was jerking because you were fucking her so hard."

I was only sixteen when I accidentally killed a slave, permanently shutting the pearly gates of heaven to my impending entry. As callus as I had already become, it was still a devastating injury to my dark soul. But I was given no time to mourn or comprehend the depth of the crime. I was in the live feed room being filmed, watched, paid, and judged for my performance. For the sake of money, Uncle had her body removed from the hanging chains and replaced with another crying young woman who I was to 'train.' Tears dripped from under my black hood as I fucked the next slave.

Father tossed a passport onto his dark wooden desk. "Adrian is to go, too."

I chuckled when studying the inside. "I am no longer Yury?"

He stared at me for a lingering moment then finally answered, "You never were."

My smile faded, and my ears began to ring. "What was that?"

As if trying to ignore the bomb he'd just set off inside my head, Father acted nonchalantly. "None of the names used in this house are real ones. It is safest this way."

Painfully, as I sat there, the illusion in which I had been raised started melting away. Dumbfounded, I asked, "But, how is this possible? I am a man who doesn't know his real name?"

He pointed to the passport in my pulsating hand. "You do now. But you are to always go by Yury. Always. I only told you your true identity because I do not wish for the U.S. to search for your true identity and find out our family business if you are to be questioned."

"Questioned?" I exhaled. "Don't you mean apprehended?"

"And you are not to mention our line of business."

My chest constricted as I imagined being imprisoned for illegally entering a foreign country. "Would you come for me, Father?"

He stared at me with his calculatingly shady eyes, then replied, "No."

Father not only asked me to sneak into a country where I had never been, and obtain unlawful documents, but to also make a delivery.

On a private jet, Kirill, Adrian, two other cousins, and I smuggled in three slaves. Two of them, I had personally trained. In actuality, the slaves' presence was how it was so easy to enter America unnoticed. Rich men, hungry for their purchases, paid off the late-night private airport employees, keeping our arrival undocumented.

Three very young women, wearing robes over their gold chain delivery attire, were heavily drugged and sleeping. It was best for travel. Their imagination with where they were being sent always made them far too nervous and hard to bear. Drugged, they were less annoying.

When the rest of us weren't sleeping during the long flight, we all sat

45

quietly. Kirill and I stared at our passports. He was older than me by at least eight or nine years, but he appeared as lost as I at the news. I asked Kirill, or whoever he was, "What does your mother call you?"

He peered out the jet window. "The only name I've ever known."

"How different are our lives versus other people's who do not train Elites?" Learning my name was false made every aspect of my life now feel magnified. Each aspect of my childhood, up to this point in my life, became something now studied in detail.

Kirill swallowed, then whispered, "How would I know?"

The private jet went quiet again. In the silence, I observed my 'cousins' and thought about how they didn't live in my home full time, unlike Kirill and myself. Neither of the men sitting across from me would meet my glare. A heavy exhale left my suddenly weary lungs. "Are we even related?"

Adrian answered, still refusing to look me in the eyes. "How does a cousin come to be?"

I could feel my cheeks heat up as adrenaline surged. Feeling like a fool, I spoke numbly. "A daughter or son of an aunt or uncle."

He inhaled and exhaled. "How many brothers and sisters does your father have?"

I leaned my head back against the seat, stunned by how blind I had been. "I don't know what I know anymore." As far back as I could remember, Father had claimed the men in my home were family—my cousins.

"Yury, you have only one true uncle."

Folding into my own lap, I asked, "Why are we being sent to the U.S. when we are so ignorant of the world?"

Silence...

Rubbing the back of my neck, I answered my own question, "Kirill and I are being tested. That is why you are with us." I didn't need to see the head nods to know they were happening. My father wanted to know if his training had stuck. I was going to be put in positions to see how I handled them. Nerves

began to shiver up my spine. If I failed? I already knew that answer. Sit in prison, quietly.

It felt like I was walking a tight rope, with no knowledge of how high in the air I was. Up to this point, I was well aware we were committing illegal activities, but I hadn't been taught the ratio of good people versus bad. I didn't know I was part of a minority. How could I? We were making money hand over foot, so many villains willing to pay for the services we provided.

There are thousands and thousands of purchasers, but *billions* of innocents. And I had been waltzing into this world of billions as an ignorant king. Lucky for me, millions of the billions were as ignorant as I, clueless to who stood in the elevator with them or in a harmless grocery store. Busy on their phones, people were very distracted with the danger circling them, eyeing them as a product and judging how much could be profited off their body.

Black sedans and SUVs waited on the runway as we landed. It was the middle of the night when groggy slaves were separated and escorted to the waiting vehicles, calling out to their Master. I explained, "I am not your Master any more."

It was a cruel time for an Elite. She or he had become so dependent; they had practically forgotten how to feed themselves without permission. I had taught them I was their life source so they would do anything I demanded. Now, that source was being ripped away. Some slaves viewed this as a brutal act and didn't adjust to their new Masters well.

Risk of the trade.

As doors slammed shut, I knew I would never see those women again. I wish I could say I prayed they would be safe, but that would be a lie. I knew they were headed to years of sexual abuse and, eventually, an untimely death because their bodies would cave. They would either age and be murdered or die during an act of violence.

In a blacked-out SUV, my one cousin, my men, and I were taken to a five-star hotel in Connecticut. Exiting the vehicle, parked in a multi-leveled

garage, the driver instructed us to leave the SUV at the private airport when our trip ended. I handed him the cash promised and took the keys.

Working a keycard at my room's door, I announced, "Everyone, get some rest. We are paying a visit to Harold Thompson first thing in the morning." Tiredly, they each nodded before entering their own rooms.

Lying in my hotel bed, I found myself processing again—the trip, my new actual name, and where I was, surprised at the notion that a foreign country could smell so different from Russia. I had been under such a veil up to this point that I had yet to experience anywhere other than my home country. Yes, the room was beautiful, but even the sheets felt different against my nude body.

Not able to relax, I got out of the bed and slipped on casual clothes. Once back in bed, I couldn't help but think of the slaves, stolen from distant places and sometimes forced into sexual circumstances within hours of delivery. They were never given the option of attire for comfort, as I just allowed myself. They were stripped and exposed, ruthlessly at times, then violated by someone who sometimes didn't even speak their language.

Frustrated with my thoughts, and an unexpected hint of guilt, I turned off the lamp and rolled over, but my mind only found more sensations of what I could only now describe as loneliness. Faintly, I could hear the television in Kirill's room next door. The voices were speaking English, a language I had learned as a child but had not heard on televisions at home. On my side, I curled into a ball, trying to rid myself of a chill, wondering what the basement sounded like to newcomer slaves. Could they hear the screaming from another room? Did they know they would soon be the one screaming?

I don't think I got any rest before my cellphone was chiming its alarm to wake me. Sitting up, I rolled my tight neck, trying to shake off the betrayal by my father and uncle clinging to my once cold heart. Even during my hot shower, I wondered why the trickery. Now that I was here, I felt I lacked the needed education before being shoved into another country to do their dirty work. Rinsing my hair, it dawned on me.

Father's curse.

Did Father believe he was still in danger? He had acted nonchalant in his office, but was he truly fearful? I thought of the night Uncle had tried to hand him the infant, and how father recoiled in fright. Either way, it was time to find out.

At closed iron gates, I smirked at the fool guarding Harold Thompson's home and explained, "It is unwise not to let me pass."

"Sorry, dude. Going to need a name," the security guard barked.

"Dude? What is a dude?" asked Kirill.

The guard lifted a brow. "Damn, you have a strong accent. Where're you guys from?"

I snarled, "*Russia.*" Awareness crossed the man's expression. "My name is *Yury.*" The fake name now tasted rancid on my tongue.

Beep! Beep! Another guard put a handheld radio to his mouth. "Sir, we have a visitor at the gate. Says his name is Yury."

"Right now?" replied a stunned Harold Thompson.

"Yes, sir."

"Jesus-fucking-Christ." The guard tried to lower the volume of the radio, but I still heard, "Let him in. Stay out of his way. These boys don't play nice." The guard paled as he studied my annoyance. He quickly gestured to a man inside a tiny building next to him.

The gates rolled open as I got back into the SUV. I told my cousins—my men, "*My opinion of Americans has not changed.*" Their arrogance was thick and untamed.

Once the SUV rolled to a stop, another guard quickly greeted us by opening my car door. He said nothing and barely dared to take a glance in my general direction. I was pleased my presence was causing nerves to rise. I was in need of a boost of confidence.

Inside the house, I was satisfied to see that my family made far more money than Harold. I observed the rounding staircase with wood railings.

Everything wasn't white and pristine as in my own home. This house had more of a lived-in feel. I was surprised to suddenly be envious of the vibe exuding from picture frames on the walls. In Russia, I was accustomed to priceless artwork on our walls. Studying the numerous headshots of Junior, I instantly recognized Marina within him and wondered if he knew his biological mother was a sex slave.

The American, Harold, came from a side room he referred to as the den. "Why wasn't I told you were coming to the U.S.?"

"Because I didn't want you to hide Marina."

His Adam's apple nervously bobbed. "I already told your father she's dead."

"How did she die?"

"Fucked to death."

"Where is she buried?"

Harold's body seized. "What does it matter?"

"*Where?*" I roared at the top of my lungs to make a statement.

"We burned her!" Harold yelled in return with lying wide eyes.

Composing myself, I asked, "Where?"

I watched as his mind raced, searching for a believable lie. "My backyard."

"Show me."

He winced. "Been years. Nothing left."

"I will find bone fragments. Take me now."

A female voice drifted down the stairs. "I had her sent away."

Peering up, Harold groaned, "Babe, stay out of this."

Ignoring her husband, this woman studied me intensely as she took each step with purpose and poise. "You are clearly not blind and know my husband had feelings for her."

This woman was one like I had never seen before. She was very tall, elegantly so. Long legs expertly owned the high heels on her feet. Perfect toes

with red nail polish shined from the floor. My eyes drifted up to admire the whole view. My mouth salivated as I dipped my chin. "Thank you for your honesty and observation." I realized she was different from any of the slaves because she was strong. Her height alone would have made her a challenge to control. I got hard just thinking about how good it would feel to experience every ounce of her fight.

High heels clicked on the marble floor after leaving the stairs behind. Harold grabbed her elbow, but she yanked it away, demanding, "Don't touch me."

After a moment of locked eyes, silently reading each other and the anger pouring off her skin, he shook his head and stopped interfering.

Mrs. Thompson pushed her long, light brown hair back over her shoulder. Surprisingly, her hazel eyes then raked over my clothed body, as if wishing for a better view herself. "You are from Russia?"

I set my shoulders back and firmed my stance as if hoping to impress. "I am."

"My husband works for you?"

Because of her willingness to honestly answer the question her husband would not answer, I paid her the same respect. "He works for my father."

Her stare fell to the floor, and her voice trembled. "The man who killed my son?"

My head tilted. "Pardon?"

Eyes brimming with tears met mine. "Harry is my youngest. My eldest… was shot… in cold blood… in *Russia*." She said Russia with an undeniable hatred.

Before I could stop myself, my mouth gaped open. I suddenly remembered the conversation when Seafoam was dying while giving birth. My eyes shut in remorse. "Yes. I believe it was my father who ordered his death."

I waited for a slap, some sort of punishment for being related to a monster, but it didn't come, so I dared to open my eyes. And what I saw was grave pain. Harold Thompson's wife was experiencing a slow death, by the death

of her son. "My son was innocent."

Even though I knew his death was retribution for Harold's betrayal, I replied, "I was too young to know the reasoning."

"You are not too young now."

I understood her innuendo.

Her fight was either a façade or the result of a hard life. "Will you hurt my Harry?"

I wondered if my mom ever loved me as much as this woman loves her only living child. With more regret, I replied, "We both know he is not *your* son."

She clutched her stomach as if I had wounded her with words. "Not from here." She patted her chest. "But here, he always will be."

My throat tightened. Father had sent me to a foreign country without any hesitation. This woman was facing a hard criminal for her heart. "So far, due to your honesty, Harry is safe."

"Babe, go back to bed," growled Harold Senior.

She refused to acknowledge him and kept staring at me, her chin once again defiant and proud. "And how do I *keep* him safe, Russian?" Mrs. Thompson made it clear all options to obtain her son's safety were available.

In Russian, I told Kirill, Adrian, and my men, "*I'm going to rattle a cage.*" Their hands slowly went to their guns. In English, I told Mrs. Thompson, "You look... hungry."

Mr. Thompson stepped forward as his wife, again, regarded me in a fashion a married woman should not regard another man. My men pointed their guns at Harold. Harold's men pointed guns at me. Mrs. Thompson and I ignored them all.

She licked her lips. "I am. I'm hungry for," her eyes met mine again as she stepped closer, "revenge."

My sight followed as she slowly reached out then caressed my crotch, much to the dislike of her husband, who was now being held back by his minions, yelling profanities at his wife.

Accepting her silent offer, I wrapped one arm around her narrow waist, tugging her slender body to mine. Face to face, I told her, "It must have hurt you, knowing he was fucking her and not you."

Her hands seductively moved up my arms. I tightened my hold to inform her I was extremely willing to play her game. With her hands on my shoulders, open lips brushed mine. "Pure. Torture."

"What the fuck are you doing?" screamed her cheating husband, only to be ignored.

She removed one hand to start lifting the hem of her dress. "Are you shy?"

Mr. Thompson struggled to get free from his employees, growling through his growing rage.

My balls started to ache with hunger as a bare leg caressed my pants. "No, never been known to be shy."

The leg then slightly curled around me. "So, you don't mind an audience?"

I thought of how many times I'd fucked on film. "Never has affected my performance before."

Her eyes slid shut as if I were entrancing her. "It's been so long since I've had it right."

Momentarily removing my stare from her tortured eyes, I grinned at her fuming husband. "Is that so?" In my mind, Harold stole my pet when I was a little boy. Now, as a man, I was going to steal his wife, right in front of him.

With me guiding her body backward, she hiked her dress up completely. Smooth, long legs were mine to touch. Her confidence was enticing. As soon as her back hit the wall under her stairway, I let go to unbuckle my pants.

Harold was foaming at the mouth, screaming how he was going to kill me.

His wife lifted a leg as I approached her with a naked, raging hard-on.

I wrapped that hiked leg around my waist and slammed inside her. I

could barely hear her moan over her husband's roars and my men's laughter. But I could feel her wetness in my trim pubic hair, something I usually had to force from a woman.

Not this time. Mrs. Thompson had not told a lie.

She was starving.

I was too.

So, after hoisting her up and wrapping her other leg around my waist, we primal-like fucked each other, fast and hard. One of my hands reached around her pert ass to hold her up, and my other reached between us to massage her clit, knowing exactly how to make her feel wanted. As her core pulsed around me, over and over, and she screamed out her ecstasy, I came inside her with the vocal vengeance she needed her husband to hear.

Once Mrs. Thompson was more than satisfied, orgasming in front of her husband twice, I gently let her legs down from my naked and drenched waist. She was breathless and unsteady on her feet, so I held her to me while asking, "Can I buy you breakfast?"

Sated and spent, she smiled. "Young man, you can do anything you like."

I buckled my pants, then, like a gentleman, gestured for her to head for the door.

She sneered at her husband, who had angry spit hanging from his chin. "I'll be back later, *dear.*" She walked out the door and into the waiting sun.

Smirking at Harold, I followed her. "I'll be back after dessert." I licked between my spread fingers so he understood what I would be eating.

Harold fought to be set free from his guards, who were truly guarding his life. Had he been set free and come at me, my men would've killed him where he stood. Then, all witnesses would have had to have been eliminated. That would have been unfortunate because I truly wanted another round of being inside Mrs. Thompson, not her blood.

Kirill and one of my men slid into the rear seat of the SUV. My other man took the driver's seat, and Adrian, the front passenger. I sat in the middle

row, next to the woman I had just pleasured. Her demeanor was much different now. That didn't shock me.

Solemnly, she stared out the window, her fingers touching her lips. "Thank you for not rejecting me in front of my husband."

I grinned. "Trust me. I enjoyed myself."

The revenge fuck did not seem to be bringing her much solace. "You are the only person that I knew who could get away with what I needed to do."

As the SUV began to move, I jokingly feigned hurt feelings. "I do believe I've been used."

Deadpan, she said, "You continue to be honest with me, and I will continue to be honest with you. I know who you are and what you want to know."

After a moment of thought, I conceded. "Honesty? Here it is." I blew out a labored breath. "You are the first willing partner I've ever had." I had never experienced it, so was clueless to what I had been missing in an eager partner.

Her wince was full of sympathy and disgust. "No." She glanced at the other men in the vehicle for conformation. None disagreed. They knew where I grew up and how I was never alone except for the slaves in my home.

My shoulders felt heavy as I shrugged.

Mrs. Thompson lectured me, "This human trafficking is awful. You do know this, right?"

It may sound odd, but I felt we had a bond over her son's death. I know I had just fucked her, but in my profession, sex was part of breathing. It was present at all times. So, the recent act didn't stop me from opening up to her. "I'm not sure what I know at this point."

Mrs. Thompson touched my face in an endearing fashion, something I had craved on such an unknown deep level. "It is why I couldn't let your father sell a baby into the trade."

The curse.

I exhaled disappointment. "So, she *is* alive."

She took hold of my hand and squeezed. "She is. In fact, Whitney is ten

now."

Whitney. Nodding, I said, "Yes. I was there when she was born. April ninth."

"Sounds like the date is burned into memory."

How could it not be? The curse had been a fetus in her mother's stomach when her mother was forced to take my virginity. And she had been an infant about to be born when her mother had been murdered right in front of me.

Mrs. Thompson squeezed my fingers again. "That date is burned into my *soul.*"

Her son's death. I exhaled through a twitch of feeling in my chest. I didn't like it.

Maybe she saw the opening—a glimpse of sympathy. "The people she is with, unfortunately, have not given her the most loving home. Please, leave her be. No more punishment for her." I could hear the hope in Mrs. Thompson's voice, to save one child, since another was tragically lost.

With all Seafoam's child had been through, before even being born, my interest was piqued. "Where is she?" She shook her head, eyes full of worry. I squeezed her fingers back, hard. "Don't make me show you the rough side of my fucks."

Slap!

I sat there, stunned that this woman had the nerve to strike me.

Kirill laughed from the back seat. "No blood in the rental, Yury."

Mrs. Thompson faked bravery. I could tell by her trembling voice. "That was rude."

I touched my burning skin and smirked. "*I'm* the one being rude?"

"You don't say those things to a woman after having sex with her."

A disturbed chuckle escaped me. "I thought you said you knew who I was."

She recoiled. "I feel like I just slept with the devil."

"Only his spawn." Aggressively, I leaned into her. "Now, *where* is

Whitney?"

She swallowed. "Can you promise me she will live?"

"Shouldn't you be more concerned for *Junior*?"

Her eyes slammed shut. "So young, yet already so cruel."

My spine straightened as her words sizzled against a sensation I would eventually learn to be my growing conscious. I warned, "Don't forget it."

The vehicle came to a stop before Adrian turned to face me. "I do believe you two have built up an appetite. Let's eat."

We had arrived at a restaurant, but I still needed to know the whereabouts of Marina. "You guys, go in. Mrs. Thompson and I have more to discuss."

While Kirill exited the SUV, he patted my shoulder. "Discussions? Is that what we're calling it now?"

With everyone out and entering the local restaurant, except the two of us, I softly spoke to her. "Where is Marina?"

Mrs. Thompson rolled her eyes. "Of course, you know her name." I waited. She exhaled, I believe, for many reasons. "As much as I despise her, she is not to blame. Harold treated her as if merely a toy."

I was confused because that was Marina's purpose. "But she is for his entertainment."

Mrs. Thompson cringed. "Yury, she is human! How can you treat her with such disregard?" She grabbed at her chest with a desperation that lured me in. I watched her actions, completely intrigued. "We humans have hearts. We have emotions. We have *souls*. Ones you men are damaging with heinous crimes."

"You speak as if you are a slave yourself."

"Aren't I, in a way? I mean, I sold this damaged soul of mine to the devil by standing by and watching, not turning anyone in."

In a knee-jerk reaction, I grabbed her hair and the nape of her neck, yanking us face to face again. "That is a deadly threat."

"It's not a threat." She trembled, but I was quickly learning that it was

not I who scared her, but her guilt. "It's regret." I couldn't move. This woman was baffling me every time she opened her mouth. "You're hurting me." Again, her point was moot to me. As her eyes filled with water, she sighed. "Hurting a woman is like breathing for you, isn't it?"

Some foreign sensation in my gut was becoming annoying, so I released her to get back to what I came for. "Where is Marina?"

Water in her eyes spilled over and dripped down courageous cheeks. "She was resold—"

"She was never Harold's property to sell."

Her eyes slid shut as if I had physically injured her. "—to a very decent man. One who cherishes her." Mrs. Thompson opened her eyes. I believe she wanted to read my reaction. "This man married her."

It was like losing Marina all over again. Under my breath, I whispered, "Pet."

In surrender, she said, "She got to you, too?"

I waved off Mrs. Thompson while sitting back in my seat. "No. I was only a child."

Mrs. Thompson spoke as if she knew I was lying and was full of sympathy that I felt I had the need to lie in the first place. "That's too bad. You should allow a woman to show you a soft side and love you someday."

My mind flashed to pet on her knees, starving for the bread I had placed in her mouth. Leaning my head back, I forced a smile, trying to change the subject. "Isn't that what you just did to me?"

Pity crossed her expression. Resting her head against the seat while facing me, it appeared she was swallowing down more emotions. "No." Her palm laid on my chest. "But I will try now, if you're willing." We stared at each other for a while as I tried to understand what she meant. The grudge fuck we had just experienced was on the beautiful side of sex for me, possibly the most beauty I had ever known during a sexual experience. *What more could there possibly be?*

Slowly, and with much reservation, I nodded. "Show me."

Her hand, ever so gently, left my chest and touched my neck, then tender fingers ran through my hair. My eyes rolled back, closing, as I faced forward. Never had I felt such kindness. It was soothing a part of me I had not known to be unhinged.

Shortness of breath is what I experienced next as her fingers continued to touch and explore me. When lips softly touched my ear, I was shocked to find my mouth blindly searching for her warmth. Mrs. Thompson didn't refuse the monster. She let me in.

She let me devour her teachings—her lesson.

And offered more.

Never had I had a tongue in my mouth. It was delicious. *She* was delicious, creating an unexpected hunger that arose inside of me. That hunger craved gentleness, something I had never offered another.

During the most sensual kiss in my life, she softly grasped my face while rising to her knees. I tensed because it almost hurt, her taking control by straddling my lap. The tall beauty's face hovered over mine. "Shh," she whispered, reminding me of Seafoam. "You will be okay."

It was then that I learned there was much strength in surrender. As if a scared child again, my arms raced around her waist, needing to be cemented to an earth that was violently changing from what I thought it was.

Her arms wrapped around my head as if trying to protect me from the shift that had to be felt. From within, I was trembling. I was desperate for shelter and searched for it in what I knew best. Lifting her dress, I was shocked to hear, "Ask."

I kissed her clothed chest. "Why?"

"It's an act of kindness."

I grabbed onto her ass with both hands and peered up at her. "I'm not kind."

Soft, feminine hands caressed my face. "You are." She kissed my forehead. "Somewhere inside you." She kissed the tip of my nose. "Be brave."

She kissed my lips. "Let it show."

Our faces, so close, I felt her breath brushing my lips. It was like an angel's blessing. Permission to not be Yury for a moment. In it was as if time stood still. Everything I had been taught screamed that this was a mistake, but the angel's breath was too heavenly. I shook as I spoke a fear out loud, for the very first time. "What if there is nothing in me for someone to love?"

There was a pause. "Then your life is even more pathetic than mine."

My throat closed as my eyes welled. It was clear now. There was nothing in my soul to be saved.

Her lips kissed my numb ones. "But you asking that, Yury, tells me there *is* something to love."

I gaped at the woman and the hope she just offered me. "My name... it is not truly Yury."

Affectionately, she brushed hair from my forehead. "Does it really matter?" Her finger drifted down my face. "Look at all we've just shared." Her eyes met mine. "And you don't even know *my* name."

CHAPTER FIVE

Shameful Threats

In front of Harold, I gave Mrs. Thompson my burner cell number. I made it *very* clear to her husband that she was to experience no repercussions for our actions, then kissed her hand. "It was an honor meeting you." I stood upright. "I never would have chosen her over you."

She opened her mouth to speak but was silenced when we heard, "Mom! You're home!" Junior, a.k.a. Harry, was only thirteen when I met him for the first time. He happily ran down the stairs for his mother's embrace.

"How was camp—" She held him tight while staring at me from over the top of his head, "—my son?"

I wonder if I could've changed all that was to come had I only took a second to feel our lives intertwine. But I didn't take the time. I had a number in my pocket, and I needed to dial it.

Back in the SUV, Adrian laughed. "*Smells like a fuck-factory in here.*"

Pulling my cellphone to my ear, I faked my amusement, continuing the banter in our native tongue. "*She couldn't get enough of Yury. Anyone blame her?*" Through all the laughter and comments, I heard "Hello?" over my cell. I motioned for them to go silent. "Is this Mr. Summers?"

"It is. Who am I speaking with?"

"The owner of property you have acquired."

"I'm sorry? Property?"

"Miss Whitney."

Click!

Calmly, I placed my cell in my pocket. "*He asked us to come over for a*

As more laughter erupted, I handed Adrian, sitting in the front passenger seat, a piece of paper with an address on it. *"Mrs. Thompson was useful in more ways than one."*

Facing me, Mr. Summers grumbled about needing neighborhood security. At the time, there was none present to prevent us from entering his privileged neighborhood. Sitting inside the office of his residence, I glanced about, studying my surroundings. "Unlike you, Mr. Summers, I do not have a security issue." I gestured to my men standing behind the chair I was presently lounging in.

Mr. Summers appeared to be in his forties and was in the beginning stages of greying, noticeable through his dirty blond hair. He had dark green eyes, not the frosty shade of Seafoam's.

Frustrated, Mr. Summers sat down heavily behind his desk. "A bunch of lowlife thugs."

I raised a hand, stopping Kirill as he took a step forward, not appreciating the insult. "As much as I enjoy Americans' sense of humor, let's get down to business, shall we?"

Behind Mr. Summers was a huge open window showing off the lake he lived next to. He responded, "I have no business to discuss with you."

Beyond the lake was a massive white home I would come to know well, but that isn't what caught my eye. It was the two boys treading water. One looked to be an older teen and the other younger.

Condescendingly, I teased, "Oh, this is where you are mistaken." In his suit, Mr. Summers stubbornly crossed his arms, so I picked up a picture frame to explain I was fully aware of his lies. "Your wife is beautiful." She had brown hair and brown eyes—also no relations to Whitney.

"Thank you."

"Where does Whitney get her vibrant red hair?"

Mr. Summers coughed. "Uh, my mother's side of the family."

I set the frame back on the desk. "I see," I gestured to him, "we like to

play games." Making a smacking noise with my lips, I leaned back in the chair. "Unfortunately, that is not my forte. So, let's get back to business. Your *illegally* adopted daughter is my property."

"My wife gave birth to her."

"And the hospital bill is where?"

Silence.

"Return her to me." This child needed to be placed with Harold again and be sold properly.

"Not a chance. I paid for her. The deal is done."

Is this so? Harold failed to share the profits. "You're making money off her?" I leaned forward and retrieved the gun tucked in my pants. He was not to profit off our investment.

Ignoring my weapon, he winced. "Jesus, you sick fuck. No."

These Americans kept baffling me. "Then why the attachment?" I tapped the barrel of my gun to his wife's picture. "And no more games." Mr. Summers studied the men around me, growing impatient for my cue.

He exhaled. "Whit is part of the image I have developed."

My brows scrunched. "You are kidding, no?"

His jaw locked. "I have future plans in politics. I've spent *thousands* on our presentation. PR has made sure the public sees what they all wish for—the 'perfect' family."

My upper lip snarled. "So, this is not a moral issue of selling her or wanting to save her life from me?"

A hand with a diamond wedding ring waved through the air. "Absurd."

Resting my gun in my lap, I mumbled in disgust, "No attachment to little Whitney." Mrs. Thompson had been correct. This kid was a mere pawn in a political game. I couldn't help but feel she was a distant kindred spirit of mine. Father's game wasn't political in the public's eyes, but we dealt with politicians and had agendas that would be far more lucrative than any goal Mr. Summers may have set for himself. And my own father was willing to risk my well-being

to further his objectives. Hence, where I was. It was then that I realized another clue as to why I had been sent to America. Father didn't want anyone else knowing of his connection to Whitney. That is why I was instructed to remain quiet if apprehended. He knew I was facing a strong opponent in Mr. Summers.

I had a job to do, and I wanted it done efficiently so I could return home, no handcuffs. Re-staking my claim on Whitney wasn't a concern—we abducted people all the time—but I also needed her false documents.

Looking past Mr. Summers and out the window, my attention was rerouted when catching a glimpse of a girl around the age of eleven running down a wooden dock, headed toward the lake. She was celebrating. "I finished my homework!" My chest tightened as I recognized who I was seeing; a younger version of Seafoam in a little yellow bikini, wild red hair flowing in the wind. In my mind, I heard Seafoam whisper, "Shh… you will be okay…" and felt phantom hands from the past take hold of my virgin dick.

Splash! My sight focused on the noise—Whitney disappearing in the blue water.

Resurfacing, the little Whitney said, "Timothy, did Reether tell you…"

Her voice faded as Mr. Summers opted to play another dangerous game. "Whitney was brought into this country with falsified documents."

I'm well aware. I shrugged. "Your point?"

"They lead back to your organization."

I hadn't even had a chance to request the documents, yet I was now faced with words that were a full out threat to my family. Not a wise strategy for Mr. Summers. It activated my instilled way of life and the need to protect it. In America, the land of the fat and selfish, I sat up straight, my trigger finger tightening.

As Mr. Summers gloatingly smirked, not understanding who he was attempting to intimidate, I gained my composure and took another gander around the office for more intel, because this man had made Father nervous. I wasn't going to take his power lightly. On a shelf, I found what was needed. I pointed

my gun to a picture frame. "Strapping son you have. Timothy, is it?"

Sweat built on Mr. Summers' upper lip in no time at all. Anger that he was failing to hide radiated from his whole body.

Now, I was getting somewhere, so I stood because this meeting was coming to an end. "I would hate for your perfect image to be tainted if your daughter and son were to disappear with no logical explanation." In a relaxed manner, I stretched then sighed, knowing I would have the last word. "You have two days to get your lies in order and hand her and the documents over." Heading for the office door, my men following me, I said, "If I must return, the visit will be far from pleasant." With my gun, I knocked Timothy's picture from the shelf. It hit the floor. "Have a good afternoon, *Mr. Summers*."

Almost to the SUV in the driveway, Adrian mumbled, "*Your father and Uncle would be proud, Yury.*"

That was pleasing to hear. I felt pride in my chest.

Loading into the vehicle, Kirill asked, "*Now what? Just wait?*"

Seated, I pulled a device from my pocket. "*And listen.*" Turning it on, I heard Summers yelling curses and throwing things in his office.

In amazement, Adrian peered over his shoulder from the front passenger seat. "*No.*"

As we drove out of the expensive neighborhood, where we knew security detail would be in place soon, I explained, "*I placed a bug on his wife's picture frame.*"

Everyone appeared astonished except for Kirill. He grimaced, probably knowing he would never lead because he was more muscle than brains.

Over the device, we could hear Mr. Summers' fingers punch numbers into a phone on his desk. Then he growled, "The problem we hoped wouldn't arise just rose. From hell! They want me to hand over the documents and her. Of course, I'm not giving her to them! I have an image to... What? Yeah, you do that. Call that fucking drug dealer and tell him to get these assholes off my back..."

Knowing who the "asshole" was, I rubbed my chin. *"Who is he speaking with?"*

Mr. Summers then said over his phone, "He's fine. In the water with Tim and Whit."

Sitting back against the seat, I pondered. *"Another boy was in the water with Timothy. I believe Whitney called him Reether."*

There are parents who would die for their children. There are parents who will unknowingly teach their children horrible cycles, such as abuse. There are parents who let their child become a human trafficker. And there are parents who will do nothing if threatened.

Timothy had the latter.

Timothy's parents chose not to protect him. It appeared that they had sent Whitney away right after we left their home. That gave me no choice but to add heat and abduct Mr. Summers' son, but someone had beat me to it. According to the newspapers, Timothy supposedly had a drug addiction the 'perfect' family had hidden from the public in an attempt to shield his privacy, and had been placed in a facility for treatment. The false portrayal of a family at their wit's end had an outpouring of public sympathy. Mr. Summers was correct. He had quite the PR firm behind him, and his money was well spent.

To make matters worse, I wasn't able to find this facility or any trace of Timothy.

"Yury, why are you calling me?" I hadn't heard her voice in days.

Back at the hotel room, I rubbed my tired eyes. I had yet to adjust to the time difference and was frustrated that Mr. Summers was already covering his tracks. "You never texted. Does that mean the American behaved?"

I could almost hear Mrs. Thompson's smile. "Yes. In fact, I got the opposite treatment."

Jealousy snaked into my ego. "He fucked you?"

She moaned, "Brutally."

"I can help cause another vigorous session with your husband."

As if happy for the first time in a while, she giggled. "Aren't you here on business?"

"Business with no play makes Yury pent-up and frustrated."

"Although a young stallion taking out his frustrations on me sounds delicious, I better not. I have my husband's full attention now. Don't you have slaves stored in your hotel room?"

"No. They have already been delivered."

"Yury, I was joking."

"I don't see the humor."

"That is sick."

"You're the one trying to find my line of work as a laughing matter."

"A mistake I won't repeat."

My father was growing impatient. I needed answers and was running out of time and options. Mrs. Thompson was my only other inside connection to this situation. Desperate women will do desperate actions, so I decided to cut deep and use what tools I had at my disposal. "So that you will not lose your husband's attention again, I will teach you why he craved Marina."

Her breath caught over the phone, but she said nothing.

"I train them. I train in her specialty."

"Her... s-specialty?"

"Everyone has an itch. Learn what to scratch, and he will always be yours."

After a pause, I heard Mrs. Thompson sniffle. "I would be using you."

Not wanting to admit that I was somewhat also craving her touch, I only said, "That's okay, as long as you do it in my bed."

Silence...

I wondered how her mind was trying to convince herself not to do this and how her ego was begging for the secret to her husband's deepest desires.

A strained voice finally replied, "I will be there in an hour."

INDIA R. ADAMS

"You do not have to ask where I am?"

"My husband runs this town. You're on *his* turf."

"Yet, I am fucking his wife."

She exhaled. "So young and already so cruel."

A sting to my unknown conscious had me growling, "Short skirt. I want to see your legs at all times."

She hung up, but I knew she was coming. I had made a hell of an argument.

Room service had already arrived by the time Mrs. Thompson, in a full-length black trench coat, quietly entered my room. Her hair was tied back, exposing her long neck. As I closed the door behind her, I noticed how unhappy she was to be in the room. There was no sexy smile trying to tempt me. She was indeed using me and, according to the anger growing inside me, I did indeed care. I needed the sense of control. Everything that had transpired as of late and my encounter with Mrs. Thompson had me thinking too much. It had me doubting my responsibilities and loyalty. My confused state of mind was pissing me off even more. I sneered. "You can leave if you like."

In a flash, Mrs. Thompson turned to face me and hid her face in my neck, her body pressed to mine. I was used to slaves getting confused and looking to me for comfort, but I had never had the desire to fulfill the request. In fact, the pitiful expressions usually excited me.

This was different. My heart started to pound, but I was unable to lift my arms.

She almost cried, "Please, hold me."

My eyes closed. My fingers twitched.

I pushed her away. "Let's get on with your lesson, shall we?"

Like the woman she was, she smoothed out her trench coat and lifted her chin, accepting the harsh rejection. I suppose she'd had much practice with her husband, and that's why her voice was deadpan. "Of course. Why else would I be

68

here?" Her hazel eyes bored into mine. "It wouldn't be due to caring for you."

I bit the inside of my cheek. "Why are your legs covered?"

Her jaw rigid, she unbuttoned the black coat and let it drop to the floor. She wore a black leather corset that zipped up the front, her perky breasts overflowing. A black skirt that barely existed hugged her hips and firm ass. Long legs teased me like a cold glass of water on a Russian summer day. The whole package of all woman, not an inexperienced scared slave, beckoned me in a daring manner. I licked my lips. "This outfit is derailing my plans."

"Then I'll leave." Believing my words to be only another rejection, she spun around and bent over, reaching for her coat. Her short skirt was not enough coverage and ended up exposing her mature core. Like a bull, I rushed forward, taking possession of her body.

Slamming her front to a wall, I growled in her ear, "Master has not given you permission to leave yet." I stepped between her legs, forcing them apart. "Understood?"

I could almost hear her heart racing in the silence of the room, but she coyly repeated, "Master?"

Kissing her exposed neck, I explained, "I do not like repeating myself." Between her legs, I surged my hips forward. "Yes, Master. Let's try again."

"Yes." She reached behind and around my waist, grabbing onto my ass to pull me into her.

I loved how her long fingers finally felt hungry for me. "Yes, what?"

Her hand stilled. The side profile of her face scrunched in confusion. "Pardon?"

Confused about her confusion, I felt slightly deflated. "Yes, *Master*."

With no understanding of this process, or of the pecking order, she angrily groaned, "Yes, *Master*. Better, you little *twit*?"

I smelt her hair as I relished in the fact that she wasn't willing to play. Usually, this brought immense joy because I would get to break her, but deep down, I hoped she would never bow to me. Her older essence was intense. Her

strength was something I was quickly learning I craved in a woman. "Careful, your husband is not here to protect you this time."

She chuckled with no humor. "If I remember correctly, *you* won that round. Not him."

Again, I kissed her neck that smelt of flowers. "I believe you were the true winner, no?"

Her hips tilted back for me to have better access. "In more ways than one."

I pumped my erection against her while my hands searched up her corset. Once her breasts were found, I pulled on her nipples. "I need a repeat performance. Should we invite your husband this time?"

Mrs. Thompson was breathless, her body arching into mine. "Can't. He and Harry are off to a father and son retreat for two weeks."

I stopped moving. Everything suddenly made perfect sense. A phone call to a certain drug dealer had an unpredicted outcome. There was no rehab for Timothy, nor a retreat for Harry. That was only one lie to cover another. I was starting to suspect Timothy didn't even have a habit to cure, and that Harold was trying to save Timothy while fearing for his own son's life due to interfering.

Mrs. Thompson peered over her shoulder. "What's wrong?"

My eyes met hers, and I lied to her face. "Nothing." My hands released her and went for my belt. "I just need to free my dick so I can fuck you."

She turned to face me, her back against the wall. "What about my lesson?"

Suddenly feeling like the rejected one, I released my belt buckle. Mrs. Thompson wasn't here for me. She was here to learn how to hold on to her lowlife husband, the one fucking with my livelihood. Swallowing the unexpected injury to feelings I didn't know I had, and burying them with irritation, I stepped back from her. "Of course." My eyes now bored into hers as I repeated words. "Why else would you be here?"

Concern crossed her expression as she tried to explain, "Yury, I love my

70

husband."

I snarled, "And I should give a fuck, why?"

Her chin rose as her shoulders set back. "I just wanted to be sure you understood what is happening here."

My anger grew as I stalked over to my bed and walked around to the nightstand. "It is *you* who is unaware of what is happening here." I gestured to the room service cart. It contained a display of butter, coconut oil, and lube, as well as a bottle of champagne on ice.

Paling by the second, she grabbed her throat. "Oh…" Hurt eyes found mine again. "He… Harold liked to fuck her in the ass?"

"Meh." I shrugged. "She doesn't have an ordinary ass."

The scorned woman's nostrils flared. "What the fuck does that mean?"

I smirked. "Jealous?"

High heels spun on the carpet and headed for the door.

Watching her soon exit, I merely said, "This is a one-time offer."

Those heels stopped. She slowly faced me, her jaw painfully locked.

I held up a prescription bottle. "Want to relax before we get started?"

Her stare raced and locked onto the bottle with a ravenousness that surprised me. That stare didn't cease while she told me, "No. I don't touch drugs anymore. Harry needs me."

Toying with the bottle in my fingers, I watched her eyes light with a desire that no longer included anything her husband or I could offer. Mrs. Thompson was an addict.

Did I take pity or pride that she was trying hard to make the right decision for Junior?

No.

I blamed her for my numbness that was fading away, not my father's actions and horrid guidance. I blamed her for awakening a conscience in me, not the fact that my father didn't even bother to tell me my true name. Not only did I eventually convince Mrs. Thompson one pill wouldn't hurt, but I sent her

71

on a downward spiral that she would never recover from. Never. Inadvertently, affecting Junior's very future.

I deserve all of God's fury and judgment.

In the morning, Mrs. Thompson awoke in my bed on her back, confused with the loss of time and events. Her makeup was smeared, and she was fully naked. Propped on her elbows, she blinked and blinked, trying to clear hungover eyes. On the room service cart, there were opened jars, used butter sticks, and an empty bottle of champagne. She fell back to her pillow, groaning. "Tell me I at least had a good time."

Fully clothed, I crawled into bed next to her. "Oh, you had a very *fulfilling* evening." I held up my cellphone in the palm of my hand. "Want to see?"

Her jaw dropped. "You filmed us?"

"My cousin did."

The color drained from her cheeks. "What?"

I winked. "He filmed *all* of us."

Mrs. Thompson's chest started to heave with nerves. "No."

"Oh, yes." I tapped the play button on my phone. "See?"

I had witnessed much shame by that point in my life. I had caused much shame, too. My slaves were always trying to redeem themselves after being lost in forced sexual acts. But I had never witnessed a loss of fervor from a woman's soul. That is what happened that mournful morning. Mrs. Thompson lost all her fight as this certain video played.

With a pillowcase over my head, I was naked, on my back, on the hotel bed. She was also bare, face not shielded like mine, with her chest laying on top of mine as I fucked her. But she and I weren't the only ones moaning with pleasure. Adrian, also concealed, was fucking her mouth from over my shoulder. With a pillowcase over his head, Kirill's bent legs were on each side of my thighs so he could properly fuck her in the ass. He had requested that hole since it was the tightest of a woman who was far too old for his true needs.

72

In the video, from under her used body, I asked, "Everyone ready? All at the same time."

Soil. A lesson my father had taught me well.

As trainers, we were experts at climaxes, others and our own, so we all came at the same time, filling every open orifice Mrs. Thompson had to offer.

Now, lying next to me on the same mattress, tears streamed down her face. "Why?"

Ignoring her, I pointed to the phone. "Look how my sperm is leaking from you like that." We never used condoms when training slaves—most buyers wanted their new pets to perform without and would refuse the sensation-killing material—so had not provided that respect to Mrs. Thompson either. Her eyes closed as if she were resisting the urge to vomit, seeing all our seminal fluids leaking from the available holes we had used and abused. "I wonder if that is how your *husband* will react."

She was barely audible. "What do you want, Yury?"

I chuckled, referring back to the video. "I think we got it, no?"

As if all her energy had been zapped, she got out from under the sheet and stood. Reaching for her trench coat, she said, "I see now that you are a true manipulator and have a purpose behind all your actions." She slipped her limp arms into the coat. "I have learned my lesson well." Buttoning it, she stared at me. "So, I will ask again. What is it you want?"

I sat up, angry that her words were having any effect on me. "I'm supposed to double-check properties owned by your husband but can't find them."

Her whole body drooped as she pointed to my cellphone. "You put me through *that* for an address I would've given you freely in trade for knowledge to save my marriage? One you have now ruined?"

My mouth opened, but I couldn't force more angry words because anger was slipping from my grasp. My emotions had become as erratic as my horrible reasoning for my horrid actions. I felt like I had disappointed a mother I only

wanted to please.

With shame I was unfamiliar with, I said, "I won't show him the video. I… will delete it."

She exhaled, but there was no relief in the released breath. "So young, so cruel, and so utterly stupid." Mrs. Thompson shook her head, almost laughing at me, yet there was no comedy in her tone, only sadness and loneliness that would haunt her for the rest of her days. "I am simply a woman wanting to be loved by her man. I felt I wasn't good enough to hold on to the love he once had for me, so I was willing to do whatever it took to be worthy of his affection." She wiped at tears with exhaustion that was heart-wrenching to witness. "Now, I am tainted, never to be worthy of him again." She inhaled the most labored breath. "Your family stole my husband with an expertly trained slave. Then your family killed my son for retribution for the child that slave bore. Now, the same family threatens that same son I have graciously raised, one not truly mine by all opinions but my own." Slowly, she faced the closed door. "I am paying for every sin committed by staying silent." Her bare feet took tired steps forward. "Show my husband the video, Yury. It doesn't matter now." Her hand on the doorknob, she exclaimed, "There is no saving the damned with you and your kind involved. We will all burn in hell with you." She opened the door. "Our other home is under my maiden name."

Completely unaware she was informing me of where her husband and son were hiding, she told me the address I needed and left me to sit in a deafening silence.

CHAPTER SIX

Behind the Curtains

Does it matter *how* change takes place, as long as there is change? From my own experience, I'd have to say yes. The next ripple I was about to cause in innocent lives would be everlasting.

Kirill, Adrian, and I quietly rowed a small boat across a lake to observe the address Mrs. Thompson had provided. We didn't need to use our cellphone flashlights. The moon was shining the way and reflecting off the water.

At the dock, we hid the boat and ourselves off to the side behind some shrubbery. It was about ten PM, and the only noises were Harold on his cellphone and a loud but muffled TV inside the home. Harold's lake house was a solitary house. Lights were on in the basement, which was partially underground, making it easy to see two young men, Timothy and Junior, sitting on a large, dark, L-shaped couch, watching the blaring TV. There were snack wrappers and fast food bags scattered about. Timothy, who was seventeen, was not being ill-treated. Harry, thirteen-years-old at the time, was playfully popping candy into his mouth, laughing at the movie the two young men were watching.

Harold was pacing the wooden decking outside the basement's sliding doors leading to the lake. He growled into his cellphone, "These are not the guys to toy with for your career. They've already killed one son. Yours will be next. I swear it." He angrily tapped on his phone's screen, hanging up on one person and calling another. "It's me." He rubbed his stressed face. "I can't get him to cough up cash or the certificate… No, I know we can't hand over Whitney, but I figure they only want to make money off her… No. You already paid for Marina, so I'll offer them five-hundred K for Whit… Okay. Good to know you'll match me if

Yes, good to know.

"—but there's more... Summers reminded them about her Russian certificate... But he threatened it can lead back to them... Yes, he thinks he's untouchable with his career to hide behind... Yep, a damn fool is right. Did you read the paper? I know! Tim on drugs? I'm a dealer, and even I know that would never happen... Yeah, that's why I'm calling. Can you get one that looks real?"

Not appreciating their efforts to save young lives, I only focused on the trickery and snarled.

Harold continued, "When can you have it by? That'll work. No, why would they? Your son has nothing to do with this... Well, they don't know that! No, I still have him hidden... You know Tim, smart little bastard... Yeah, he'd do anything for his little sister, and that's what I'm afraid of. He didn't put up a fight when he saw me coming. I suspect he ordered his father to hide Whit." He plopped into a patio chair and rubbed his face again. "Okay, I'll call Yury now."

After working his phone again, mine vibrated in my pocket. Kirill had to muffle a laugh as Harold, frustrated, hung up when I didn't answer. Harold went back inside and said something to the teenage boys before leaving. Once he was driving away in his Mercedes, I was free to make noise. Retrieving my cellphone from my pocket, I returned the missed call. Harold answered on the first ring. "Hello?"

"American."

"I have an offer for you—"

"Where's the boy?" I asked while staring at Timothy through the glass. It was imperative to see how far Harold would take his lies—his disloyalty to my father.

"What? I don't have him. He's at a facility—"

"I'll kill Marina."

Silence, then, "Okay. I have him, but be reasonable. That kid has *nothing* to do with this..." The liar proceeded to offer me a birth certificate—the imitation of the one my family gave him years ago—and five-hundred thousand to leave

Whitney in Connecticut.

To go along with the ruse, I accepted the offer. "Double the price."

Harold exhaled relief. "Done."

After discussing the wire transfer and birth certificate to be delivered in one week, I waited for the two boys to fall to sleep. The TV still blaring, I snuck up to the house, slid the sliding glass door open wide enough to reach my arm inside, and planted a bug behind the nearest piece of furniture which happened to be a little table holding a bowl for keys.

For the following week, my men went to American 'strip clubs' while I stayed back in my hotel room and listened in on conversations. Naked females were a part of my daily job. Watching them swing from a pole, faking being aroused and wanting men to gawk at them wasn't appealing to me.

Due to my recording device, I listened as the two young men, Timothy and Harry, became very close in a short amount of time. They spoke of sports and cars while playing video games, but what held my attention was the subject 'Little Treasure', the nickname Timothy had given to his sister, according to conversations. The young man, Timothy, spoke with a knowledge *far* beyond his years, *far* beyond what a normal teenager would comprehend in his situation, and was very aware of his parents' mistreatment toward his 'Little T.'

Harry, even being raised in such an environment as a drug trafficking ring, was also quite observant for his age. "Is that why you let my dad take you?"

Timothy, chewing on popcorn, offered, "I *treasure* one life more than my own."

"Why?" asked the astonished kid while he made noise, digging into a popcorn bowl.

"That's what you do when angels appear out of thin air."

On my hotel room bed, I shook my head. *He knows Whitney was illegally adopted. His mother was never pregnant.* I was surprised to be envious that Whitney had someone watching over her. The closest I had was Kirill, who I

77

believed hated me.

Timothy went on to explain, "My parents suck, and she is the sweetest girl. Someone has to look out for her. She has a best friend, but he's still too young for the job."

"He? Her best friend isn't a girl?"

Timothy beamed. "Link is a good kid. He lives across a lake we live on."

Harry was flabbergasted. "*Wow*. I would *never* have a *girl* as my best friend."

"You say that now, Junior, but she's special. And, apparently, I'm not the only one who knows it." Timothy added, "That's why I have her hidden away while I lay as bait."

Harry promised, "My dad will make whatever is happening go away. He makes everything go away."

I could hear Timothy trying to be careful with his next words. Harry was painfully naïve of the treacherous man his father was. Harry was unaware he was only a couple of years away from being forced into the drug dealing industry. Timothy spoke as if not wanting to be the one to burst the bubble Harry was presently living in. "It hurt to learn my dad wasn't what I thought him to be."

"What do you mean?" asked Harold Junior.

Timothy further explained, "As a child, we tend to believe lies easily. We trust the elders in our life. As we get older, we sometimes finally see what's been in front of us the whole time. Or, at least recognize a lie when told one."

I did my best to ignore how his situation mirrored my own, but there was no denying it. I had just experienced the same realization.

"Like Little T?" Harry almost cheered, completely missing the hidden message.

Softly, Timothy replied, "Yeah, Little T is actually the reason I learned the truth. But that's okay. I'm glad her coming into my life opened my closed eyes."

Harry's mood shifted. His voice also got quieter. "I used to have a

brother like you."

There was a pause before Timothy found the courage to ask, "Used to?"

"Yeah." I could hear Harry struggling to share more. "He was shot... I, uh, saw it."

"Fuuuuuck," Timothy hissed.

"Yeah." Harry sniffled. "We were in Russia. It was cold. I wanted hot chocolate." His voice was almost a whisper. "He waved to me from the sidewalk outside, way below our hotel room... He never waved to me again after that." Harry took a deep breath. "Have you ever seen hot chocolate and blood mix?"

It sounded as if Timothy was fighting for composure, his voice tight and constricted. "No. No, I haven't. I'm sorry you have."

Already showing signs of brushing off emotions, a survival technique some have to learn early on, Harry casually replied, "I guess the baby was to replace him, but my mom refused her."

"What baby?"

Shit. Kid, stay out of it.

"An infant that screamed on the plane, always wanting a bottle." He sounded somewhat annoyed with the memory.

As if scared of the answer, Timothy cautiously asked, "When did this happen, Harry?"

"My mom cries it's been over a decade but feels like yesterday. That's all she will say about it."

"Holy shit." Timothy mumbled, "That's where she's from."

Already with regret for the kid with a good heart, my eyes slid shut. Harry didn't reply, probably lost in the memory, but Timothy had now connected events that would cost him his life.

I turned off the device because my stomach started churning. I sat up in bed, fighting my sudden nausea. "Stupid American food." I even paced my room, trying to shake it off.

Food poisoning or not, we had work to do, so I got on my cellphone

and called Kirill. When he answered, music from the strip club blared over the receiver. "Yeah?"

"Yeah?" I asked, annoyed and still feeling ill. "Stop sounding ignorant and get your asses back here." After hanging up on him, I grabbed four syringes from my nightstand full of the product we bought from Harold.

They were full of the drug needed to snuff out a promising life.

Back on the lake to further spy and listen to what was happening inside the lake house, I was very agitated when calling Harold. Believing the deal was complete and the threat was over, since I had received the false document and a bank transfer of a million dollars, he casually sat on the couch with the boys while eating dinner from white To-Go boxes. He had planned on returning Timothy home that very night, not knowing his actions to involve Timothy had irrevocably changed the course of my mission.

Harold eyed his vibrating phone, then answered, sounding concerned, "Hello?"

"Do you think I like to play games?"

His expression fell to despair as he continued to lie. "What are you talking about?"

"The trickery in my hand. Worthless paperwork."

"I—"

"No, no. No more lies. You have one hour to deliver me the truth." I hung up on him.

My men and I listened as he made another call, but his whispers were too hushed for us to hear. Once off the phone, Harold then claimed, to the boys, that he was leaving to meet up with Mr. Summers.

Timothy continued to show wisdom dangerous for his health. Patronizingly, he asked, "My father is actually doing the right thing?"

Harold nervously retrieved keys from the bowl. "Uh, yeah. Great news, huh?"

"Dad?"

"Everything's fine, Harry."

As soon as the drug dealer raced off into the night, my cousins and I rushed into the basement, baffling the two young men. Harry begged us not to take Timothy. "Please! He's my only friend!" Harry's infatuation with the new relationship was a blatant reminder that my family stole not only his own older brother but also the adoration Harry was clearly craving himself.

Kirill rolled his eyes as he restrained the child. In Russian, he told me, "*How pathetic.*"

I smirked, but it wasn't sincere. I couldn't help but realize Harry had one up on all of us. Kirill, my men, nor I had one true friend. Not one man in that room would've begged for my life like Timothy, who was yelling, "Leave him alone! It's me you want!"

Unfamiliar feelings zipped through my body as I observed Harry, terror blanketing his young face, while my men and I overpowered a struggling Timothy. I told Kirill, "*Tie the American's kid up.*" We were expected to kill him, as another lesson in betrayal; Harold earned money by selling Whitney.

"*But—*" Kirill stopped when my jaw locked, and my nostrils flared in warning. "*Whatever you say, Boss.*"

"No!" screamed the boy, catching on as he saw us taking Timothy toward the sliding door. "Take me instead!"

Timothy demanded, "Harry! Shut your mouth. I mean it."

Harry did. It appeared to break his heart, but he did it. In front of the couch, Kirill laid Junior down and hogtied him, then gagged him with a handkerchief tied behind his head.

Being shoved toward the sliding door, Timothy begged me, "Please don't hurt him. Please don't hurt *her*. She's good. She's kind. She knows nothing about all this…"

Peering over my shoulder, I watched Harry staring at me from the floor, his eyes full of desperation and helplessness. I think he knew Timothy's life

was coming to an end. I think he instinctively knew I was about to obliviate his last shred of innocence. I felt sorrow for robbing him of another brother, but I believed I had no choice. There were already too many threats present with the Summers. This one could be disposed of. The newspapers already had provided an alibi with the drug addiction stories.

Timothy, unlike his father or mother, had heart, a good soul, and most of all, courage. That made Timothy the most dangerous kind of threat. I felt trapped between mercy and my duties. Pulling my cellphone to my ear, I angrily spit out, "You may want to check in on your son," and hung up on the now frantic American.

Sheltered by the darkness shadowing the boat dock by the lake, we watched Harold's car race back to the lake house. The car was practically still in motion as he jumped out and ran to the front door. I gazed down at Timothy, who was tied and sitting on the dock's wooden planks, leaning against a bench. I grinned at the hatred in his eyes. "Your fight is admirable, kid."

"Fuck you."

I shrugged. "You know my job, yes?"

His brows bunched. "No. I have no idea who you are."

"I train sex slaves. You sure you want me to fuck you?"

Appalled, the back of his head slammed into the bench. "Stay away from me."

"No worries. Your ass is safe with me, but," I gestured to Kirill, "maybe not with him."

Timothy was eyeing his possible rapist while lights were being flicked on in every room of the lake house. Harold rushed about, searching for his kid, screaming his name, "Harry!"

Once he found him in the basement, he didn't even have him fully untied before attempting to get me back on the phone. As if I hadn't caused havoc and an abundance of fear, I answered, "Kidnapping services, may I help you?"

"You sonofabitch!"

"Meh, that title belongs to the one who tried to fool me. Dumb American." I gestured for my men to lay Timothy down and hold the syringes to his arm.

Timothy immediately started to struggle and plead, "Don't do this. No. Stop. I don't do drugs…"

Meanwhile, Harold was becoming frantic, "What's going on? What are you doing to him?" There was a slight pause as he tried to disguise his fear and calm his tone. "Don't do anything you will regret, Yury. Talk to me. I'm trying to save young lives here."

I took a picture then sent it to him. "Maybe you should stick to selling drugs—*ruining* lives." I knew my next words would kick him in the balls. "Obviously, this present circumstance shows that it is what you are best at." Being careful not to show my location, I pointed my cellphone toward Timothy to show Harold the view.

With knees and hands, Kirill, Adrian, and my men were putting their full weight on the teenager, who had yet to reach his full strength, making him an easy target for the experienced.

Harold yelled, "No! What do you want me to do to save his life? I have what you want!"

"You don't. We both know it is another false document."

Harold begged, "Please, listen to me. I swear I'm not trying to piss you off, but this man Summers, he's impossible. He thinks he's above everyone. He's not home and won't answer my calls…"

As he continued his plea, I looked down to see Timothy, staring at me in a horror I instantly recognized. It's the moment you realize you are dispensable, not important enough for your father to fight for your happiness or safety. I think I stopped breathing as I witnessed Timothy's eyes glaze over in a numb awareness. His struggle ended, and he laid flat on the dock, awaiting his sentence. I think he realized the man who had the true power, his father, was sacrificing

him. Timothy, staring at the dark sky above him, now understood he was merely a pawn in a circumstance beyond his control.

My ringing ears finally heard Harold again. "…I know what you're capable of. I'm scared. You have all the control. Please, spare this good kid. It's Summers you want. Just tell me where you are, and I will come to pick up the kid."

Again, being trapped between duty to my father and my developing conscious, I became unstable, confused with what to do. Unbeknownst to Harold, his wife was on a downward spiral due to my actions and his. Now, I was about to make him witness another failure of ours. I struggled with my next words. "I, er, just… want to, uh, remind you of what we do to traitors. How we will teach a lesson."

With his alarmed eyes watching me through his phone, Harold nodded. "I've already learned that lesson well." His next expression suddenly showed him getting lost in thought of the son we murdered. I was sure of it. His step faltered as he pulled his untied son from the floor. "Tell me what to do, and I will do it."

There was nothing he could do at this point. I had a father to appease. And I had to damn my soul further. The only mercy I could offer was for Harold not to watch my next cruel move, so I lied. "I want the correct copy."

Harold's eyes closed in frustration. "Summers was bluffing. That certificate will not lead back to you."

What Harold didn't know was that my cousin's wife was about to use her copy against us. If more connections were made—if officials found the same document in Summers' care—it wasn't going to be difficult to find us. I was being trained to eliminate any potential hazards to our profession. Even though I knew Harold couldn't get his hands on the hazard, that I would have to do it myself, I wanted him gone before he recognized where I was and was forced to witness a murder in which I wished I didn't have to commit. "Go get it or *Timothy* is going to the bottom of this lake."

After a long pause, Harold nodded in defeat. He had been in this business

for a long enough time to know that now, it was time to protect what he could. Holding his son's arm, he guided him toward the stairs.

"Tsk. Tsk. Leave the boy as my insurance policy."

Harold jolted, his eyes darting around to the windows and sliding door. He stared through the glass and into the night as if finally understanding how close I truly was. With much determination, he told me, "No."

"Then I will shoot him as he heads for your car."

"Fuck!" yelled Harold after a moment of silence.

Then he hid his son somewhere in the house before racing his car away from the boys he was trying to save. I didn't care. Him hidden didn't change my plans.

Kirill asked me, "*So, now we wait?*"

So aggravated with what I had to do, I punched him, right in the face, knocking him off his feet. As he stared up at me from the dock, I growled, "*Maybe you should spend less time at the strip clubs and do your fucking job instead of fucking whores.*" I pointed to Timothy while continuing to speak in my native tongue. "*He knows where Seafoam's child came from. Killing him is not a bluff, you idiot!*"

Kirill rubbed at his jaw. "*Why does this bother you so?*"

I roared, "*I don't know!*"

"Just tell me she gets to live."

We all looked at Timothy. He was full of surrender to his upcoming death, yet had the dedication to plea one more time for his sister's life. At the moment, his righteous actions, as noble as they were, made me even more irate. So, I lashed out. Squatting in front of him so we could be face to face, I sneered, "Remember my profession? If you don't, it's okay. Your sister will soon." He gaped as my palm cupped my groin to be sure my message was clear.

The loyal brother mentally unraveled. He had been ready to die but now fought to live. He was a tied-up ball of pissed hysterics. He started screaming at such a loud tone; the inevitable had now arrived. He had to be silenced, once and

for all. I took no pleasure in giving out demands while trying to hold him still as needles were inserted one by one. Drugs were forced into veins that didn't want to stop fighting for life, and they were forced to carry death throughout his whole body.

Timothy's struggle slowed.

His expression showed understanding as the drugs took hold…

His dazed eyes met mine. "She's… good. She's… good."

The rest of my men loaded the small boat as Timothy's gaze held me in a frozen state. Maybe I sensed what I had done—what wheels of destiny I had started to spin with this murder. Attempting to permanently sever the bond between Little Treasure and her brother, I was unknowingly creating another bond. A bond only death would see part.

"Timothy!" Harry screamed after opening the sliding door off in the distance.

Yes, the wheels of fate had begun to turn.

The boat carried me across the lake while a promise was being made between two young men, one dying, and one to fight on for Little T.

On a night neither would ever forget, because of me.

CHAPTER SEVEN

Accountable Actions

Chain reaction…

My father had sent me on this wild goose chase to snuff out any threats, but it only strengthened Seafoam's curse. Chain reactions had begun with such a force; nothing would end the madness until I stopped what I had started. But the true power behind Seafoam's curse was yet to be in my personal care, so I freely continued to inflict life-altering damage to all those unlucky enough to cross my path.

I had a young man murdered.

Chain reaction…

Now, a broken mother was on a warpath because of her surviving son's shattered heart and determined promise.

Chain reaction…

Knock! Knock! Knock! After looking through my hotel room's peephole and seeing Mrs. Thompson in her long black trench coat, I willingly opened the door. Intrigued, I did not expect the knife she shoved into my chest. I fell back against the wall with a heavy enough thud to alarm my men in the next room. The shallow blade in my skin—my flesh—didn't compare to the burn her evil stare seared against my soul. Eye to eye, while she was pulled away by my men, she growled, "Now, my son is fulfilling a *promise*. He's searching for a little girl, unaware that his mother sold her!"

Chain reaction…

Another threat…

Another demise…

Hatred seethed off her body, and her expression was like steam from a

boiling kettle on a lit gas stove. Fighting Adrian's hold, she growled again, "You are the devil's spawn. Killing that boy made you just as horrid as your father when he killed *my* son."

My throat tightened. Stunned, I stood there, hearing her confirm my suspicions.

Kirill was yelling in Russian, trying to gain my attention, as he pushed a hotel hand-towel against my stab wound, after removing the blade. But I couldn't pull my eyes from hers. I was entranced by her revulsion. It was that intense— that absolute.

Even though I was having more than a glimpse of a notion that my actions had been horrid, I couldn't bring myself to admit it. I should have opened my mouth to say how her loathing cut me deeper than her knife, but instead, my mouth—my training—told her, "I should order your death for this." I gestured to Kirill, who was trying to stop the bleeding she had brutally, and justifiably, caused. It was a standoff, her daring me to make my next move. But, cruelly, I decided she had served her purpose. Her dilated eyes spoke of the drugs rushing through her system, one I had personally rebooted her to crave. Then I sighed because I had another problem. I couldn't have Harry investigating, searching for my illegal property, so cruelty prevailed over compassion. "But, instead, I shall scar you, as you have me."

Mrs. Thompson stilled in Adrian's firm hold as if just realizing the magnitude of her actions. Her eyes spoke of awareness to the impact of the dangerous animal she had provoked.

In Russian, I told one of my men, *"Grab a syringe."*

He didn't ask questions. He went to retrieve the vial I would need in mere seconds.

Still leaning against the wall, where Mrs. Thompson's slice had sent me, I told her, "Harry will travel with me to Russia." She paled, and her mouth fell open. "I will train him myself," I licked my teeth, "so he can be of more use to your husband's growing business in the sex trade." Her shocked mouth tried

to speak, but I had stolen her breath and her reason for existing. She could only shake her head no, so I continued, "He will be returned as deadly…" I pulled the white towel, now red, from my chest, "as his mother," and held it up for her to see. Before the woman had a chance to react, I nodded my head. *"Drug her."*

I couldn't go to the hospital and draw attention to myself from authorities. My best chance was to close the wound and go home. As Mrs. Thompson's body went limp from the effects of the syringe emptying a drug into her veins, I directed, *"Lay her in my bed."* She wouldn't die. She'd merely slipped into unconsciousness. It was a merciful thing to do.

Breathless from pain, I pointed to Adrian and my men. *"Go. Retrieve her son. We leave tonight."* As they left without another word, I swallowed, then told Kirill, *"Heat a blade and stop my bleeding."*

When Mrs. Thompson finally awoke, my men and I would be in the air, flying home with her son. This would bring about another chain reaction that would come with heavy consequences. Mrs. Thompson was going to have to explain to her husband why we took his child and how she knew where I had been staying. How, when the drug dealer thought more danger had ended, his wife had actually stirred the hornet's nest. Their marriage would not recover from this blow. Mrs. Thompson would fall deeper into her addiction and would never be fully drug-free again.

She was right. I was just as evil as my father.

In the private jet, Harry appeared petrified, buckled in an ivory leather seat. Sitting across from me, he stared at my chest. Even though Kirill had cauterized the wound, there was still seepage. Blood lingered on my shirt. I didn't bother to tell him his mother was the one who inflicted my injury. I only said, "You will be staying with me for a while."

He peered around at my men. "In Russia?"

I nodded.

"Do I get to go back home someday?"

"Of course. Why do you ask?"

A surprisingly daring glare shot from blue eyes that mimicked his father's. "Because I recognize you from that little boat. You killed my friend. I thought maybe you would kill me, too."

"Meh." I shrugged through exhaustion. "He was no longer of use for me. You are."

Tears streamed down his young face as I explained that his father was a drug dealer and also dabbling in a "trade" business and that Harry himself was being groomed to join our line of work. He asked, "Do I have a choice?" I shook my head. I wasn't lying. He had been born into a family that would, eventually, be his demise. "Can this training wait?"

I was shocked to feel a bit of respect for the young teenager not trying to run from his destiny. "You have something more important to do?" He nodded. Intriguing me, I gestured for him to explain.

He finally conceded. "I made a promise." I hand gestured for more. "Timothy has—" With a touch of regret I didn't miss, Harry corrected himself, "I mean, *had* a little sister." His expression of dismay faded into sadness. "I-I held Timothy as he died where you left him." I watched him swallow as he fought more tears. "White foam." He pointed to his own mouth. "He had white foam—" Then he shook his head as if refusing to relive the gory memory of witnessing his new friend's overdose. "His last words were him begging me to watch over his Little T-Treasure." Tears finally fell as he spoke with hopelessness. "But I don't know how to find her. Dad won't tell me who Timothy was. Can you tell me, so I can find her?"

Clueless to all the hearts Whitney Summers would capture, I asked, "You are rather young for such responsibility, no?"

Angrily, he wiped at his wet cheeks. "But not too young to learn about how to sell drugs?"

I didn't answer because his point was sound and not one I could argue with, nor could I let him know who 'Little T' was. "No. I don't know who

Timothy's little sister is."

Harry's shoulders sagged. He believed me and moved our conversation along. "Does my mom know what my dad is doing?" I nodded. His Adam's apple bobbed, but no more tears were shed as he stared out of the plane window. "I don't believe you."

I laid my seat back, so in need of rest. "You may not believe this either, but I understand. I, too, had to learn that my father and mother were not who I thought them to be. I felt very alone."

Hope laced his next question. "But you don't anymore?"

If only. "I wish this were the case." With sorrow, my tired eyes slid shut. "Now, I know... I *am* alone."

With Harry being so young and overwhelmed in a foreign country, there was no need to blindfold him. As Adrian drove us from the airport, he shrunk his body to avoid touching us. We contained him between Kirill and me to keep him from leaping from the moving vehicle. His eyes darted to the door handles with every breath he took.

My other two men had taken separate vehicles to go to their homes.

I told the boy, "Where we are going, there are men that are not as kind as I." Harry stared at me as if he did not think that possible. "So, it would behoove you to stay close to me, so I can protect you."

My cellphone was vibrating in my pocket, yet again, so I finally answered it, not even checking to see the caller's name. I already knew. Mr. Thompson bellowed, "You motherfucker!!!" Bored, I stared out the window and hung-up on him. "That is why your worried father keeps calling." In the silence of the drive, my cell again vibrated.

"C-Can I talk to him?" asked the scared and trapped child.

"Not at the moment. If you earn it, then yes."

"E-Earn it?" he asked as if sensing there was no good meaning behind my words.

He was correct.

Walking through the front door of my home, my father greeted us. He was beaming. I actually smiled in disbelief, thinking he missed his only son and was concerned for my injury. But that smile fell as he cheered in Russian, "*The American is so angry! What possessed my son to be so brilliantly conniving?*"

My cellphone continued to vibrate in my pocket, a painful reminder of just what a concerned father looked like.

Mine approached the alarmed Harry and switched to English. "Hello, dear boy. Welcome to my home." In Russian, he told me, "*Go to your room. I have surprises for you.*" He put an arm around Harry's shoulder. "I will care for our guest."

Another wave of exhaustion flowed through my consciousness as I realized it was time to start formally training again. It was time to establish who Harry's protector was so that the delusional trust between the two of us could begin. I removed my father's arm from my subject and replaced it with my own. I was sure to speak in English so that Harry could comprehend who I considered dangerous for him. "That is not necessary, Father. I do not wish for anyone to mistreat Harry."

Right on cue, the young teenager leaned into me, ever so slightly.

Chain reactions…

It was almost surreal, guiding Harry up the stairs I had seen his biological mother travel many times, sometimes on her knees, always as a slave, especially the night Harry was conceived. Harry was not to be a slave. My goal was not to have him on his knees, but he needed to understand the life of a slave in order to train them properly back in America.

Due to his biological mother's petite size, Harry was also on the shorter side for his age. He was timidly observing everything around him, especially the front door. I couldn't help but remember the first time his mother walked through

that passage, before being abandoned and dragged into the basement, to have her first of many experiences of gang rape.

Entering my bedroom, I coyly asked Junior, "Think you can find your way back to the airport?" He wasn't going to have the opportunity, but I was curious about his answer under such duress.

"I'll figure it out."

There was no denying how brave he was trying to be. Unfortunately, there was no time to appreciate it. Across the room, a woman was frantically trying to open my bedroom window, not knowing that they had been designed to prevent slaves from escaping. As soon as she heard us, she peered over her shoulder then rushed from the window, slamming her back against the nearest wall. Then she shimmied as far away from me as possible, into a corner. Her dark hair stuck to the stucco of my wall, her expression filled with desperation. In Russian, she told me, "*This is not what I signed up for. Release me.*"

Exhaling, because I was far too tired for a panicked new slave, I pulled keys from my slacks and locked my bedroom door. It was the only way to get rest when having a slave or slaves in my room with me through the night. Escaping was not part of their training; only fucking, sucking, and obedience.

After the door was secure, I gestured for Harry to sit in a lounge chair in the opposite corner of the frantic woman. His chest was panting as hard as hers while he stared at the locked door. Disobedience in my bedroom was not permitted, so I sternly commanded, "Now."

Junior jolted, then locked stares with the woman, almost tripping over his own feet as he rushed toward the chair. "W-Why is she so scared?" He didn't speak Russian yet, but you didn't need to in order to recognize pure fright— something he was also presently experiencing.

In Russian, I replied to the woman with brown eyes, "*What you signed up for?*" No abductees ever had signed up for such vile treatment. I slowly walked to my bed and removed my blazer.

Her gaze rushed to monitor my movements, which is exactly why I

was moving in a calm manner. With her hands gripping the wall behind her, she swallowed. *"The dangerous situation I asked for."*

Neatly laying my jacket on the bed, I lifted a brow and smirked. *"Danger you have found, Pet."*

"Rainbow!"

Hiking one leg up, I casually sat on the edge of the mattress, my smirk now forming into a very entertained smile. *"Rainbow?"*

Her shoulders heaved with her labored breathing. *"My mercy plea."*

I shrugged. *"No such thing as mercy exists here."*

She suddenly, angrily, screamed, *"Rainbow!"*

Harry pushed back against the chair he was sitting in, clearly desiring distance from the situation he was far from understanding.

Coolly, I pointed to him, while telling the woman, *"You are scaring the child."*

To know what kind of person I was dealing with, I studied her reaction. After observing Junior, she immediately tried to compose herself. It was shocking how quickly she was able to calm herself for appearance's sake. This told me her line of work was a stressful one. She was far too accustomed to immediate role reversal. She inhaled through her nose then stood, no longer leaning against the wall she had viewed as a safety net. Even her tone had changed dramatically, as the woman told Harry, *"I'm sorry. There has just been a misunderstanding. Please, do not be afraid."*

Harry looked at me, clueless of what was spoken to him due to the language barrier. I raised a hand to him, asking for silence, but asked the woman, *"Your profession?"*

Her shoulders proudly set back. *"I am a nurse."* Her gaze dropped to my bloodied shirt.

My eyes tiredly closed. This was making much more sense now. Father had kidnapped this woman to help with my stab wound. I knew this meant Uncle was out of town. Reopening my eyes, I stood. She slammed her back to the wall,

not sure where to run. Exhaling, I raised both palms to show a truce. It was a false truce, but exhaustion had me temporarily bending the rules.

She eased before nodding in surrender.

I patted my chest, over the red blotch. *"You are here for this."* I gestured to the bathroom door. *"Will you join me?"*

Attempting to smile at Harry to keep him calm, yet epically failing as her lips trembled, she started toward me. *"The door is locked?"*

I nodded. *"Yes. You saw me lock it."*

She shook her head and pointed to the bathroom. *"No. That one."*

Reaching back into my pocket, I explained, *"That must be due to having medical supplies present."*

We both headed to the bathroom door, the woman behind me. I strategically did this to earn her trust.

"Yury?"

As I turned to face my American guest, who was confused by the whole conversation in Russian, the woman backed away, continuing to watch my every move. Now, I was inhaling for patience. I had not given her permission to move. Trying not to lock my jaw, I told Harry, "It is okay. She is a nurse. I was… stabbed yesterday," *by your mother,* "and need to have it looked after."

In the bathroom, the nurse took in her surroundings. My bathroom was large. To the right, after entering, was the long counter with two sinks, and a mirror covered the whole wall. To the left was a walk-in shower with tan marble and glass walls. Straight ahead was a large sunken Jacuzzi tub. In the left corner, between the tub and shower, was the toilet. It was best to have it exposed to gain control over my slaves while training. Most of the coloring was beige because I found it soothing—something needed after a long day in the basement—for both me and my pets.

Sitting on the edge of the tub, I pointed to the ample amount of medical supplies in a box, then removed my white button-down. *"What is your name?"*

The nurse fingered through the necessities while telling me, *"I wish to*

keep my name private."

I had to force down a chuckle. She believed her name would matter after being in my presence. This delusional woman thought she was going to return to her normal life. "*Do you work at a hospital?*"

"*No. A pediatric office.*"

Now, I understood her affection toward Junior. I also understood her wanting her twisted fantasies being kept private. I tossed my soiled shirt into a corner, knowing a slave would retrieve it in the morning. "*Oh, yes, back to this 'agreement.' Can you please explain?*" I knew what it was but wanted to hear her voice her stupidity.

As if trying to appear confident, the nurse walked toward me, but I could smell her fear. And I liked it. "*Shouldn't you know?*"

"*Possibly, but I do not.*"

Her educated eyes scanned my chest, then her eyes widened. "*You had your wound cauterized?*"

With my hands resting in my lap, I confirmed, "*Needed to stop the bleeding.*"

She took a step closer, then stopped. "*Please, do not touch me.*"

I linked my fingers together, planning on doing so much more than merely touching her, but the game was amusing and keeping me awake.

Accepting my silent promise of lies, she dared to step closer. As her fingers grazed my chest, my dick hardened. Her inner strength reminded me of the woman who had stabbed me earlier. My mouth watered for revenge.

The nurse's hips naturally swayed while heading back to the bathroom counter. She fiddled with the box of tidbits then returned to rub a solution on my burn. Bandaging me, she explained, "*There is not much I can do for you here. We should go to the hospital.*"

Clearly, that was not on the agenda, hence her present predicament, but I admired her effort for reasoning with the unreasonable. "*Tell me more of the agreement,*" I peered up at her, "*Rainbow.*" Fear crossed her face for an instant

before she hid it. I was toying with her by making her 'mercy plea' her new pet name.

Attempting to appear unfazed, she replied, "*My friend had a wild scenario she wanted to experience.*" Her cheeks blushed before whispering, "*I did, too.*"

"*Did?*" My curiosity was building by the second.

She threw the bandage packaging in the trash, next to the toilet by the shower. "*I didn't expect the kidnapping to feel so… real.*"

My tongue sucked at my teeth, hunger growing. "*You were expecting it?*"

As if trying not to sound like the moron she was, she dismissively said, "*As to our emails, our 'agreement,' of course, I did. I have the weekend off from work, so it was perfect timing for the—*" Her eyes snapped to mine.

I waited, but she said nothing more. "*So, you and your friend discussed this scenario, yet you are the one who sought it out? To actually go through with it?*"

This woman had signed up for a fictional kidnapping, not realizing when she was online, she was speaking to one of my employees. We have men who speak with all kinds of girls and women, searching for love. Occasionally, we get a woman who is looking to fulfill a fantasy. There are possibly kind pretenders, willing to abduct and follow rules and guidelines. And then there is us.

With regret, Rainbow glanced to the floor. "*I did. I was looking for…*" Her eyes closed. "*I'm not sure now.*"

"*What was the kidnapper supposed to do with you?*"

Rainbow shook her head.

"*Oooooh.*" I leaned back, acting surprised. "*Rape.*"

"*Tell me this is all part of the act. Tell me I'm not in real trouble.*"

As gently as possible, my fingers grazed hers. "*Of course, this is all part of the coercion. I just had to be sure you truly wanted to use your mercy plea.*"

She dropped to her knees, squeezing my hands. "*Thank God.*" Her eyes opened to see me as she grabbed her chest with one hand, desperately holding on

to me with the other. *"I was so scared."*

I smirked. *"You paid good money, no?"*

She nodded emphatically. *"A whole paycheck."*

Yes, we took her money—that she would no longer have a use for—tricked her, and planned on selling her. *"We also had to be sure you and I are a good match. Are you attracted to me?"*

It is amazing to watch someone lie to themselves. Her reality begged her to see all the signs, but her mind was so terrified it chose to believe my deceit. The truth was simply too much for her to comprehend; the child in my bedroom, the bolts on every door, the windows that would never open, the wound on my chest, the fact that we allowed her to see where we resided, and her instincts screaming for her to run.

All. Ignored.

Still on her knees, she scooted closer to me. *"Now that I know you're not a real rapist or murderer, yes. You are very handsome."*

I smoothed down her hair and fed her more lies. *"True rapists are out for control, not the sexual act. Clearly, I have no control here, yet I have an erection."* Her cheeks lit up with a shade of rose, and she smiled bashfully. *"And I bet the sex is not what you are truly after either. You want to be dominated."* Her eyes slid shut as her breathing picked up. I slid a thumb over her nipple to check if she was aroused by my insight. The bud was hard as could be. This flower was ready for the picking. My free hand slid up her neck then lightly fisted her hair. *"Touch my dick."*

Without opening her brown eyes, her hand blindly searched for my crotch. When she found my hard-on, her head fell back slightly, as if she needed to believe I wanted intercourse. I did want it, but for the control I spoke of rapists desiring. I had every intention of owning her against her will. I had every intention of taking out my frustration with Mrs. Thompson for making me *aware*. I wanted my numb state of mind back, something I would now chase until my demise.

Her lips rose to touch mine. I yanked on her hair. *"Rapists don't kiss. We must keep your fantasy as real as possible."*

She moaned, completely unaware of how real all this was going to get.

CHAPTER EIGHT

Strong Wills

Falling... How far do you descend into hell before feeling the fire?   How many flames need to singe your flesh—your soul—before you realize there is a desperate need to escape the heat?

For me, I had to fall so far down; most don't literally have the strength to climb back up from the pits of hell. Seeing what you have become is the most painful part of the journey. The reflection in the self-imposed mirror is nothing short of a demon. Not many want to look into the eyes of the horrendous and see their spirit laughing at all the suffering of others.

Opening the door that led to the basement, my cellphone vibrated. It was a message from Kirill saying he had the filming room ready. I was sure to hide my phone's screen, but halfway down the stairs, Rainbow finally started to acknowledge her instincts. Unfortunately, it was far too late. When she didn't follow me down the next step, the monster in me smiled. My fun was about to begin. I was finally going to get to break the strong woman in her. Shredding her independence and forcing her to need me for the basics of life was going to give me immense pleasure. I knew my eyes were gleaming satisfaction as I faced her, planting my feet, preparing for the delicious battle to come. My nostrils flared to inhale as much of her fear as possible. The scent seeped into my devil-spawned pores, fueling my hunger to epic levels.

Sensing the evil before her, a visible tremble racked her whole body. *"You lied."*

"As did you, to yourself, thinking this prepaid sexual scheme was a good idea." I licked my lips while staring her down, daring her to deny it. Like a

vampire needing blood, I watched her throat as she swallowed.

I beamed with dark desires as she stubbornly set her proud shoulders back, ready to defend herself. *"Who are you, and why am I here?"*

"Who am I?" My hands opened and closed as I fought for control. I wanted to throttle her for her lack of respect. *"I am your Master."* I didn't need to look behind me. Rainbow's eyes widened, let me know Kirill and Adrian now flanked me on the stairs. *"Why are you here?"* I could feel their hunger, too. I was delivering an unexpected treat, after a long time on the road. *"To be fucked, as requested."*

After silence hung between us, Rainbow spun on her toes and rushed back up the stairs. Three chuckles followed her as she pounded on the door that automatically locked after being shut. All masters had a remote in their pockets to allow exits and entries.

At the top of the stairs, there was nowhere for her to go, so I pursued. Once to her, I pressed my chest to her back, pushing her stomach against the door. In her ear, I whispered, *"Is this the rape scenario you were hoping for?"*

An elbow crashed back, slamming into my mouth. My upper lip split on impact. Blood gushed as I cursed in Russian. Kirill and Adrian reached over my shoulders to try and subdue the enraged woman. The four of us struggled in the confined area, but soon, Rainbow was subdued. Her legs tried to kick, and her arms fought to swing, causing us to make our way back down the stairs clumsily. When she saw a naked female slave on her knees in the hallway, properly submissive, her rage doubled. When we got to the door of the filming room, Kirill and Adrian held her still so I could remove my clothing and put on a black hooded silk robe that covered my identity.

Rainbow was one of the strongest willed women I had ever had the pleasure of breaking. It was as if she blacked out. Fear was gone, and rage was present, all feeding my dark soul. Once properly robed, I grabbed her by the throat. Not being able to breathe was the only action that refocused her will to fight. She pulled at my men's tight hold, trying to break free. At my mark, they

released her, and her hands clutched at my tight grip around her neck. I told them, "Robe up. Meet you in there. I'm having her first."

Peering at the light above the door, I waited. When the light bulb lit up, I knew we were recording. Flashes of Mrs. Thompson's face kept entering my line of sight as I shoved Rainbow backward into the cold block room that consisted of only a mattress. My voice was muffled under the thick hood, better disguising me. "*I hope you scream for me. I hope every man who jacks off to your pleas knows that you wanted this.*"

She was trying to speak but had already run out of oxygen. I had yet to release my vice grip blocking her airway. When I finally released her, she was so busy gasping that she didn't see my strike coming. I smacked her across the face so hard she slammed to the concrete floor. I gave her no time to collect her wits. I dragged her back to her feet by her hair.

With an arm wrapped around her waist from behind, I put my mouth to her ear while holding her face to the camera. Blood from her busted lip dripped to my fingers as I whispered, "*Your family will search for you, but you will never be found. The only ones to ever see you again will pay top dollar to watch me violate you in whatever way they choose.*" Her chest panted from under my hold as I now pointed her view to a monitor. Text appeared through the web feed as men typed what they wanted to witness…

Close up of her cunt as you…

Double penetration…

Come on her face…

Bite her nipple…

She tried to pull her face from mine as I licked up the side of her cheek, salty tears dancing on my tongue. "*Be careful what you wish for.*"

Her head leaned back against my chest as she wailed at the ceiling, where more cameras filmed me breaking her with only words… to start with.

Harry was asleep in the chair when I reentered my bedroom. I was back to being exhausted. The lack of sleep from the trip had me in need of a shower and a good night's rest. Without turning on bedroom lights, I slipped into the bathroom for a shower.

Hot water was jetting against my back when Rainbow entered, naked. Through the glass, I studied her dragging her feet as she headed for the toilet. Makeup was smeared under her eyes and down her cheeks from all the tears I expertly pulled from her. Wiping a hand down my face to see past the water, I watched her. She winced as she cautiously sat. When I left the film room, Kirill and Adrian were almost done fucking her at the same time. They knew to bring her back to me when done so that training could continue.

The toilet flushed as she slowly walked toward the sink. Fresh water wet her face before she stared at her broken reflection in the mirror. The glass wasn't broken, but her spirit most certainly was. Her eyes were shadowed with wisdom she now wished to be without.

When she reached into the medical box, I snapped through the opening of the shower, "*Did you get permission?*"

Hips, bruised from being manhandled, lazily scraped against the countertop, due to the lack of energy to turnaround without support. Her shaky hand held up a prescription bottle.

With no sympathy at all, I grinned. "*Need another round to help you sleep?*"

Her bloody and swollen lip kept her mouth from moving much, but she managed, "*I hurt.*"

Suggestively, I grabbed my dick. "*I bet you do.*" Her eyes closed as she looked away, almost as if feeling ill. "*Open your eyes.*"

When she did, I finger-gestured for her to come to me. With a blank, almost dead expression, she did. I held my wet hand out for the bottle. After reading the label, I told her, "*Only two,*" and handed it back to her. "*I don't want*

103

you to try and overdose."

Standing before me, she sneered while opening the bottle and popping two pills in her palm. *"Who would ever want to kill themselves instead of spending the evening with you?"*

Those words sliced a nerve I didn't know was exposed. With blinding speed, I grabbed the nape of her neck and jerked her close. Leftover cum rubbed from her chest to mine. *"Be careful, or you will anger me before training even begins."*

Face to face, I could see tears flood her eyes. *"Training?"*

"You didn't think I was going to let you go, did you?"

Her terrified, panting breath brushed across my lips. *"Please?"*

"Your ride has only just begun." Her brown eyes started to slide shut again, so I jerked my fingers in her hair. *"Did I give you permission to close your eyes?"*

Rainbow's jaw locked. *"No."*

"No, what?"

She refused to speak, her eyes defiant, so I pinched her nipple. After a squeal, and a hand blocking any further attack but not breaking free of my hold, she replied, *"No, sir."*

"Master."

She winced but gave me what I wanted. *"Master."*

"Good, Pet. Now, open your mouth." I glared at her until she obeyed. Her tongue was exposed as I pulled her head back by her hair and guided it under the streaming water so she could fill her mouth. After pulling her head out from the water, I tapped her hand. She popped the two pills in her mouth. *"Swallow."* After she gulped them down, I pulled her whole body in the shower with me, pill bottle and all. Putting her back to my stomach, I reached around her hips. *"Spread your legs."* I knew she didn't want to be one but loved that she was already a better student. It didn't bother me that we had to fuck obedience into her.

Cupping her sore core, I spoke into her ear. *"One of the worst parts of*

being my pet is coming on command." Her body stiffened. *"I just fucked you against your will, but I still didn't make you mine."* I rubbed two fingers against her nub, knowing it would respond, no matter how much she hated me.

After a few moments, I slipped a finger inside her. The moisture spoke of her own betrayal. *"There. See? She wants me,"* I cooed, positive the sound of my voice was like rubbing her skin against a cheese grater.

She shook her head, trying to gain control I was denying, always would. Her voice now trembled for other reasons than fear. *"P-Please stop."*

"I love to hear you beg."

She fought it, but soon she was panting, her head hanging forward. *"I-I don't want to do this."*

My touch became more vigorous. *"Because fucking you is nowhere near as bad as me making your body perform for me."* With her so close to her orgasm, I said, *"Your body is listening to me now, not you."* My hand expertly sent her over the edge, against her will, robbing her of so much more than another sexual experience. *"Now, it belongs to me."* As she came on my hand, she shed tears of regret and shame.

Before she could even recover, I pushed her out of my shower. *"There's a bed on the floor. Be sure to find it and stay out of mine."* She stumbled to the counter. Not facing me, she held up the bottle by her slumped shoulders, needing permission to leave it. Already, she was learning more. *"Leave it in the box."* Her hand lowered as she tiredly nodded before leaving the bathroom.

A towel was wrapped around my damp, naked waist as I exited the bathroom, leftover steam filling the cold air in the bedroom. I had stayed under the hot spray of water until I could barely stand any longer. In America, my stabbing, killing an innocent, and grudge-fucking my new pet had sucked me dry. The only thing I desired at this point was my mattress, not the distant sniffling.

Teeter-tottering whether to go to sleep or get pissed, I turned on a nightstand lamp. "Harry, it is late. Can you please cry tomorrow?" He didn't

answer, nor was he in his chair, so I walked around my bed to see him sitting on the floor, in the corner, with Rainbow, naked, lying limp over the thighs of his stretched-out legs. "Fuck!" I raced to him and dropped to my knees, clamping my palms over her bloody wrist, her inner thighs...

This nurse knew she needed to slit her jugulars and major arteries to create the greatest damage. Blood soaked the carpet, me, and Junior.

Rainbow's eyes were open, her head facing the young man, but she was far from him now. Her empty stare told me so. I roared, "Why didn't you call for me?"

Affectionately, his bloodied hand wiped at her hair. "Sh-She..."

"Are you cut?" I grabbed at his hands, quick to examine him.

Harry cried, "No. No. It's hers." His eyes were full of confusion and sorrow. "What did you say to her?"

I blinked. "What?" I had never been asked to be responsible for my words by anyone except Mrs. Fucking Thompson, who was still haunting me from across the world. It somehow seemed ironic her son was now asking the same.

"Sh-She..."

"Fucking speak, Harry!"

"I think she wanted me to let her die! Every time I tried to help her, she stopped me!" Gasping for air and reason, his chest heaved. "What happened to her? Why is she hurt?" He stared at the scalpel on the carpet, lying next to us. "She kept handing it to me, wanting me to cut myself." His terrified stare found mine again. "But I can't. I—" He started shaking his head "no" as if headed for a mental breakdown.

I laid my hand on his shoulder. "Junior. Tell me."

His breaths were uneven as if his lungs were seizing. "I couldn't do what she wanted... because I made Timothy a promise." Tears and heartbreak burst from this kid. He was holding his second dead body in a matter of days. "I must find Little T! I don't want to fail him!" On the brink of hysterics, Harry wailed,

all while petting Rainbow's bloody hair. "Timothy is dead, and I have to find her!"

The naked woman in his lap, her blood, snot dripping from his nose, and his utter distress had memories of my murdered mother pelting me and my still forming conscience. Harry was beyond distraught, just like I had been the night that doorbell rang. Harry was young, unbelievably sheltered, considering his upbringing. It made me feel compelled to help him, as I wished someone had helped me the night I found my mother's naked, butchered body. So, I got up and went to my cellphone on the nightstand, and texted Kirill and Adrian.

Returning to Harry, I began to pull the corpse from his legs. His hands gripped but lost purchase, due to me coldly insisting he let go. He asked me to stop, but I kept dragging her across the room. "Learn to let go, Junior."

Holding the sides of his head as if to prevent an explosion in his mind, he cried, "Let go of what? I don't even know her name! Do you?"

My Rainbow's body stilled as I realized I'd indirectly caused a death, not even knowing the name of the dead body. I remembered Mrs. Thompson in the SUV, in my lap, telling me, *"And you don't even know my name."* In our line of work, names were obsolete. By Junior's expression, that was a horrid fact that disgusted him.

The young man I had forced to join me in Russia, Harry Thompson Junior, began to mature right before my eyes. His hands rubbed down his face, aging with every passing second. "You said I'm here to learn, to be trained." His voice lowered as he shifted into manhood with only one unwavering mental step. "To become like you." His blue eyes filled with determination and promise of future wisdom as they glared at me. "I won't. I refuse to *ever* be as cold as you. I have no idea what happened to you, and I don't think I want to know what made you like this." He gestured to the dead hand in mine. "But that? You? I will never be." He rose from the floor, lifting his chin with an admirable might. "I may be no match for you now, so I will train, but I promise to save some young girl someday to make up for all this." He pointed to Rainbow, who no longer shined

with the colors of life. "For all your destructive, reaper ways."

Time stood still for me as another promise he would later fulfill was made.

CHAPTER NINE

Continuing Cycles

6 Months later

Can danger bring about puberty? The answer is, yes. Did nature sense the need for immediate growth? Did nature know Harry needed muscles and *iron* balls in order to survive me? I would've once answered no, but that was before I witnessed Junior's transformation.

Living with me and my men, Junior was under constant threat. Danger caused his body to race to maturity, so he could defend himself.

For the rest of us in the mansion, being strong was a job requirement. We handled both women and men. Young, strong men, we had to overpower and turn into submissive slaves. So, we exercised vigorously. Not with actual weights, but with our own unique program. On one end of the house, we had a gym made of obstacles. Concentrated arm, core, and leg strength were needed to get from beginning to end. Using long ropes hanging from the ceiling, we climbed flat walls with only a slight tilt and rocks walls, and would then body roll to our next challenge.

This room became a perfect distraction for Junior. He loved it and strived to be an expert in strength and mobility. He would ask to be permitted its use for extra hours every day. It seemed to be his outlet from all the confusion driving him mad. His circumstance, being held captive at such a young age, was beyond comprehension for him. So, we attempted to ease him into the whys of the Elites present. We explained what we had been taught, that the Elites liked this treatment, but he was not easily convinced. In fact, he wasn't convinced at all as

he witnessed women having to earn meals with sexual favors. He would gesture to the Elite in a submissive position. "She's not smiling."

Kirill would smirk while unbuckling his pants. "That's because she hasn't had breakfast yet." To the slave, he demanded, "Open your mouth…" Junior would recoil and turn away. Kirill would only laugh. "Junior, try it before you judge."

Junior refused every available Elite. I refused to force his first sexual act. I needed him on board. I needed him to enjoy his new job so that he could lead this training in America. Until he was willing, we taught him every detail we knew of the drug trade. Adrian had been involved with it for years before joining our force. We also taught him about guns. He was an impressive shot.

Entering the kitchen, where I was sitting, Junior demanded, "It's my birthday. I want a tattoo."

Junior was now fourteen-years-old. "And you're telling me this, why?" I took a sip of coffee while nodding to Adrian, who had escorted Junior so that I could take over watching him.

Junior further explained, "I want you to make it happen. You killed my brother and stole me from my family. I'd say you owe me."

Unable to deny the kidnapping, I sneered. "That murder wasn't mine."

He countered, "Well, Tim's murder was."

Ignoring guilt, I shrugged. "I don't see your point."

Junior stepped around the slave I was feeding and took a seat across the table from me. He pointed along his neck. "I want 'Life' with the date 'Nineteen-eighty-two,' the year my brother was born."

I placed cheese in the Elite's mouth. "Aren't those numbers along your jugular a bit dramatic?"

Resting his interlocked fingers behind his head to stretch his growing biceps, he stared at me, seemingly lost in thought. "I can't believe I am going to say this, but I feel sorry for you."

That pissed me off, causing the Elite to cower while I growled, "Never

pity the devil. It's dangerous."

No longer crippled by daily fear, Junior ignored me. "So, you'll make it happen?"

Fighting a grin of respect, I asked, "How are your studies coming?"

He switched to Russian. *"Very well. Thank you for asking, asshole."*

I caved and smiled. *"The Elite teaching you Russian is doing a fine job. Has she sucked your dick yet?"*

Junior not answering me *was* the answer. No.

Rounded shoulders moved as Junior reared back his arm. His fist soared forward with such speed, Kirill was stunned as he dropped to his knees. My laughter boomed throughout my father's large living room, filled with wall to wall windows. The sun was shining off the snow on the ground outside; hence, the living room now a boxing ring. Kneeling slaves stayed off to the sides, near the furniture. They were to keep their eyes down, as always, but I ignored their peeks. I dare say I enjoyed them finding entertainment beyond servitude training. I blamed the new irrational thought pattern on the young man I was coming to appreciate. His youth and drive to survive was so similar to my own story, it almost saddened me to know his outcome would be no better, no kinder, than mine.

From the ground, Kirill wiped his busted lip while speaking in Russian. *"This is not funny."*

"Yes, it is."

Kirill snarled at Junior. *"Stop speaking my language."*

Adrian bellowed, *"Junior's fist crashed into your skull!"*

Junior repeated a word he had yet to learn, *"Crashed?"*

I explained in English, "Ram. Hit. Crash."

Light on his feet as trained, Junior bounced around, fist ready for another

target. He was smiling at his accomplishment—Kirill on the floor—and his next opponent. "Adrian, ready for me to *crash* into you?"

Staring at Junior's tattoo, *Life 1982*, I uttered, "*Crash*." My eyes lit up. "New name?"

Smirking, Adrian lifted his fist and took a fighter's stance. "How about it, Crash?"

Crash appeared proud. "I think I like it."

Adrian shrugged. "The name is appropriate for dealing drugs. When an addict crashes after a high, they will search for the one to save them."

'Crash' charged Adrian and rammed his fist into his face. I guess he didn't appreciate the sentiment.

It would be encouraging to say we had many enjoyable times like this during Crash's stay in Russia, but it is not so. These light-hearted moments were few and far between. Moments Crash wished had never happened. He had become somewhat accustomed to Elites in his presence, yet still always left the room when sexual endeavors were demanded of the slaves. He hated when I brought trainees to our room. I may have fed him well, a mistake I would later not repeat in order to keep my hostage much weaker, but I made him sleep on an Elite bed on the floor to remind him of his place.

While plowing into a slave on my bed to get Junior accustomed to witnessing sexual acts, I would peer over my shoulder to see him lying on his side, hands covering his ears, eyes slammed shut. His right bicep was bandaged due to his new tattoo.

In the early mornings, while pretending I was sleeping, I would watch him, lying on the slave bed on the floor, staring out the window above my desk, as if longing for freedom. In years to come, another American would lay there with the same longing stare, wishing to be anywhere but there.

Even though a part of Crash liked me, most of him hated me. We had a very twisted relationship that skirted between respect, curiosity, and a desire to not be lonely. We both were. We were both trapped in a hidden world only the

deprived and corrupt were daring enough to willingly be a part of. And, as much as I cared for Crash—saw him as a younger brother—I kept abusive cycles in proper working order.

Repeat...

At the basement door in the foyer, Crash shook his head. "Don't make me go down there."

My hand nervously tinkered with the remote in my pocket, deep down, knowing what I was doing was wrong. "But you do not know what takes place there. Why fret?"

"Because I see the girls you bring up from down there. I see the emptiness in their eyes. Something down there robs them of hope."

I shook my head, dumbfounded by his wisdom at such a young age. "Crash, it is a profession you are acquiring. You must face this."

"But it's not one I've agreed to!" His now longer legs started pacing across the white marble. He brushed his dark, now longer hair from his eyes. "I've learned everything you have asked. I know the contents of Crack, Meth, Coke, Molly... I know prices in most countries. I know how to smell out a snitch or cop, but there are certain things I can't *un*know, Yury. Don't drag me into your hell. If there is any part of you that gives a damn about me, at all, don't make me see the Elites before they become so..." he winced, as if not sure to be disgusted or filled with mercy, "obedient."

If you care about someone's opinion, you don't want to hear it when you know they're right, yet you hope they're wrong. "Meh." I shrugged and repeated, "They like what we do to them."

"You sound like Kirill." Crash stopped, his shoulders deflating. "Tell me it's an act." His hands jerked through the heavy air drowning me. "Tell me you don't really believe this bullshit!"

I sneered. "Are you saying my life is bullshit?" My hands now started to tremble with anger.

Crash heatedly inhaled then exhaled. "You put leashes on human beings

as if they have no rights. So, yeah, I guess I am." I stormed forward to get chest to chest. I was still taller so I was sure to hover, reminding him who could win if we were to exchange blows, but he didn't retreat. In fact, he lifted his chin and continued his stubborn streak. "I don't care what you do to me. Beat me down if you have to, but I'm not training and selling sex slaves."

Taking one step back, I licked my drying lips. "What if I gave you the opportunity to save one?"

"You're lying."

"I guess you'll never know." I turned, clicked my remote, and opened the basement door.

Proud of my trickery, I smirked, hearing Crash race down the stairs to follow me. "H-How can I save one?" His eyes were racing around, studying his surroundings.

Passing closed doors, I simply replied, "Pick one. And claim her." I peered over my shoulder. "Or him, if that's what you're into." I winked.

"Fuck you. I'm not gay."

"Neither am I, but I fuck men." Crash's mouth opened as if he had just tasted a rotten lemon. I chuckled. "A hole is a hole."

"Bull. Shit."

In front of the door where Crash's prize was being kept, unbeknownst to him, I stopped and faced him. "How would you know? Ever been inside *anyone*?"

He tried to lift his chin again, but his eyes couldn't meet mine. Crash was a virgin.

I nodded toward a closed door. "One I think you will want to claim is in there."

"Claim? Jesus, Yury."

After pulling a blue-jeweled collar and leash form my other pocket, I dangled them from my finger, hoping to tempt the saint. "*Claimed* ones are not permitted to be touched by anyone other than their owner. Up to you. Kirill has

114

been eyeing her. Maybe she likes older men." It was a lie. She was far too old for Kirill's true likings.

Crash's whole body flinched. "How *young* is she?"

Acting bored instead of showing a pained reaction to his disappointment, I repeated, "A hole is a hole. What does it matter?"

Crash shoved me backward. "I fucking hate you!"

Stumbling back a couple of steps, I laughed while tossing him the leash and collar. "Go walk your straight and narrow path, Savior."

He gawked at the items in his hand before turning toward the closed door. Then he stood there staring at the bland, dark grey door while stuffing the jeweled restraints in his back jeans pocket. His eyes slid shut in surrender as a new abductee, down the cold hallway, cried out through training she was yet accustomed to. I had instructed for rooms to remain quiet to not spook Crash before we began, but it seemed to be perfect timing. His forehead fell forward and rested on the cold door, as if he might pass out at any moment, again aging before my eyes. Mother Nature was calling on all powers to toss him deeper into manhood so he could possibly save an innocent. But not even Mother Nature was that powerful.

After locking Crash in the room, I raced to the viewing room. TV monitors were all over the walls, showing us the inside of each captive's quarters. Kirill and Adrian were already watching the one where Crash was slowly approaching a terrified girl, huddled on the floor in the corner. In Russian, I said, "*Turn it up.*" The room was barely lit, but I could hear Crash gasp at her torn clothes. "*Nice touch,*" I told Kirill.

On the monitor, Crash held up his hands. "*I won't hurt you.*"

I asked Adrian, "*She's Russian?*" I wanted an American for Crash, as that was what a waiting client had requested. Normally, Father left the children

115

training to other organizations, but we'd acquired a client who refused to work with any other business due to a "friend" highly recommending us. I was about to start yelling at my stupid minions but then heard the girl cry, "I don't know what you're saying."

"Oh, shit. You're American," said a startled Crash.

As she sat up, long blonde hair fell from her hidden face. Her left cheek had a cut from a firm smack, but, other than that, she was absolutely stunning. She looked as if she'd just stepped out of the magazine titled, Every Young Man's Wet Dream.

Crash's step faltered.

My eyes widened at the screen, and then I gawked at Kirill. He gestured to Adrian at my other side. *"He is the one who picked her out."*

I clamped Adrian's shoulder and shook it. *"My God, man! She is perfection. I will own Crash with this girl."*

Father entered the viewing room. *"And our client will devour her. He has requested Tanner stage four."*

Some would say our client had a mental disorder, due to his craving of children on the older side. We claimed he simply had a sexual preference. It just so happened his preference was to witness the completion of puberty, and possibly grope and have sex with them along the way.

Adrian bobbed his head left to right, appearing somewhat proud of this rare find, as her smooth voice echoed over the monitor. "You're American, too?"

Crash covered his mouth, I think still in awe of the gorgeous creature in front of him, but he asked, "How old are you?" She searched behind Crash as if doubting whether or not she could trust him. He assured her, "I'm alone."

"I'm fourteen." Her eyes were huge, crystal blue doe circles of innocence. "How old are you?"

Crash ripped a piece of his shirt free and went to her sink. "I'm fourteen, too."

She studied him. "Your voice… You sound older."

"I feel like an old man after being here for so long." He wet the cloth then faced her, holding it up in an offering. "Can I come near you?"

After a long pause, and observing Crash top to bottom, she nodded.

Slowly, he approached, then squatted in front of her. They both winced as he dabbed her bloody cheek, but she was the one to speak. "I don't know why he hit me. I wasn't fighting back or anything. He just came in and hit me a couple of minutes ago."

Crash practically growled, "What did this asshole look like?"

"His hair was too light for such dark, scary eyes."

In the viewing room, I lifted a brow at Kirill. He shrugged while grabbing a chair. "*You said to make it appear convincing.*" He sat down, watching the monitor again. "*Look. It worked.*"

I grabbed a chair also. "*He already cares. Well done.*"

Father told me, "*She is to be delivered in four months. Another boy is being trained elsewhere. Our customer likes to watch the young fornicate, then join in.*" As if not just announcing a grim future for the two teenagers, he left the room.

On the TV screen, I studied the newly forming friendship while the girl studied Crash's expression. She asked, "You know him?"

"Yeah," he replied, still dabbing at her wound. "If it helps. I spar with him sometimes and hit him hard."

She nervously smirked. "Can you hit him harder next time?"

Crash smiled for the first time in weeks. "Consider it done."

"Do you know why I'm here?"

His hand fell from her face as he sat back on his bent legs, nodding in a gloomy manner. "How much did you see when you got here?"

She shook her head. "Didn't. But I know I've been tricked. I was supposed to—" She glanced down in shame.

"What?"

"I can't. I feel so stupid now."

"Hey, I have a feeling you are far from the only one these guys have tricked into being here. I won't judge you. I swear it."

Her head leaned back to the wall behind her. "There was this guy I was talking with online. He seemed to get me. I believed he cared for me." Her eyes welled. "He said he loved me." She sighed. "I was going to run away with him. I snuck out my window. Waiting for me in the car was not the hot guy who loved me. By the time I realized what was happening, I was shoved in the car. I felt a poke." She rubbed her arm where the needle had stabbed and drugged her. Choking on a whisper, she said, "Now, I'm here." With hopelessness, she shrugged. "Where's here?"

Crash's shoulders folded in. "Russia." She paled as her mouth gaped, and her eyes spoke of knowing she was in grave danger. He nodded and touched her knee. "I'm sorry they tricked you."

"Who are they?"

Crash swallowed. "Traffickers. They sell… girls."

"Oh, no." Her eyes slid shut. "Sexual slavery. My teacher spoke of this in class." A couple of tears slid down her smooth skin. "Running from one problem, I found a worse one."

"Problem?"

"My stepdad—" her eyes opened then deadened "—likes *me* more than my mom."

Repulsed, Crash cringed. "No."

As if used to the truth of abuse, she replied, "I so wanted to believe Chris loved me."

"Chris?"

"My boyfriend—online guy. I thought he was my boyfriend."

"Oh." Crash played with the shoelace of his sneaker then froze. "How long were you talking to him?"

"About three weeks. How long have you been here?"

"Over six months." After a couple of lingering moments of silence, Crash

asked, "What's your name?"

"Sam."

Sam was my last attempt at forcing Crash to become a trainer, a Master, in America. My father was able to desensitize me at a young age by taking away my very first pet. I was hoping to do the same with Crash. His father clearly wasn't the material for the job—hence, fucking Junior. But, I guess, their father-son similarities ran deep. Harold Thompson fell for his first slave, too.

Two days later, I rolled my eyes while unlocking the door Crash was banging on. I wasn't surprised he was irate when I finally opened it. He charged me. "We are fucking starving!" I let him shove me across the hallway and into the wall so that waiting Kirill could make his move. Crash froze when he heard the door behind him slam shut and lock. Then, he spun around to see Adrian smirking, leaning against the wall—right next to Sam's room.

Crash was already in protective mode. That tends to happen when someone inferior is looking to you for shelter. Sam was afraid her door would never open again when we refused to answer Crash's insistence to be set free, but she also feared what lay waiting in her future.

Once the drugs from her kidnapping had worn off, the cold room seeped into her body as if she'd been soaked in a tub of ice. She was from Florida and craved heat like a coldblooded snake. I had sat in the viewing room, witnessing some important physical bonding in the middle of the night. Sam had asked for Crash to leave the floor and lay in bed with her. Crash may have been only six inches taller than her, but he managed to wrap his growing body around hers as she burrowed close, anxious for warmth. The thin, dingy green blanket we provided was inadequate, as planned for all slaves. Hungry and cold for endless hours tended to make them desperate for options. Only providing cold water for showers also made them willing to partake in 'trades.' And so, the process of earning their keep began. Hence, no food for two days.

Frantic, Crash scanned the hallway. "Where's Kirill?"

Perfect timing had Sam screaming, "Get away from me," from inside the

room.

Crash was now ramming his shoulder into the door to get back in. I scoffed, "Do make up your mind, Crash. You wanted out. I'm starting to suspect you're unstable."

He ignored me, yanking on the locked doorknob and banging on the metal. "Kirill! Stay away from her!"

The two innocent young souls had truly bonded during their duress. Would they have done so in normal circumstances—a boy taking a girl to the movies? Fuck no, but that is not where I had them locked away. Being confined can be lonely, the unknown terrifying. So, they had talked and brought each other comfort, a connection that would prove to be hard to break.

Crash looked to Adrian. "Please. Give me a key." Adrian pointed to behind him where I was waiting for an audience. Crash smacked the door twice, more in frustration than trying to get in, then told me, "I won't be you."

"She's beautiful. What is the delay? Leash her."

Tiredly, he rolled along the door as he turned to face me. "It's wrong."

"Only according to you."

"I... I can't hurt her like you hurt the others."

I threw my hands into the air. "Who is asking you to mistreat her? I'm only asking you to claim her before someone else does."

Crash jerked when Sam beat on the door behind him, crying out, "Crash! Help me!"

He spun again, his forehead to the door, telling her, "You don't understand what they want."

"H-He's trying to pull down my pants!"

Crash roared to the ceiling, then to me. "Stop him!"

It was now or never. I had to push the kid over the edge of his morals. "She is free game! We have rules! Ones you are refusing to follow."

Another scream came from Sam as the doorknob jiggled, a clear sign of her trying to escape. Then it stopped moving. I was impressed by Kirill's

ingenuity when I heard the springs on the little cot squeak, Sam begging for help. "Crash! Do whatever they want! Please!"

"Kirill!" screamed Crash. A fist opened up long enough to pull the leash and collar from his back pocket. He held it in the air above his head. "I'm claiming her right now!" He faced me with a rage that was impressive for such a young man. He screamed in Russian, *"Call him off her!"*

Delighted to have won this round, I nodded. *"As you wish."* To the door, I shouted, *"Kirill. Well done."* I head-gestured for Adrian to unlock the door.

As soon as Adrian opened the door, a disheveled and horrified Sam flew through the doorway, running straight into Crash's chest, burying her face from all surrounding witnesses.

Crash's arms blanketed her as they panted together, backing away from us. "I'm so sorry, Sam."

"H-He almost—"

Crash wrapped his arms tighter, her long blonde hair getting tangled around them. "He won't again." When his back hit the wall behind him, the three of us men slowly closed in, being sure his promise—his claim—was solidified. Our unified approach was intimidating. Crash's wide eyes told me so. He may have been trained, and a natural fighter, but no fourteen-year-old had a true chance against our extensive experience and icy hearts.

Swallowing, Crash raised a palm, silently begging for us to stop. We didn't. We only prowled forward. Kirill even added a tug at his crotch to remind Crash of his capabilities. Crash blew out a shaky breath then finally said, "Keep your eyes closed, Sam." Her head bobbed as she nodded, refusing to let him go. When his arms released her to open the collar, she pushed into him. He laid his head to the top of hers. It was impressive how fast the simple gesture settled her tense body. In what felt like only hours, they had become emotionally intertwined.

Crash ran his hands under her hair and up her back, his eyes filling with water. Her hair moved as his hands started wrapping the collar around her neck.

Sam slowly peered up at him. I don't know what those doe eyes were asking him, but Crash whispered, "If I don't," he moved his stare to Kirill, "someone else will."

I explained, "You two will be staying in my room from now on."

As Crash's mouth fell open, he pulled Sam to his chest again as if he suspected we were about to steal her from him. "But you only have Elites in your room." He tightened his hold on her, Sam most willing to be protected. "I claimed her as you asked."

I took a step back to offer confirmation. "And no one will touch her." Kirill and Adrian took a step back also. "Only you."

Sam's body moved with Crash's as he started to struggle for breath. He switched to Russian while growling words at me. *"Yury, you said she's mine. That I could save her."*

I lied. "And she is." I was sure to speak in English so Sam would know Crash was trustworthy. "You *can* save her, as long as you want her, but she still has to be a part of what we are."

Crash argued, *"That means 'training.' Not part of our deal."*

"What exactly do you think you're claiming her for? Cupcakes and tea parties?"

"You fucking prick."

"As long as you use yours, she will be safe. Now, speak English."

His jaw locked, and his nostrils flared. "I don't trust you."

You shouldn't. "Why? I have kept my word."

"What happens when I go home?"

"Meh." I shrugged. "What do you want to happen?"

His hand sheltered her head. "Take her with me."

"Done." *Never going to happen.* "Just follow the rules while you're here. Example," I gestured down the hall in the direction of the stairs, "she is always to follow you. She cannot be treated as your equal."

Crash's voice shook, "Yury, you know I can't—"

He stopped when Sam grabbed the front of his shirt, peering up at him again. "Get me through this and back to America." Her eyes welled. "I want to go home."

I internally smiled, listening to her plead. I knew Crash couldn't deny her, even though he was the wiser of the two. His expression was already apologizing for all that was to come while he forced a slight smile and nodded. Taking hold of her leash, he told her, "Upstairs is going to shock you, but I won't let you become one of them." Their stares locked on each other as she, reluctantly, released him and moved to stand behind him. Crash inhaled and stepped away from the wall. "No one is to touch her."

Seeing naked, kneeling slaves did make Sam gasp. I was surprised when Crash demanded, "Eyes down," as he led her up the marble stairs toward my bedroom. Sam appeared startled at his harsh tone, but she did as told.

Behind the two, I nodded to Kirill and Adrian, impressed that Crash had learned more than suspected. No wonder he feared for Sam and knew what was going to be asked of her.

In the bedroom, after locking the door, I poked the young bear with a reminder. "Clothes are not an option." I laughed as Crash barreled into me, knocking us both off-kilter and into my nightstand, the lamp falling to the ground with a thud. "I guess I need to train *you* first." Grabbing the back of his neck, I tossed him off me. Backing away in the direction I threw him, Crash corralled Sam behind him, not daring to turn his back to me. Picking the lamp off the ground, I smirked while telling Sam, "He does not get to eat until you strip."

Before she could respond, Crash growled, "I'm fine with starving."

I answered in a casual tone as I headed for the door, "That is irresponsible training, Crash. It has already been two days. How much longer can your pet last?" In the hallway, I turned around. "I'm going to the kitchen to eat my dinner now." And I shut the door.

They lasted two more days…

Sam was the one to cave. She had to be. Crash was never going to ask her to strip for me. He begged her not to, probably knowing it would eventually lead to more, but she touched his concerned face then unbuttoned her shirt. Her breasts were small and lacking fullness that comes with age; hence, why her future Master wanted her. When she took off her pants, it was confirmed I wasn't into bodies that had yet to mature. I seriously doubted I was going to be able to complete this training.

On her knees in a submissive form, she waited to be fed. Crash couldn't seem to lift his hand that held a piece of cheese and place it in her mouth. Not until she softly said, "Please. I'm so hungry." Shaking his head no, Crash placed food in her mouth. Her eyes closed as she moaned, chewing as fast as she could, relishing in substance soon headed to her stomach. She claimed, "This cheese is sour, but I don't care."

Avoiding staring at her body, he offered her more. "No good ol' American cheese here in Russia."

Sitting on my bed, observing the lack of technique and discipline, I explained, "Americans know nothing about good cheese. And, she should be punished for speaking without permission."

Crash eloquently told me to mind my business. "Fuck. Off."

A chuckle, full of admiration, escaped me.

It was a surprise, but while Crash gave Sam more food, he slightly smiled back at me. I guess he appreciated that I found his disrespect humorous.

The sincere moment had me trying to muster through guilt for creating more deceit. "How about we make a deal?" It may have appeared I was being kind, but I was only attempting to gain more trust.

Crash's whole body perked up, hope gleaming from his expression. It felt… nice to know I could make his shitty predicament a tad more tolerable,

even if it were a lie. "How about she gets to wear a shirt—"

I didn't have a chance to finish before Crash ripped off his T-shirt, shoving it over Sam's head. It was somewhat comical, especially with Sam's hungry mouth following his hand—even through the cotton—for more food. Crash and I started laughing as he popped her head through the neck-hole. He said, "Oh, damn. Sorry," and rushed more cheese to her mouth.

Covered, she seemed to relax, too, giggling, as Crash stuffed crackers in her mouth. When she spoke, "You ea' too," cracker crumbles puffed from her lips, causing us all to laugh even harder.

Catching his breath, Crash asked me, "So, what's the price to keep her dressed?"

"Only a kiss."

Crash snarled. "You want to kiss me?"

I recoiled. "What? No!" I pointed between them. "You two."

Crash studied Sam, who was gruesomely still chewing. He asked me, "Now?"

"I don't think that wise." I threw him a bottle of water.

Rising to his knees, he caught it, but he suddenly appeared very distracted in thought. I'm sure many scenarios raced through his mind. "Why do you need me to kiss her?"

I was stealing the tiny laughter reprieve they'd just enjoyed. "If things do not work out between you two, she will be sold."

Sam rushed to her knees, facing him, horror blanketing her face.

Crash, still distant in thought, brushed a crumb from her lip but asked me, "*The kiss will lead to more, won't it?*"

Sam's eyes found mine, so many questions present, especially with us reverting to Russian. I found it hard to look at her while answering the truth, so I stared out the window. "*It will lead to the end.*"

"*Don't take her from me.*"

"I won't," I answered him, telling myself, this time, I wasn't lying. I told

125

myself that it was my dad who was going to rip Sam and Crash apart. I also told myself I wasn't feeling guilty for all the empty promises I told the two souls I was leading down a path of destruction.

Crash stared at Sam's young, full lips. "I've never kissed anyone before."

She stared at his. "I have."

The room became so quiet I could hear him swallow. "Your dad?"

It felt like I was violating them in so many ways as I watched their private moment, one that I was literally forcing.

She whispered, "Yeah."

"I don't want to be like him."

As the predator, I watched their first intimate moment, the first of so many to come. Father was right; the awkwardness between the two eventually disappeared over time. Due to the encounters becoming more frequent, and the kisses and touches progressing, it was like a relationship between the three of us, even though I never physically participated. I didn't become aroused watching the tenderness, but I started to recognize the infatuation with such a sight. The man who had already paid for Sam, he desired an unusual rawness. It was there. It was very present while two young people were learning their bodies together.

Again, I witnessed maturity at a stupendous rate. Crash kept Sam by his side, night and day. They slept on his floor bed, her against the wall where she wanted to be. She only got privacy in the restroom. Only my restroom was allowed, per Crash's orders. No complaints came from her, and she loved to be in his T-shirts. I think the coverage gave her the ability to forget she was completely naked underneath.

Crash was caring for her at such a level I had to feed him extra, or he wouldn't eat. He insisted on giving her part of his portions. I had no choice. I needed him strong and healthy to do his job—the one he had yet to admit was his.

I found his dedication mystifying, so I allowed it. I could've forced a different outcome, but I had other things to force. And, I was curious to what

126

Crash's reaction would be once he finally noticed his sacrifices were not being reciprocated. It was blatantly obvious, but Crash was still far too naïve for such grim thoughts. He couldn't even see my betrayal, truly.

A heaping plate of fruit was in my grasp as I unlocked my bedroom door. When I entered, Sam's eyes locked onto the sweet, juicy delights, just as I had hoped. Crash? Sitting on the floor, he glared at me, not the sweets in my palm. When he saw the Elite following me, he pulled an entranced Sam into his lap. Her mouth was gaping, her tongue almost reaching out for the fresh peaches promising juice from the heavens. I walked past her to be sure she could catch a whiff of vitamins on a plate. Her body was begging for what cheese, crackers, water, and bread weren't providing. Sam hadn't felt sunbeams in many weeks. She was starving in more ways than one.

In the middle of the large bedroom, I faced the two young spirits. The Elite kept her eyes down as she sunk to her knees next to me. I praised, "What a good girl," as I sat next to her, placing the plate in my lap. I was sure to pick an Elite who spoke English. "Would you like some delicious fruit?"

"Yes, Master."

"Open your mouth."

She did, so I placed a slice of peach in her mouth. The Elite tried to fight it, but her eyes fluttered shut. That was all Sam could take. Crash tried to stop her as she rushed from his lap on her hands and knees, eyes watering and silently begging.

I ignored the disobedient pet and asked the Elite, "Would you like more?" Of course, I knew she would, and she would do anything I asked. Her nod was with a gasp of anxious need. I could hear her stomach growling, persistently. "Okay, then lie back for me. Show me what I will get in return."

"Stop this," growled Crash. He had caught up to Sam and was practically hovering.

The Elite slowly laid back. With her feet flat on the ground, she pulled her heels close to her buttocks so that I could easily view between her thighs.

Crash covered Sam's eyes with his shaking palm. She didn't fight him, but she did make a mistake by blindly reaching out to the plate of forbidden fruit. In a flash, I smacked the top of her hand. Sam barely had time to retract before Crash reached around her, yanking her hand from me. He held it to her chest, so angry with me. "You're not allowed to touch her."

My jaw locked to confirm I was done with his games. "Then tighten her fucking leash."

Crash wrapped his arms around her and pulled her closer to him. He was panting as Sam fell into his chest, crying, "Please. I'm so hungry."

Holding her as if she were priceless, his nostrils flared as his eyes slid shut. "Sam, this is what he wants."

Practically in a fetal position, curled in his lap, she held her starving stomach. "Just ask what I need to do to eat."

With his stressed face to the ceiling, he rocked her. It was gut-wrenching to watch him battle his morals against her pleas for food, something so many take for granted. He begged, "Yury, please don't do this."

Swallowing down guilt, I attempted a casual tone. "All I want in exchange for the fruit is for her to have pleasure." Sam peeked out from Crash's chest. I nodded at her. "That's all."

Trembling, she peered up at him. Crash refused to open his eyes nor stop facing the ceiling. Her body trembled as she touched his face. "I won't make it on cheese alone." She had no sympathy for him having to be the one to force her body into submission. She lacked empathy for him having to be the one to literally take charge of her, beyond the handling of her leash.

Who am I to judge her? I suppose I was doing the very same thing.

Sam was rewarded with fruit for lying on her back, for placing her legs like the Elite, and for every orgasm Crash was forced to wring from her body with his hand. As her belly filled with food—something Crash was still refusing, as if punishing himself—and her body was sated with pleasure, the young man in charge of her wiped away his tears.

A depression took the place of all the food Crash denied himself after that day. He began to deteriorate. Sam began to flourish. She was eager for any new lesson, as long as food and pleasure were involved. The young woman's body began to crave the highlights of ecstasy, what her upcoming Master had paid for. The man wasn't into forceful sexual acts, unlike most of our patrons. He preferred underdeveloped bodies spurred into desire at his whim. Then he wished to watch the orgasm between the young teens he owned. Once lust was in the air, the new Master would join in with the heated bodies, having both at his fancy.

Once four months had passed, Sam's new Master wanted his purchase delivered the next day. That is why I didn't stop Sam in the middle of the night when I heard her trying to steal kisses from Crash. Unbeknownst to her, it was her last innocent moment. It was to be his first. All Crash knew sexually, up to this point, was forced acts. He had yet to find any arousal that I could see, during Sam's orgasms, so I kept my eyes closed for once and let them share a night to hold close to their hearts, since I was just a few hours away from ripping those same hearts apart.

There was a glimpse of pride, knowing I could give Crash this one gift. I refused to let him lose his virginity as I had, bleeding all over the older female underneath him. Escalated breathing from Crash and Sam lulled me back to sleep as I wondered what it would be like to have such true affections.

The next morning, sitting next to the slave bed Crash had put to good use the night before, Crash was devouring his breakfast. In the bathroom, the shower was running. Sam was humming an American tune I didn't recognize. I teased, "Crash, you cannot stop smiling this morning." His eyes widened, his mouth full of cheese and bread. I teased again, "Huh. I wonder why."

I observed his joy, watched him storing it into memory, knowing he

would never smile at me again.

In the hallway, I waited for Crash to get a clean Sam into his T-shirt. Kirill and Adrian stood with me, also in their gym clothes. We needed to tire Crash out for the battle to come. I carried a casual smile, but somehow, I felt ill inside.

Kirill elbowed me, calling my bluff. *"You like this kid."*

"Does it matter?"

He exhaled regret, losing his smirk. *"No. I guess not. Still have a job to do."*

In the gym, Sam stayed in the corner in a submissive position. It was like she recognized how out-powered Crash truly was, so she tried to stay off the radar of the deranged. She was right to worry. Much danger surrounded her, like starving leeches, except it wasn't blood that we craved. It was control. Maybe, because we knew, deep down, we had none. Not one ounce. And, Sam and every other trained sexual servant paid the price of our frustrations. The cost trickled down from the top of the pile of shit we pretended to own.

Crash was sweating, climbing the rock wall, still smiling, blissfully unaware of the nearing tragedy. What I didn't know was how killing a part of Crash would harden a part of my own soul. Not until we were both fighting for the same girl, again, would we both be brought back to life.

Hanging from Monkey Bars, Kirill met Crash's eyes in the floor to ceiling mirror. "Young one, you are looking winded."

"Yeah? Well, it hasn't been a vacation I've been on while here, fucker."

After the workout, Crash kept Sam leashed but held her hand in an endearing fashion, close to his back, as we left the house gym behind. In the narrow hallway leading to the foyer, Crash was still catching his breath from the vigorous training we'd pushed him through to exhaust his fight. Getting closer to judgment time, Kirill and Adrian flanked Crash. He noticed immediately and yanked Sam against his back. Again, she asked no questions, always so willing to follow his lead.

So young…

Crash started breathing hard for a different reason when he saw my father and two handlers waiting for us. He stopped walking and tried to backtrack. Sam almost yelped when Crash backed her up, accidentally, into my chest.

"Yury?" Crash called out, sounding lost and most definitely scared.

"*I am sorry, kid.*"

His shoulders rose and fell with his exasperated lungs. "*You're killing me?*"

I stared at the back of his head, energy draining from me by the second. Then I nodded to Kirill and Adrian to grab Crash's arms. His knee-jerk reaction had him struggling. "Wait! If I'm dead, what happens to Sam? No! Yury! If you kill me, what happens to Sam?" Believing he was about to be murdered, something he knew firsthand we were capable of, he still attempted to protect his pet, not himself. "Sam! Come here!" yelled Crash, as I pulled her leash out of a panicked, sweaty from the workout, hand. Crash didn't have a chance to defend her.

She simply stared at Crash as if in shock he was to be murdered.

Kirill and Adrian hauled Crash forward. I forced Sam to stay with me.

Crash pleaded, "Don't kill me in front of her! Don't let her see this!!!"

Once Crash was out of arm's length, I proceeded toward my father, who snarled at Sam's coverage. "*My son is weak once again.*"

Crash stilled as he watched me, understanding crossing his expression. "No." His sight was locked onto the slave being handed over to my father. "Wait." As a handler took hold of her arm, he unraveled. "Wait!" Crash yelled, finally comprehending that he was not the one leaving my home. "Where are you taking her?"

Internally, I begged my heart to ice over and ease me of the betrayal that was eating me alive.

"Yury! You promised!"

My father smiled. "I see I am not the only liar under this roof."

Please ice over. Ice over, dammit! I replied, "Isn't life one big lie, anyway?"

He shrugged. "Maybe so. Either way, we have a sale to complete."

"Nooooo!" screamed Crash. "She's mine!" He told my father, "Kill me! Take my life for her freedom! Please, goddammit!"

Father exhaled his disappointment, asking me, "He is never going to train, is he?"

Not able to look into the desperate eyes behind me, I glanced to the floor. "It is time for him to return home."

"Home?" squeaked a confused Sam.

Father cupped her chin. "You, my dear, are a beauty, and your home is now in Germany."

With unexpected strength, Crash broke free of Kirill and Adrian's grip and charged forward. Father's minions caught him before he could reach us and proceeded to beat him down to the ground. It was violent. It was gruesome. It was how things were done. Yet, Crash kept reaching out for Sam. "Yury! Don't do this!"

Sam shook violently, watching Crash epically lose this fight. She barely reacted when I removed her collar and leash. Tears fell from her eyes as shock took hold of the young girl. "C-Crash? I-I don't get to… Where… Who will I… C-Crash?"

Kirill and Adrian stepped in and called off Father's dogs. Beaten to the point of delusion, Crash fought for focus. Blood seeped from his left, busted eyebrow, that would become a well-defined scar, as he stared up from the floor. Weaker than I had ever seen him, Crash reached up. "Sam."

"C-Crash? W-What's gonna happen to me?"

As ice wrapped its wonderful crystals around my tampered heart, I thought ill thoughts of Sam and what I portrayed as selfish, when she only worried for her future.

Crash tried to sit up, to get to his feet and help the sold slave, but his

body refused and fell back down. His tears mixed with his blood as he cried, "Yury! Please, don't let this happen."

I was as helpless as he. So, the ice completely took over. It was a merciful relief.

My father and his mutts escorted a shell-shocked Sam from my home, as Crash, in absolute agony, wailed from the floor. It was a horrific sight to witness. It was a horrendous sound to hear. Had I not iced over already, the bloodcurdling pleas would've been my undoing.

But I had a corrupted life to lead.

And, there are no happy endings in human trafficking.

Crash was never the same after that. I had broken him that fateful day. He only spoke one more time to me, and it was only to ask for another tattoo. I stood behind him and watched the gun ink *Death 1995* on the back of his neck. It was the year his brother left this earth. Crash didn't even flinch as the gun needled directly over his spinal cord. I guess I had already caused the worst pain he would ever endure. During the whole agonizing inking process, his hand gripped Sam's collar and leash, another way he had been marked forever.

There was no point for Crash staying any longer, so I called his father to come and retrieve him. When the man who once treasured his son arrived, I was stunned to witness him lift Crash's chin to get a good view of the *Life 1982* tattoo. The kid was now almost fifteen, but there was no warm embrace, only hatred and disgust. "Now, every time I look at you, I have to think of my lost son."

A menacing grin formed on Crash's face. "Appropriate, since it is your fault he's dead." He switched to Russian, "*You fucking drug dealer.*"

Crash saw the punch coming but never moved nor protected himself, even though most capable. No, instead, he fell to the ground where he had been when his Sam-world fell apart.

After recovering, he got to his knees, facing me, not his father. He pointed to the tattoo on the back of his neck while telling his father, "Now, you

can be reminded of his death every time I walk away from you to sell drugs."

He stood, then turned to the man who'd spawned him, something Crash clearly regretted. Again, he reverted to Russian, *"You piece of shit."*

After Crash left, I sunk further into my role as Master, soon to take over this organization. There was no more light within my world, so I let the darkness win, positive it was where I belonged, anyways.

Six years later…

Lying in bed, it was in the middle of the night when my cellphone rang. I fumbled in the darkness, searching my nightstand, then answered, *"Hello?"*

"Yuuuury?" I heard ice clink in a glass.

I sat up straight. It was Mrs. Thompson. "Yes." I was dumbfounded when I heard myself asking, "Is Crash okay?"

Her drunken exhale echoed over the receiver. "I nee' you to protect him."

"Why? What happened?"

She started to cry. "Who… does this leash belon' to? It was hidd'n in his room."

I was still groggy from waking up in the middle of the night—opposite hours of America. Rubbing my burning eyes, I simply replied, "A friend of his. One he lost."

She slurred, "He foun' another one."

My ears perked. "Who? He found who?"

"Whitney."

I shoved my blankets off me and swung my legs off the side of my mattress. "You said he had given up the search."

She cried even more. "He had. There were too many S-Summers in the US with s-sons named Timothy."

134

"Then, how?"

"M-Movies. Accidental meeting at the movie theater. Popcorn. She likes butter on her popcorn…"

At the age of twenty, Crash had finally found his promise to Timothy.

Mrs. Thompson was too intoxicated for me to get much more information, but one thing was for sure, the Curse had been brought back to life. Mr. Summers had never made another threat, and Uffe's wife stayed in hiding. Father and I decided to let snakes lay where they rested. But this news, I knew this was going to bring complications. Crash had broken one promise to himself by not saving Sam. There was no way in hell I'd live to see the day this kid broke another. His stubborn streak gave me no choice.

I was headed back to America.

CHAPTER TEN

Complicated Secrets

Moving forward, I felt as if I were running in circles, chasing an end that kept eluding me. I had been tucked away in my pretend world once again, blissfully far from guilt. Now, I was being boomeranged back into a conscience.

Father was livid with the news. He was back to wanting Whitney to be either dead or making him money. Since I felt I had already left America in disarray, I never told him that Marina was still alive, supposedly living a dream-life with her husband. Father believed she was dead, burned to ashes. I wasn't about to be truthful now.

"Would you like a private dance?" The stripper's swaying hips and voice attempted to lure me, but she was unable to pique my interest. The false promise actually revolted me.

She wanted cash. I wanted tears.

We were never going to find a meaningful compromise.

From my chair in the establishment in Connecticut, I glared up at her. "Why make it private? Let's fuck right here."

Her movements slowed as she stuttered, "I-I don't do that."

"Then cease your false seduction. My money doesn't come cheap."

Pleased I'd made my point, I grinned as she walked away. I needed the humor since Kirill had convinced me this nightclub, *No Cherries Here*, would be a discrete meeting place for Mr. Harold Always-A-Thorn-in-My-Ass Thompson. The lights were low, but I could still easily see Kirill had picked the youngest of the strippers. She may not have had a cherry to pop, but I would have sworn she was no older than fifteen. Kirill was spellbound as she gyrated in his lap.

Long, blonde hair danced along her back as she cupped his face, saying things I couldn't hear over the annoying thumping music.

Facing me from across a little cocktail table, Adrian nodded that my guest was approaching. I was facing the entrance—not the stage with an abundance of disobedient slaves to their trade—eager to get this meeting over with Mr. Thompson, who, apparently, had back door privileges.

He sat in the empty chair at my side. His tone was far from pleasant, understandably. "Not watching the show?"

Nodding to Adrian to follow through with our plan—put a tracker on Harold's car—I reached for my American top-shelf vodka, which tasted more like piss water. "Not interested in bullshit tonight."

Harold observed as Adrian disappeared out the front door. He sneered, "And what *are* you interested in tonight?" He sat back in his chair, attempting to appear casual and unconcerned, but his leg was bouncing with nerves, not the beating music the dumb bitches were dancing to.

"Loose ends being tied up as they should've been long ago." After taking a pull from my glass, I set it back on the table then crossed my hands in my lap, staring Harold down the whole time.

A waitress strolled up to our table and delivered a bourbon and Coke to Harold. "Here ya go, stranger." Then she whispered, "Can I see you tonight?"

"No, but their tab is on me." Harold waved her off.

With no humor, I chuckled. "I see you are still loyal to your wife?"

"My wife is none of your business."

"We'll see if she feels the same when I call her to inform her I'm in town."

A few patrons glanced at our table when he shouted, "Why are you here?"

Pleased I had him angry and unstable, I gestured about. "Not to cause a scene, unlike yourself."

"I thought you said no bullshit tonight."

I leaned forward, closer to him. "You're correct. I'm actually here to spy on your son, Crash."

He paled. "The fuck for?"

"He has acquired a new friend. Maybe you know her. Miss Whitney ring a bell?"

Harold grabbed his cocktail and drained the whole drink down his throat before setting it back on the table. "Impossible. He's always being guarded."

"Do they know of our—" I, condescendingly, tapped my chin. "How should I put this? Complications?"

He swallowed as his jaw went rigid. "No." Before I could ask more, his phone rang. Sternly, he answered, "What? Why was he at a skating rink? A date?" His eyes met mine, then closed. "Where are you headed? I'll meet you in the alley." He slipped the device in his front pocket as he stood. "I will take care of the problem. Crash won't see her again."

As he exited from where he had come, I quickly called Adrian's phone. *"He's coming."*

After chastising Kirill for not paying attention to the business we were in America for, we left his child-like stripper and the dirty establishment behind to follow Harold Thompson. Kirill was in a foul mood since he didn't get to buy the dancer for the night and was being forced to work. Reading a sign above a building, he snarled, "*Mug and Pour*? The owner could pick any name for his establishment, and he chose *Mug and Pour*?"

Scanning a parking lot for Harold's blue Corvette, from our black SUV, I remarked, "As if 'No Cherries Here' is any better?"

He finally smiled. "Little Yury, clever is clever, you must admit."

"Yes, I suppose so." Then I told Adrian, who was driving, "Circle the block. The Tracker says he's here."

Harold was. His blue corvette was sloppily parked in an alley behind *Mug and Pour*. Adrian was sure to drive slowly so we could gather intel with

what we were seeing. On each end of the alley were two of the guards Harold had assigned to watch his son. I couldn't help but smirk at the larger men, as if their size meant a damn thing. They were protecting a kid who could probably beat each one to the ground with his training. That is why it was disturbing to see Mr. Thompson punching Crash in the face. Crash had grown and filled out to be the man he now was, yet he still allowed his father to have the upper hand.

"Wait a minute," said Adrian as he drove away from the alley entrance, only to pull back into the parking lot. I was about to ask what he was doing when he pointed to a dumpster. Crouched behind the dumpster was another young man, spying. He had dark hair and was very focused on the conversation in the alley.

Growling, due to witnessing yet another complication, I asked, *"Now, who the fuck is this?"* Suspecting Harold was yelling at Crash for his involvement with Whitney, it was easy to predict this new stranger was overhearing details to a situation I was in the process of taking down.

As the young man snuck back to his dark Beamer, Adrian commented, *"Parents have money."*

Exhaling, hoping not to have to kill another unfortunate rich kid, I nodded. *"Follow him."*

When the kid pulled to the security gate of Mr. Summers' neighborhood, we all chuckled. Kirill said, *"Security now in place? Check!"* But my jaw dropped when he was waved through, clearly known by the guards.

I thought to myself, *Who are you and what kind of a threat do you bring?* My thoughts were interrupted when my cellphone vibrated in my pocket. It was my father. *"Hello?"*

"We have word that Uffe's wife is becoming too friendly with a policeman here."

"Shit. She is talking?"

"Or fucking, the whore. Either way, it is too close to business. I want that document of Seafoam's spawn. But first, I have a client you must meet with. He has chosen the location 'No Cherries Here.'"

Overhearing the conversation, Kirill practically cheered in silence.

"*Now?*" I asked, "*I'm in the middle—*"

"*Of course, now! Big money waits for no one.*"

"*It is not a set-up? I prefer to stay out of jail tonight.*"

"*A man of his wealth is untouchable by police, Yury. Do as you're told.*"

After a long night of negotiations with a particularly nervous billionaire client, Kirill, Adrian, and I ate dinner before we made our way back to Mr. Summers' home. Since there now was security at the entrance, we took our "off-road" vehicle off-road and made a rear entrance through the woods on the outskirts of the neighborhood.

Parked in a discrete spot still hidden in the woods, we made our way through the trees to find the lake. It was easy to recognize Mr. Summers' home after that. There were only a few homes to choose from. So, we crossed the green grass of Whitney's backyard. It was plush, thick, and extremely well-groomed. Money was present everywhere. More so than when I was there years earlier. Mr. Summers was doing quite well for himself. I guess that is one reason he was not willing to save his son. The sacrifice for future status was well worth it. He and my own father had much in common.

The problem with money? It offers more power. Mr. Summers was now becoming more than a legitimate threat to my family's business. He was becoming a hurricane that could blow us away. Mr. Summers would soon have the resources and clout to come after us while keeping himself appearing as the savior, not an acquaintance.

No lights were on as we quietly studied the house. Unbeknownst to Whitney, her parents had another home in California. They claimed to always be traveling, but the truth was, they chose to live without her in their constant presence. It was a well-hidden secret that the media never caught wind of. Whitney was alone. Or, at least, that is what we had thought.

Standing at the edge of the back patio, the three of us stared at a tall,

young man sleeping in a lawn chair. Dread filled my stomach as the three of us eyed each other in dismay. I shook my head, now completely convinced much had been overheard in the alley. This kid was here to protect Whitney. Therefore, he was neck-deep in a shit storm that had only begun for him. Again, or so I had believed.

Three Russians circled the sleeping form, wondering what to do with our new obstacle. I couldn't help but somehow recognize that he looked familiar to me. I gestured for Adrian to go find the kid's car in case we needed to dispose of him immediately. Kirill stayed with me, deciding it was time for an American "selfie." He crouched behind the sleeping young man, then held up his phone while making faces by the kid's shoulder.

I smacked Kirill.

Putting his phone away, he shrugged and mouthed, "*May come in handy.*"

Within moments, Adrian returned only to inform me no Beamer was present, not even in the four-car garage. Stumped and baffled, I crossed my arms while peering around, trying to figure out where the kid hid his car, and why. My only choice was to wait until he woke to see what he would do next, so we snuck back to the woods for cover and to get a few hours of sleep. Being from Russia, the cool evening air didn't faze us in the slightest.

I woke as dawn made an appearance, lighting my face. Rising to my feet, I was surprised to see the sleeping guard now awake and swimming across the lake. I kicked at Kirill and Adrian to wake. Before the kid reached the middle of the lake, he dove under the water and disappeared. Kirill and Adrian stood in time to see him resurface and climb a ladder on the dock that was in front of the very large white home, directly across from Whitney's home.

I glanced back to the Summers' home, remembering the day I was in Mr. Summers office, watching Tim play with a younger Whitney and a boy named Reether. Then I remembered after we left, how we eavesdropped, overhearing Mr. Summers saying to someone on the phone, "*He's fine. In the water with Tim*

and Whit." I was starting to suspect that whoever Mr. Summers was speaking to lived across the lake and was possibly the same person who Harold was on the phone with when I was spying on him at Harold's lake home; *"Your son has nothing to do with this... Well, they don't know that!"*

Watching, who I was suspecting to be Reether, walk up the dock, his body mannerism again triggered a recognition I couldn't yet place. I whispered, *"Does he look familiar to either of you?"*

They both shook their heads no.

After grabbing a towel and wrapping it around his waist, the kid snuck through the back door, baffling me further. I was about to go investigate when I suddenly heard music coming from within the Summers' home. When I saw fluid movements in the rear living quarters, it was like luring the devil to an angel as I crossed the space between us, not caring who saw me.

Adrian rushed to follow me, shoving me behind a tall potted plant so I could still watch Whitney, eyes closed, become one with the music. At first, muscular legs worked with such precision that even a non-dancer such as myself had to appreciate the craft. One limb would extend impossibly high into the air while the other stayed grounded as if giving permission—stability—freedom to soar. I had never seen balance in such rare form.

In Russia, we have the best of the best. Our ballet dancers were once known to be untouchable. Miss Whitney was attending a high school that offered a dance program, but she was not only dancing; she was *screaming* of pain in her soul. She was petite, not as ravishing as Mrs. Thompson, but her body moved like a beautiful song of agony and the fight for survival. Her evident internal ache spoke volumes. And it fucking spoke to me.

I envied her ability to have such an outlet, like I had with sex, but also saw her release not being enough. She was as hungry as I. An instant connection was made from one hungry entity to another. The kindred spirit I had once felt toward Whitney, after speaking with her father years ago, was now blooming into unknown soulmates of sorts.

And then… her eyes opened. It may have only been for a second, but it was enough time for me to find the eyes I had been, unknowingly until that moment, trying to replicate in other redheaded slaves. Seafoam. I gasped and jerked back at the magnificent sight, bumping into Adrian. He quickly leaned forward to see what I was captivated by but was snared by Whitney.

Wild red hair flowed, following every turn and gracious bow of her body. Fingers fisted and stretched, full of emotions begging to be unconstrained. Her eyes were closed, again as if she was lost in the sentiment of her inner battle.

I don't know how long I stood there before Adrian was pulling me away and into the woods once again, trying to warn me, *"He's coming back,"* but my stare was locked to the back patio window, watching the rawness of her every move. *"You are staring at her like a starving man seeing his first glimpse of a steak."*

Adrian couldn't have been more correct.

Soaking wet on the back patio, the young man was now watching her, too, as her hands slammed against her chest. He was as enthralled as I had been and jolted when she finally stopped dancing and dropped to the floor. She laid there for a moment then screamed her frustration instead. *"Whyyyy?"* I grabbed my chest. I had heard a bloodcurdling plea before, the night little Harry rushed to Tim's dying side. With her recently meeting Crash, I knew—just *knew*—this scream had to do with him and her brother. Therefore, it had something to do with me. It caused me a twisted physical discomfort, mixed with pleasure, to know I was personally responsible for that beautiful dancing.

I instantly wanted to inspire more.

Is this desire where Seafoam's curse truly began? Was this the beginning of my family's fall? Or, were all souls linked by the crime of sexual slavery destined for a much bigger picture? The answer would soon be a marvel and would reach far beyond what I could see or comprehend at the time. Maybe it is true; if you look hard enough, there is always beauty present within the ugly. That beauty may not be within your grasp but may benefit others also in dire need.

143

Either way, what was to come would prove an undoubting connection between myself, those I knew, and those to come.

A prime example was about to present itself.

Adrian, Kirill, and I made our way around the lake, staying hidden, as the young man finally swam back across the lake. My head tilted as I observed security cameras everywhere on the white home. The head of this household was on the border of being highly paranoid, so we didn't dare break from the trees. We stayed shielded and studied the young man jogging around the side of the house when he heard the garage door opening. "Mom?"

As a woman came out, stretching. Her attire and pulled-back hair informed me she was about to run for exercise. "Reether, I'm here, baby."

Meeting her in the driveway, Reether said, "I'm gonna hang with Whit today."

She beamed up at her son with such pride. "And why would I expect anything different?"

He kissed her cheek, "Love you," then jogged into the garage.

As she watched him with an abundance of adoration, I quickly recognized the large brown eyes hiding under long bangs. The eyes were older, but unforgettable, just as she would always be to me.

Well, I'll be damned.

This woman was my very first pet.

Back at the hotel, walking through the front door and into the lobby, I snarled at Kirill. *"Why the fuck is there a stripper waiting for you?"*

There was the little blonde who stood no taller than 4'11", shyly smiling and waving at him.

"Little Yury, don't you prefer I fuck her rather than find my usual?"

I was too tired to even respond, but yes, the willing stripper was a much

better alternative to him raping a child.

After the elevator ride to my floor, walking down the hall toward my room, my mind spun with Marina being Reether's mother and how all the scenarios would play out. Loose ends were multiplying every day. Was it time to reach out to my father and inform him of another revelation? That I never even told him she was alive? I didn't have the moment needed to come up with an answer, because Mrs. Thompson was pacing outside my door.

I was about to turn to head back to the elevator, but she noticed me before I had the chance. "Is she going to get him killed?"

I stormed her, concerned that hotel patrons would overhear the conversation. "Shut your mouth."

"Is she?" Her pupils were small, informing me of drugs in her system.

The nape of her neck was in my grip as I growled in her face. "What are you on?" She had lost weight and had dark circles under her eyes. The last time I had seen her, pain killers were her drug of choice. I quickly pulled out my key while telling Kirill and Adrian, "*I'll handle this. Go to your rooms.*"

Kirill quickly opened his hotel room door and scooted his little stripper inside, but Adrian shook his head as he approached. "*Must check for knives.*"

Mrs. Thompson's worried stare held me as she was patted down. Kirill held out one of her arms for me to see needle tracks. "*Shit,*" I swore.

Heroine.

Her runny nose was possibly not from tears.

Once proved weaponless, Adrian went to his own room as I shoved Mrs. Thompson into mine. "Not planning on stabbing me again?"

She stumbled on her high heels. "Why? So, you can steal away another child of mine, then return him coldhearted?"

"You have none left." I closed the door behind me. "Besides, it is not as if the life you've offered him is so much more appealing."

"Fuck. You."

Grinning, I said, "Now, *that* is an appealing offer."

As if preparing for me to attack her, Mrs. Thompson bent her knees, slightly crouching. "Never again are we having sex."

"No?" My dick hardened at the challenge.

She rushed for the door.

She didn't make it.

Wrapping an arm around her midsection, I had her fancy shoes off the ground in no time and was headed for the bed. She fought me, which I took as foreplay until I threw her down to the mattress to be met with angry swinging fists. Capturing her wrists, I forced them above her head, then asked, "What the fuck is wrong with you? Is this the heroine talking?"

"Whatever it takes to forget you!"

Exasperated, I winced. "Last time I saw you, you stabbed me. I should be pissed at *you*, not the other way around."

From under me, her body arched and struggled to be set free, all the while, she screamed, "That was after you drugged and raped me!"

I laid my weight on her to subdue her efforts. "It's not rape if she's begging for it."

"You are worse than your father."

My chest rumbled anger. My voice instantly became a grave warning. "Then why are you here?"

"To save what's left of my son."

I didn't want to hear her affections for Crash because I was in denial that I too cared for the kid. I got off her and turned away. "Then go home and try to be a better mother."

Instead of noticing how my last words triggered quite the reaction, I assumed the drugs in her system simply took control. She slowly stood from the bed, appearing dazed and confused. "Yes, I need to be a better mother." Then she clumsily walked toward the door.

In need of rest, all I wanted was to sleep, but I feared Mrs. Thompson was too inebriated to find her way home, so I watched her stumble into the

hallway. Without her knowing, I followed to see if she was going to try to drive. Her long dress flowed against her legs as her hand lazily touched the wall all the way to the elevator, never glancing back to see if she were alone. She didn't react to the moans of pleasure already coming from Kirill's room.

My concern grew as she kept mumbling about needing to be a better mother as if slipping into a trance. I asked, "Are you all right?"

Mrs. Thompson didn't respond. She didn't even notice when I entered the elevator with her. She leaned against the mirror to her right and closed her eyes, repeating, "Let me be a better mother," as if praying.

When the elevator *dinged* and the doors slid open, she numbly exited and headed straight for the hotel entrance. There were cabs parked under the overhang. I was only going to make sure she got in one safely, but then she told a hotel doorman, "I need to go find him."

"Who, ma'am?" he asked in return. When she stared at the doorman, clearly intoxicated, he asked, "Would you like a cab?"

Her head bobbed yes in reply. The doorman guided her to a waiting cab.

I slid into the next waiting cab and directed the driver to follow her. Something told me she was not going home. As we pulled up to a house in an unfamiliar neighborhood, I knew I was right. It was approximately 3 a.m., but that did not stop Mrs. Thompson from walking up the manicured walkway and through a picture-perfect, low, white picket fence. I stayed in the cab as she banged on the door, claiming to want to see "him."

A porchlight turned on. I couldn't hear the conversation when a woman answered the door in her robe, but her body language appeared sympathetic and not judging the lost and confused woman at her door. Gently, the kind older woman guided the now crying Mrs. Thompson back to her cab. Mrs. Thompson nodded the whole way as the woman spoke to her. She even held her hand as she slipped back into the cab.

The cab's taillights lit up, and then he pulled away. As instructed, my cab followed until I saw Mrs. Thompson had finally made her way home.

Rubbing the bridge of my nose, I told my driver, "Back to the hotel, please."

I had no idea what had just occurred, nor did I care. A decision I would one day regret, in the worst way possible.

CHAPTER ELEVEN

False Security

Since I had not told Father about Marina being alive, it was challenging to explain that she had another son. *"Yury, please explain how a dead woman keeps having children."*

"It was before she died." Why did I not tell the truth? I can only say that it felt wrong to disrupt her life more than I had to.

"And the father?"

"A ghost so far."

"Well, I want him dead."

I chuckled, *"Father, it is not wise to kill everyone who annoys you."*

"It will prove annoying me is not a wise move. Besides, this world could benefit from one less American."

This was hard to argue, but… *"So, kill the kid?"*

After a moment, Father replied, *"No."*

After his instructions, there I was, now standing outside Miss Whitney's bedroom porch door. I was still bewitched to know exactly what I wanted from her. Watching her sleep, I kept thinking of how her body had moved with such passion. It was like a magical drug for my aching, crushed spirit. That enchantment had me craving more ease and peace for the never-ending chaos in my crooked world.

Suspecting what she could offer me, I became angry knowing there were no live security cameras to protect her. Earlier, Adrian had checked the system set in place and showed me all wires had been cut. Standing outside her home, I commented, *"But she sets the alarm every night."*

Adrian had held up the cut wires. *"Then it's rigged to give her a false*

sense of safety."

It was as if her father was paving the way, making it as easy as possible to kidnap her. Was he completely clueless to her value? Did he already have another PR story lined up to gain votes and public sympathy? It didn't matter, because it wasn't Whitney I was there for. It was the young man lying in bed with her. Reether, being Marina's son, made him our property.

Father said Reether was to be trained and sold.

Approximately 3a.m., again, Kirill and Adrian were waiting on the ground for the signal that I had successfully drugged Whitney. I needed her unconscious while trying to lug out a subdued Reether Jones, who was much larger than his mother. I was doing the job myself because I wanted to be the one there if she were to wake up. I wanted to see those eyes, then decide how to react next. I wasn't sure I could leave her behind, even though that is what Father had decided until I had her fake certificates in hand.

All was planned as well as could be, under the circumstances, except for one thing: fucking Crash. My stupid cousin thought it fun to taunt Crash by sending him the 'selfie' of himself behind a sleeping Reether. My hand was on the doorknob as he barreled into my side, sending us both over the railing, flipping in the air, plummeting one-story, and slamming to the ground. Kirill and Adrian started to rush forward but stopped when hearing Whitney's porch door swing open. Kirill and Adrian pressed their backs to the Summers' home, as Crash and I tried to stay quiet while suffering from the oxygen being knocked from our lungs.

Once the door shut, we both rolled over quietly, gasping for air. Kirill and Adrian dragged us to our feet then into the woods. Still breathless, Crash took a weak swing at me. "You fucking knew who she was!"

Kirill easily blocked the effort and said, *"Knock it off, imbecile."*

Crash and I fell to our butts, resting until our lungs cooperated again.

He leaned against a tree. "Why didn't you tell me so I could've watched over her this whole time?"

150

I coughed, "Because I do not need you interfering with my business."

He swallowed, trying to breathe properly. "How the hell does she have anything to do with you?"

"Nothing. Her father has a document I need to be returned to me."

He paled. "So, you want to use her as leverage or something?"

Or sell her body. "Something like that."

"Yury." Blue eyes bored into me. "She means something to me."

Knowing that he was asking me to spare her for him, I teased, "Trying to make good with this promise?"

"Stop toying with me. Timothy was a hero of mine."

I rolled my eyes. "You only knew him for a few weeks."

"I was a fucking kid, you heartless bastard."

"Meh." I shrugged.

His lips flattened. "Maybe I'm trying to make up for the promise you broke. Have you heard anything about Sam?"

He was chasing ghosts. He was chasing a redemption he would never find. "You can't save her. She's gone."

Crash stared off into the darkness in more way than one. "Is she alive?" I stayed silent. "Has her owner bought another?" Crash was smart. If her owner bought another, chances were, she was being replaced due to being deceased. When I still didn't answer, he quietly said, "Please."

I did my best to remind myself I was a professional and not emotionally involved. "He has bought another."

Refusing to look at me, Crash nodded, sadness blanketing his expression. "I will never forget what you did." Then he pointed to the house where we just came. "You should know, I'm fighting for her."

"I can see that." I exhaled a long breath. "Then let me take Reether."

His reaction was intense, and I was clueless about what I was dealing with. "Are you insane? He has *nothing* to do with this!"

"He overheard a 'conversation' you had with your father."

Crash blinked but stayed stubborn, shaking his head. "No way. I just met him. Never knew I had another brother." He glared daggers at me. "So, fuck you, Yury. He stays with me. Reether doesn't even know who I am to him. He's innocent."

In the corner of my eye, I could see Kirill and Adrian trying to reattach their jaws. Not only was I now understanding why Reether looked so familiar to me, but I was captivated by the fact Crash was clueless to who his biological mother was.

Barely recovering from the shocking news, I sneered, "A drug dealer's son is innocent?"

"Are you listening to me, fucktard? He doesn't know who his dad is. My dad doesn't know about him, either. The woman he fucked must've kept the pregnancy to herself. Can you blame her?"

Pet has been a very bad girl.

For many nights, we watched as Crash kept his word, sitting in the Summers' backyard, literally watching over Whitney and his brother. I say literally, because Reether was there, too, clueless of his impending danger. All the while, Whitney was oblivious to the triumphant efforts taking place below while she slept.

From the woods, I was too far away to hear but was so curious to what Crash and Reether talked about for all those dark hours, how they found Whit to be enough of a common ground that they learned to join forces against her threat. Their undying dedication spurred curiosity in me. I had never experienced such devotion and wanted to understand something I could only witness in other's actions.

There was something else I wondered about, also—if I were going to be able to watch Whitney dance again. Still entranced and desperate for more, I found myself preparing to sneak into her high school. Adrian hated the idea. "*And if you get caught?*"

At the hotel, I had asked Kirill to get his little stripper to call the school asking for a Whitney Summers. She was told she was unavailable due to being a part of an audition in the auditorium.

I got out of the SUV parked across the street of the school's parking lot, but before I could shut the door, Kirill chuckled. *"Look who likes them young now. No?"*

Ignoring their remarks and accusations, I traveled across the school's property. Since the school doors were locked and ringing the bell to say, "Hello, my name is Yury, and I am a human trafficker. May I please come in to spy on one of your students?" didn't seem wise, I decided to be patient and wait. As a student exited, I smiled and held the door open for her, then slipped inside to follow signs to guide me to the Auditorium.

A piano was just starting to play a haunting song as I approached a side door to a stage. Peering through the little window above the handle, I found her; the one who made me ache for peace. On the stage, all by her lonesome, was Whitney. With no self-control, my hand opened the door. Before I knew what I was doing, I was standing in the wings of the stage, completely enamored. Fire burned from her soul as she danced from one part of the stage to another. Grabbing her chest through expression, I found myself once again grabbing my own.

In disbelief, I glanced down to my hand. It was the first time I had felt my heart beating in years.

I would've watched her to the end of times, but I was suddenly in the presence of another. Crash glared at me as we stood shoulder to shoulder. Causing a scene wouldn't have benefited me in the least. It was time to exit, even though it was the last thing I wanted to do.

I mouthed, "Fuck you," to Crash before I left.

As I slipped back through the stage door, the music came to an end. In the school hallway, I pressed my back against the wall to catch my breath from seeing her so close. Within seconds, the door started to open, so I raced around a

corner. I could hear Crash quietly growling, "Tell me I'm still not alone in this! Ignore me if you will, but don't fucking lie to yourself."

My stomach soured to know he was already so close to the dancer who silently sung to me. So, when I heard a door opening and saw a teacher exit a classroom, I approached him, acting as if a concerned bystander. "Sir, I think there is a student being rough with another."

As if on cue, Whitney shrieked, "You're still not alone! I shouldn't, but damn..."

The teacher's eyes bulged before he thanked me, then ran toward the ruckus.

I left, promising myself I would someday, somehow, see the magical one dance again.

Back in my hotel room, Kirill, Adrian, and I did research on the man Reether believed was his father: Ted Jones. Being forced to leave the fire dancer, I was already annoyed. Then I learned more bad news. *"He's a fucking lawyer."* Kirill and Adrian watched as I slammed my laptop shut and rolled my hotel chair backward. *"He's the one making the false birth certificates."* I picked up my cell and tapped a phone number on the screen.

Harold answered, "What?"

Not appreciating his attitude, I coldly replied, "Ted Jones."

Silence...

"I see. How is he 'enjoying' your slave? Apparently, she fucks him well enough to have a son." That was a lie he had yet to learn.

Silence...

"Since she is my property, it means her son is also mine." My self-control slipped away right before I screamed, "And I will be collecting!" *Click!* I stood, smoothing out my blazer. "Let's see how fast Mr. Ted Jones can squirm. Shall we?" I knew Harold would be calling him with a warning.

Back in the SUV, Adrian was driving, and Kirill was in the front passenger seat showing me pictures on his cell. *"Look, Yury. See how tight she is?"*

Staring at his stripper's pussy, I said, *"What are you doing with her?"* I hadn't meant it in the literal sense, but Kirill carried on to show me another picture. This time, it was a close-up of himself being inserted inside her. I shook my head and sat back in my seat. I couldn't help but wonder what my little Fire would look like naked while her body stretched and danced. I rubbed the back of my neck when I thought about how angry my father would be if I brought his curse back home, along with Reether.

Kirill snickered, *"I have the answer to your question, Little Yury."*

Apparently, Ted Jones was a fast mover. Tailing his car loaded with my pet and her son, we followed them to another house. We kept a good distance away, to stay undetected, as Reether rushed from the barely stopped car to hug a blonde waiting in a driveway.

As Reether picked the young woman up and swung her around, Kirill snapped yet another round of pictures. *"I'd fuck that."*

The girl appeared to be Reether's age and madly in love with him, the way she smiled at him then kissed him, mouthing 'I love you.'

While Adrian teased Kirill for being willing to "fuck anything with two legs, or even one," I knew I had found my sweet revenge for Mr. Jones running away with my property. It was time he learned a lesson about with whom he was dealing.

As I said, money is power. And I had lots of it. Money was what it took to have Reether's little blonde girlfriend disappear in a deadly car accident.

After hearing of the murdering of an innocent, my father sent two more men to 'help' me clean up his Seafoam curse. I was annoyed and felt disrespected but

acted unaffected by his lack of confidence.

Mr. Summers refused to answer any of my calls to discuss the wanted document. His only response was from a burner phone in text form, claiming: *What you want is inside the house.* I thought again about no cameras and the fake security system, a clear invitation to enter, but couldn't help but feel he was setting me up for a fall. I wasn't willing to take the bait quite yet, so I thought one more threat was needed to see if I could force him to react accordingly; give me what I wanted.

Alone in my hotel room, I peered at my vibrating cellphone. I recognized Crash's cell number, so I answered, "*Hello?*"

"Tell me you had nothing to do with his girlfriend's death."

"*I thought you didn't appreciate lies. How is our little dancer?*"

Silence…

"I figured out who Whitney is to you, and you can't have her back."

I wanted Whitney. Crash's demand pissed me off. "*Then get me the fucking certificate!*"

"Her father is an asshole!"

I tried to calm myself. "*Finally, something we agree on.*"

His voice sounded strained when he said, "Please, Yury. This girl… She… I need her, man."

Crash was no longer watching her out of duty to Timothy. He was falling for her. I heard the hunger that had also been affecting me. Owing him made my eyes slide shut as I tried to feed more ice to my cold heart. "Her father says what I want is in her house."

Crash's voice filled with hope. "I'll search every time she sleeps."

My head felt so heavy I let it fall back and hang for a rest. "*Search well, my friend.*" I hung up. After letting the phone rest in my lap for a few minutes, I finally picked it back up, dialed another number, and pulled it to my ear. My chair on wheels slowly spun in a circle as I waited. After two rings, I heard, "Ted Jones here."

Still gently spinning, I stared at the ceiling while attempting to sound cheery. "Mr. Jones, I presume you got my message?" One of Kirill's pictures of Reether hugging the blonde girlfriend had come in handy after all.

"You *sonofabitch*, you did not need to kill anyone to get my attention."

I stopped moving my chair. "But it got you to stop running from your crimes and secrets."

"I am an upstanding citizen who has committed no crime—"

"You are a slave owner who is hiding the identity of a drug dealer's son." When there was no reply, I asked, "No?"

"Who are you, really?"

"The proper owner of your wife and son."

"They are human. They cannot be owned."

"Then why do you sound so scared?"

"Because you clearly do not follow laws or reason."

This I could not deny. "Then you understand the grave danger your family is in."

"Which is why I am speaking to you."

I liked Mr. Jones. It may sound odd, me being in the profession I was in, but I found honesty to be refreshing. "It should please you to know your son, Harold's son, shows your bravery, not the drug dealer's."

An exhale echoed over the phone. "It does. Thank you." I waited as he coughed then choked out his next question as if the answer may end his life, "Is my son safe?"

Again, I rewarded honesty with honesty. "My boss prefers him to be trained and sold."

I never knew a lingering silence could slice someone, but that is what happened to Mr. Jones. Me, by not adding to such news, stabbed him in the heart. His voice was so restricted I wasn't sure he was breathing properly. "His life... his safety... is priceless to me. Do you understand?"

Jealousy pinged my ego. This man adored a son that wasn't even his.

"Sir, do you have children?"

I could barely talk myself. "I do not."

"If you did… you could possibly understand how desperate I am right now. I will give you my home, every cent in my bank accounts, even my own life, just please, leave my wife and son alone."

In order to do this, I would have to lie to my father. Weighing my options, I pondered over what other deceit my father had lurking. I was willing to bet the truth would sadden me greatly.

Mr. Jones reminded me, "I am in this mess quite deep. I'm sure you have figured out how."

I nodded to myself. Mr. Jones made Whitney's American false birth certificate. "How much does your son know?"

"Not enough for his death."

"Says his father."

"Says a lawyer."

I understood what he meant. Reether would not be a strong witness. "Can you keep his curiosity to a minimal?"

"I can."

After more thought, I decided, "For now… I will leave your son be."

I can't be sure, but I may have heard a sob from Mr. Jones before he asked, "Marina?"

"She is thought to be dead."

Another strangled noise of emotion escaped Mr. Jones before he timidly asked, "Whitney?"

"She will not fare as well." I debated how much to say. "Her father has made it clear he is not protecting her. Quite the opposite, unfortunately for her. But don't fear. Crash is taking care of it."

Regrettably, Crash had come up empty-handed, night after night, so it was time for a profound statement. My father was starting to lean in favor of Whitney's death. His thought process was "no girl, no problem." Since I was far

too infatuated with an unrealistic notion between Whitney and myself, death was yet an option I was prepared to consider. I had to get creative to buy me more time. So, when the perfect moment presented itself, Whitney was to take the hit.

The blow was profound.

For her… and for me.

It was eerie to feel your vehicle run over a part of a body, one so small and defenseless. Kirill laughed as he sped us away. In the back seat, I vomited in my mouth then swallowed it, never letting my comrades know of my weakness. They couldn't know that I had single-handedly snuffed out the fire I so yearned to witness, with the hope it would save her life.

Whitney's mother finally acted as a mother should after the extensive surgery on the dancer's foot. I told myself the crutches and pins sticking out of her ankle and foot weren't the end of her dancing career. I told myself many lies. I even told myself Crash didn't deserve to be Whitney's first. It was actually my fault. I had accidentally provoked him when in his father's den.

He had overheard a part of a conversation not meant for his ears. "Dad, don't do this."

Harold, aging by the day, snarled, "Do *not* start with me again. I don't give a shit about your feelings. This girl has been nothing but trouble since she entered my life."

Crash screamed, "Yury will sell her!"

His father stood from the couch and screamed in return, "Good riddance! At least someone is going to get something good out of her!"

"You don't understand, Dad! I was there! I saw what they do to these girls—"

Quite efficiently, Harold practically flew toward his son. Face to face, he sneered, "I was there, too. Where do you think I was when your brother was

shot?"

Crash lost all color in his face. I don't think it was the harsh comment that made him appear ill. It was the realization that his father was so willing to disregard a young life into my care, even when knowing her fate would be nothing but doomed.

The young drug dealer nodded with a gaping mouth while backing away. "Okay, Dad. You're right. It's probably for the best."

Crash seemed incapable of ever giving up a fight until he was sure the battle was lost. So, I should've known, should've seen what was coming. But I was Yury. I felt I didn't need to explain myself or my actions to anyone, except my father. Therefore, I didn't tell Crash that he was mistaken, that I had not made up my mind on what path to take with Whitney. Had I been the wiser, maybe I could've stopped the upcoming earthquake.

I didn't know Whitney's mother had already left the half-crippled girl to fend for herself and returned to her husband in California. But Crash knew. He watched that girl's every move and not only slipped into her heart but between her virgin thighs.

I had yet to dream of sex with Whitney, only her dancing, but now that Crash had taken something that I saw to have extreme value, something in me snapped. I seethed at the sight of Crash holding Little Treasure in her place of rest. Standing on her bedroom porch, I once again found myself on the outside of her world. A place I was quickly tiring of being.

Someone had to pay for my discomfort.

As Crash kissed the forehead of the sleeping dancer, my decision was made.

Him.

Witnessing his sincere affections toward Whitney, I knew just how to capture him.

CHAPTER TWELVE

Escaping Numbness

Setting traps and luring the prey, that is what I was doing. It was a vicious sport that spun out of control before I could comprehend my actions. I was a hunter, out for revenge. I told myself I was angry with Crash for stealing part of Whitney's worth. It would take time to understand the truth; I was acting on the whims of an unreasonable infatuation.

Not that I thought any infatuation was reasonable.

I asked Harold, "So, another son, yes?"

Having never contemplated children of my own, I had no idea what it was like to learn I had a son; a fully grown, almost a man son. Therefore, I lacked the compassion it called for.

Apparently, it was just as shocking for Mr. Thompson. Sitting in his den, Harold stared at me with a bewildered expression. "I swear, I didn't know."

With elbows resting on my thighs, I sat there on his couch. "So I heard," was my response while texting Crash, unbeknownst to his father.

My skin felt heated as my resentment stirred. *You took something that was not yours.*

Crash's response was, *Nothin u dont do every day with yor profession.*

Harold ran his palm down his exhausted face. "Junior knows Marina is his mother."

Crash seemed as enraged as I. *Did u fuck my mother?*

I was seven.

And that means what in your world? Fucking more money!

I do not fuck children!

He had me seething, so I decided to punch him back. *Now that you know*

who I own, you will know why I'm collecting. Maybe I will take your mother, too.

I fucking hate you!

Sarcastically, I typed, *Now, you are breaking my heart…*

What heart?

You shouldn't have fucked Whitney!

U gave me no choice. I saw how u were— I winced at the set of eyeball emojis staring at me. *—at her. And I kno how you operate. Whit has been soiled. You wont want her anymore.*

My teeth begged for mercy from my tight jaw. *This is where you are mistaken. I sell non-virgins daily.* I peered up from my phone to see Harold— who wouldn't stop staring at me—so I asked, "What?"

"I find out I have a long-lost son, only to worry you will think he's your property—"

I held up a finger. "Which he is."

Harold yelled, "—and you can't get off your phone for one fucking minute?"

Adrian, waiting for me in the foyer, lifted a brow at Harold's tone. Kirill and the other men were waiting in the SUV. Harold had no minions present as I stretched and sat back in my seat. "No need to get hostile, American." I texted, *Tell Reether to pack his bags. I'm selling his ass, too.*

Touch my brother, and I will kill u dickhead!!!

Harold blinked in shock. "No need? We are talking about my son's blood being spilled!"

Angrily I typed, *I should kill you for what you have done!*

Fine! Do it! Just leave them the fuck alone!

Done! Your life! Their peace!

Now, *I* was the one blinking, wondering what I had just agreed to. Dazed, I lied to Harold, "I have not mentioned anything of the sort. It is you who is speaking of blood and death."

As if sensing I was lying yet again, he raced from his chair to a little

bar along the wall. Pouring whiskey into a glass of ice, he mumbled, "You are a deadly, impossible asshole."

In my already confused state, my brows bunched. "It could be a language barrier issue, but that makes no sense to me."

He threw the full glass against the wall, then roared. "*Are you going to kill my son?*"

Frustrated with myself, as much as with my conversation with Crash, I stood, preparing to leave. "Reether? No. His *father* and I have an arrangement."

Harold appeared as if he were either going to implode or explode at any second. The pressure of possibly losing another son was clearly a breaking point for him. Maybe my snide remark helped push him over the edge. As I exited the den, he yelled, "What about Junior?"

I peered over my shoulder, "Crash? We, too, have made an arrangement." I winked before walking out the American's front door.

Adrian followed me as Harold, still in the den, screamed into his handheld radio, "Get my fucking son home, you ignorant, useless bastards!"

Harold's minions found Crash at Whitney's home when they returned from a doctor's appointment about her foot. Leaving a stunned Reether and Whitney behind, the minions returned Crash to his father. Harold put the kid on lockdown in an attempt to keep him safe, but Crash had learned how to outsmart his father long ago and delivered himself to me.

A hotel room was not a good place to hold a hostage, so Adrian had arranged for us to rent a secluded house a couple of hours away. Harold and all his minions searched and cashed in favors to gain any information to our whereabouts. Apparently, five Russian men in Connecticut is quite memorable. After being found twice, by Harold's hired guns, and after successfully shooting our way free both times, we managed to keep Crash in our care.

The men Father had sent me came in handy.

"Hello?" I answered my cell, knowing exactly who was calling.

"You motherfucker! You killed four of my men!" Harold was livid.

"It was actually five. I can only recommend hiring more competent help or stop chasing us."

"You have my fucking son, you Russian asshole!"

I disconnected the call, laughing. "Your father is pissed." Crash was sitting next to me in the middle row of seats in the SUV. He had blood on his face because I had shot the thug that tried to take him from me. As if lost in his circumstance, he stared out the window. "You didn't have to kill him. I had almost broken free."

Kirill laughed, still exhilarated from the fight. "Did you see that guy's expression? He kept saying 'I'm here to help you!'"

Crash's eyes closed, as if trying to block out the image and the choice he had to make. Had he let that man take him, nothing would stand between myself and Whitney.

Trying to ignore more annoying sensations in my chest, I did my best to be casual about an unsettling situation. I rested my arm around his shoulders. "What would you like one of your last meals to be?"

He shrugged me off him. "Jesus, Yury. You're such a dick."

"What? At least I am feeding you."

His head fell back against the seat. "Why bother? I'll be dead soon."

The reality of the situation I had created—the hasty deal I made with Crash while still angry—started to sink in even more. Then came a feeling of dread in my gut. I couldn't help but quietly ask, "What does it feel like to choose to die for someone?"

Crash blew out a weighted breath, his shoulders showing exhaustion. "It's sad."

Not being able to back down due to exhibiting weakness in front of my employees, I figured this was a perfect way out for Crash. "Then, why do it? Just let me have her."

His head leaned against his window. "It's not sad because I will be dead. It's sad because I will no longer," his voice changed as he became choked up,

"get to see her."

The SUV went quiet. I was trying to understand such dedication. It was mystifying and unsettling to me, all at the same time. Crash was willing to no longer breathe or exist on earth so that someone else could. Not only was that confusing, but frustrating, because I couldn't relate in the slightest. I felt as if I'd missed out on some sort of secret of life—some sort of 'knowing' that didn't apply to people—traffickers—like myself.

Adrian said, "I hate to interrupt this uplifting conversation, but where are we going to take Crash now?" He examined his gun. "I'm running low on ammunition."

"Let me think for a minute." I observed Kirill staring at his naked stripper on his phone. "How old is she?"

He touched the screen as if lost in thought. "Valerie? Twenty-two."

My mouth fell open. "Kirill, she's legal?" I was almost proud of the child molester.

He smirked while glancing over his shoulder at me. "Yeah, and willing to let me fuck her in the ass any time I want."

Running out of options, I tapped my fingers on my knee. "You trust her?"

He glanced back to the phone. "I trust no one, Little Yury."

Every Russian nodded. This was how we survived.

After an exhale, I asked, "If she rented us a house, would it be imperative I kill her?"

Kirill's upper lip lifted in an animalistic snarl.

Even though Adrian was driving, he saw it. "Oh, shit. Protective?"

"No." Kirill's brows bunched in confusion while he stared out the windshield. "Am I?"

"Can I fuck her?" I asked to gauge how hard Kirill had fallen. When he twisted in his seat to punch me, I had my answer. I blocked his blow with my arm. "No?" I laughed. "No need for violence, Kirill. You could just deny me that sweet, tight—" I wasn't able to block the next blow in time.

But he never got to land his punch.

Crash shook as he held Kirill's fist in his own.

Junior having my back was sure making it much harder to kill him.

None of us Russians, nor my hostage, were in sight when Valerie rented a large house with plenty of bedrooms. We wanted no trail back to our location. Valerie was so enamored with Kirill; I knew she wasn't going to tell anyone. After every dancing shift, she would come to Kirill, and they would keep us up all night with their sexual endeavors.

Crash had his own bedroom in the beginning, but it became harder and harder for me to see him. He was a walking billboard of self-sacrifice. It was nauseating to wonder constantly if I would ever do the same. Plus, as annoying as it was, the kid was funny. It reminded me of how fond I was of him, only complicating the fact that I had to kill him. So, I had him put in the two-car garage so I wouldn't have to see or hear him. That made me feel even worse. I hated the weighted sensation sitting on my chest.

So, I drank a shitload of vodka to numb it. Once I was seeing two of everything, I finally went to bed, only to be kept awake by another hard-core fucking session between Valerie and Kirill.

I hadn't had a release in weeks, so I burst into Kirill's bedroom. Stumbling, due to alcohol and confusion as to how I fit into this world, I pointed to my raging hard-on. I slept nude, so there was nothing left to the imagination. "I can't take it anymore. I'm wound so tight I'm losing my shit, Kirill. So, both of you, shut the fuck up!" I needed quiet so I could fall asleep and stop thinking.

In his bed, Kirill rolled off his naked girl and onto his back, laughing uncontrollably.

Valerie's head tilted after propping herself up on her elbows, as if reading me. I wanted to look away, but recognition crossed her expression. Her eyes saddened, as if what she saw in me was something that caused her pain. Her pity spoke to me before her words did. "How about a blow job?"

166

Kirill stopped laughing. "What was that?"

My eyebrows rose as I swayed on my drunk and uncertain feet. "Truly?" It was a sexual promise, but those of us in the sex profession understood the power behind each act. It was for control, bravery, giving pleasure, or causing pain—even mental instability, which I was presently experiencing.

Kirill rolled to his side, resting his hand on her stomach. "Explain yourself."

She didn't. She simply said, "Look at him."

It felt like I was waving a white flag. It was like begging for something to ground me to the earth I no longer could feel under my feet. Sex. Sex was something I knew. I prayed the act would quiet my mind. I put my hands together, and in a rush, reverted to Russian. "*Please.*" I was desperate for him to hear my need, so I said anything that might convey my urgency. "*I won't soil her mouth. I'll pull out. I swear it.*" We had shared many slaves. I hoped a girl he liked would be the same.

His eyes studied me intensely, like never before. I think he saw past my persona and into my fear. We had our differences, but that didn't take away from the fact he probably knew me best. I grew up with him watching over me. Even as an adult, he was still watching over me, hence being in America together. It was a raw moment. Silently, I was so exposed.

Fortunately, he heard my insecurities that were also waving my flag of mercy.

Not removing his stare from mine, Kirill's Master's tone resonated as he commanded, "Val, on your knees." Without question, she slid out of the bed and onto the floor, landing on her knees. As she waited, I stayed back, to be sure Kirill was going to let me do this. Our stares still locked, he left the bed and stood in front of her. Blindly, he fisted her hair then growled, "Yury, soil this mouth and I will shoot you. Twice."

Relief. Pure relief eased from me as I nodded, greedily. "Not a drop will touch her."

I had never accepted the submissive role, but tonight was like no other for me thus far. So, when Kirill demanded, "Come," I did, thankful someone was taking charge of my erratic thoughts. I was desperate to feel wet, soft lips around my cock, yes, but also some sort of steadiness that I couldn't seem to find on my own. I was being haunted by a dancer and the one who loved her—the same one I was soon to murder.

Once next to Kirill, he yanked on Valerie's hair and showed her his veined erection. "You will come back to my dick. Understand?"

Her mouth, agape with heavy breathing, had me suddenly realizing she also needed someone to control her. In that very second, I finally comprehended her expression in the lobby of the hotel and every time I saw her waiting for Kirill. She craved his dominant ways. She was like me, hoping for something or someone to connect us to this life, whether we wanted it or not, because there were times when it was just too much to bear. The thought that her 'stripping' may not be what she wanted, and that her life was also out of control, had me feeling an unfamiliar empathy for another.

Chills broke out across my skin as his hand took hold of my hip to pull me in front of him, never letting go of Valerie's hair. When his chest pressed against my back, his erection slid between my legs, which were propped apart to keep me on my feet. He wasn't prodding my ass, but I still stiffened. Both of us being close to the same height put his mouth at my ear. His Master's tone commanded, "Breathe. I'm not going to fuck you."

I exhaled.

"That's right. I have you, Yury."

My eyes fluttered shut to the words I needed to hear.

His free arm wrapped around my ribs, his palm to my chest. "Breathe."

Valerie waited as air filled my restricted lungs. The release that fresh air brought me had my head falling back and landing on his shoulder.

Kirill repeated, "I have you."

Trust, what we had all claimed not to have, had me melting back against

him. That's when I was finally rewarded. Kirill pressed Valerie forward… and her little lips blanketed me. My legs almost gave out with a fantastic and much-needed sensation. Kirill's arm tightened around my waist. He had not lied. He had me and wouldn't let go.

Her tongue pulled on me from underneath. The warmth was heavenly. I found myself softly saying, "Thank you."

The gratitude was well received. Kirill started working her head, which in turn worked me. It was unlike any oral sex I had ever experienced because it was almost as if Kirill was the one truly getting me off. And, him being a man, he had perfect timing, yanking her head back to tease me when my balls were tightening up. When he would press her lips flush to my base, I was deep throated with skill. Kirill slowly started pumping his erection between my thighs, finding friction under my sack.

I was lost…

Now found.

All three of us started panting when Valerie reached between my legs to massage my aching balls and his hungry dick. She moaned as we all started gyrating and moving, desperate for climax. Kirill leaned his forehead to my shoulder, gasping for air. I reached behind me, holding his head to replicate the comfort he was offering me. The heat from his every exhale only ramped up my desire.

Maybe he sensed the heightened sexual tension because he kissed my shoulder, his mouth open, then my neck, all while bobbing Valerie on my dick, daring me to accept more. When I didn't shy away, he kissed the side of my mouth. It was then that I knew what he wanted.

I tilted my face toward his.

Kirill leaned forward and set his lips to mine.

When I opened my mouth, he dove in, yanking Valerie forward to deep throat me again. My whimper echoed in Kirill's mouth. Then a battle of male tongues took place. Both being Masters, we each fought for control. Neither, or

maybe both, winning.

Seeing what was happening above, Valerie moaned more pleasure. The vibrations revved up my desire, having me pulling on the back of Kirill's head to get deeper into his mouth. His hips pumped against me. It was all so arousing; I pulled my face from him just enough to say, "I'm going to come soon."

He kissed me again as he pulled Valerie from my dick and from her knees. His lips released mine as he yanked her between us, her chest to my back, then he hoisted her tiny body, saying, "Hold on to his neck." Little arms came over my shoulders from behind and wrapped around my neck. She gasped in my ear as he slammed inside her... Her soft breasts rubbed against my shoulder blades. As they both started grunting, I thought I was going to be left out, but then Kirill reached around and took a strong hold of my dick. It was so intense; I stumbled forward. Kirill followed until I could place my hands against the wall and hold us all up. His hips would thrust forward, pushing her harder against me, all while his fist pumped me into a frenzy.

"Harder," I demanded. My head fell forward as my dick was beautifully abused. "Yes. Fuck. Don't stop." My whole body began to shake as I was taken on the ride of my life.

But what took me right over the edge of the slippery cliff was Valerie in my ear. "I think he's fucking you by fucking me."

In the family business, my position was dominant over Kirill's. He knew it. We all did. I think he needed one over me. That night, I let him have it, and I let myself enjoy it.

I roared through a heart-stopping orgasm that shattered my mind into blissful numbness.

The next morning, I was still with them, with Valerie in between us. Everyone was still naked. No longer drunk or feeling vulnerable, I woke, pissed at my

surroundings. Anger poured from me as I left the bed behind, needing to brush my teeth to remove my cousin from my mouth.

Exiting the room in a shameful rush, I ran right into Adrian. He had clearly just woken up himself and seemed shocked to see me naked. "The fuck, Yury?" Then his eyes raced to where I had just come. With the door wide open, he saw the bed, then smirked. "Oh, and Adrian was not to receive an invitation?" I shoved him out of my way and entered my own room down the hall.

Clothed, I stared at my reflection while brushing my teeth in the bathroom. What I saw—the weak being I had become last night—enraged me. I punched the mirror. As the pieces crashed to the counter and floor, I charged toward someone else I blamed for my fall.

In the garage, where Crash was tied up, he cussed, "Here we fucking go again," when he saw me storming for him. He did his best to block but was the recipient of a kick at full force. He rolled across the cement floor and laughed at me through his grimace of pain. "You're just mad that I slept with her and you didn't."

At the time, I wasn't sure if his statement was true, but I was positive his mouth was pissing me off further. "I'm mad because you stole her value." Maybe it wasn't even about the sexual intercourse. Maybe it was only the disgust I had for him and his dedication to her, and that I was completely and totally incapable of such devotion to anyone but myself.

From the ground, he smiled up at me. "We both know her virginity is way low on her 'value' list. And you killed the one who knew this first. Tim was well aware of the rare being she is."

My skin, boiling from all the rage inside me, begged to be set free and bring about a wrath to be felt for all the ages of time. I didn't want any more reminders of the hell I had rained down on her life, so, with trembling fists, I sneered, "And, now, I will be killing the second?"

A tortured laugh burst from his soul. "Nah, clearly, you haven't been

paying attention. The second would be Link."

Pausing my rage, my brows scrunched. "Who is Link?"

Crash smiled, as if knowing the best secret the Universe had to offer. "That would be her very best friend in the whole wide, motherfucking world." He smiled wickedly. "Reether. My fucking brother. Her strongest link. You break that—you kill him? You might as well kill her." I recoiled in horror. Snuffing out her and what she brought to my miserable existence was beyond comprehension. His laugh was different this time. It was confident. "That's right, dickwad. Checkmate. I'll soon be leaving to save the girl I love, but she and the only brother I have left will continue to walk this earth. Together."

His supreme truth sent me into a blind rage. I didn't wake from it until Adrian and Kirill were pulling me off of Crash. He was bleeding. He was already bruising.

But the bastard was still fucking smiling.

"*I am bringing her home with us.*"

I gawked at Kirill. "*This is not possible.*" Valerie was an unknown marvel, and I understood his fascination. Her perception was quite impressive to the heartless, such as Kirill and I, but she had no place in our world back home. Whatever purity that lurked within her would be stolen the moment she set foot in our hell.

Frustrated, he told me, "*If you support this, our fathers will allow it.*"

From the dining room table, I watched as Valerie carefully and quietly set a plate of Taco Bell in front of me, as if aware of what Kirill was asking me in Russian. She knew I didn't like to eat in front of the television. She also figured out I hated to eat off paper plates or To-Go boxes. I appreciated her attentive ways. We had no slaves present to tend to us.

Adrian and the other men were also sitting at the table, but their dinners

were not plated like mine. They were not nearly as refined as they shoved food into their hungry mouths.

As Valerie set down a glass of water with no ice in front of me, the way I preferred my beverage, I grabbed her wrist. "Do you know his profession?"

Not trying to pull from my hold, she glanced at Kirill. "It doesn't matter to me."

"No?" I asked, amused. "What about him continuing to be a Master to other women." Her eyes slid shut as if my words were painful. "That is correct. It is his job and will not end because you have captured his interest."

Her eyes opened as her jaw ticked. "It is more than that between us."

I licked my upper row of teeth. "Yes? Then why did he let you suck my dick."

Everyone stopped, with tacos hanging from their mouths, and looked to Kirill, who was fuming. "Little Yury, be careful."

Leaning forward, I barked, "Don't forget who it is you are speaking to!" He needed to remember his place, even after all that had transpired the evening prior. "I am your boss." I glared to Valerie, "That means I am also yours." Turning my chair slightly to face her, I glanced at the carpet, then to her. "Kneel."

Her nostrils flared as she settled onto her knees. "I see through you. Being exposed was a deal-breaker for you."

Before she could register me moving, I had her hair in my fist. Adrian, already out of his chair, restrained Kirill with an arm around his neck, practically choking him, and placed a gun to his temple. Valerie, not able to move her head without pain, peeked out from the corner of her eye to find her boyfriend. As soon as she caught a glimpse of the gun, she grabbed my knees. "Don't hurt him. I'll shut up."

Trying to ignore the fact that Kirill might actually have someone to care for him, I warned Valerie, "That is correct. And the only weakness you are going to witness today is yours and his." I released her and sat back in my chair to take a bite of my burrito. I also pulled off a piece. "Open your mouth." I didn't know

eyes could spew hatred and gratitude at the same time, but hers did. I placed food on her tongue. "I learned this mouth well last night. No?"

As she chewed, she angrily replied, "Yes."

"Therefore, you earned this meal." I gave her another bite. "What are you going to do to earn your flight to Russia?"

Kirill stopped fighting Adrian, asking, "*You mean this?*"

I shrugged. "There will be a price."

His eyes raced to hers, then back to mine, his face showing understanding as it took place. The price would be high. "But, why?"

Casually, I wrapped a leg around her, crudely pulling her off her balance so that she would fall into my lap. "As you said, you trust no one."

He winced. "But... last night—"

"Is never to be spoken of again."

Not caring about the gun to his head, Kirill eagerly, and nervously, nodded. "Okay. Done, Yury. Just do not take this too far."

"She needs to know what she is going to be surrounded with. How many girls she will witness you fuck, rape, and train."

Kirill shouted, "I won't do it in front of her!"

"You really think that takes away the sting? Have you forgotten Mrs. Thompson and me in front of her husband?" I took a bite of my food. Speaking around my mouthful, I asked Valerie, "Can you envision his dick sliding in and out of many pussies, for the rest of your days together?"

As if I had sucked her dry of energy with my words, she laid her upper body in my lap. "Why are you doing this?"

I patted her hair. "Because this is our reality. One that only death will end, for all involved."

Roles had switched. Kirill was now as lost as I had been. "Yury! You're scaring her!"

"If only *hearing* the truth is hard for her to handle, imagine what seeing it will do."

His eyes closed.

Adrian lowered his gun.

I lifted Valerie's chin to peer into her eyes. She needed to understand I was not exaggerating. "And you are not wearing a collar, Little Pet." Confusion crossed her pixie face as I sneered to my comrade, "Isn't this correct, Kirill?"

Nervously, he swallowed. "Yes, but—"

"But what? Already, she has you not following the rules?" While he was tongue-tied to the trap I led him into, I explained to Valerie, "If a slave has not been claimed, he or she is free game."

No barrel to Kirill's head made her braver again. "I'm not a slave, you pig."

My face invaded her personal space. "That is where you are wrong, yet again. No woman taking residence in our home is free of this title."

She recoiled. "Stop it."

"Stop what?"

"Treating me like this."

"Like what?"

She screamed, "A piece of meat!"

Fed up with her disrespect, and trying to get her to acknowledge the godawful circumstances she was willingly joining, I shoved her body to the ground in front of my chair, then followed her descent. Kirill roared to be released as the rest of my men assisted restraining him as I was prying her legs apart. Holding Valerie down, I lifted her dress, ripped her G-string from her body, then shoved two fingers into her cunt. "But meat and walking dollar bills are all you are in my establishment."

Getting to my feet, I dragged Valerie with me. It was easy to toss her over my shoulder. She kicked and smacked my back as I faced Kirill, pointing my wet fingers in his face. "Leash her, or I will do this over and over!" After trapping her legs to my stomach, I stepped closer to Kirill and growled, "Never try to fuck me again." I slammed an aggressive kiss to his non-responsive lips.

"*And, now, because you have involved her to this level, I have to take her back with us, you stupid shit. Either that or kill her.*" I stepped away, reared back, and punched his chest. "*Decide. Now. Do I fuck her or kill her?*"

Adrian jostled Kirill to snap him out of shock. Kirill blinked, then exhaled a regret all men present could feel. I was sure of it. "*Fuck her.*"

With Valerie still hanging over my shoulder, I smacked her ass. "Good choice."

As I started to walk away, Valerie slipped into a panic. "Kirill? Stop him!"

In record speed, he grabbed the SUV keys from the dining room table. "Valerie, fight as hard and as long as you can."

I didn't slow my pace either. "Tick tock, Kirill. Tick tock. I'm already erect."

Valerie whaled in horror as tires screeched out of the driveway.

CHAPTER THIRTEEN

Mental Scars

Valerie clawed at the shirt on my back while I shut my bedroom door. Still perched over my shoulder, she screamed for Kirill, who couldn't hear her. He was too busy rushing to the nearest store that sold pet supplies. Since we were hidden away in the countryside of the small town, I knew I had plenty of time.

As pain seared my skin, I grabbed the tiny girl and threw her across the room, aiming for the bed. She bounced on the mattress, then onto the floor. Feeling the carpet for only a second, Valerie scrambled to get to her feet and run toward the door.

"No, little pet."

"Stop calling me that!" she screeched as I expertly wrapped an arm around her waist to hoist her into the air where she was, once again, powerless.

"The less you fight, the better chance of you enjoying yourself."

"Fuck you!"

Coyly, I explained, "I'm trying to let you, but you are not cooperating." I tossed her back on the bed, this time holding her down. Clasping her wrists together, I effortlessly held her hands to the mattress above her head. My knee slipped between her legs as I used one hand to lift her summer dress, once again, to see her core. "Open up for me, little flower."

"Noooooo!"

"If you calm yourself, it won't hurt so much."

"Yury! Stop! I tried to help you last night!"

I started unbuckling my pants with my free hand. "This is not about you

She cried, "Why? What did he do wrong?"

I pushed down my slacks. "He let you into his heart."

Even with me partly naked, she stilled underneath me. "But… why punish him for that?"

I sighed. "It is a hazard to his job and health."

"H-His health?"

Now, I stilled. Twice, she had shown compassion for his well-being. I wasn't sure if I was jealous or confused about such affection. Maybe both at the time. "You really care for him?"

With determination, she looked me directly in the eyes. "If I stop fighting, will you believe me?"

I think I was already starting to believe her. How could I not? I was presently preparing to rape her, yet she was more concerned about Kirill's health. Sadly, none of this had the power to stop the lesson I had been taught long ago, one I now had to instill into Kirill's psyche, so I answered, "Yes."

Valerie stared at me for a slight moment, then her legs fell open, exposing what she thought I craved. Her arms released the tension against mine. Then she quietly spoke, "I don't know what love is, but I feel something so strong for him. So strong."

Suddenly feeling terribly drained myself, I rolled my body off of hers and laid next to her, both of us now facing the ceiling. "It's not love. He's a Master. We know how to fuck your mind as well as your pussy."

She wiped tears from her cheeks. "You don't sound happy about your profession."

I gestured to my exposed flaccid penis. "What gave it away?"

"Does that mean," she pointed to me, "we don't have to have sex?"

My palm rubbed down my face as I exhaled regret. "No."

Accepting her fate, she choked on more tears and bravely said, "Okay."

My head fell to the side so I could see her. "We are conditioned to not fall in love. If we think we are doing so, another must soil her."

Sniffling, Valerie winced. "Is that why he didn't want you to come in my mouth?" Her expression showed how hard she was listening to me and trying to understand. It made my chest ache a little, so I didn't have the courage to lie. I nodded. Swallowing, she nodded also. "And if you 'soil' me?"

Commenting about this horrid theory out loud, for the very first time, had me realizing how absurd it truly was. "It is supposed to be a deterrent. It is supposed to make you no longer desirable. He should no longer want you." She gasped as if I'd just sliced her with a blade. I closed my eyes and faced the ceiling again. "Does it sound crazy?"

"It sounds… hurtful."

I stayed quiet, hoping she would explain.

She did. "If another man, one raping me, is enough to make him want to dump me—"

I glanced at her. "Dump?"

"Oh, umm… Break up with me."

I raised a brow. "Break you?"

Her eyes widened. "No. I mean… uh, end our relationship."

"Oh."

She rushed, "My point is, I want to know if he will let me go after such a horrible thing."

"Why?"

"Because, if after I was to be raped, soiled, if he still wanted me, then I would know we are the real deal."

I thought for a moment then asked, "But why should it matter?"

After her mouth gaped open and she stared at me as if I were baffling her, she finally asked, "Have you ever had a girlfriend?"

Absurd. "What for?"

"What for?" She blinked. "Well, to love someone."

I gestured to our present situation. "Are you not comprehending what I'm about to do and why?"

179

Shaking her head no, as if to clear her mind, she closed her eyes in dismay. "To fall in love is a dream. At least, that is what cartoons have taught me."

"You are starting to sound more confused than I."

Opening her eyes, she whispered, "My mom's pimp wasn't the best role model. He handed me a remote and told me to watch cartoons while he sold my mom in the bedroom."

Now, this was a lifestyle I knew, so I asked, "When did he start selling you?"

"He never got the chance. By fourteen, I was his girlfriend."

Her attraction and acceptance of Kirill's profession were now making much more sense. It's all she knew. She grew up in a similar environment.

Valerie continued, "He didn't want to share me at first. That changed after his 'partner' raped me." She rolled to her side, drawing her legs into her stomach. "Yeah, so I know what being soiled is all about. I thought my boyfriend would kill his partner, not turn me out to the streets." She wiped away more tears. "On my first run, that's exactly what I did. I ran. Never looked back. Not even for my mother, who was too hooked on crack to notice anyway. I've been dancing ever since." She wiped snot from under her nose. "So, that is why I need you to—" She blew out a trembling breath. "I can't handle Kirill treating me the same as him. I need to know a rape won't change how he feels about me."

I guess I should've been thinking about the upcoming rape, but instead, my mind wondered on my own slaves. If one were to somehow make it home, I wondered how their family would receive them. Tainted? Soiled? Dirty? It was the first time I considered that surviving my training wouldn't be their only battle. Surviving the mental scars I caused would be another mountain to conquer. And, if any boyfriend, girlfriend, or family weren't supportive, it would be nearly impossible.

I could no longer rape Valerie. Our conversation had gone far past a sexual act. Actually, knowing some of her history somehow made her more

CHAPTER FOURTEEN

Whiplash Emotions and Fantasies

Hearing the SUV's engine roar toward the house, I stared at Valerie. She had a choice to make. Here was the moment that would change her future's outcome. Here was the very moment she could have saved herself. I exhaled regret as I watched her little bottom lip quiver.

Sitting on the edge of the bed, facing the door, she shook her head. "I... I want to be with him."

Tires shrieked into the driveway as I said, "I should be killing you for what you already know about us, but I am giving you one chance... to run."

As if sensing the dire mistake she was making, tears dripped from her eyes. "I can't. Not from him."

Surrendering to her fate, I nodded. "Now, the chance is over."

The door swung open...

Kirill, frantically holding a collar and leash in the air, yelled, "Here is my claim—" He stopped when seeing Valerie clothed and unsoiled. His eyes raced to mine.

I shrugged. "Meh. I don't like to fuck strippers—" I never got to finish. Kirill had me in an embrace, whispering, "Thank you."

He shouldn't have thanked me. I wasn't worthy.

Valerie would join him on our journey back to Russia.

And, Valerie would be dead in his arms within one year.

human to me. Surprising me, I could no longer view her as the meat I had claimed her to be earlier, so I stood and started pulling up my pants.

From the bed, Valerie gasped. "What are you doing?"

"Warning you about us. Go home, Valerie. Live a better life. What your pimp boyfriend did? Kirill and I make him look like child's play."

The billionaire client I had to meet in *No Cherries Here*, to whom I was to cater, according to my father, had hand-picked his slave during an operation he recently experienced. Yes, while this man was home recovering, he was high on painkillers and dreaming of his young surgeon in a sexual sense.

Had the fresh-out-of-his-internship doctor only known.

Leaving one man behind to watch over Crash, I went with Kirill and Adrian to observe the risky slave we would soon apprehend. Generally, we preferred young adults who didn't have many loved ones to search for him or her. A doctor, from a prominent family that moved from Holland to Connecticut for their son's education? Not wise. They were going to bring lots of media attention. But seven-hundred-and-fifty-thousand dollars is quite swaying; hence, we found ourselves sitting in the SUV watching the doctor leave an apartment building that was not his.

Was it ironic that we were judging his affair while contemplating how to proceed with his upcoming abduction? *Meh.* Maybe so, but it didn't stop us from searching for a weakness—clearly not his young wife waiting at home. My money was on his three-year-old daughter.

This educated man, who was somewhat arrogant with his accomplishments and stunning appearance, was not going to be easily fooled, drugged, and taken to another country for training. In fact, we were so confident he was going to be beyond reasonable that we were giving ourselves four extra months after his abduction, to break and rebuild him into the perfect sexual machine.

A full head of dark hair blew in the wind as his car lights lit up after he pressed a button on his key chain. His hair was shiny, straight, and fell past broad shoulders.

With binoculars, Adrian sharply inhaled. *"Are those contacts?"*

Now, we understood why our new client was so taken. The young doctor had grey eyes like I had never seen. It was as if they were beams of light, piercing with magical power in the night.

Kirill patted my shoulder. "*You will have your hands full, training the Soul Reader.*"

He was correct. Those eyes were for reading souls, and he would soon be reading mine.

Back at the rental house, we were greeted by an apologetic guard. He was trying to explain that he didn't know Valerie had been in the garage and spent time with Crash until she emerged, crying.

Kirill quickly asked, "*Where is she now?*"

"*In your room. Packing her duffle bag.*"

Kirill ran down the hallway toward his bedroom as I faced the door that led into the garage.

I have many regrets when it comes to Crash, and the times we shared, including this time. I regret I was yet to have a better hold of my temper when he provoked me. I regret I was unable to recognize all there was to learn from such a selfless person. And, I regret what I did to him for three weeks in that garage. Once again, I was mistreating him with starvation, mental abuse, and most certainly physical abuse.

After entering, I tossed a burner phone at him. "Call your brother."

Crash, filthy from being chained in the garage, sneered, "Why?" but quickly picked it up, knowing this was his last chance to speak to a family member.

"I need inside the Summers' home. Tell him to let me in with no interruptions."

"Fuck you, dude."

I knew Mr. Jones would behave, but my suspicions told me this Reether character would not be so obliging. So, I pulled out my gun and aimed it at his head. "You have two minutes."

"To say what?"

"The Jones family is not to interfere with my plan to get back

documents."

"But—"

I held up my hand to silence him. "I will not be leaving this horrid country empty-handed. Do you wish I take your brother and girlfriend, or two pieces of paper?"

Crash panted as he started to tap a number he clearly knew by memory. His voice violently trembled, but he tried to disguise it when he spoke into the receiver. "Link." He listened then gave a shaky smile that spoke volumes, such as: this may be the last time we ever speak to one another. "Where've I been?" Crash eyed me and replied to Link, "Oh, you know. Catching sun rays in Hawaii."

After the phone call to his brother, begging Link to allow us into Whitney's home for a thorough search, all chess pieces were back on the board. I needed one more thing. "Whitney's cell number."

"Bite me."

"Do you not think she would prefer a call versus me barging into her home?"

To my pleasure, he eventually agreed.

Now, it was time to address another issue. "What did you say to Valerie?"

Crash pretended to be more like me. "How do you know I didn't hurt her?"

Suddenly drained again, for reasons I was yet to realize, I sunk into a folding chair. "As absurd as it sounds, because you are surrendering your life to save another's." Before I could say anything else, Kirill stormed in and set his fists free. I yelled, "No!" while pulling him off of Crash.

Kirill was seething mad. "Now, she doesn't want to go to Russia!"

While I shoved Kirill back into the house, I told him, "*It is probably for the best. Have her killed if you can't stomach doing it yourself, weakling.*" I shut the door. If she was already backing out of the arrangement, there was no point in taking her.

185

Sitting on the floor, Crash leaned against a concrete wall, wiping blood from his bottom lip. "Someone had to warn her." He had old and now new bruises all over.

Hiking up my slacks for comfort, I sat back down. "And you assumed it should be you?"

He dabbed his swelling cheek. "Who else? One of your rapists that's getting to sleep in beds, not this luscious concrete?"

"Let go of this crusade, and I will take Whitney back where she belongs."

"With *you,* to Russia? Oh, sure! Good times, Yury. Maybe she can share a room with Valerie, and they can have gang rape parties!" He clapped his bloody hands in fake glee. Then he slumped back to the wall. "No, thank you, deranged foreigner."

Against my will, his sarcasm and insults still entertained me. I found myself fighting a grin. "So, you still choose death?"

He smeared blood from his hands to his grungy jeans. "I'm not sure you have the capacity to understand, so why bother explaining?"

"What if I promise to give you my best effort to 'keep up'?" I did quotations in the air as if an American, causing us both to chuckle. Then, I propped my body up by my elbows against my thighs, ignorantly unaware that Crash was about to speak words that would punch me in the gut.

He gazed at me as if we were once friends, then he swallowed and spoke from his heart. "I'm sorry your life ended up shittier than mine, Yury."

There was no pity present, only a regret that was losing the strings that once held me together. That, too, was pissing me off, so I pulled out my cellphone. "Let's film which of us has the shitty life."

"Then you need to point that camera at yourself."

I was exasperated. He wouldn't see reason. "But you die tonight!"

"I don't care! She's worth it!"

"Tell me why!"

"Fine!"

The garage went quiet except for our stressed breathing. I was to kill Crash within hours, yet I was dumbfounded by the constant burn in my chest. Everything in my immediate surroundings felt as if it was unraveling. At the time, it seemed it was imperative that I stood strong, for the sake of leading our enterprise, and for the sake of my sanity. If I could convince my own self that I was in charge, I foolishly believed it would be true. So, I tapped record and aimed my cell at Crash. "Tell me."

Leaning against the garage wall, he paused so long in thought I had time to reflect on the surroundings. Due to being in a rental, there weren't many tools or items, but I could smell leftover oils that had dripped from a car or lawnmower. I could almost sense the memories that had taken place there. Now, it was tainted with Crash's blood and my draining ego.

"Have you ever listened to someone sleep?"

I blinked, being pulled from my own thoughts. "What the fuck for?"

"Think about it. Have you ever slowed your world down enough to take the time to appreciate someone else's very breath? I know I hadn't."

I hadn't either, so I was already becoming annoyed with his insight that was far above my own. My nostrils flared as I stared at him.

He didn't care. He was already staring at nothing but a memory in his head. "Not until a fiery little redhead entered my world—my life—my pitiful excuse of an existence that ran aimlessly from one miserable day into the next."

It had been the same for me. Seeing that girl dance awoke something inside me.

Still lost in thought, he said, "I'd become so complacent, so unaware, yet so absorbed in my actions, and my action's results, that a numbness overtook me and my thoughts."

My hand tightened on the phone while my other one gripped at my leg as my nerves lit ablaze.

"Not even an action-packed movie could hold my attention, so I left the

theater in search of water." Crash's fingers touched one another as if he were longing for something. "I say water, but I think I was truly searching for air."

Sweat broke out across my back.

"For relief from the dead feeling in my soul."

I could barely swallow.

"The unseen weight, crushing my chest, begging for the nightmare that was my life to end."

My mouth opened as I panted for oxygen.

"A breath of fresh air is exactly what I got as I turned the corner, seeing Franky eye that popcorn machine with nothing but pure determination."

As if I had been there, experiencing his same relief, I exhaled. "Who is Franky?"

His brows bunched. "Whitney."

"Oh."

"'Oh' is right, Yury. More like *Oh boy*. I stayed back, watching her mind debate whether or not to take advantage of the old employee's absence. I had to muffle my laugh, which was a shame because it was my first in more years than I can remember. I kept watching as Franky decided the prize was worth the risk, and clumsily dove over the concession counter."

I then covered my mouth to muffle my laugh, totally thrilled she was such a rule breaker.

But Crash heard or saw me, because he chuckled at me. "Yeah, it was that night she woke me, but the night *you* want to know of," his eyes finally met mine, "that was the night she *stole* me."

At first, I thought Crash was saying that having sex with Whitney was absolutely beyond all comprehension, but I had missed his true meaning. It wasn't the sex he was speaking of.

I had stolen freedom many times in my life, but never had I seen someone taken like this. By the knowing in his blue eyes, Crash had been altered where I had no access. No matter all I had done to slaves, their heart could

always be theirs, if they chose it to be. Whitney would soon teach me this very lesson, just as she had this young man who sat mesmerized in front of me.

I stopped recording, desperate to know. "Tell me." His mouth opened, but no sound came out. Teeter-tottering on the brink of suspense, I moved to the edge of my seat. "Tell me why I shouldn't kill you both and be rid of all this hassle."

His eyes welled before he whispered, "Because... she is everything."

So hungry to feel what he was feeling, I growled, "More."

In a sweet surrender, he told me, "She let me in."

"To where."

"The unknown."

I inhaled for control of my aggravation. "It was only sex."

His body sulked. "Yury, the sex was just on the outside. It was what was happening in her heart." He gazed at the floor. "Happening inside mine."

I snarled, disappointed to where I thought this conversation was headed. "You fell in *love*?"

He chuckled, but it sounded to be more out of pity. "People who say you 'fall' in love are wrong. You float... You float right into the safety of someone who would *never* let you fall." Fingers grazed his lips as if still able to feel her lingering kiss. "Franky and I... we floated to each other." His eyes met mine, and they filled with dominance.

A Dominant knows when confronted with another, like an alpha to alpha confrontation.

He sneered, "And *that's* why I am here. *I* will *never* let her fall." His eyes bored into mine, challenging me. "Even after you kill me."

After I adjusted to his insult, thinking he was more dominant than I, a laugh escaped me. I sat back in my chair, believing Crash had no power in the afterlife. I lifted my camera and said, "Let's take it from where we left off. How shitty is your life?" I tapped my phone and started recording.

Crash, being the young man I would come to admire for the rest of

189

my days, was once again stubborn. It was his last night to exist, so he taunted me. Instead of getting past the emotional message I was refusing to hear, he continued, "Her breath exhaled across my chest as we laid together, naked in her bed, her innocence now gone."

My chest rose and fell...

"It was wrong of me to be the one who took it. I know who deserved that first more than me. I know who loves her, even though he claimed Constance was his girlfriend. Link would give his life for the girl who was clinging to me in her sleep."

All this loyalty was making me uncomfortable. "You speak of your brother giving his life, yet you are the one going to die for her."

"Yeah. Good point." He shook his head. "But I saw the look in Link's eyes. He was going to turn himself in to you, for her—for us."

"Why did you stop him?"

"He's my brother. I can't let him go down like that. Not for me." Crash's eyes welled. "And... because I love her... And... she loves *him*."

I was confused. Crash had just told me he and Whitney "floated" to one another. "She does not love you?"

He wiped under his eyes. "She thinks she does. But it's Link who truly has her heart. Ya gotta see them together to understand. It's like they are an extension of each other." Crash chuckled. "They blended long before I arrived. Franky is just stubborn, and my brother is just a dumbass."

I was done with all this love babble and was getting back to what needed to be addressed. "Crash, we have a problem. You stole from me. Her virginity was already sold for another to take." It wasn't a complete lie. I think I wanted it.

Nodding, Crash studied me. Anger crossed his expression. "I've been to your home. I couldn't let you take her to that godawful torture chamber you call a training facility."

I felt Crash was playing dirty and forgetting I was holding all the cards, so I decided to remind him of something. "A debt is a debt."

Crash knew me well enough to hear my underlying threat. Maybe he started remembering other promises I had not fulfilled. His voice was suddenly strained, not confident as it had been seconds earlier. "Paying my debt with my life keeps her alive, though, right?"

I licked my teeth. "It will keep her *alive*." Then mouthed, *like you did Sam.*

"Wait. We had a deal." Crash was referring to me being the one who cost Sam her life.

"And I am keeping it." From behind the camera, I shook my head no, so Crash knew Whitney was going to be all mine.

"Is that why you're recording me?"

From my pocket, I pulled out a red collar and leash. I had already prepared myself for my father's wrath.

"You sonofabitch!" Crash got up, wanting to fight me. "No! She is not going to be one of your fucking pets—"

There was no more holding back all my pent-up rage. It simply overflowed as if a rapid river, no longer cooperating with the built damn. I was yelling at more than Crash. I think it was my father, too. "You stole what was mine…"

This young man was, throughout the years, constantly willing to face my wrath and be burdened with my insanity for the sake of others. Nothing was any different that unforgettable, fateful night.

When I was forced to stop beating Crash and go back into the rental house, I broke free from my men. I smoothed out my jacket and my hair with my hands, trying to gain an ounce of composure. "He dies… and Whitney goes with us to Russia… tonight."

"What does he keep mumbling?" asked an annoyed Kirill.

Crash had been so severely beaten by me that he was barely conscious. They rolled his tied form into the back of the SUV with our suitcases. We were headed back to Russia after visiting Whitney's home.

I stared at my bruised knuckles, then swallowed guilt that tasted like acid and death. I'd lacked the courage to look in the back since we placed him there, but I could hear him, clear as day. "He's praying." I exhaled a sentiment that I was unable to understand at the time. "He's saying 'Save her, Link. Save her, Tim'."

Adrian peered back at me from the front passenger seat and studied me for a moment before saying, *"I'll do it."*

He meant kill Crash. I shrugged my weighted shoulders. *"Meh, whatever."* My stomach stirred with a storm of emotions that were threatening to be my undoing.

Adrian's wise eyes were seeing through me. *"Are we still taking the girl tonight?"*

I was already doubting that decision also, but I snapped, *"Is that not what I already said?"*

Adrian gave a knowing nod before turning up the radio and facing forward, maybe to give me a break from hearing Crash's hopeless pleas. Maybe they weren't hopeless at all as they ate away at me. Maybe God was intervening the whole damn time.

Kirill and the other two men were so engrossed in their casual conversation; I was surprised Kirill was handling Valerie's death so well. She was not with us. I had presumed Kirill had done what was told. I didn't seem to have enough energy at the moment to inquire why his mood was not sour.

After we drove down a hidden back road through the woods surrounding the Summers' neighborhood, we parked at the edge of Whitney's vast backyard. Unloading the SUV, Kirill studied across the lake, where Link lived. He chuckled, *"What do we have here? Amateurs 'R US?"*

Link and his parents were poorly hidden in bushes, using binoculars to watch over Whitney's home. They had yet to even notice us. I knew they would do nothing when they did. Mr. Jones had an illegal alien wife, therefore a false marriage license, and a son produced by the human trafficking trade that they had allowed to continue without notifying the authorities. That would be almost as much trouble for him as me. If nothing else, he would lose his license to practice law, although falsifying government documents held a hefty punishment. Mr. Jones and I could share a prison cell if he wasn't cautious.

Walking toward the back of the SUV, I commented, *"We stick to the plan."*

"Sounds good, Boss." Kirill stepped in front of me near the tail of the truck. *"I'll retrieve* Crash."

"Boss?" I lifted a brow at Kirill. *"And since when do you volunteer your services to me?"* His shrug was a pathetic lie. I sneered, *"I see."* I pushed him from my path, suspecting my cousin was up to no good. Lifting the hatch of the SUV, I saw I was correct. I stared at a dead Valerie lying next to Crash. Facing Kirill, I whispered with anger, *"You brought her fucking body, you sick fuck?"*

Kirill winced. *"Not exactly."*

Adrian joined us, then recoiled. *"Oh, shit."*

If we were to get pulled over by an officer, it would have been hard enough to explain Crash, beaten and tied, but I had a plan for that. I was going to tell the officer we found him and were rushing him to the nearest medical facility. The dead girl? *Meh.*

Madly, I gestured to her, demanding Kirill explain.

His head bobbled on his shoulders. *"She is not dead, per se."*

Fisting my hands, I whispered my growl. *"Why the fuck not?"*

He put his palms together. *"Because she is mine. I claimed her."*

This was true, and we did have rules, but I was still about to lose my composure. *"Then why is she unconscious?"*

Kirill exhaled as if preparing for my rage. *"She was unwilling to join me,*

193

so I drugged her."

Even though we kidnapped on a daily basis, I slammed my fist into his mouth, sending him to the ground. There was no time for such a distraction. I had Crash to kill and a different girl to kidnap. Now another one to sneak out of the country? Kirill was being extremely selfish with his actions, so I kicked him, too.

He accepted my abuse, wiping his bloody lip, but stated, *"She has been properly claimed, little Yury."*

Kirill knew he had backed me into a corner. If I didn't follow this rule, a trust issue would wave throughout all the men I was soon to govern.

After telling Adrian to get Kirill off the ground, I told one of my men to retrieve Crash. Crash hung over his shoulder as we crossed the yard, his tied wrists dangling.

Adrian whispered, *"They see us now."*

I peered across the lake in time to see Mr. Jones, Reether, and Pet. Mr. Jones was pushing down Pet's binoculars; I'm sure so she couldn't see her beaten, semi-unconscious son.

Staring at the back of Whitney's home, I could see her in a white nightgown, sitting on a couch in a stoic state. The cast on her leg pinged my already annoyed stomach. As I had no time to spare with Kirill's nonsense, the same went for my own needs. So, I lifted my cellphone to my ear...

"Link, I just need the night to think. Stop worrying." Her voice was glorious and had me refocused in a second flat.

"Maybe it is not Link who should be worried." After her marvelous slight gasp, I said, "Ah. Already worried?"

Her vibrant voice was now laced with fear. "Yes, I am worried."

The Master in me was pleased. "Good. I love to have someone's undivided attention."

Blood rushed through my body as her obedience sang to me like her dancing. "You have it, sir."

I had to restrain a groan. "No wonder little Crash likes you so. You are a

194

smart little cookie. Do you know what it is that I am looking for?"

Her hand anxiously rubbed her thigh. "No. No, I do not."

I desperately wanted to see the face I was speaking to. I craved for those eyes to burn me with their brilliance. So, I hung up on her. It was risky, but, in an instant, I decided a video call was in order. As soon as her face appeared on my phone's screen, my whole body eased, and a smile crossed my face. All I could do was become enamored by her close-up appearance. Of course, her eyes were beyond magnificent, but her button nose fit perfectly between high cheekbones. A tiny, pink tongue darted out every now and then to wet little, pouty lips that were red from her nervously nibbling on them.

Trying to collect myself, I regarded, "Forgive my rudeness. I just thought this way would be more persuasive for you."

She was standing now and jerked when an automatic timer of sorts turned on lights inside her home. Even with fear riveting through her, she nodded, trying to catch her breath. "Again, you have my full attention."

Her willingness had me lost between the trainer and the man who enjoyed Mrs. Thompson so much. It only intensified my hunger for her and my unwarranted jealously. I was a bastard, through and through, as I peered over my shoulder to say, "You hear that, Crash? We have her full attention," hoping he could hear me and know she was practically mine.

It was so dark; I was confident Whitney wouldn't be able to place Crash's location, but I could still see his lips moving in his repetitive prayer. His bloody finger twitched above a carving in the wood on the dock.

I told Whitney, "Crash is… oh, how do I put this? Uh, indisposed at the moment."

"Sir, I will do whatever you ask of me. Anything. Absolutely anything, just give me a chance before you hurt him anymore."

So willing… I sighed. "If only your father had been so easy to work with."

Long eyelashes fluttered shut as she said, "I wish the same. If he had, my brother would be alive. Because of this, I hate my father beyond words and do not care what happens to him in order to keep you happy and Crash alive and well."

Her perseverance had me pondering if this was why Crash was so loyal to her. I surely didn't believe in the 'love' notion, yet Whitney appeared and sounded equally committed. I told her so. "I do think I believe you." *Mind-blowing.*

"My actions will prove you are right to do so. What do you want or need, and where can I find it?"

I exhaled out all of the pent-up frustration from this whole endeavor. "This is where our troubles begin. I cannot tell you what I want—or I have to kill you both." I jolted when I realized I had just told her Crash was as good as already dead, but she didn't catch my truth. Luckily, she was blinded by fear.

With beautifully wide eyes, she nodded during an adorable shrug. "A dilemma I'm willing to work around, seeing how I wish to live."

Laughter burst from my delighted lungs as I spoke to myself. "I really do like this American girl."

As if hearing this brought about an opportunity, Whitney added, "Would you believe I have a thing for Russian men?"

Intrigued, I leaned back. "You don't say?"

She tucked a curl behind her ear. "It's true! If we had the time, I would show you where I wrote it in my diary under 'foreigners to conquer.'"

I grabbed my chest because she was making it tingle. "You are impressively quick on your feet, especially at such a dire time."

"Not as quick on my feet as I used to be." She peered down at her injury.

I thought of what it felt like for the tire to spin over her. "Now that I know how charming you are, I certainly would like to go back in time and rectify my error." I would have found some other way to make my point to Mr. Summers.

A slight grin appeared. It was nervous, but she faked her bravery, admirably so. "Well, thank you, Russ. Do you mind? I have a thing for nicknames."

I dipped my chin, absolutely stunned by her resilience. She had figured my accent to be Russian. "And your charm continues. I now feel we are bonding, for me to have acquired a nickname from my American friend."

"Maybe someday we can laugh over all this with a cup of tea—wait, I bet vodka is more your speed, huh, *Russ*?"

"Vodka is from the gods. Tea is from shit."

Her fear almost took over as she attempted a chuckle, but lost to what sounded more like an anxious dry throat. "So, can you at least tell me what the thing you're looking for looks like? Do you know if it is here?"

"Again, I do not wish to kill you."

"Again, we agree R.U.S.S. Tell me, what's rambling around in that magnificent brain of yours? You must have a plan. Don't all mob leaders *lead* because they have great plans?"

I snickered, "I am not head of our organization. This work is beneath *him*. But the answer to your question is, yes, there is a plan, though you may not like it."

"Well, you're clearly *leading* this mission, and I'm not liking my boyfriend," I could tell she was fighting tears as she played the game well, "looking a bit mistreated there behind you, so try me. I'm open to suggestions."

I paused. "I wish to send one of my men inside your home," I said to keep her calm, but had every intention on sending more in because the house was massive and I needed it searched swiftly.

"Oh." She swallowed. "Now, I see why you assumed I wouldn't be too excited. Can you at least promise your man doesn't have a young-girl fetish?"

Umm, not really. "When I like someone, I tend to become violent if this person is mistreated. The men I'm in charge of do not like putting me in this state of mind. It causes bodily damage to them and their loved ones."

197

I stared at Kirill then the back of the SUV, so he understood my threat; if he touched Whitney, Valerie was as good as dead. Kirill dipped his chin and raised his hands, not contesting or willing to put Valerie in danger.

Whitney showed more charm by saying, "Now don't I just feel all warm and fuzzy inside. Hey, Russ, if I say yes, can I come outside and see him?"

I froze. *Smart little girl.* "I slipped up, eh?"

"Don't beat yourself up about it. I'm just a good listener, and there were *signs* everywhere."

Signs... I thought of Crash's finger. It hadn't been twitching at all. He was telling her where he was. I wanted to go and kick him, but truly, especially now conversing with Miss Summers, couldn't blame him for still trying to watch over her. I soon was going to be doing the same for her in Russia. "I do believe you *are* a little treasure." Then I explained, "My insurance shall stay separate from you." Dangling a chance to see Crash in front of Whitney was how I was going to control her.

Her eyes welled, but she ignored the tears and smiled weakly. "Can't blame me for trying, right?" She then said, "I'm turning off my alarm and will meet your man at my back sliding door."

I silently cursed her father as Whitney hobbled over without her crutches to hit buttons to an alarm that was not connected to any online or phone security company. Whitney was a sitting duck, and her hunter had arrived.

For the hours it took my men to search all through the house, I watched Whitney. She watched Crash. I don't think she could see him blanketed in the night on the boat dock, but she stared as if sensing him, all the while believing he had a chance. The only time her eyes strayed was when I had the SUV brought closer to the house. After killing Crash and kidnapping Whitney, we needed to leave immediately, due to the Joneses still watching. Mr. Jones may have let me leave with Whitney, but I was still concerned whether or not he could convince Reether of the same.

At one point, while Whitney paced—hobbled—back and forth in front

of the back sliding glass door, her injured foot accidently kicked a wooden chair leg. She grimaced before screaming and flinging the chair across the room in an unexpected rage. Whitney had dangerous criminals all around her at that moment, yet she still had the capacity to be filled with anger without the fear to express it.

From the shadows of her backyard, I stared at the crutches she seemed to be refusing to use and smiled. After her dance in that same living room weeks earlier, she had screamed her anger.

Yes, the fire in her was incredibly deep, and I desired those flames, but I had taken a chance of snuffing out those flames when we ran her over. Fortunately, I'd failed. But would her flames still burn after the loss of Crash? Whitney adored Crash. That was clearer than the sun that was starting to rise in the sky. Killing him was going to alter her. I wanted her as she was…

At that very moment, I decided to give her adequate time to heal before retrieving her.

Taking a break from searching, Adrian joined my side, quietly saying, *"We can always come back for her if you think it best for now."*

Was he reading me again? Was I staring too long and hard at the little redheaded pistol? Either way, he was giving me the out I needed. I wanted fire… or nothing.

Nonchalantly, I shrugged, *"Kirill has indeed complicated our travels already."*

He bowed his head. *"Just let me know."* Then he headed back inside.

I called out, *"Have Kirill check Timothy's room."*

Moments later, Kirill swiftly came down Whitney's stairs, nodding to me through the glass while putting the certificates in his pocket.

Father's request was finally fulfilled. It took years, but it was now done. Who could have known two little pieces of paper could cause such irreversible destruction, that all lives involved would forever be changed? Including mine.

Whitney continued to stare past me and into the dark for Crash, while my

men headed for the back door. Adrian observed me as he approached Whitney from behind. I silently kissed her in my mind, *Goodbye, Fire,* then shook my head no to him.

As men loaded the SUV, I stepped into the light and raised my cellphone to my ear. Watching me, Whitney slowly did the same. "Hello?"

Solemnly, I told her, "I wanted to thank you personally for your honesty and cooperation."

She stared at me as if sensing something was amiss. "You're welcome. May I come outside now?"

I nodded.

Her eyes did not leave mine as she grabbed her crutches then opened the back door, slowly making her way onto the patio. I think she sensed there was something I wasn't telling her.

There was. "But it saddens me to not return the favor."

She stopped walking but still spoke into the phone. "I don't understand. I did all that you asked."

There was far too much to explain, not that I felt she deserved any explanation. "Yes, but Crash's father did not." Even though Harold was responsible for not telling us Marina was still alive, I blamed Crash for making our twisted friendship come to this end. "A debt is a debt." My stomach started to turn when I realized the horrendous moment had now arrived. I had known Crash for years now, was a part of him in ways most had never experienced. And, now, I knew I had to kill him. Some moments are ones I wish I could relive... to change.

I shook my head before looking to the young man, tied up on the dock, for the last time. His finger was still tense, lying next to the carved symbol in the wood. Only loud enough so he could hear me, I told him, "You saved her... my friend."

It was a lie, but one I felt he deserved before lifting into the sky to where good people go.

He *was* good. He was one of the best.

I watched as his hand relaxed. He had heard me.

Then, like the coward I had become, I slipped into the SUV parked in the back yard. I simply couldn't watch the needle being inserted into his vein, emptying death into his bloodstream.

I wanted to cover my ears as he called out, "Franky!" but my men would've reported my weakness to my father.

Franky was a nickname Crash gave Whitney. Why, I did not know, but the way he yelled it was full of so much admiration and desperation, I instantly understood her fascination with them. They were a personal connection in times so exposed.

My hand gripped the doorknob when I heard Whitney fall down the patio stairs, due to her crutches and cast, but I didn't open the door. Reether was nearby and would be to her soon. If I got out of the vehicle, it would only prolong the rescue she deserved. That knowledge didn't stop my eyes from shutting as Whitney screamed in horror before I heard Crash's body splash into the water. Adrian had rolled him into the lake as planned. Leaning my head back against the seat, I couldn't help but swallow down more bile as I felt all the lives unraveling because of me.

My eyes didn't reopen until after a door shut, telling me my last man was in the vehicle, and we were driving across the grass then back down the dirt backroad we had arrived by. There was no need to rush. We knew the Joneses would not be calling the police.

With a drugged stripper in the back, the drive to the airport was quiet. Nobody was asking why I left Fire behind, nor willing to speak of the heinous crime just committed against someone we trained and shared a home with. We drove past trees as the sun was rising, but everything else felt as if falling. Not even Kirill had snide comments to share. Maybe we all knew—sensed—we had all just sealed our fates.

CHAPTER FIFTEEN

Soul Reader

"Who fucking sent you?" I practically spit in the old man's face because I was boiling mad. Two weeks earlier, my men had returned to my home country with the doctor slave. Did this old man have something to do with his abduction? Had the doctor's family already hired someone to find him? Had my men been sloppy and left a trail to follow?

I needed answers.

Kirill thumbed through the man's passport then researched his name with his cellphone. He read something then explained, "This American is a PI."

A fucking private investigator. *Fuck!* After punching his face, again, I screamed my rage, more directed to myself than anyone else for allowing myself to be distracted in daydreams about Fire. "Who sent you?"

What kind of intel did this Private Investigator collect before we noticed him?

Adrian had spotted our tail, so we led him to one of our abandoned warehouses. In a chair with hands tied behind his back and blood dripping from his bottom lip, he stared at me, no fear present. His eyes spoke of hatred. "You hurt women and children."

I paused at this, because if he were there for the doctor, why not mention men? An exhale of relief escaped me before I stood up straight. Then I walked away a few steps in an attempt to regain composure. "I fuck them, yes." Of course, I was lying, I still didn't fuck children, but was hoping to get a reaction out of my now prisoner. The youngest I had ever wanted was presently finishing high school. As soon as she was done healing from Crash's death, I planned

on having her in my bedroom, dancing for me. That thought had my mind envisioning what she would look like, moving soulfully, for only me—

"Yury! Can you hear me?"

I snapped out of my daydream that was soon to come true. *"Yes. What is it?"*

Adrian handed me a larger yellow envelope. *"This was on him. You might find the recipient interesting."*

He was right. This package was addressed to someone who should know better. Inside was a picture of me crossing a street in Saint Petersburg, and the name Yury. Fortunately for me, this private investigator lacked needed talents. He had no picture of my home, nor did he even know we also abducted men. Feeling a little cheery, I grabbed my cellphone and tapped to find a needed number.

After two rings, a man answered, "Ted Jones, here."

"Tsk, Tsk, Mr. Jones. I leave your son alone, and this is how you repay me? A stupid Private Investigator?"

"You killed my wife's son! She's distraught, you animal!"

"Meh." I pushed an image of Crash on the dock far from my mind. "I kill many sons. A debt is a debt. Now another one has to be paid—"

"I felt I had no choice! I have to protect these kids!"

I ignored his outburst and stated a fact instead, "The PI is returning to America. In a box." After ending the call, I slipped my cell back into my front trouser pocket and asked the PI, "Are you married?" His non-response told me, yes. It told me he didn't want me to hurt her, but that could no longer be avoided. I pressed the envelope to Adrian's chest. "Mail it to Jones, so he gets what he paid for. Then send his," I gestured to the PI with brimming eyes, "body to his wife."

I left the warehouse behind as the sound of a gunshot rang into the night.

The doctor's grey eyes were so mesmerizing I had named him Wolf. Most appropriate. He paced within his confinement as if a caged, wild animal. I loved to hear him speak. His wording, his slang, was like an American at times, but it was all laced with the slight leftover accent he still carried from Holland. Agitated, he kept asking questions about his abduction. He seemed irate, as if we caught him off guard.

Handlers, as per instructed, found the best time to capture my new pet. They were trained to find times there were no witnesses, no cameras. The handlers explained that Wolf had two gyms he visited. A public one that many attended, but also a private one. They said the private was an hour away from his home, but that he had a key and would go in the middle of the night. I assumed the doctor had odd working hours and wanted some privacy.

After a solitary workout, handlers apprehended Wolf in the dark parking lot. Drugged and unconscious, the doctor was flown to Russia on a private jet. For extra precaution, due to the doctor's family, many cars were switched and different routes were taken to get him back to my home undetected.

Since then, Wolf's determination to not be broken proved to be my perfect distraction while I waited for my chance to abduct Fire. It was especially true since Wolf was not to be marked, scarred, starved, or damaged in any way, per his new owner's instructions. He was to be left as pretty as when he was found. That made previous training techniques null and void.

"Why are you showing me this?" From under his long hair, Wolf glared at me, holding a burner cellphone. He was full of pure hatred while propped against the walls at the other end of his bed. It sat in the corner directly in front of his door. His toilet—which he didn't deserve—was in the opposite corner with a sink next to it. Of course, the water had been turned off so I could control his thirst.

In the beginning, he had requested hair bands, but I refused. All slaves were refused requests, but that isn't why I did it on this occasion. It was merely

me being selfish. I loved to see his hair in its uninhibited sense. It was like having a true Tarzan in my captivity.

Standing in his dark cell near the door, enjoying being in his presence, I shrugged. "I just thought you would like to know who is going to pay the price next for your constant disobedience."

It had taken four men, but we had eventually stripped him of his workout attire. I had been stunned to see him fully unclothed. His body was nothing if not art, with its perfection. Every part of him, every muscle was defined and full of strength, without being too large. His essence spoke of determination, which made him even more stunning.

Wolf still refused to sit on his knees, informing me sex was never going to happen willingly. Fortunately, where there is a will, there is a way. And the way was being delivered right now.

Wolf's perfectly sculpted shoulders stiffened. "What do you mean next?"

To give him a taste of my sinister side, I acted appalled. "What? I did not tell you who has paid for your insolence?"

"My insol—" Angrily, Wolf stood from his bed. "You asshole, what are you talking about? I've been abducted. Of course, I'm going to fight." Wolf wasn't as tan as he had been when he first arrived, but the one light in the ceiling shined off his body, exposing what his soon owner would be admiring for some time. His defined stomach muscles continued down and between his hips, leading to a penis that hung in front of finely trimmed pubic hair.

"Asshole?" As if he were merely a child, not a marvel for the eyes, I lectured, "No, no, Wolf. What are you supposed to call me?"

I witnessed his internal battle between his ego and need for knowledge as he stared at the phone in my hand. With his teeth locked together and his jaw muscles thick, he finally said, "Master."

With a pat to my chest, I cooed, "Now, wasn't that easier? You just doing what you're told, versus this?" I tapped the cellphone's screen and showed Wolf my special video—my demand for him to behave. The screen was dark,

due to the evening. A handler pinned Wolf's tied up mistress to her living room floor, but her muffled cries could be heard. The other handler, who was filming, was sure to get a close-up of her gagged mouth and tear-stained face, while the hooded attacker and his erection was seen sliding in and out of a vagina.

As Wolf charged me—something I was completely expecting—I slipped the phone back into my pocket. We wrestled for a few moments so he could wear himself down before I made it clear I had full control by wrenching his arms behind his back. To prevent scarring, I had to be sure his head didn't crack against the blocks when I shoved him into the wall, my chest to his back. Leaning my weight into him to hold him still, I couldn't help but notice how he felt up close. Yes, he was firm due to being in excellent condition, but there was a softness I didn't expect. Or maybe he smelled so good it softened his hard edges.

Pushing my unusual thoughts aside, I sneered. "We have been over this, but let me explain again. You are no longer in America. Your family will never find you nor rescue you. Now, here's an update. We have obviously found your family. Your mistress is used up, but we still have your wife, your mother, and your daughter to hold over you." He resisted my hold, but I pressed forward. Eventually, his eyes slid shut. "You have already been sold. There is no changing this. However, I am offering you an opportunity to go through the process without dragging more of the women in your life down with you." When he once again tried to get out of my trap, I pushed harder, physically and mentally. "So that you and I are clear, this is your one chance to save your daughter. I will fly to America to personally rape her three-year-old cunt if you piss me off."

"You fucking bastard!"

I had won. So, I grinned with us cheek to cheek. "Fucking bastard, what?"

His back expanded with every sob I tore from him. "Master. You fucking bastard, Master."

Leaving a distraught Wolf behind in the hallway, I watched as my father happily

approached. *"I have wonderful news,"* he said. *"There is now a bidding war going on with your new pet. Three billionaires are fighting over him. We are at a million so far."*

Wolf had been chosen and sold, but money is money. Father must have purposely bragged to other customers about the prized slave. Let the price dance begin.

He patted my chest before waltzing toward the hallway that led to the stairs. *"None want him damaged, and all want only for him to be an incredible lover. Yes, I said lover."*

"Fuck." I had just played hardball with Wolf. Completely wrong approach. *"I could have used this knowledge moments earlier."* Training an Elite to be submissive, able to handle the whip, or good at oral sex is one thing, but to train one to be a true 'lover' is something else altogether. I exhaled, long and hard, sensing the unknown of the upcoming direction of Wolf's training. *"He is not a homosexual."*

Father's voice echoed as he climbed the stairs to enter our home. *"Not my problem, Yury."*

"It is your problem. You have given me an impossible task."

"You pull off this sale, and I will give you twenty-five percent of profit."

There wasn't enough money in the world to force someone to prefer the same sex if it wasn't what they truly desired. Staring back at Wolf's door, I wondered if the money was even worth the effort. I was sure to fail. *"How long do I have?"*

Father's voice faded. *"The hungry men will wait for as long as it takes."*

To make Wolf into an enthusiastic lover—one to blow the minds of millionaires—I was going to have to make him desire men. Since that was not an option, I decided on another approach. Not from personal experience, but from novels I had read, I learned love and sex can be two different entities. Even though they blend incredibly well, you can have one without the other. I pondered on the thought of finding a way to make Wolf fall in love with me. As

it had worked with other slaves, when emotions were involved—one-sided of course—sex became something they did to please me. I hoped to convince Wolf he wanted to please me, also.

My mind raced to figure out how to first rectify the damage just done. Since using his weakness against him had worked, I figured it was worth using it in my favor this time. From my front pocket, I retrieved a little pink elephant, then unlocked Wolf's door. He was sitting in the dark room, propped on the floor in the far corner, appearing emotionally spent. Even his bare feet were a balanced beauty with his perfectly proportioned toes. Legs bent with his arms resting on his knees, his face was still wet from tears over his daughter. I picked a wall and sat next to him. I thought it better than looming over him while in my chair or standing. He needed to view us on the same level, in more ways than one.

Shielding the elephant in my closed palm, I leaned my head back against the wall. I wasn't faking my own exhaustion. This lifestyle was taking a toll. "I'm sorry you are going through this."

He wiped the wetness from under his nose. "Bullshit. I'm nothing but money to you."

Changing his mind was crucial, but it would take time. So, I started us off with some honesty before my trail of lies. I nodded. It was true. I was only interested in profiting off of him.

Wolf's hands turned into angry fists. "I want to kill you."

Staring at the floor, my shiny dress shoes, his bare feet, I nodded. "I understand that, but her safety remains the focus. Yes?"

His voice cracked. "Yes."

I opened my palm to expose the stuffed toy.

Wolf inhaled sharply, then his eyes raced to mine. "No. You don't understand—"

"Do you? Don't force our hand."

He swallowed then exhaled a shaky breath, his eyes staring at the floor, completely lost in thought. He blinked. He shook his head. "You... You truly

found her?"

"It wasn't difficult. You left a trail."

His eyes raced to mine, and they were full of guilt.

"Why are you so stunned?"

"I, um," he blinked again, "thought you were bluffing."

He stared at the toy. "You don't understand. You can't." He palmed his face. "Please, don't hurt that innocent child."

Should I have noticed that was an odd way to refer to his own kid? Most likely, but I had nothing to refer it to, so I handed him the toy. "Your daughter is safe for now, and your mistress won't be harmed again." I pointed to the elephant. "But you have to help me protect her."

He couldn't stop nodding, gripping the item. "Yes. Just don't let them hurt her."

"You have to do as I ask. There is no other choice."

Letting his head fall forward, he closed his eyes. "I don't even want to know what I'm agreeing to, but I will do what you ask." He blew out a stressed breath while lifting his head. "Is my partner—my girlfriend, is she okay?"

"I do not know. She disappeared after that night."

He blew out rapid breaths as if all this was finally becoming real for him. "That's good. She's safe now."

"But—"

Wolf held up a hand as if my words may push him over his mental edge.

Nodding, I left the subject of his mother, wife, and daughter alone, and let him gather his wits. I wasn't sure how long it would take since I had never been in his position before. The closest I was to caring about a woman was Fire. And since I planned on abducting her and making her my personal slave, I felt it was a moot point.

Wolf finally sighed then sat back against the wall again. "Will you hurt my family if I escape my new 'owner'?"

I had never been asked that before. His mind was racing for solutions.

"Once you are out of my hands, I am no longer your Master; therefore, you are no longer my responsibility."

He kept nodding as if he needed a plan—a goal to strive for—and now had one.

Hoping Wolf had recovered enough, I decided it was time to proceed. I figured, what place better to get started than the basics? "Why did you become a doctor?"

His chuckle was not sincere. It was patronizing. "Like you care."

"I'm still trying to apologize."

"You suck at it." He tucked his long hair behind his ear closet to me. I was thankful. It made it easier to see his face, even though I wasn't sure why I wanted to.

"It should. I've never tried it before."

That got his attention. "You've never been sorry?"

Half of my mouth smiled. "Didn't say that. I simply don't believe I have ever voiced it before."

"Not even to your victims?"

"Victims?"

His full lips parted. "The people you *sell*?"

"Oh." I looked to my hands in my lap. They rested on my outstretched legs. "No. Not once."

Wolf gazed at me as if I repulsed him. "Doesn't that bother you?"

Quietly, I replied, "No."

"You lunatic."

I looked him in the eyes. "You prefer I lie?"

His shoulders sagged him further into the wall. "No. That would make this conversation meaningless."

I smirked. "You do not like to waste your time?"

"Time is precious." In disdain, he gazed about the room. "You never know how much of it you have."

The profound thought was one I had never considered. I was young. I was rich and felt as if this would all last forever. Now, I was wondering if I even wanted it to.

"What?"

I looked at Wolf. "Excuse me?"

He rolled his eyes. "What, *Master*?"

I laughed. I actually laughed. "No. I meant, what are you referring to?"

"Oh. I just saw you in thought and wondered what it was about."

Exhaling, I answered, "Just wondering... what it is I want with the time I have."

His perplexed expression was somewhat comical. "Did a human trafficker just have a deep thought?"

I teased, "Don't expect this to be a common occurrence."

Patronizingly, Wolf snapped his fingers. "Oh, darn, and here I thought you were going to be my savior out of this hell hole."

I tried to smile at his joke but lacked the will. "No. No saviors exist here."

"What *does* exist here?"

"I don't know how to answer that."

"It's a simple question."

"Fine. What do *you* think goes on around here?"

"You rape, kill, and sell people."

"That is what I mean. My perspective is much different than yours. I say I train people who were stupid enough to get caught."

"Your logic is beyond disturbing, but let's play it your way. What do you train them to do?"

That answer was easy for me. "Whatever we are paid for them to do."

"You mean whatever some sick fuck wants them to do."

"You say sick. I say someone who knows what they desire."

In disgust, Wolf offered, "Someone against their will?"

I bobbed my head. "Force. Yes. This is some customer's preference, yes."

"What about that person's rights?"

His point had no logic to me. "Someone is going to kidnap the imbeciles. Why should it not be me that profits?"

"Besides it being tragic and wrong? How about this. Believe in Karma?"

"I was only taught the 'dollar' rules. Not a fairy tale."

"Then you have been brainwashed."

"Maybe so. Or maybe our way of life is the right way."

"Said Hitler."

"Meh. How will we ever truly know he was wrong?"

Wolf gawked at me as if I was Hitler himself, and I had just come back to life. Once recovered, he said, "Let's try again. Please get me a knife, so I can cut off your finger."

Amused, I asked, "What do you need with my finger?"

"I want to sell it." He thumbed over to a fictional person. "I have a buyer who will pay me a hundred bucks for it."

"Sorry. I choose to keep my finger."

He raised a brow. "Must be nice to have a choice." My head almost cracked against the wall as I jolted. "That's right, life stealer. Now, guess why that guy wants your finger." When I didn't ask, he answered for me, "Because he likes to store them in his ass."

I winced. "Why?"

Wolf lifted his hands in question. "What does it matter to me? It's his 'preference.'"

My eyes squinted as I studied this slave with a strong mind. "Do you wonder what you have been bought for?"

"I'm not stupid. Model agencies have chased me all my life."

"He doesn't only want to stare at your rarity."

Wolf recoiled. "He? Fuck... Like, a guy?"

212

I chuckled. "Not what you were hoping for?"

"Hell no. More like a rich MILF."

"Milf?" I was stumped.

A *pff* exited his mouth. "That's right. American slang may not be your strong suit."

"Not at all. Americans are dull."

"Then, why kidnap us?" He kept referring to my job as something he was familiar with, so I stared at him, trying to comprehend his angle. Wolf rolled his eyes. "MILF stands for a Mom I'd Like to Fuck."

This I could understand. "Oh. I have fucked a mom. Well, she was almost a mother. She was pregnant."

Blink. Blink. "You completely missed my point." After staring at me again, as if I were mystifying, his nervous palms rubbed at his thighs. "I've been with many women, but I, uh, I don't have sex with men."

"I didn't think so."

"Is there any way out of this without getting Bentley hurt?" Bentley was his daughter.

"There is not."

"Shit."

"But I will do my best to buy you time." I joked, "Although, you *are* the one who dislikes wasting time."

"I have been kidnapped by a comedian." He exhaled… "Buy me time before I'm sold?"

"No… Before your training begins."

CHAPTER SIXTEEN

Chance Attraction

Exiting the basement of my home, I was confronted with quite the sight. A guard was standing in a corner, laughing at someone else's expense, of course. Wild screams were shrieking throughout the foyer. Feeling as if I were the parental figure needed, I sneered, *"Father,"* seeing Valerie hanging in the air, over the railing, from the second story.

Holding the tiny girl from under her frantic arms, Father peered around her, then smiled. *"Yury!"* Knowing he wasn't smiling at the sight of me but that I had perfect timing, I walked forward while he asked, *"How was the private session with Wolf? Invigorating, I hope."*

Valerie wore a T-shirt but nothing else. I had quite the view from below. Father's hands released Valerie as he laughed at his horrid humor, not caring whether or not she survived the fall. My arms stretched out as Valerie wailed in terror, anticipating her upcoming death. When she landed in my embrace, she gawked at me, then threw her sweaty arms around my neck, wrapped her bare legs around my waist, and howled her tears.

She wasn't adapting well. Seeing her present treatment, it wasn't exactly shocking.

I glanced up with a tad of irritation, due to the weeping in my ear. *"Father, must you mistreat our guest?"*

He switched to English to further terrorize Valerie. "Oh, Yury, always with the dramatics." He headed down the stairs. "This vile creature is not our guest. She is a whore that has bewitched your cousin."

Walking past us, he tugged on her hair.

Valerie squealed and tightened her hold on my neck.

Choking, I scoffed, "Not appreciating your humor, Father."

He headed down the hallway toward the kitchen. "She needs to be soiled."

To keep Father from getting any more ideas, I lied, "Has already been done."

Valerie jolted in my arms, confused by my lie.

Father spun on his Louis Vuitton shoes. "By whom?"

"My semen leaked from her womb and core, yet here she is." Confident Valerie wasn't going to release me, seeing how her life literally depended on it, I lifted my arms to show how she was glued to me. "See? Now, will you please stop your childish games? They are tiresome."

The lie worked. Father pondered, his finger to his mouth. "Is killing her an option?"

His overpaid minion in the corner dared to step forward. Valerie whimpered. I pulled the gun from the back of my slacks and pointed it at the minion's head. We locked eyes. He stopped moving, trying to read how serious I was. With a double meaning, I warned the minion while telling my father, "Kirill did not choose to follow that order, due to his claim." The minion retreated to his corner. Putting my gun away, I glanced back at my father. "*If you wish not to respect Kirill's claim on her, hear mine. She is not to be harmed.*"

He closed his eyes and dipped his chin. It was a false agreeance. I was sure of it, so I retrieved my cellphone and texted Kirill:

> *Valerie is with me. My father was terrorizing her again.*

As I walked up the stairs, he texted back:

> *I need a better lock on my door*
>
> *Agreed*
>
> *Almost home*

Valerie whimpered in my shoulder. "Your dad is awful."

I unlocked my bedroom door. "This is truer than you know." As I walked

us inside, she pulled her face back enough to see my eyes. Her expression was full of shock and horror. "Yes. Stay clear of him, if at all possible."

She lifted the black rhinestone leash attached to her collar. Kirill had given her 'bling' in attempts to buy back her love. Understandably, she was irate to wake in another country; one she had specified to no longer be interested in. The bribe was not a success. Valerie had been sneaking about, trying to escape ever since. That is why Father had her over the balcony.

I nodded at the leash. "That is the only reason you are still alive." Then I stared at her, hoping she would cease her futile attempts.

A burst of tears broke free before she could muffle them. "I hate it here. Crash was right—" I dropped her to the floor, causing her to yelp. From my mauve plush carpet, she studied me. "You regret killing him, don't you?"

Done with the conversation, I left her where she sat. "I'm taking a shower." I stopped entering my bathroom when I heard her scurrying behind me. "Valerie, what are you doing?"

On her hands and knees, she scrambled past me and into the bathroom. "Following my best chance of survival. You didn't lock the bedroom door." She crawled to my tub and planted her naked butt on the floor as if refusing to move.

I didn't lock the door so Kirill could retrieve his property without bothering me. "I don't wish to bathe with my clothes on, and Kirill may not appreciate my naked dick anywhere near you."

"I'd rather him being pissed versus dealing with that crazy old guy."

Continuing into the bathroom, I shook my head. "You have clearly yet to face the dark side of Kirill."

"Maybe so, but until then, shower." With drying tears on her fairy face, she dismissively waved her hand in the air. "Bathe. I've seen you naked. Fuck Kirill. He's an asshole anyway."

I chuckled. "I hope Fire is as entertaining as you—" I jolted when I realized how distracting Wolf truly was. I hadn't thought of Fire for days…

"Who is Fire?"

Removing clothes, I growled, "None of your concern."

Wisely, Valerie stayed quiet. It allowed me to enjoy the hot water spraying on my back as I tried to rinse away the hunger my shower couldn't reach. I couldn't even reach it because I was yet to understand what I was craving. Flashes of Wolf's eyes kept appearing behind my closed ones.

As I was rinsing the shampoo from my hair, Kirill stormed into the bathroom. Seeing me naked in the shower, he yelled at Valerie, "Why are you in here?"

She raced to her feet and charged forward. It looked like a hamster trying to be intimidating as she shoved at his broad chest. "Because he just saved my life, you fucker!"

Appearing a tad concerned with her claim, Kirill peered at me through the glass of my shower, looking for confirmation. I shrugged. "Meh. She may have survived the fall from the second-story balcony."

"Fall?" she shrieked in a godawful high pitch that almost made my ears bleed. Kirill and I were still frozen in a wince as she shoved at Kirill's chest again. "I didn't *fall*. I was dropped!" She smacked his chest. "On fucking purpose! Your family is a bunch of deranged psychopaths!" *Smack!* "If they weren't insane, I would march out of this bathroom and ignore you and teach you a lesson!" *Smack!* "But he may toss me out a window next time!" *Smack! Smack!* "The worst part?" She screamed, "*I'd be happy to find a fucking window that opened in this godforsaken hell hole!*" She blinked in dismay as Kirill and I burst into a fit of laughter. "Ass. Holes."

Still laughing, Kirill pulled her to his chest. "Yes, we are, but you warm my cold heart."

Valerie melted to him. "Kirill… I want to go home."

His large hand sheltered her head to his breast. "It was selfish of me to bring you."

My whole body went still in the shower. I had never heard him speak of someone else's needs, especially placing them before his own. I guess you could

say miracles do, in fact, happen.

Kirill tucked his head over the top of hers. "And, now, it is too late to remedy."

It was impossible to not think of Fire, to realize I would soon be stealing her life. It was impossible not to see judgment in Wolf's eyes. And, at the time, it was impossible to know why I gave a fuck. My miracle hadn't happened yet.

Due to Wolf's unique training, I allowed him privileges without him earning them. He now had running water, a toothbrush, and an operating toilet. Entering his room, I was surprised to see him getting off the floor, his chest riddled with sweat. "What are you doing?"

He wiped his hands on his dirty blanket. "Push-ups." He bounced on his feet, in a circle. "I'm fighting for my sanity in here. Need some movement." Muscles bounced with every landing. "Dude, can I get a shower or something? Anything to get out of here for a few minutes."

"Showers are to be earned."

He stopped and faced me. His head tilted. "What the fuck does that mean?"

Still distracted by his sweaty body, I struggled for words. "It... means..."

Wolf looked down at himself, trying to see what I was seeing. Then he slowly peered back at me. "Are you checking me out?"

That snapped me from the trance he had me in. "No."

"You don't seem gay."

"I'm not," I growled.

"Ain't judging. Relax. I just know when someone is giving me a look over. That's all."

I marched to him, but he didn't retreat. In his face, I declared, "I don't want you."

We were the same height. That put his soul ⸻
They peered into me, through me, and read my future⸻

Trying to disguise my urge to throttle him, I sa⸻
your shower or not?"

Chest to chest, he angrily replied, "What I want i⸻
truth."

As I inhaled for patience, I could feel my nostrils fl⸻
matter?"

"Because you are the closest person I have here. And ⸻
you for your word. My family is safe? I need to know if you've ⸻
me."

"I didn't."

"The only way I can be sure of it is to know I'm right. Tha⸻
now."

This was a pivotal moment for us. Trust could gain me much⸻
his training.

My mouth sucked in my lips while I debated on admitting som⸻
powerful to a slave. Would it give him the upper hand? "I…" *Am I attrac*⸻
you? As he adjusted his stance, his leg grazed mine. Chills raced up my b⸻
"Okay. I'm attracted to you, but it means nothing."

"Are you the one who will be 'training' me?"

I swallowed to keep my voice from sounding gravelly, but it didn't w⸻
"Yes."

He lifted his chin. "I'd rather it be you than anyone else."

"Your preference is no concern of mine."

He smirked. "You just lied again."

"Last chance for a shower."

"Okay, okay. I'll leave you alone. What do I have to do to 'earn' some
soap?"

His demeanor, for his circumstance, was unexpected. He wasn't begging

ed. It was as if he had accepted his fate and wanted it over with as
possible. As if he was sure he had the mental capacity to survive
ome time with his new Master, and the wits to break free at the first
should've recognized such skill, but I was too busy seeing other
like Wolf on his knees before me.

Gazing up at me, he asked, "Now what?"

I had so many scenarios rushing through my mind, but said, "That is it
."

ding to Wolf's scowl, he didn't particularly appreciate the comments being
regarding his nude body as he walked the hallway to the shower room.
though the words were in Russian, he understood the gestures.

He wasn't leashed. He was somewhat free game. Only the strict
ructions about his training kept him safe.

In the grey cement block bathroom with three showerheads, Wolf teased,
his room is so uplifting."

o comments. Just shower." I told myself that I watched him wash himself
make him uncomfortable, not because he looked as if he were a god under a
vaterfall, bathing in a spring instead of a shower. His mere presence made my
cage fade away completely.

Yes, the gloomy block walls melted away as I watched soap suds drip
down his chiseled back and into the crack of his ass. He turned to rinse his long
hair, leaning his head back to spray his face with water. In a relaxed fashion,
the corded muscles in his neck stretched and bowed as he demanded. It was
mesmerizing.

After turning the water off, he asked, "Are us slaves permitted to have
towels?"

I threw him one. "Dry off then it is to go in that basket." I pointed to one
in a corner.

At first, I spent hours a day with Wolf. I told myself it was all about the

training—developing his mind into having a new viewpoint on the male gender. I needed him to see me as so much more than a trainer or man. In fact, I didn't want him to view me as one at all. I needed him to desire affection, and desire it from me, since I was all he had.

No other trainers were permitted in his room because of this. When I was to start eventually cutting his visits back, he would long for the company. In turn, hopefully, he would long for me. Isolation can twist a mind. I needed his warped so that I could convince him he wanted me to console his loneliness.

Our discussions ranged from minuscule subjects to the present situation. I knew about his first girlfriend in the third grade. He knew that I wet my bed for a couple of years after my mom was killed.

Wolf assured me, "It's no surprise, with all you have been through."

Was it risky to confide in him? I didn't think so at the time. I always left out important details so that I gave him no true leads on me. Besides, there was barely any record I even existed. My true identity was buried in lies. I wasn't even confident I was born in a hospital. As far as the world knew, there was a Yury who appeared from time to time. In truth, I was a ghost—a very dangerous, haunting ghost that was impossible to track.

Squished in the corner, I sat on Wolf's bed, the wall propping me up. He was next to me. Both of us together barely fit, with our broad shoulders, but for long conversations, it was much more comfortable than the cold floor.

He no longer asked why I was a trafficker. He knew this life was all I understood. But he did repeatably ask why I stayed. Wolf was baffled. "Just get in your car and go." He moved his hand in the air as if leaving my whole life behind was as easy as driving away.

Watching his hand, I was actually tempted. I was tired. Really tired. Even though I wasn't positive as to the reason why, Wolf had me suspecting it was my environment.

I asked him, "If I left, where would that leave you?"

His face was so close to mine; I could see his lips quiver as he softly

said, "Take me with you."

Anger filled my chest in record speed. "Is this what all these conversations are about? You're trying to trick me?"

He gawked at me in total dismay. "Me? Trick you?" With surprising speed, he got on his hands and knees in front of me, putting his face in mine. "Have you forgotten I'm not here willingly?"

I had. Wolf had, once again, made his confinement feel more like a true bedroom where we just happened to prefer lounging about. "Of course not. You are only a job to me."

It was only for a second, but there was hurt in his entrancing eyes. "Then get on with your 'job' so I can get the fuck out of here and away from you."

"You want away from me?" As I quickly maneuvered to my knees to take the dominant stance in the argument, Wolf lifted his hands to match my aggression.

On our knees, chest to chest, face to face, we stared at each other. His panting breath mirrored my own. "I want away from anyone who only views me as a 'job.'"

At that very moment, I felt so off-kilter and confused, but I didn't care, because his words were telling me something; he was longing to be more to me. It was a perfect moment to pursue.

My hand felt alive, tingling as I reached under his long hair to touch him. Wolf didn't move as my palm grasped the nape of his neck. In fact, he slightly leaned into my affection.

An incredible sensation fluttered in my stomach as I whispered, "I'm apologizing again."

The quarrel was ending, but we were both still, very much so, locked in an intense moment. Wolf's eyes went half-mast. "Don't use our friendship against me by twisting up my words."

The closest I ever had to a friend was Crash.

And I killed him.

Wolf was becoming so much more than a slave, but he was also a silent redemption to the wrong I'd committed against Crash. Unconsciously, I craved the forgiveness needed to move past a murder that was drowning me with guilt.

I leaned my forehead to Wolf's. "I won't again."

His forehead tenderly rubbed against mine. "What is your name?"

My lips hovered above his. "You know what you are to call me."

His eyes squeezed shut as he pled, "No. For moments like these." His hand touched my hip. "When no one else can hear us, let me call you something else."

His reaction to me was all wrong—against what he should be feeling—but I was already so enraptured, so lost in how Wolf pleasantly puzzled me, I was missing key details.

It tasted sour to speak my false name to him, but I lacked a choice. "Yury."

His eyes drifted open. "The last thing I expected was to care for my abductor."

My heart raced, hearing that he cared for me. No one had ever claimed to feel that way for me. It was almost paralyzing. Only one thing kept me moving. "What do you mean, 'expected'?"

He jolted. There was something in his eyes again. This time, it was deceit.

Wolf quickly left the bed as he looked away. Then he walked toward a wall. "You're twisting my words again."

I followed, in prowl mode. Smirking at his back, I sneered, "You have nowhere to hide."

He turned, but when he saw me, he stumbled back against the wall. "What are you doing?"

I continued my hunt. "What did you mean by 'expected'?" Face to face again, a menacing growl left me. "How can you expect something you do not know is coming, unless you did know?"

"W-Wait."

"Are you an agent?"

His otherworldly eyes widened. "W-What?"

I pressed my body flush with his. "You have only seconds before I kill you." My palm search for his neck, not in the affectionate way I had moments earlier.

"You're getting me all wrong." His hands gripped at my wrist as my fingers wrapped around his throat.

"Two seconds." I started to squeeze.

"There was a time in school that I—" His voice cut out, and my fingers tightened.

Curious to the rest of the sentence, I released, slightly. "One second."

He was gasping for air, but his eyes didn't show fear. Again, they showed something else. "His name was Chance."

"Whose name?" I could feel Wolf swallow from under my hands. I noticed because I suddenly envisioned my cum slipping down his throat. I slammed my eyes shut, desperate to not be distracted by the man. After reopening them, I shook him. "Who is Chance?"

His strong hands pulled on my wrist, but I was too angry to be overpowered. "My boyfriend."

Instantly, my ears began to ring. Even though we had a sexual tension brewing between us, this was the last thing I expected to hear. And I took it for a lie. My fingers tightened again. "Do not play with me, my little pet." I felt he had been this whole time.

He struggled to say, "I was young." He winced under my grip. "I was scared." His hands finally fell in surrender. "I broke his heart."

My fingers loosened. "But... You had me admit to being attracted... You said—"

"I said what I've been telling myself ever since Chance, what's supposed to be heard from a guy like me who has family that doesn't accept—" He sighed.

224

"My parents, they don't... My dad, he doesn't... I didn't want to be the son that he was ashamed of."

Baffled, because my father pays me to fuck men, I asked, "What about your wife? Your girlfriend?"

Now, looking back at this time in my life with Wolf, I see his lie for what it was. A cover for all he was hiding. "Girls are hot to me. I love fucking them. But I never forgot Chance." His eyes closed as if in pain.

"Why lie about it to me?"

His eyes opened. Their beams of grey light warmed me to the core until he said, "I've lied to my *family* about my sexuality. Why would I confide in a human trafficker?"

It wasn't a question. It was a statement.

As much as it made sense, it still hurt. I released his neck and backed away. "Yes, that is what I am."

"But all our talks... Now, I see you're more."

There was such regret in his voice; I misread him and chuckled in a cruel fashion. "Not even close. I've only been fucking your mind before I fuck you."

With a touch of lust in his expression, Wolf swallowed.

I gave him a warning glare. "You only think you will enjoy it."

With the wall still holding him up, he said, "Kiss me, and let's find out."

Like a coil wound tight enough to break, I rushed forward, slamming my hands against the wall on either side of his head. At that moment, that very second, there was nothing I wanted more than to taste this beautiful creature, but... "I don't kiss. It's best you remember that."

That fucking sexy smirk reappeared. "You're lying." His hands went to my hips. "Who have you kissed?"

The touch was simple but sent my body into a typhoon of wants and needs; nothing I had ever experienced compared. Barely able to inhale without gasping through desire, I informed my slave, "I have work to do." And, I left him alone in the cell he was trapped in.

In the hallway, I leaned my back against Wolf's door to catch my breath. From the other side, he sadly whispered, "Please, don't go."

He was burrowing too deep in places I had denied all my life. I needed free of this dangerous grasp he had on me. The line between us was so blurred; I wasn't even sure what side I belonged on anymore.

Instead of replying, or going back inside Wolf's cell, I went to the monitor room. One of our 'conversationalists', A.K.A. someone prowling the internet for slave prospects, spun in her rolling chair to face me when I entered. "How's it going, Yury?"

She spoke English and was great with talking to young women. They trusted females so much faster than males. She could even fake cry in a second flat. Young girls would believe her lies, that she cared, and she could help them run away and work for her. She would promise a grand life that was far more appealing than the dull or abusive one the child was presently in. She was also now our Prepper. When there was to be a delivery, she would prepare the slave by doing any essentials needed—showering them, doing their hair and makeup, and waxing their bodies.

Lying, I replied, "I am well. Thank you."

Another conversationalist turned in his rolling chair. "*Hey, Yury. You told me to let you know if a Whitney Summers was catching a flight anywhere.*"

He had my full attention. "*And?*"

He sipped from his coffee mug. "*She bought a ticket.*"

Frustrated with Wolf, and this employee not offering more information, I barked, "*To where, you imbecile?*"

His eyes widened as he leaned back in his chair for some distance between us. Then he quickly said, "*To Saint Petersburg, Russia. She will be here in three days.*"

Reether was leaving for Harvard to be a lawyer like his father. With Fire's best friend moving on, it made perfect sense she was on the run again. And why was she headed to Russia? I knew that answer, too; Mr. Jones and the

226

fucking PI.

Grabbing my chest, I stumbled back two steps. Whitney Summers—Seafoam's spawn—was coming for revenge. *Yes, my Fire. Come and try to burn me with your angry flames.*

Wolf jumped to his feet when I entered his room, his hair falling over his shoulders. Again, I tried to overlook how gorgeous he was. He was doing some ignoring of his own. He paid no attention to the tray of food in my hands. He only said, "I'm sorry I made you mad."

"It matters not." I placed the tray on his bed.

"It does to me. Yury, please let me explain—"

"Explain what? That you played me for a fool? Got me to admit my attraction to you?" I marched to him. "I fuck men as a job. Never had I actually wanted one. But, when I finally get my chance with you, I'm going to... I'm going to—"

"You're going to do what, actually enjoy yourself because it won't be forced?" He shook his head. "It won't be. Not with me."

I knew it wouldn't be forced with Wolf, and I knew I was going to love every moment of being inside him, but I also knew I would have to let him go to the highest bidder. That was a pain I wasn't willing to endure. "Falling for a slave is the worst thing I can do."

His jaw locked tight. "I'm not just a slave to you, and you know it."

Deadpan, I stared at him. "Maybe a couple of days of solitude will help you understand your place."

Not wanting anyone with me, I snuck out the front door and was flying down the

driveway in my car. The hours I waited for that plane to arrive were pure agony. It was the same as being lost at sea and knocking at death's door. Even though I was surrounded by water—sex slaves and Wolf—I felt I was without the water needed to truly quench my thirst and keep me alive. Whitney had become my unreasonable obsession, one I felt I could no longer live without.

In a ballcap, something I never wore, I disguised myself and blended as best as I could with the crowds in the Pulkovo International Airport. I even wore jeans, something I saw as degrading, but I wasn't going to allow another trafficker to abduct my Fire before I had the chance to myself. Yes, any travel station has us. We lurk, we spot their weaknesses, then we pounce, physically or mentally. We snatch you up by force or convince you to come with us by a mastered mind game.

Sitting, I groaned when flanked on the bench. Selfishly, I wanted this moment to myself.

Kirill chuckled as he sat next to me. *"And you tease me for Valerie, Little Yury?"*

Groan.

Adrian sat back, laying his arm out across my back. *"You do know you live in a home full of cameras, yes?"*

Groan.

"We saw your tail lights in the driveway and knew where you were headed."

I was about to tell him and Kirill to fuck off, but, through a crowd, I suddenly saw that red hair. I leaped to my feet. Abruptly, Adrian stood, grabbing my arms. *"Security cameras."* He was right. Once she went missing, all video would be scanned and studied.

I inhaled... then exhaled...

There was no longer a cast on her leg. Only jeans were covering the skin I desired to see. She had a bag over her shoulder that dwarfed her, and ticket stubs in her hand. Her small appearance and evident youth—and her constantly

asking, "Four Seasons' shuttle?" was practically screaming "Abduct me, please! I'm an American idiot!" so I was staying close to her. We followed behind, staying a couple of people deep. When she asked, "Four Seasons' shuttle?" again, I told a man—who was staring at her as if she was an American moron, "*She is inquiring about shuttles.*" The man nodded and politely pointed which direction for her to go.

Like a shark to its prey, I followed, eyes locked on a silver charm that I immediately recognized. It was the same symbol carved in Whitney's boat dock. The same symbol that Crash had been touching the night I killed him. Even after death, he was still interfering.

After gathering her suitcase, Whitney loaded onto a shuttle. I told Adrian, "*Get on that shuttle.*" He opened his mouth to offer his unwanted opinion until I got in his face. "*Now.*" He nodded. "*Then text me her hotel room number.*"

After I was in her hotel room, having a delightful—maybe not to her— conversation, I drugged her.

Then, I stole her.

Now, she was *truly* all mine.

Or so I thought.

My father had been sent into a tirade of a fit when he saw me carrying his personal curse through his training hallways. Then he spotted the scars on her legs, and he went ballistic. "*I can't even sell her with those heathen marks, you fool!*"

I was flanked by Kirill and Adrian. Kirill, probably due to Valerie, paid special attention to the argument, as I yelled, "*I have no intentions on selling her!*"

Father was appalled. "*You will leash this creature?*"

"*Consider it already done!*"

"*What is happening to the sons in this family?*"

I glanced at Kirill next to me. His eyes spoke volumes without one word.

He was keeping Valerie and needed my father off his back over it. So, I told the irate man, "*Maybe we are tired of being under your reign.*"

Adrian had no family ties to me, but he stayed firm by my side as he and Kirill observed Father's minions. I had made a strong statement. I would be taking over soon. It was ironic that this all came at a time I was no longer sure of what I wanted.

Still deeply affected by the drugs in Fire's system, she had only stirred as my father screamed. I was surprised he hadn't caught on to my plan sooner. After learning that Whit would be in my care soon, I immediately dispatched men that were already in the States. They were there to capture soon-to-be slaves, so I had a couple of them go to Harvard and inspect Reether Jones' living conditions. I asked for videos of personal times, such as entering his dorm building, showering, and I even asked for a gun to be held to his head while he slept for good measure and threats. Fire was not going to become my slave without a fight. So, as human traffickers do, I searched for her weakness. Since I had already killed her brother and her lover, that left her best friend, Link, someone I had every intention of exploiting to get what I wanted.

The dance.

Crash gave his life to save Whitney's. Now, I was going to ask Whitney to relinquish her freedom to save Link's. These young adults were so easily manipulated through their loyalty and refusal to abandon each other. I guess that meant not only poor kids growing up in poverty are at risk when it comes to my profession. And, I guess that meant I was a heartless bastard who took advantage of them all.

Once I had her on her new cot, I stared at her sleeping—unconscious—form. I found it ironic it was in the same room that I had stored Crash's pet, Sam. But this girl didn't have long blonde hair. No, she had curly, unruly hair that was fitting as could be for her spirit. It laid all over the stained pillow under her head that I wanted to replace with a brand-new one, but I still had to stick to training. Dirty pillows were an excellent way of beginning the transformation from free

human to slave.

Touching her soft red curls, I sighed, somewhat regretting the road I was about to force her to travel. "I will see you when you wake, Fire."

In the hallway, I told Kirill, "*When she wakes, let the fucking begin.*"

Still dressed, he asked, "*Can I give Wolf a go?*" Not meaning to, I delivered a scrutinizing glare over my shoulder. His brows scrunched, but he didn't ask more about my other special slave. "*Filming?*"

Walking toward the monitor room, I responded, "*Want to get paid for it?*"

"*Do Russians like vodka?*"

Telling myself I was strong again, I collected a food tray and unlocked Wolf's door. Entering, I immediately recognized his soft scent. I inhaled, already becoming entranced.

"Where have you been?" He sat up in his bed as I entered.

As happy as I was to now have Fire in my care, I was still somehow relieved to see Wolf. He was that stunning to me. One glance at him, and I was undone all over again.

I sat next to him, placing the tray in my lap. "I had to pick up a friend." Then I examined his face because it was a little peaked. "Are you okay?" Not pulling from my hand, he lifted a brow as if I had asked the most idiotic question in the world. He was being held captive. I grinned while nodding. "I see your point." I offered him a cold cut sandwich.

He took it but refused a bite. "Are you still mad at me?"

I studied his soulful self, then shook my head. "Eat your sandwich."

While he devoured it, I watched him. Wolf's mouth would stretch open to shove in far too much food. The muscles in his face and neck strained as he chewed with much effort. Dark eyebrows and lashes encased those intense eyes that were locked on his sandwich.

After swallowing the last bite, he sighed. "Thank you." His sturdy hand grasped at his stomach as if relishing in the full sensation.

I handed him a bottle of water. "Thank you for not trying to break free while I was gone."

His shiny, straight hair slipped from his face as he leaned his head back to gulp down the water. I watched as his throat worked before he told me, "We made a pact, right?"

If he were to behave, his family was safe.

Sighing, I thought about how, when I first saw the doctor, I believed he was arrogant. Maybe he was. Maybe being caught in the snares of human trafficking can humble the best of them. I appreciated him standing by his word. "Right."

"I've had a lot of time to think while you were gone." Hope then sadness passed through his eyes. "Are you actually trapped here, too?"

I took a gander around at his block walls and realized I did have walls, too. They were just invisible to most. "In a way, yes." That answer may have been the first time I spoke the truth about my predicament.

"That's what I thought. You wouldn't bring anyone here if you didn't have to."

I peered down, surprised to feel an ounce of shame. The hand in my lap had just played with the hair of a girl I single-handily forced to be here. Too uncomfortable to hold still, I got up to leave.

"Wait." Wolf also stood, in a bit of a panic. "When are you coming back?"

I watched as his hand fought to not reach out for me. He was lonely. I didn't like how that made me feel. So, I reached out and took hold. He looked away with a hint of humiliation, but his hand didn't release mine. For the first time, it was awkward to admit. "I have another... to tend to."

"Oh." He pulled his hand from mine as if scorned. "It wasn't a 'friend' you had to pick up. I thought—" He blinked, then plopped back onto his bed. "I don't know what I'm thinking anymore."

He was unstable, just the opening the trainer in me was looking for, so I

squatted in front of him, sure to rest a hand on his knee. "Listen. Don't lose your mind in here. Stay strong… for me."

"I…" He brushed his fingers through his hair. "I've never felt so alone. I've always had family around me." He ran a palm down his stressed face. "I'm freaking out, dude."

"You are not alone."

"I am!"

I grabbed the nape of his neck with my free hand. "I'm right here, watching over you and your daughter. You're not alone."

He stared at me as if I was his only hope, which I was. His eyes bore into me with such intensity; I felt it in my stomach. When I realized my tongue was wetting my lips, I jerked back and stumbled to my feet, away from him, slamming my back into the wall.

He jumped to his feet, racing forward. "Wait!"

I rushed to the door.

"Please!"

I grabbed the doorknob.

"Master." Wolf sounded as if in despair.

To this day, I am still unaware of where my speck of pity came from, but it was the true beginning of my surrender to Wolf. How, in such a short amount of time, he wedged himself between my reality and what I, unknowingly, wished for, is still a mystery.

My head fell forward. "I'll come back to you tonight."

He was so close to my back; I felt the vibration of his breath. "Thank you."

Leaving his room, I was now feeling as unstable as my slave. I rushed to the monitor room for balance, or maybe the grounding I knew only one could offer. As soon as I was in the monitor room, I saw her. Just like that, my insides went from simmering to a soothing hum. I stared at the monitor—that was solely

for my Fire—like a child dying to open his presents under the Christmas tree. Cameras in her room surveyed her even breathing as I waited for hours…

She was tiny. I think her dosage was a bit much for her weight.

When Whitney finally began to stir, my heart started to pound. Those incredible green eyes opened, then scanned her surroundings. Her expression said everything; she was well aware of the hell she was now in.

Sticking my head into the hallway, I announced, "*She is awake.*"

Robed in a black hooded garment, Kirill nodded, then started guiding a naked male slave into the room next to Fire's. On a monitor, I observed her scurrying from peeking underneath her door to rushing back into her dreary bed. On another monitor, Kirill already had his slave tied up to chains that hung from the ceiling. He took no time getting started. Valerie had recently pissed him off with more whining of wanting to go home. The slave was the recipient of Kirill's frustrations.

Screams echoed over the speakers as Kirill cracked a whip across the slave's bare back. When the slave finally tired, Kirill decided it was time to open his robe and expose his raging erection. He went to a table and lubed before approaching the slave from behind. His feet pushed the slave's apart, taking a firm stance. The slave had already been taken in the ass many times but still grunted as Kirill thrust inside him. I had instructed Kirill to be swift and loud. He was both. Grunts had now replaced the whimpers. Due to the slave being trained to enjoy the torture, Kirill reached around to make sure an erection was taking place. It was, even though the slave's expression showed remorse.

As Kirill stroked the slave's dick, I thought of the night we shared. I had felt disgraced to have enjoyed the roughness of his palm. Now, due to Wolf, and realizing the possibility of myself being bisexual, I started to forgive myself for the indiscretion. I realized I had never been given the choice of my own preference because I was only trained to prepare slaves for others.

I suppose Kirill's slave was experiencing a similar regret because he begged, "Please, no more," but lost the battle. As he ejaculated onto the cold

234

concrete floor, Kirill groaned through his own climax inside the slave's rectum.

Setting my self-pity aside, I stepped back and clapped my hands together once. *"That should have Fire ready to cut a deal."* I grabbed my blazer to look nice for my pet's introduction to her new life.

A handler walked into the room. *"Yury, the delivery is minutes away."*

Perfect timing. *"Her room is ready. Tell him to take her there first and strip her."*

"Will do." He handed me a Mini iPad. *"Edited video of the Harvard student you requested."* He went to leave but stopped. *"Oh, I almost forgot."* He pointed to the iPad. *"I saved some links. That kid is starting a video blog that may interest you or at least be useful with controlling your Elite."*

As he left, I mumbled, *"She's not an Elite."* If she were, that would mean she was for sale. Annoyed, I tapped on the screen and saw a self-video of Reether talking about human trafficking. I stopped the video, not sure how to handle the kid, but was sure I'd somehow use this against Fire.

Without inspecting the edited video from my men—because making threats to slaves was common, I knew it would be adequate—I pulled out my cellphone and sent the video of Crash to the iPad, then I slipped the item in my inside Blazer pocket. Energy buzzed through my whole body. *"Back to my special—"*

The technician pointed to her screen. *"She's asleep again."*

"Fucking drugs." I pulled a remote from my pocket and hit a button. The monitor went blank. I did not wish for our private moments to be anything other than that. Then I grabbed a folding chair and demanded, *"Time for her to wake."*

Only wanting in that room to start breaking down my new pet's spirit, I was most disappointed to see Valerie, in hysterics, while being dragged down the hallway. As soon as she saw me, she whaled out, "Yury!" She was with her black collar but no leash, so I asked the handler what he was doing.

Groping at the struggling, tiny form, he eagerly replied, *"Your father said Kirill no longer has a claim to her. I want a round with this little tart."*

I stared at Whitney's door, debating whether or not to take the time to save Valerie from this lie. There was no way Kirill was ever releasing his favorite toy. My father was up to his shenanigans again.

"Yury! Please, help me!" begged Valerie while fighting the handler's hungry touches.

It wasn't her plea that convinced me. It was Kirill having my back earlier that day when I stood up against my father. After a long exhale, I finally leaned my chair against the wall and reached out my hand. *"Give her to me. Kirill has not revoked his claim. My father is trying to get you killed because he is bored."*

Since Kirill was ruthless and had not one issue with killing a man, the handler released Valerie as if she had just contracted a deadly virus. Valerie rushed to me, throwing her arms around my waist. I growled at the affection and refused to hold her in return, but warned the handler, *"I am tiring of these games. I highly suggest you inform other employees to stop interfering with claimed slaves."*

He raised his hands while backing away. *"I will not touch her again."*

Gripping a fist full of blonde hair, I yanked Valerie's head back and stared down at her. "Did you try to escape again?"

Even though I was causing her pain, she refused to let go of my waist. Tears leaked from the corners of her eyes as she whispered, "Please, try to understand."

"It is *you* who needs to understand." I shook my fist. Her head jostled, yet she held on to me. "The only way you are leaving this house is in a body bag." Her eyes closed. "Do you truly believe we will let you walk the streets knowing all that you do about us?" When she didn't answer, my fury got the best of me. I pried her arms off me and dragged her toward a training room.

A technician was coming down the hall, aiming for the monitor room. *"Film?"*

"No. Just beating her ass." I shoved her into the room.

Frantically glancing around at all our training supplies, she asked,

"W-What am I doing in here?"

I didn't bother shutting the door because I knew who would be running in soon. He was showering off the slave he had just fucked.

Handlers gathered at the door. Valerie saw them and backed away, blindly searching for me behind her. Once she reached me, she gripped at my thighs. I had no pity for her fear because she was keeping me from my prize, my Fire. So, I pushed her forward then, face first, against a training wall, grasped a wrist, and locked it above her head.

Onlookers chuckled.

Valerie didn't fight me but sounded very confused and somewhat alarmed. "Y-Yury, p-please stop."

Grabbing her other wrist, I told her, "It is Master now. Say it."

"Y-Yury—"

"Master!" I locked her wrist above her head in a handcuff bolted to the wall.

Panting fear against the cold concrete blocks, she said, "M-Master, what are you going to do?"

"Treat you as you should have been treated." Admiring her ass, I squatted and locked both ankles to the remaining cuffs, spreading her legs apart. "Like the slave you are." Then I retrieved a leather whip from the wall. "Your disobedience is exhausting."

"Y-Yury—"

Whack! I struck her backside.

Her knees gave as she screamed. Hanging from her wrist, she cried, "I'm sorry!"

Whack! I struck her ass again, enjoying how it wiggled.

"Oh, God! Stop!"

Whack! I tapped that butt again, then readjusted my growing erection.

About to strike it again, I stopped when Kirill barreled through the horny bystanders. His hair was still damp from his shower. *"What the hell are you*

237

doing?"

"Kirill!" screamed his girl, believing my torture would end, but when Kirill got a long gander at the red marks on her ass, his eyes rolled back in his head like a shark before it attacks.

When he focused again, he slowly prowled forward. I started laughing, telling Valerie, "It looks like your boyfriend is about to fuck some sense into you."

Back on her feet, Valerie began to struggle, trying to break free of her entrapment. "Kirill, don't you dare, you bastard."

He dared. His hand appeared so large against her perky little ass as he tenderly touched it. "Shh, my little pet."

"I ain't your fucking pet!"

His clothed penis gyrated against her butt. "Seeing you like this is making me realize a pet is exactly what I want you to be."

"Stop this!" She growled, "Get off me."

His eyes drifted shut, and he nodded behind her while smelling her hair. "Yes. Fight me." Then he told me, "Have someone fetch a robe."

Laughter burst from me again. "Oh, Valerie. I think you should have let me continue to whip you." I head-gestured to a handler. "Robe. We are getting a show."

Valerie rambled on but was ignored by all. Kirill stripped, his eyes locked on his prey while everyone gathered around. He was breathing heavily and totally ramped to fuck Valerie, audience or not, but already robed, Adrian entered, asking, "We are filming with Valerie? I thought it was with the new delivery."

Kirill actually pouted. His shoulders caved. "*No.* There is *another* one today?"

"What?" shrieked a tied-up Valerie. "Another one? You already fucked someone today?"

Again, she was ignored.

I shook my head. "That's right. I got distracted, and I need my *own* pet to witness the introduction." It was an effective way of scaring the hell out of a trainee. After witnessing a brutal rape, they tended to be willing to do anything to avoid becoming a victim themselves.

"I'm not a fucking pet!"

Kirill smacked her ass cheek then reached around Valerie's thigh and slid his hand over her mound while casually telling us, "Okay, I can't fuck three times in twenty minutes." He slid fingers inside Valerie. "Let me get her off, then I'll join Adrian."

I gestured to his busy hand. "How is you giving into her whim ever going to teach her obedience?"

"I'll take care of my woman. You go deal with yours."

Due to my frustration with Wolf, my voice dropped octaves. "Fire is a slave. That's it." Then I stormed out of the room.

Valerie was yelling out demands for Kirill to stop fingering her, but as I collected my folding chair and headed to Fire's room, she was already moaning through a forced release.

Onlookers cheered.

CHAPTER SEVENTEEN

Influencing the Master

Even though I had chastised Kirill for implying Fire was more to me than a slave, I ignored the fact I was rushing to get into her new home. "Good morning, Little Treasure." It wasn't morning, but the greeting seemed appropriate since my new slave had slept for so long. *Meh.* She would never know the difference, having been locked away in a basement.

Angels were far from being a part of my world, but I felt as though I was witnessing one wake as Fire sat up and pulled the dirty blanket to her clothed chest. Fantastic eyes blinked and peeked out from under perfectly disheveled long, red curls. She looked petrified, yet I could sense her inner strength. I pushed away Wolf's theory that I was a good man and smiled because this felt right to me. This, torturing a new slave, was what I knew best.

"P-Please, don't call me that."

I had no intention of continuing to do so. It was only said to rile her and to open conversation for the new name I had already picked. But I truly enjoyed her will. She was dazed with the substance I had drugged her with yet still had the capacity to make a demand.

After shutting the door, I unfolded my chair and sat down, eager to finally learn about the one who had undisciplined me. "Since you said please, I will grant your request. Any suggestions on what I *should* call you?"

"A cab?"

I'm not sure how long I sat there, stunned at her bravery, before I chuckled with pleased laughter. She was far more entertaining than I even expected under these circumstances. "I'm afraid that cannot be, but we could

come up with another name. So far, I've been enjoying Fire."

She was beyond frightened; I could tell by her slight tremble as she wrapped her toned arms around muscular legs and pulled them to her chest, but that didn't stop her audacity to shrug as if my nickname was acceptable. My hunger grew. "You can call me Master." Fire was proving to be my most fascinating pet as she stared at me with disdain. "No?" I winked. "Don't fear. You will see it my way, eventually. Until then, Fire, do you have any questions?"

"My chances of escaping?"

My mouth watered with her twisted humor because it was a sign that she may, someday, handle my lifestyle. So, I reciprocated. "Alive?"

She mumbled, "Yes, being alive would be a plus."

"None." This was the truth. I wasn't giving her up unless she was in a body bag and her beautiful figure was decaying. *Fuck Wolf and his assumptions.*

"My chances of you having a change of heart? Setting me free?"

I thought of Wolf and how he was hoping for the same chance that I knew would never come. "It is very possible I have no heart."

I believe my honesty spoke to the fear she had attempted to hide. She finally sounded vulnerable when she said, "Yury, why am I here?"

Instead of continuing to focus on her desperation, I internally jolted. "You know my name?" *Fucking Mr. Jones and his goddamn PI.* "How unfortunate. Refrain from using that name. Only Master."

Her throat bobbed as she swallowed. "In the hotel room, you said you wanted to profit off me. There is no way you could make enough to make all this hassle worthwhile. So, tell me the truth. You got the paperwork you wanted from my house. And you've killed two people dear to me. What else do you want?"

I stared at her as I thought of how unpredictable I had become since I'd seen her dance. I thought about how much power she truly had over me, and we had yet to begin. I thought how much I didn't want her to have such influence, but my desire for her had become too debilitating. "Wants and needs are not the same."

"Then what do you *need* from me?"

Freedom. I think, deep down, I appreciated her vigor because I lacked it. Yes, I had a gun and was considered deadly and dangerous, but deep down, I was realizing I was as much of a slave as my pets were. Yet, I didn't know how to change my circumstance, nor was I confident I had the courage to do so. I couldn't just drive off into the sunset like Wolf suggested. The cost would be detrimental. All I had known would then change. Was I prepared for the unknown path? How were Timothy and Crash so willing to step into that unknown, death, for the sake of another? I explained, "Someone made the ultimate sacrifice for you. I... *need* to know why?"

"What are you talking about?" Her cheeks went crimson, telling me she was well aware of what I was asking. And that she was carrying much guilt for the sacrifice I was questioning.

To be cruel—to start getting her adapted to her training that would soon be underway—I pulled out the iPad, tapped the screen on the correct video, and handed it to her, then sat back to study her reactions. Watching what was playing—the conversation between Crash and myself that had sent me into a tirade in the garage—she immediately burst into tears.

Fascinating.

Crash's voice echoed in the confined area. "Have you ever listened to someone sleep?"

While the video continued, I took notice when Fire let out a slight moan of agony. At one point, her eyes raced to mine. Too entranced with her reactions to hear what Crash said to get her emotional, I gestured for her to keep watching.

As her whole body started to shift, her legs rubbing against each other in some sort of measure of anxiety, I focused on what Crash was saying. "...Link would give his life for the girl who was clinging to me in her sleep."

It was as if Fire was reliving the memory with him, and it was making her skin crawl. She abruptly pushed pause, leaned her head back against the wall behind her bed, and struggled to breathe. Anguished, she asked me, "Why? Why

is he telling you this?"

I was mystified to how a memory could bring forth such emotion. I was also mystified at how hearing Crash's voice was like walking through a desert full of blazing hot sand with no shoes. I asked, "You are in pain?"

"So much pain." She grasped at her chest as if trying to remove something I couldn't see.

I observed her stressed fingers failing at their task. "Why?" My thinking was, if she could explain her discomfort, maybe I could end mine.

She screamed, "*Because you fucking killed him!*"

I warned, "Do you wish to finish the video, Fire?"

Fire now guarded the iPad as if it were her only link to the dead as she protectively pressed it to her chest. "Yes."

"What does the pain feel like?' I mirror touched the place where she was massaging the pain on herself, on my own chest. I wondered if it was the same annoyance I had been experiencing. "In here."

She stared at my chest as if searching for a sign of hope—a heart that didn't exist. "It, uh, feels very tight. The tightness grows into a sharp, stabbing feeling."

Literally, I had been stabbed, so I was attempting to correlate the two wounds, mental and physical. "Like with a knife?" I asked this because both Wolf and Mrs. Thompson had jabbed me with shocked glares. Those made me uncomfortable, also.

With much hesitation, she replied, "I don't know. I've never been stabbed." I unbuttoned my shirt to show the scar above my left breast. She paled. "You were... stabbed?"

Her voice faded, and the memory of Mrs. Johnson wanting me dead suddenly had me feeling disconnected. "Finish the video."

With Fire's little red nose sniffling, she tapped the screen. Over the video, I heard myself say to Crash, "You speak of your brother giving his life, yet you are the one going to die for her."

243

Her dancing was my drug, but would I die for her? At that point? No.

As she continued to watch the video, tears streamed down her face. She tucked a curl, exposing a perfectly proportioned ear. There was nothing hanging from it. The only jewelry Fire had on was the silver charm necklace from *fucking* Link.

She gasped when she heard Crash speak of knowing how much Link loved her and how much she was truly in love with him, even if she didn't know it. I wanted her to argue those words, say it wasn't so, but her expression spoke what words could not. Crash had once again been a Whitney expert.

When my voice resonated from the device, "Crash, we have a problem. You stole from me. Her virginity was already sold for another to take," Fire started to shake while making a high-pitched *hiss* noise. As Crash spoke about feeling like he had no choice but to sacrifice himself to me so that I wouldn't bring her to my training facility, Fire peered around the room as if it were haunted. Maybe she now understood Crash had once been here, too.

Her eyes met mine.

I smiled.

Along with my voice over the recorder, I mouthed, "A debt is a debt."

There was a bit of an overly dramatic reaction from Fire when she continued to watch the video and witness Crash being severely beaten by me. Crash's pleas over the iPad must have been too much for my little slave because she vomited. I took advantage of her weakness, of course, and made a deal. I would turn off the iPad if she obeyed and called me by my name. Fire finally caved and called me Master. It was a euphoric moment I will never forget.

Now, it was time to introduce her to how I planned on keeping her in my constant control. "Fire, I need to understand Crash's meaning and the why of the willing sacrifice. I figured the best way is to see it first-hand. You will show me."

Wiping her mouth, she asked, "How the hell am I going to show you how to sacrifice?"

Waiting to see how deep her affections went for her best friend, I uttered, "Link."

Fire's skin seemed to melt from her skull as she stared at me. That is how strong her silent, unmoving reaction was. I knew, instantly, she was mine in a whole new way—one I had not imagined. She was going to endure anything I wanted for the young man she loved.

That was the moment I knew I hated Reether Jones.

I wanted my pet to desire only me.

Reasonable? I suppose not, but my goal, never-the-less.

Trying to put aside my jealousy, by reminding myself Reether Jones would never see her again, I simply stated, "Crash said your heart is limitless. I say everyone has their limit." *And I will find yours.* "You see, due to who Reether's mother is, he is technically my property, as are you—"

"You're insane."

"—so, in trade, for keeping him from experiencing what you recently overheard—"

Her eyes raced to the wall at my back, in the direction she overheard Kirill whipping and fucking a male slave.

"—I want…" I waved my hand dismissively. "No, I *need* to witness your sacrifice."

"Link's father has him very well protected. Plus, Link's at Harvard." Her sneer was as if the mere thought of someone violating her friend was atrocious.

It was exhilarating to witness her fight return. And to squash it. "Expecting you not to believe me, I have another video for you." Even though I never took the time to see what my men recorded, I knew it was dire. Fire's eyes were locked to whatever she was seeing, and her hand was slowly rising to cover her appalled mouth. Then I heard water running. When I heard a male's voice singing some song about "time after time," I knew they were filming Link in the

245

shower. It was right after that, that Fire cried out in horror before slapping her palm over her mouth even harder, her eyes filling with terrified tears.

Taking a gander, I was pleased to see a gun being held at Link's head while he slept. Glancing back at Fire, I saw her now staring at me. And, just like that, her eyes told me she no longer trusted Link's father to protect him. It was now all up to her.

I asked, "Do you wonder what I will ask of you?"

Fire's flames evaporated. Tiredly, she leaned against the wall at her back. "I do, but it doesn't matter." After a pause, she added, "I would live or re-live any horrid event to have Link... safe." Her words were as sacred as a vow, just as Wolf's had been to protect his family.

Without lifting her head from its resting place, she studied me. "You don't look like the monster you truly are."

I sighed, thinking of how my looks had Wolf believing I wasn't evil. "Appearances are a façade we profit from hourly. Young girls believe our lies, and then we sell their bodies."

Hurt exuded from her. "Am I to be sold?"

How could I explain she was only there for my selfish reasons? "You already have been." It wasn't a total fabrication. I was indeed paying a high price to have her with me, including alienating my father. "But, Fire, you pique my interest."

Baffled, she uttered, "Why does it sound like this is a good thing?"

I continued my lie, "I'm debating on going against Father's orders and keeping you for myself."

I was hoping she would be satisfied with my answer—find me to be the more pleasing option, but she replied, "What are the chances that my illegal human buyer is better than you?"

So, I chose to make myself appear more appetizing than her fake purchaser. I got creative and described past customers. "Seeing how your new owner has gone through one redhead with green eyes every six months, for the

last decade or so, I would say you will be dead in, let's say, eight months."

She locked her jaw, "I thought you said six," almost implying she didn't want to live the extra two months.

"Two months of training."

"Training?"

I had to swallow more saliva as I hungered to torture her. "We sell anything that can be imagined in the trade of sexual servitude."

Her upper lip snarled as if my job was repulsive. "Meaning?"

"Some deliveries go straight into sex farms. Others, our Elites, are trained for certain perversions." I realized, with this reasoning, things I wanted to do to her, would now be explainable. "Your soon-to-be owner has paid a very high price for you to be an expert in oral sex and bondage. I have to build your endurance. The non-written agreement says you have to last as long as possible."

As it was with Wolf, Fire had been mystifyingly easy to converse with. And, as had happened with Wolf, Fire's presence seemed the only other chance of me ever being a decent human. Something inside her had the only ounce of my humanity fighting to the surface, desperate for her to hear my silent cry for help.

I dare say she heard that plea.

Maybe that is why, by the end of the conversation, Fire chose to win me over rather than be sent to her fictitious owner. Maybe it was the fact that I only gave her two horrid options to choose from. Either way, it was time to move us forward, but she had another demand: warm water.

Not for Wolf, but showers for slaves were always cold. It was a technique to break them down even more so. Washing your body in cold Russian water was a torture of its own. So, Fire and I made a deal. She stared at me as she spoke over my burner cellphone. "I'm calling to say goodbye, Mother. There is no need to continue the façade. You don't love me, never will. Be well."

I needed to cut ties that I could control, and I knew her parents well. I knew they would happily accept Fire exiting their life. I knew they wouldn't ask questions. And they didn't.

When she handed me back the burner cellphone, her voice sounded defeated. "You are literally using against me the only person who cares for me on this earth."

As I had with Wolf, another weak moment took over, for the sake of a slave. In disbelief, I watched as my hand reached out and took hold of hers. "You are lucky to have *one*."

I relished in the sensation of her fingers clinging to mine until she asked, "Will I ever see Link again?"

Thinking of the blog Reether was presently working on, and realizing my recruiter was indeed wise, I replied, "Frequently, if you behave."

Her gasp was almost pathetic as she cheered at the idea of the boy anywhere near her. "How? Will you fly him here?"

So, I sneered, "Only if I plan to profit from him."

She stared to the wall where she heard Kirill manhandling a slave. "No. I don't want that." I was done with hearing her caring ways for Reether, so I got up to start our training. It would be a distraction for her. "Wait!" I should've corrected her insolence as she rushed toward me. "How will I get to see him then?"

After opening the door, I placed my chair in the hallway. "You will earn it."

"But—"

I held up my hand to silence her while returning to her room, shutting the door behind me. I needed to instill a very important lesson. I didn't need any more rumors of my obsession spreading. And, it was already clear she was going to be as special to me as Wolf was. "Conversations are not protocol between slaves and masters. If you wish to continue them, they must be kept private."

Fire eagerly nodded. "What about being monitored?"

I had told her that I was watching. I pulled my remote from my front pocket and held it up for her to see. "At my discretion."

"Oh… May I ask how I will see Link?"

Now, she was poking at a raw nerve. Not wise. "I've already answered that question. You will earn it, as you will everything I give you. Now, take off your clothes." *Maybe being naked will get you more focused on me.*

She took a tentative step back, away from me. "S-So soon? I-I-I'm scared."

Now, I had her full attention. My eyes euphorically slid shut. "Music to my ears."

"Hey!"

My eyes snapped open to discipline the hell out of my unruly pet, but what I saw was too magnificent to snuff out. Tiny fists hung next to taut thighs that were balanced on trembling knees. Her shoulders were full of false power I decided to respect. Fire was taking a stand. "You *promised* a warm shower before we…" She couldn't even say the word "sex" to me. Her hands nervously fluttered about between us to finish her sentence silently.

She was so wonderfully innocent; I couldn't wait to taste her. "I thought my word meant nothing to you?"

She readjusted her nervous legs. "Well, here is your chance to prove me wrong." For a few moments, I pondered the complications that could arise if I gave into her. Not wanting another Valerie on my hands, I was about to refuse her. But then she almost whispered, "Please, prove me wrong… Master."

Two slaves, in one day, obeyed me. Their obedience, which I didn't deserve, struck me in the chest.

CHAPTER EIGHTTEEN

Raw Survival

Mind manipulation is an art form I had absorbed from the very best. Who more appropriate to learn from than people who can trick a person into selling their body? The whores on the streets can testify to such deceit. Not many grow up aspiring to believe someone cares to be raped or tortured, but we captured them every day.

Fear? One of the most powerful manipulations one can generate; hence, why Fire was already vowing to give her body to me. She was terrified of what would happen to Link if she didn't. To solidify that control tactic, I purposely had Fire overhear a conversation as I directed her to the shower room.

Fire's feet had stumbled to a stop as she watched an interaction in a holding cell: a recruiter with his delivery. The girl, still in her drugged haze, was asking the normal questions. "Where are we? How did I get here?" Her American accent resounded loud enough for Fire to hear.

The recruiter, probably anxious to get home to his wife and kids, was beyond irritated due to the long enlist and trip home. "Shelly, shut the *fuck* up! Damn."

Because she was very accustomed to him removing her clothing to 'make love' to her, the American was stupefied at his present attitude. There was no romance behind his touches this time, only purpose; to get his pay and go home.

As planned, I shoved Fire forward so we could head further down the hall toward Kirill and Adrian, already robed and ready. Her body tensed. I think she recognized them from her hotel room. Kirill and Adrian had been surprised that she didn't recognize them from her home, but I wasn't. Fire had had her

sights honed in on Crash the whole time.

In the hallway, Adrian teased, "Good evening, Seafoam's spawn."

Her little bare feet had her halting and going in the opposite direction. Not daring to remove them from her sight, she backed away until she ran into my chest.

Anger charred me to a crisp when she immediately leaped forward so that I couldn't touch her either. I grabbed her shoulder and forced her against me. "They are not here for you, Fire."

To keep our charade in full swing, Kirill stomped his foot toward Fire as if about to attack her. Looming over Fire, I pretended to appear protective to instill who she should start trusting.

As soon as she melted back into me, very willing to accept my offer to keep her safe from the men in black robes, Kirill chuckled. Our strategy had worked, as always. "Easy, young one. Just playing the game."

From over Fire's head, I smiled, knowing she believed Kirill was talking to me.

Adrian entered the filming room while Kirill waited for the recruiter and his abductee. Shelly came up from behind Fire and me, but once next to us, she asked Fire, "Do you know what's happening? I-I don't understand what's going on."

From over her head, I watched Fire's sight race to Adrian standing by the mattress in the room. Fire stepped back into my chest, shaking her head no to Shelly. Was she telling Shelly she didn't know? Or was Fire already figuring it out and shaking her head no to me, silently begging for me not to allow this to happen? Either way, her little back against my stomach had my eyes almost shutting with satisfaction. Fire was already acting accordingly, and her dancer body was touching mine, causing havoc to my groin.

It entranced me to the point that I had a difficult time staying focused— keeping to the plan. Adrian, and now Kirill, were in the room beginning to rape Shelly. I had to push my own desires for Fire aside and hold her chin, forcing

her to watch. But, when her little hand nervously gripped at my pant leg, and she whispered, "Please... Master," I gave in and moved us toward the shower room again.

The shower room consisted of three stalls with no walls or privacy. There were no candles or scented oils. We kept the room as unemotional as we were. Fire stumbled into the next concrete room she would become accustomed to. All the slaves did, eventually.

My voice rumbled against the block walls. "Put your clothes and shoes in the garbage can." I was so hungry for this point in her introduction.

She had still been examining her surroundings but was now gaping at me with a horrific look I truly appreciated. "Wh-what will I wear?"

"Nothing." I tightened my jaw, trying to hide my eagerness.

"Ever?"

"I warned you about people overhearing our conversations." Was it fair for me to charge, then smack her so hard with my open palm that Fire fell to the ground? She appeared horrified. No. But I did it.

The poor girl held up her hand as I swung my shoe back to kick her. She begged, "Hours. I've only been here hours. Please, give me time to learn your rules."

Blood dripping from her lip onto the grey tile had me thinking of my father while holding my own lip. He had struck me over and over to fuck the mother of the young woman I just hit. It was an eerie moment that made me truly pause and reconsider who I was and what I was becoming. I didn't want to be my father, as much as Crash didn't want to be like me.

Fire was now standing in front of me, so close that it felt as if we blended on another level. We both stood there, silent. Me holding my old scar, she holding her new.

Back in the hallway, I had allowed Fire one tiny washcloth, but I wouldn't allow her to cover her now naked self with it. She was to experience what every other

slave did: humiliation. Any employees lurking knew the routine; if present, make lewd comments to the naked newcomers.

That wasn't the only lesson for the day. We had Fire stand at a doorway to witness what was left of Shelly. It was meant to cement the lesson of 'behave or be fed to the hungry rapist,' but the lesson fell apart on me.

I watched as Fire quietly left my side, and without permission, went to the traumatized girl draped on the mattress. Fire had a bravery about her that couldn't be taught or bought. It was simply a part of her spirit. I can't be sure if Kirill and Adrian also fell quiet, or if I was the only one that was mystified watching Fire kneel next to the raped girl. She exuded such tenderness I couldn't look away. She took her only protection—a tiny washcloth—and used it to wipe Shelly's tears and the cum off her breasts. It was then that I first started to truly understand that fear wasn't the reason behind Fire's choices. It was compassion and kindheartedness—something I knew nothing about.

Crash was indeed knowledgeable when it came to this rare treasure. He had said Fire's heart was limitless. For the next couple of months, I was going to put his theory to the test. I began by letting Kirill and Adrian harass her, to the point that Fire was willing to do anything to get a lock on her door, one to which only I had a key. The price? Link's necklace. Fire appeared physically ill as she handed over the gift, in trade for a collar of red rhinestones. But, once again, I had truly not given her a choice.

It was the act of raw survival.

Fire moved as if crawling to her death bed after I forced her to her hands and knees, then commanded she come to me. And she seemed to have lost all fight for life as I taught her how to sit like an Elite, exposing her core to me.

Somehow, it all made me feel like shit.

That night, after leaving Fire stunned and overwhelmed on the floor in her room, I crept into Wolf's. His light was off, and he was sleeping. I tried to shut the door quietly, but he sprang up. I could feel him intensely reading my body language. My soul reader was showing his expertise as he pulled down his

blanket, inviting me in.

Drained, I slipped off my shoes and jacket, and accepted. Crawling into his bed, I felt dismayed. "I'm not who you think I am."

His stare never left mine as he opened his arms. "The problem is, *you* don't know who you are." His voice was gravely due to having been awakened, and I loved it. It wasn't gentle, like Fire's, but it was perfect for what I needed. I needed him. His bare chest, his embrace, was too alluring to deny. I settled my head against him before he laid us down. On his back, he held me comfortingly. It was the first time I had ever experienced such a sensation. "You have to make the decision to see who you really are, Yury, and decide if you like what you see."

His beating heart was a rhythm I held on to so I could be brave enough to soak in his words.

I finally admitted, "My real name isn't Yury." Although I did not offer him my real name, he gently ran his fingers through my hair. It is probably a simple gesture to most, but it was heavenly to me. My body melted to his as I inhaled his soft scent, finding a relief I didn't deserve. I asked, "Can I kiss you now?"

I could feel him staring at the top of my head, but he lacked the courage to meet his eyes.

Maybe he knew me asking was a first. Maybe he knew he was seeing a side of me no one else ever had, certainly not to this level. Maybe that is why he answered, "I'm afraid, once I kiss you, I will never want to stop."

Was it a leap of faith? I couldn't be sure, but I jumped anyway.

Lifting my face to his, I begged, "Never stop," and moaned as he took my mouth.

I didn't know much about kissing, but I was certain no one had ever been kissed like this. I felt it through my whole body, from my toes to the ends of the hairs on my head. Strong hands clutched at my face, grounding me, while I was preparing to run. His tongue told me to stay with him, not to be afraid of the unknown.

We kissed until our lips were swollen, and my eyes finally shut. We fell to sleep in each other's arms. It was the most beautiful night of my life. And it only got better.

I was awakened by his lips. At first, I jolted back, not used to kissing anyone and not wanting a slave's mouth on mine, but then I saw his heavenly eyes, asking if it was okay to kiss me. I rushed forward to lie on top of him, seizing his mouth in approval. I wanted him so desperately, it almost caused pain in my chest and stomach, yet it was superb agony. My breathing became erratic as his tongue caressed mine.

With me on top of him, he opened his legs, where I slipped in between. Breathless, he told me, "Time. We never know what we have left."

Again, my mouth possessed his, because his point was so valid it scared me. I didn't want this to end.

He was naked, and his erection was prominent. It felt heavenly against my stomach. I was clothed, but still, my hips bucked forward, desperate to find my way inside him.

Not moving his mouth from mine, Wolf's hands slipped between us to unbuckle my pants. I was gasping for air, so eager to feel his touch. When he finally grabbed hold of me, I stopped breathing altogether. I literally had to pull my mouth from his to see—to understand—why it felt so fucking good.

With my pants still around the lower part of my hips, I gawked at the male hand stroking my dick. "Wolf, I might come before we get started."

"Wolf?" He chuckled through his heavy breathing.

I nodded, "Yes, that is what I call you—" until I caught a glimpse of his own erection, laying on his muscular belly. I had touched many but only during torture or training. Never had I held one in my palm because I wanted the man to have an orgasm with me.

Watching me, Wolf gazed down. He gritted his teeth while I worked him as good as he was giving me. And, if his hand felt this good, I knew the rest of him was going to be glorious.

My eyes drifted away… then back to him.

Wolf's hair spread all over his pillow. Sweat built on his chest. He whispered, "It's been a long time." I nodded. I understood to go slow. He smiled. "But I want you naked. I want to see what has been hidden." Again, starving, I nodded. I kicked off my pants and socks while he unbuttoned my shirt. "I like the name you have given me—" That had me kissing him even harder. He laughed against my mouth, half-kissing me back. "As much as I want my mouth on yours, I want something else, too." He stripped my shirt off. Staring at my chest, he said, "Damn." Then took my nipple into his mouth.

It felt so incredible; I slammed my palm to the wall above his head. He laughed again, his breath brushing across the wetness, stirring me into a frenzy.

His hands grasped my ass and pulled.

"Let me have you." Naked, I knelt between his legs again, then spit on my palm. I was sure to spread it well before directing my erection right where it needed to be.

Wolf started to shake, his hands gripping at the mattress, so I leaned down and kissed him. "I promise not to hurt you."

In between kisses, and breathing impossibly heavy, he assured me, "I'm not scared. I just ache for you."

Another first. My head dropped to his shoulder as my mouth opened, and I gently bit him, fighting for air in my heated lungs.

Wolf groaned and lifted his knees, giving me full access. This was it. I was finally going to feel this man, inside and out. Ever so slowly, I worked the tip of my shaft inside him, giving him time to adjust. Soon, he was pulling at my thighs, so I surged deeper, absolutely seeing stars that only blended into blindness. Yes, having sex with Wolf made me go blind, yet I could see perfectly all at the same time. I wasn't fucking him like the slave he was; I was joining— blending—with him like the lover he had become.

There was no need for dominance or control.

We just… were.

I didn't feel the need to protect or own, overpower or control.

We just… were.

The ease, the naturalness of it, was beyond what I could ever have imagined.

Crash had told me, 'you float to the one who will never let you fall…' He was right.

The more I realized what I had taken from Crash, the more my rage grew. That magical night with Wolf would be the last for some time. Angry at myself for all the wrongs I could never right toward the young man I had murdered, my sanity slipped. Wolf and Fire were both to pay the price of my mistakes.

Fire was the first to experience my unstable ways. "Dance for me."

Naked, in her room, she was forced to earn a commodity she would soon desperately need: a toilet. So far, she had only a bucket. I was already annoyed that I had hurt Wolf by leaving him in the middle of the night. He asked me not to go, but I was an asshole and explained I didn't 'sleep' with slaves.

Fire, having no choice, started to sway her hips…

So irate with Crash for punishing me from the grave, my guilt continued to push my revenge by robbing his brother of Whit. I had already taught her that she would only eat when I fed her. I continued to reinforce that I was her everything and that Link was nothing. I thought I was powerful enough to change fate, change the bond between Whitney Summers and Reether Jones, but Crash's words were prophetic.

It was never going to *fucking* happen.

So, I took what I could—every part of her that I could touch or damage. I took advantage of her every need so I could have my own fulfilled.

Her hips swayed…

This dance was also what I had been lusting for, daydreaming about.

Why was I so unbelievably infuriated with its effect on me? Because I *had* lost my mind. Not only was her dancing raw, exposing her soul as I had seen before, but it was astoundingly seductive. I had just had sex with Wolf, and having relished the act, I had practically become instantaneously addicted. How could I now crave Fire?

This siren was no fool. Her moves intended to rule my world, seducing me with her body without ever touching me. I knew I was in deep trouble when my dick hardened. I also knew that, deep down, lusting for her led me back to betraying Crash. There was no reasoning with my train of thought, yet it made perfect sense to me at the time.

I stood, desperate for space between Fire and myself.

She had won that round, got her toilet, but would always be the one to pay in the end.

First, I needed a release from the aroused state she put me in. There we many slaves to choose from at the time, but there was only one I wanted.

I stormed into Wolf's room, barely taking the time to shut the door. He leaped from the floor. He had been doing more push-ups. His body was damp from the workout, only amping my desire for him. Long hair clung to the sweat I needed to taste.

As my soul reader, he slowly backed away from me. "What's wrong?"

I followed, my mouth hanging open in a starved state. Pointing at his groin, I demanded, "I need that." Once his back hit the corner, I picked up my speed then dropped to my knees.

His head flew back against the wall as he grumbled, "Ah shit," and my mouth wrapped around him. Was I gentle? Not at all. Did Wolf mind? Not one bit. "I'm—I'm going to come." I didn't stop. I sucked harder and continued to do so as warm jets shot down my throat.

Wolf wasn't given a chance to recover. I yanked him to the ground and placed him on his hands and knees, spitting on my palm. Not until I was inside him did I start to settle slightly. His heated grunts matched mine. Eventually, his

legs gave out from under him. Not retracting from his ass, I followed him down to the ground, still pumping away.

After grabbing his hands, placing his palms to the ground, I intertwined our fingers. Using his straight arms against him, I surged harder. "Are you okay?"

In between pants, he muttered, "The best. This is the best."

I sucked on his shoulder, the side of his face, his arm, anywhere I could reach to taste more of him, all the while taking him with barely any mercy.

CHAPTER NINETEEN

Eruptions of the Heart

I had once again stayed the whole night with Wolf. I simply didn't want to let him go. In the morning, I was contemplating moving him into my room, but by then, I was unraveling again. Father was traveling more and more to help Uncle set up another location. Uncle was going to live there and build it up to be a million-dollar set-up, like ours. I guess one wasn't enough.

In Father's office, with the doors closed, he told me, *"Do not think I have not noticed you slowly wanting to take charge."* He shrugged. *"It has been the plan all along. So, let us see if you truly have what it takes. While I work with my brother, you are in charge here. If you screw this up, I will kill you."* He announced my death as if merely another deal being made. I stood there, stunned and pissed that I cared about how expendable he viewed my life to be. Then he casually asked, *"How is my retirement plan coming along?"*

I exhaled, trying to find the strength to continue this elusive and demented façade my life had become. Maybe it always was this way, but I was only now realizing the truth. *"I still need time with him, but I am pleased with what he is becoming."*

"Have you fucked him yet?"

My ears began to ring. It felt wrong to discuss Wolf like this. Never had discussing a slave's training been an issue for me. So, I swallowed and nodded. *"He... He will soon be everything our client could desire."* My stomach turned.

While Father was gone, I handled the business, monitored other trainers and Elites, trained my own, made sure deliveries went smoothly and newcomers were

housed properly, and prevented employees from abusing their privileges because damaging product meant losing money. Yet, there were only two places I wanted to be. My polar opposites: Wolf and Fire. I didn't want to be told when I could see them or how I chose to do it. They were mine. I didn't appreciate anyone else feeling they had a right to them, even the client who was waiting for one of them. A price had been accepted for Wolf. I was going to lose him within months, and it made me hostile and unpredictable.

In a hallway down in the basement, I held out the white gold collar and leash for all present employees to see. It looked more like a long silver necklace. *"He is our prized possession. He is Le Crème de la crème. So, if you see the leash, step away. One mark on him and you will be dead. Am I understood?"* They all nodded, their eyes locked on the item that represented money and death, all in one sparkle.

Now, I had to convince Wolf to wear it.

"A fucking collar?" He bit into his perfect apple. I made sure every bit of food brought to him was just that, as perfect as he.

In his dark room, I stepped close to him, hoping my touch would help convince him. Holding the nape of his neck, I kissed him, tasting the sweetness of the leftover apple. "This collar means so much more than you think. It is a protection of sorts. It shows your value and that you are off-limits."

He winced. "Off-limits?" He blinked. "What about the rest of the slaves?"

Again, he was worried about my abductees. "What does that matter?"

He pushed at my clothed chest. "Them being here is wrong. Me being here is wrong." He threw the apple against a wall. "Are you raping these people and then making love to me?"

My jaw slacked, leaving me gaping. I was dumbfounded that he thought anything else.

His eyes bored a hole into my heart. "You do." He started pacing while talking more to himself. "Why would I think you're not? It is who you are…" He

261

stopped, and looking horrified, shouted, "What does that make me?" He faced me. *"What does that make me!"*

I rushed to him and pulled him into my arms. Rocking him, I tried to calm him. "What I do has nothing to do with you. You are forced to be here. You are innocent."

Holding me as if he were scared, he claimed, "But I wouldn't leave you if I wasn't forced. If my buyer changed his mind," he peered at me, "I would still want you."

Father had just told me a mistake would have me killed. Wolf just learned I was as evil as I had been claiming, yet he still wanted me. My mouth crashed to his with a passion that had me breathless. Somehow, being with Wolf made me not care about oxygen. The way he kissed me back, forcing me to sit on the bed, was so all-consuming, sucking air into my lungs wasn't needed.

Only him.

I let the collar fall onto the bed so I could hold him, but he pushed me back to pull down my pants, demanding, "Shirt. Off." I immediately fought with the buttons while watching him undress me. Once I was free of all clothing, he pulled me back to a sitting position and said, "Hold me."

As he straddled my lap and took me inside him, I held him as tight as I could because his arms were wrapped around my neck with a desperation I had yet to feel from him. Not willing to let him fall, physically or emotionally, my arms pulled him closer, his erection planted between us. I had to make him feel safe. I just had to. My insides demanded it. "I will stop being with others."

His lips found mine in a ferocious attack. It was divine.

He told me, "Tell me, if you had the chance to walk away, you would, with me?"

At that moment, I meant my words. "I would. I swear it." And I prayed I could someday stand by them.

He deeply kissed me again before saying, "Do it. The collar. Now."

I couldn't stake a claim on Wolf because he was already sold and paid

for, but in my heart, I was claiming him none-the-less. As I wrapped the white gold around his neck, the length hanging down his perfect chest, I whispered, "You are mine."

His eyes welled as he whispered in return, "Until my new owner claims me… Master."

The pain those words brought to my chest was unfathomable. To this day, I still feel the hot lava that erupted inside me. That's why everything that happened next was part of the volcanic eruption named Yury.

Wolf was almost as desperate for natural vitamin D as were all my slaves. The only difference for him was his extensive menu and daily vitamin intake. He had the best treatment. I explained to employees it was because of his status, but I would have fed him that well anyway. No other slave had, or would ever receive such care from me. Not even Fire's treatment compared. I was starving her for control because she gave it all to Link. Wolf had surrendered to me. Also, Fire had no true new owner waiting for her. She was unbought and truly my personal slave. The agreed price for Wolf was one-point-five million dollars. He was a 'prize' in the sex slave industry.

For extra security, Adrian and Kirill helped with escorting Wolf through the house and out the back door. Since I couldn't technically 'claim' him, I did not hold the leash hanging down his perfect chest. We all were confident that Wolf wouldn't run, in fear of retaliation against his family. But if we were wrong, Father had already explained what would happen to me.

Wolf shielded his eyes from all the natural light beaming through the many windows in the mansion. Once his eyes adjusted, he studied his surroundings with such intent a warning *ping* hit my stomach, but it was quickly forgotten when I also received a sinister glare from him. He was seething when he saw the Elites, all on their knees in different rooms, waiting for instructions

as always. I was so accustomed to the sight; I barely noticed the slaves anymore. Now, seeing them, while carrying judgment on my shoulders, I could see this was possibly not the norm for most everyday lives.

Wolf's scrutiny had me wondering if there was a way to erase his memory and lock him away again so we could remain private, but the way Adrian watched Wolf scowl at me, I knew that was no longer feasible.

Once outside, for show, I told Wolf, "If you run, I will kill you then your family. Understood?"

His eyes said, "Fuck you," but his rigid mouth said, "Understood."

I never knew I could use the word glorious when describing a man, but I had never seen a man like Wolf. His naked body was designed to bathe in sunlight. Dark hair, cascading down his broad back, shined in the light. His wide shoulders lifted, then eased, as if exhaling a deep breath. So entranced with the sight, I groaned when my cellphone rang. I took my own deep breath when I saw who it was. "Mr. Jones, I presume?"

"Is she alive?"

Coyly, I responded, "Whom would we be speaking of?"

"Her flight landed. She checked into the hotel and is now gone."

"Why do you assume I have anything to do with her disappearance?"

"How much will it take?"

"For what, Mr. Jones?"

"Money. How much money do you want to return her to me?"

"I do not appreciate these allegations."

"I know you have Whitney, Yury," scorned Mr. Jones.

Hearing my false name made me itch. "Then, if she is indeed alive, you know what I am doing to her."

"Jesus Christ! I will give you any dollar amount!"

"Oh! You are still into buying slaves?"

He growled for thirty seconds before finally replying, "I only buy the carnage you abandon." I think he instantly regretted his words. Taunting me in

no way benefited the girl he was trying to save. "Please, I just want to make you richer, not bicker about right or wrong."

The damage had already been done. "The next time you call, I will be sure to have her screaming as I fuck her tight pussy." I hung up on him, thinking I made myself perfectly clear. Not only had my temper told Mr. Jones that Fire was alive, and he would be a constant pester, but it told someone else I had no intentions of stopping my slave training, something I had just promised to the most important person.

As if a statue on wheels, Wolf slowly turned to face me. What his expression said was that I had just changed 'us' forever. And there was not one thing I could do or say at that moment to try to explain. I had an image to continue in front of my men, or my father would kill me.

Oblivious, Kirill sat in a chair on the back patio of my father's prison camp/home. "*Little Yury is wound tight.*"

I couldn't respond. I just stood there in shock, staring at Wolf. I could literally feel the effects of my world crumbling. It was surreal. It was gut-wrenching.

And it only got worse. Something caught Wolf's attention.

As he stared up above my head, I slowly turned around to see what had him expressionless. It was Valerie, in Kirill's room, her hands pitifully on the window panes as if she would do *anything* to be allowed outside. She looked daunted and depressed beyond all reason. She looked like only a shell of the girl she once was.

Delivering Wolf to his room felt solemn. Not only was he not speaking to me, but his eyes stayed looking at the floor. Once back inside, he turned his face, refusing to look up, and knelt on the cold floor.

I quickly entered, shutting the door behind me. "What are you doing?"

He sat back, as other slaves do all the time, and spread his legs, his penis hanging almost to the floor. Wolf adjusted his leash to hang at his chest, then laid

his hands on his thighs, palms facing up. "I want to be treated like every other slave. It is only right—"

"Stop this."

"—that I experience the same abuse—"

"Wolf," I growled. "I mean it."

"—as all those poor victims. I am a sold slave, after all."

Racing forward to him, I begged, "Please stop." I dropped to my knees, desperately clutching his beautiful face, forcing him to look up at me. "Please."

"Then set them free."

I slammed my eyes shut, refusing to let go of his face. "Impossible."

"Nothing is impossible."

Not opening my eyes, I kissed his lips. "Do not do this to me."

He didn't return the affection. "It is you who have done this."

I opened my eyes to see his dead ones. So, I tried to kiss him again. "Wolf, kiss me."

"Yes, Master." His lips started to move in a robotic fashion.

Shaking my head, I pleaded, "No. Not like this. How you used to."

Wolf delivered a kiss that was so outstanding, I melted. He melted with me. With him now lying on top of me, we kissed like ravaged animals fighting for their last meal. That is what it was—our very last kiss as Master and Slave.

Pushing his weight up by his palms on my chest, he quietly said, "Until you release them all, you will only have the slave in me. You may fuck me or even force my body to respond, but know that I will always hate you for it." He got off me, then took the slave sitting position again, eyes down. "I may be yours in body, but not in my heart… Master."

CHAPTER TWENTY

Suspended Souls

Can insanity be diverse? In one person? Day by day?

For me, the answer was yes.

I felt lost in a darkened forest, full of hungry wolves, yet I was the leader of the pack. It was beyond baffling and distorted my every train of thought. I ping-ponged from Master, Boss, lover, and Trainer, and never found time for Yury. There was not a second to digest what happened with Wolf before I was thrust back into my unforgiving reality.

Leaving Wolf's room, my heart, that I was still clueless I had, was completely shredded. Yet I was immediately approached by a recruiter, right outside Wolf's door. The recruiter shook the arm of the terrified girl in his grasp, her red hair sticking to her tears. "There is no room available for this one."

Wolf must have heard the English spoken words. His palms, with one slap, slammed on the door at my back. I was full of regret for his suffering, but Wolf was taking the chance of making me appear weak to my employees. That was unacceptable. When I saw the recruiter staring at me, questioning what he just heard, and witnessing me not reprimanding the ill-behaving slave, anger bubbled inside me. I couldn't bring myself to go back in the room to punish him, but I felt Wolf had created the newcomer an issue by distracting me.

My resentment grew…

I asked, "*What language does she speak?*"

"*English,*" the recruiter replied.

Lifting the girl's chin, I demanded, "Look at me." I had to swallow my gasp when familiar green eyes peered up at me. This girl was not my Fire but

came in at a close second. If Wolf wanted to dismiss my affections so easily, I felt I had a right to find new distractions. Hopefully, two Fires would be the remedy. I told the recruiter, "I will take her to my room." Then I bent my knee and stomped the bottom of my shoe on Wolf's door to be sure he heard he had already been replaced.

Taking Wolf by force, punishing him—even though regular practice for me with other slaves—was not something I could bring myself to do. That didn't mean the redhead now in my grasp was safe from that fate. She would become my whipping post. Every one of my frustrations would become hers to bear. It was a horrible status to have with a madman that refused to let one more person into his heart.

As I dragged her up the basement stairs, I raced through my normal spiel. "You are so far from home you will never find your way back, nor will your family ever find you." I hit the remote in my pocket to unlock the door. "Your only chance to survive this is to do everything I ask. If you don't, I will hunt down your family and kill them." I dragged her up the white marble stairs. "If you try to run, I will kill *you*."

By the time we made it to my bathroom, she'd pissed herself.

Did I have one ounce of pity? No. I screamed, "Clean it up!"

Then I made her shower.

Then I raped her so violently she struggled to walk the next day.

"Thank you for eating," I told Wolf.

On his knees, he sneered while taking another bite. "It's not for you, as much as for when you finally smarten up."

My nostrils flared. "Smarten up?"

He peeled off a piece of his orange and popped it into his mouth that I wanted to taste again. "That's right. Let me know when you've figured it out." He

twirled his leash around his finger.

Concerned I may kill him, I left his room. As I shut his door, I heard, "Coward."

I'll show you cowardly behavior. I grabbed a bottle of water, knowing Fire would do anything for a sip. She was so dehydrated, she was practically walking sandpaper.

When I told her it was time to start her training, in brute force, I begged in my mind for her not to let me break her. To save Link, she fought. To save Link from becoming a slave, she followed me into the room in which I had punished. Fire's only weakness was fear, but she handled that so elegantly, I couldn't help but fulfill her one request; that I held her before striking her skin.

I can't say whether or not Fire was aware that the moment brought us closer, but it did. I paused, before responding as she leaned into my chest for comfort, but I eventually wrapped my arms around her, totally noticing the difference between her size and Wolf's. Even though the distinction was evident, I found her to be unique. She was nothing like me. Unlike Wolf, Fire had no chance against my strength if she ever, unwisely, chose to fight me back.

From the way she melted to my stomach and chest, her vulnerability was clear to both of us. What she didn't know was that I needed her protection as much as she needed mine. I needed her to feed my spirit and my ego what it desperately required: the tenderness Wolf had taught me.

Even as I tied up her tiny little wrists, to suspend her from the ceiling, her every movement was fluid, gentle, feminine, and full of respect for the power I had over her. Her body was breathtaking, no doubt, but so was her essence. The way her delicate eyes watched me, before I whipped her, had me staying behind her, so she couldn't see me committing such a crime against her skin.

Not since my mother's death had I shed a tear, but bringing this young, strong woman mentally to her knees had me regretting being alive. Wolf was right. I was a walking abomination that needed to be stopped. The little one trying to swallow her screams with my every strike was going to be the one who

finally set Yury free. It would just take more time for me to realize it. For me to let her. For me to let her touch me in the deepest place a person can be touched.

Before that was to happen, I made Fire dance for me to soothe my soul. When the dance would become more sensual, I would take out my sexual frustrations on the fake Whit who was still locked up in my bedroom. Fake Whit became quite accustomed to the routine. I never beat or whipped her. That was for my special pet: Fire.

With Fire's wrists restrained to the same spot as the first time, I wanted to start teaching her body that pain was good. If she was going to be mine for the rest of my days, she needed to appreciate what I liked, or at least what I thought I liked. To start her off slowly, I strapped a vibrating butterfly to her mound, between her thinning legs. With the remote steady in my hand, I stood behind her, my clothed chest against her naked back. I was careful not to irritate the skin I had enflamed with my whip.

I turned on the device to the lowest setting. Her body jerked. "Master, please, no."

She had squirmed when I put the device on her, but I kept talking in a calm voice. In her ear, I softly spoke. "Try not to fight the sensation. Let the feelings build. Surrender to what our bodies want." I gently reached around and touched her breast. She didn't shy away. The one time she did, I offered her to a handler. I wasn't going to let him soil her. I knew she would beg for me to forgive her so I would rescue her, which she did.

So, I took her back.

She'd been most cooperative since.

Fire didn't want to react to the device between her legs, but her body, as they all do, betrayed her. Her nipples went taut, and her breathing became more labored due to the erotic sensations and the fact that she was already winded from me striking her. I gave a slight pinch to her nipple. Her head fell back against my shoulder. She whispered, "I'm begging you not to make me do this."

Sweat from her face transferred to mine, with us cheek to cheek. "And I

am begging you to release this inhibition and let me show you a whole world out there that you have been missing."

I knew being on her tippy toes was getting tiresome, even for a dancer, so I wrapped an arm around her waist to help support her. Her sigh was almost audible, but when I turned the remote to a higher level, she gasped, and her body stiffened. I rubbed her stomach with my other hand, attempting to soothe her. "Let go, Fire." Feeling her so close and helpless against the erotic torture I was causing her had my own desire spiking. While my erection grew, her little ribs expanded against my chest, over and over. She continued to fight the need to orgasm as I whispered, "Let go," then turned up the intensity one more notch.

Fire groaned, as her body seized...

Beyond aroused, I buried my face in her neck as she orgasmed in my arms.

As time passed, and her training continued, her body started to light up with certain pain. Nipples were an easy way to have her silently begging for more. Tight pinches made her core wet with need. That core made me hungry, so I used her own hunger against her. She only received one or two pieces of bread, one bottle of water, and maybe one piece of cheese every three days. Her state of malnourishment made her easy to convince to do as I pleased.

Strung up by the chains, she watched as I walked in with a fresh plate of cold cuts. Tears started to fall as she quietly pleaded, "What do I have to do for a bite?"

"You know the rules. Be a good girl," meaning, let me do what I want, "and you can choose one item." Her bottom lips trembled, tears dripped from her chin, but she nodded. I set down the tray. "Has anyone ever licked your pussy?" A burst of more cries escaped her as her head hung forward, shaking it no. "It is okay, Fire. We can try another time." I picked up the tray and headed for the door.

"Please come back, I'm... I'm sorry. You can do it. Don't take the food."

Happily, I spun on my heels and went back to the table. "I do love it

271

when we can agree on our special times together." She didn't say anything, only cried while staring at the plate. "I'll tell you what. What if we eat together?"

Clueless of my meaning, her eyes widened, and her head bobbed in approval. "Yes, Master. I would love that."

I stuck a rolled-up piece of turkey in my mouth so that half of it stuck out. Her brows scrunched, but when I got close to her mouth, her eyes asked permission. I nodded.

That miniature mouth opened and stretched to take a bite, but as soon as she got a taste, survival instincts kicked in. Her mouth opened wide and inhaled all that I had to offer. Her lips, even though an accident I'm sure, brushed mine as she devoured the meat she hadn't had in so long.

Was the touch something that reminded me of Wolf? Was the touch something I mistook as affection? I can't say, because it was as if I blacked out before I dropped to my knees in front of her. She gasped around her mouthful as I stared at her mound, lightly shaded with red hair. My whole body shook, desperate for my mouth on that juncture. "I…" I inhaled. "Will give you the whole plate."

Little cheeks, puffed with chewed turkey, were blanketed with tears and regret as my Fire reluctantly nodded. While she chewed and sobbed, staring at that tray of meat, I ate at her pussy as if it would be the last time before I died.

Fire's teardrops dripped onto my face as she came in my mouth.

Back in her room, I kept taking steps backward, appalled as I watched her vomit all the meat that refused to stay in her weak stomach. What made it worse was, from her knees at the toilet, she kept reaching out to me, even though I was the cause of her misery.

Did I stay and try to ease her suffering?

No. I ran.

Straight to Wolf.

Waking, he sat up in his bed. I was surprised he was sleeping, so I

quickly looked at my watch. It was one a.m. We stared at each other, only the light peeking from under his door making it possible to see anything. Soul Reader was quietly working his expertise. Disappointment eventually appeared and crossed into a blank expression. His bent knees rose so he could rest his arms on them, then his forehead to his arms. "Who do you keep torturing with your madness?"

A lingering silence hung between us before I answered, "The little sister of a man my father wanted killed."

Wolf slowly lifted his head, appearing terrified to ask. "How little?"

My voice cracked, "Eighteen."

I wasn't sure if his exhale was relief or disgust. "Is this part of your job?"

Finding it impossible to lie to him, since he was finally talking to me, I whispered, "No."

He rushed from his bed and to me, whispering loudly, "You have a choice! Please make the right one! Please—" Once face to face with me, he stopped. "What kind of torture, exactly, are you committing?" He took a tentative step back.

I wasn't sure where I had gone wrong just as he was letting me back in, so I said, "Uh, training—"

He shoved my chest hard. I flew back against the door. "I smell her on your face!"

Bangs from the other side of the door erupted. Voices called while trying to open the locked door. *"Yury! Are you all right?"*

Again, Wolf had put me in a precarious position. *"All is well."* I glared at him… then I punched him. Wolf dropped to the ground, his hair flailing through the cold air. I opened the door wide so that my men could witness me pretending to have everything under control while I was truly falling deeper into my pit in hell. *"See for yourselves."*

Appearing profoundly betrayed, Wolf held a palm to the side of his mouth while slowly rising to the slave sitting position. Blood dripped from his

busted lip and onto his leash. Tonight, I had caused tears and bloodshed to the ones I gave a damn about.

Did I rush to either of them for forgiveness?

No. I ran. Straight to Fake Whit for another hour of horrendous actions.

As she lay in my bed, appearing numb and mentally far from me and what I had done to her, I put on workout clothes—sweat pants and a T-shirt. The release I spilled inside her did not sate my pent-up vexations. It was two-thirty in the morning when I ran down the stairs toward the workout room. I fully expected ease to take over me, but as soon as I entered, I saw Crash dangling from his hands on the rock wall. He peered over his shoulder and smiled at me. "Hey! Look what I can do! I'm stronger now."

Absolutely shaken to see him, I slammed my eyes shut, sure I was losing my mind. Maybe I was, or maybe Crash was still my friend and trying to guide me with simple words. I had laughed at him when he promised to protect his Franky from the grave. Now, I was unsure of what to believe, which only added to my growing confusion.

It was very quiet as I walked down the basement stairs, searching for an ounce of peace. Her room was dark, and the exhausted girl was sleeping as I slowly crawled into bed with her. Fire rolled into my chest, softly saying, "Will you stay with me?"

"If you will have me." I closed my eyes, almost praying she would say yes. I needed some validation in my life.

"Always."

I sighed my relief and held her close.

She burrowed into the warmth I provided her tiny body. "Always. I love you, Link."

There would be no peace for me this night and none for Fire tomorrow.

CHAPTER TWENTY-ONE

Inside her heart,

Revenge is a slippery slope into the unknown because it can become unclear when it will ever end, or *if* it will ever end. The more Wolf ignored me, the more I dove headfirst into Fire. The more she called out to Link in the night, the more I felt the need to reprimand her. The more her training intensified, the more I desired to fuck her senseless. Her only saving grace was that I wanted her willingly. Having sex with Wolf who desired me was addicting, and now he had shut me out. Fire was to be my next drug of choice.

Did that help her as I took out my rage against her for caring so deeply for Link? No. There was a beast growing inside me that still craved revenge. And, I had it, on her little body that was not to blame for all my crazy. Her breasts were red and swollen from whips, clamps, and my bites. I had finger-fucked her, easily making her come.

Fire, hanging from the chains, spent and dripping with sweat, looked divine and delicious, and ready to have me. My shaky hands ripped at the button and zipper of my slacks, preparing to yank out my raging erection, but as soon as Fire saw what I was doing, and where I was headed, her lifeless body woke up. The gag in her mouth wouldn't let her speak, but she shook her head no and her pleading, beautiful green eyes begged me not to penetrate her with my dick.

Deflated by the rejection, I leaned my forehead on the taut arm suspended above her head. I exhaled, long and hard, until I felt her face nudge mine. Raising my head, I looked at her. Her beautiful pixie face was frightened yet showed concern for me. It was a sight I won't forget. Fire and I were like the

Unbuckling the strap of the gag, I asked, "Why are you so good to me?"

I had picked the smallest ball to go in her mouth, and it hadn't been in long, so she quickly found use of her mouth. "Because you were good to me."

That made me smile, even though I didn't miss that she was speaking of the past.

Her lips trembled, but she smiled, too. "You fed me. And, you kept the others from hurting me."

Pushing her now longer hair from her shoulders, so I could see her red rhinestone collar, I told her, "I will still do all those things. They won't touch you. Just... let me have you."

She nuzzled into my hand, so I rewarded by her by cupping her face. She sighed against my palm, placing a kiss. "Thank you for claiming me."

I had, proudly, even though I knew it would cause my father to be irate whenever he returned home.

I stared at the pouty lips in my palm and asked her, "Why did you kiss me the other day?" It was right before I claimed her. I had already purchased the collar and leash, knowing I was going to make her officially mine, but after that unbelievable, simple, tender kiss, there was no turning back.

Her eyes watched my mouth as she replied, "I kissed you because I love to see your softer side. It is when you are beautiful to me."

I was rugged, I was scarred, and I was demented, by all means, yet this gorgeous creature had seen beauty in me. "I will find a way to repay your kindness."

"You can start by stopping what is happening in your room."

Moments before I claimed her, I had promised to show her Link's blog video. That's when she kissed me. Since I claimed her as a reward, she now needed another way to earn more videos. I chose a lap dance to be how she could see Link. She accepted and tantalized, while erotically moving on top of me. It even affected her. Fire had lost control as her body remembered what I could do for it. Hips moved across my growing erection, daring me to take us a step

further. I had felt sex—willing sex from Fire—was finally going to be mine. But the thought of the cherished moment being in the same room I had housed Crash's slave had me suddenly on edge. I told the hungry vixen in my lap, "Not here," and rushed us out of the room and up the stairs so I could fuck her properly in my own bed.

But, again, my life would continue to be under my father's control.

As soon as I entered the foyer, not realizing my father had just returned home, one of his minions grabbed Fire's arm and tried to take her from me, due to Father's orders. He *was* irate at the sight of her leash, screaming at me for betraying him with his curse.

I was irate that someone dared to touch my special pet, so I shot the minion, right in front of Fire. Then I pointed the gun in my father's face while explaining I was not stepping down just because he had blessed us with his presence. I then, at the top of my lungs, dared anyone to touch my Fire again. No one did, but I was still so angry I chased Fire up the stairs and into my room. Needless to say, she was appalled to see Fake Whit there and horrified to watch me rape her, as I always did.

Hanging from the chains, Fire quietly said, "I can't get past what I saw you do to her."

"You won't see it again." I kissed her soft lips. "Please, let me inside you."

Her breath trembled as she whispered, "To truly be inside a woman, you must be inside her heart."

A snarl erupted from me. "Right where Link is, correct?" Her eyes widened as if she recognized the shift in me that she had just provoked. I sneered with much menace. "Enjoy every orgasm I wring from you today. They will be your last. Whit will benefit from all my attentions… in front of you." I wrapped her legs around my waist then smacked her ass. "Tighten these strong dancer legs." She did what was demanded. My eyes fluttered shut, feeling her muscles and core pressed up against me. Then my anger reminded me to move forward.

277

Frantically, she watched as I untied her from the leather straps. "Master, please."

"The time for your begging to mean a damn to me has ended."

As soon as her hands were free, she grasped at my face, trying to calm me. "I'm sorry."

With an arm firmly around her, I pressed her chest to mine. "You have no idea how sorry you will be. Now, kiss me."

Without delay, her nervous lips smashed to mine. "Please, don't rape me."

Carrying her across the room, I growled, "My dick won't, but everything else in this room will."

Little arms squeezed my neck. "Please. I'm so sorry. I won't love Link anymore."

I stopped. "Look at me." Wet, red eyes met mine. "Then tell me I can bring him here." Fire looked away, closing her eyes, and choked on a sob. I started walking again. "That is what I thought." I set her butt on the edge of a table that reached my stomach. I pushed her upper body back, forcing her to lie down. Raising her hands above her head, I wrapped her fingers around wooden handles. "Hold on and don't let go, or I will torture you in ways you cannot fathom."

Crying, her hands gripped tight. She was barely audible. "Why are you doing this?"

Leaning over her, I roared, "Because you are to choose me!"

"B-But I'm here, Master—"

"That is not my name!"

"O-Okay, Yury—"

"That is not my name!"

She recoiled in fear but never let go of the pegs. "I don't know what you want me to do."

I grabbed a small dildo from a nearby table. "Knees to your chest."

Gasping for air through her hysterics, she did as I asked, her core stretching and opening for me. I swallowed my pleased groan at the delicious sight. "Let your legs fall open." They were tense but opened for me. Turning the dildo on, a low hum entered the cold room. After I held it to the top of her mound for a bit, Fire started to moan forcefully through her tears. I could feel my lips turn into a wicked grin. *She is no longer thinking of Link, only what pleasure I am bringing her.*

Tears faded…

With her juices flowing, I inserted the tip of the sex toy inside her. Her body was so aroused, it was soon after that I was able to slide the full length of the dildo in. Green eyes vanished behind heavily seduced lids. Since she couldn't see me, my free hand prepared a surprise sensation. As her legs began to tremble, so close to her climax, I snuck a small, lubed butt plug into her tight hole. Fire's eyes popped open, but there was no time to ask what I had done. A life-changing orgasm blew through her whole body. Her erotic screams told me so.

Little did I know, I had just witnessed the last orgasm that I would ever see from her.

My father had left to be with my uncle again. He took his minions and left me with my regular staff. Kirill kept training slaves while still devoted to Valerie. He never requested little girls again. He had found the only one he truly wanted. I wondered if I had found the same as I tortured Fire for weeks on end. I brought Fake Whit immense pleasure in my bed while Fire slept on the slave pillow on the floor, but my pet wouldn't surrender to me. I offered Fake Whit fruit and watched Fire drool… yet, no surrender. Not until I took Fake Whit out for dinner.

Fake Whit had become so entranced in me that she failed to see I was using her. She didn't even realize that me taking her to dinner was to anger Fire and show off my foolish redhead to an interested client. He didn't believe I could

get a true slave to behave in public. He wanted a beautiful one he could torture at home yet have on his arm at business dinners, and even offer her to very important clients. Nope, after dinner, and accepting payment for the privilege, Fake Whit waltzed back into my bedroom as if she were the most important Elite in my home.

Fire was literally spitting with rage. I moaned in pleasure, seeing my spunky pet had returned to me. I even told her so as she disobediently stormed into my bathroom, but she still wouldn't even kiss me. The rejection was too similar to Wolf's, especially when she said my actions made her hate me. I couldn't take it, so I punished harder. While Fire was in the shower, I took the leash she had left on the bathroom counter, in its special bowl, and went back into the bedroom. Fire treasured that leash and the protection it offered. That's why I knew placing it on Fake Whit's collar would be my best card to finally win the game.

Naked and dripping wet, Fire was so livid she practically seared everything around her, including me. And it felt magnificent. In order to get that leash back to its proper owner, Fire made an offer she knew I would never refuse; she would finally allow me inside her, willingly.

I truly believed sex with her would cure my ache for Wolf, rid me of guilt from Crash, and have me feeling more important than Link.

None of that happened.

After I had a handler retrieve Fake Whit, explaining she was to be prepared for her delivery, Fire attacked me. Her rage was not because I had abducted her or abused her; it was because those actions made her into something she despised, someone just like me.

I was confident she couldn't physically hurt me, so I let her shove me backward toward a chair. I was wrong. I had played with the wrath of this woman for the last time.

"Take off your clothes," she demanded.

As I stripped, I watched a storm like no other brew inside those seafoam

eyes. That is when it hit me. I was about to fuck the daughter of the woman who had been forced to take my virginity. I blinked. "Fire—"

"The time for your begging to mean a damn to me is over." She shoved my naked body into the chair that Crash, as a child, huddled in to stay clear of me. The leather almost burnt my skin as guilt scorched my insides. That's why I was too distracted to avoid Fire's venomous actions. Her soft palm slammed into the side of my face. Stunned, I failed to react like her Master before she snagged my penis in a vicious vice-like grip. My hands pushed off the arms of the chair to better raise my hips and follow her hand, as she lifted, literally having full control over me. "Understood?" She was repeating vile things I had said to her over the months I'd forced her to be my degraded slave.

It was pitiful, and she had every right to her own revenge. So, I made the decision to let her have it, no matter what it cost me. I winced in pain. "Understood."

"Spread your legs." When I didn't follow her directions fast enough, a tug had me quickly obeying, widening the gap between my thighs. I watched as she lowered herself to her knees. "Have you ever imagined what it would feel like for me to suck your dick?"

I had—many times. So, I nodded.

"Touch me, and I will bite it off."

Her words reminded me of why Wolf didn't want me to touch him either. I was about to tell her she didn't have to pay any more debts to me. "Fire—" My head flew back as her mouth engulfed me. "Shit!" Her warmth had blood abandoning the rest of my body as it all rushed to my dick. Her head bobbed in my blurry vision as I tried to reach out to stop this moment, the one I knew she was hating.

As soon as my hand grazed her hair, she popped her mouth free and screamed! "I said, don't touch me!" Then she turned her mouth to the side and chomped down on my inner thigh.

My skin pinched under her tiny teeth. "Fuck! Okay! Okay!"

She looked positively evil as she stared at me while crawling into my lap. "I'm not going to fuck you with anything in this room but me." Her cunt slammed down on my erection.

My upper body pushed back against the chair, so twisted between horror and pleasure. "Fire, let me—" Another smack hit my face, this time on my other cheek. My head jerked to my left. I let it lay there. "I shouldn't have done what I did to you—" I hissed as teeth sunk into my neck, her hips savagely riding me the whole time. I didn't resist. I only continued to think of Wolf and something he had told me. Holding still as she attacked me, I quietly said, "I'm sorry."

Such powerful words… when you mean them.

I did mean them, even when my hair was suddenly in her grasp and yanked with all her might. She stared me down, holding me hostage by pain and her glare. "You don't have the right to apologize to me."

We were both panting. We were both lost, but Crash taught me something wise.

So, I refused to let her fall.

I whispered, "I'm sorry for that, too."

Her eyes began to fill with tears as she tightened her grip on my hair and growled, "No."

"Fire… You never deserved all I did to you."

"You. Killed. My. Brother."

I had done so many things wrong to this young woman I had started to lose track.

My eyes closed.

"No!" she screamed, pulling on my hair to be sure I heard her. "You fucking coward—"

Wolf.

"—are to look at me. See my fucking anguish."

I opened my eyes and saw death, dread, hopelessness… and a soul worth saving. And to do that, I had to admit my wrongs, finally see them, and change.

"I do."

She opened her mouth and screamed so loud, in my face, I think I heard her vocal cords tear and bleed. I didn't move. I accepted every second of her rage and need to vent.

My bedroom door swung open. It was Kirill and Adrian with the food I'd ordered to tempt Fire. They both grabbed their chests and recoiled when Fire twisted her upper body and let out another earthshattering scream, toward them this time.

Not wanting to startle the distraught woman on my lap, I didn't move, only shook my head at them. "I'm okay. Leave."

Her body had pushed my flaccid penis from her cunt as she spun back around to see me. Her raw throat scratched as she sneered, "You are far from okay."

"You are correct."

A tray was set on the ground and the door shut.

Whack! She struck my face. "You murdered my boyfriend!"

"I'm sorry."

Whack! She struck my chest. "You took me from Link!"

"I had no right to do so."

Spit hit my face as she hollered in it. "You had no *riiiiiiiiiiight*!" Breathless, her chest heaved. She took a moment to examine us both before a horrified expression took hold, and with an excruciatingly quiet voice, she whispered, "Oh, God... Look what you've turned me into." Tears poured from magical eyes, which were now beyond haunted with too many painful memories for her to bear. She pulled a shaky hand to her gaping mouth. "I had you misuse another life to save my own." Her eyes closed as if in immense pain. "What has happened to me?" She shook as her every movement seemed to cause raw torment. "I... I can't do this anymore. Make it end. Oh, God... Please, make it end." Then her head fell back, as if she were talking to the heavens. But I knew she was asking me. "Please, let it all end. I'm so tired." Her head dropped

283

forward and rested against mine before she whispered, "Please, kill me, like you killed Timothy and Crash."

My jaw tightened as I fought tears. "I'm sorry. I can't do that."

"Please… just end my suffering." She collapsed against my chest like a waterfall finding a cliff. And she cried.

Absolute despair consumed her whole being. I felt physical pain watching the way she shattered, so I slowly wrapped my arms around her to collect the pieces I had created. In the arms of her destroyer, Fire finally allowed all she had been through since her brother's death to take hold and completely own her. It was eerie and gut-wrenching. I leaned my head to the top of hers and whispered, "Shh," trying to settle her exposed nerves, but I had uncovered them by brutal force, and I now had to pay the price by realizing her pain.

Witnessing the carnage—the death and loss—I had caused in one beautiful girl, was the beginning of the end of Yury. Every sob she released stabbed me in what I finally understood to be my heart.

How about that? I had one, after all.

Carrying her to my bed, I silently promised to somehow do right by her. I was clueless as to how to make up for all the devastation I'd generated in her life, not knowing if it was even possible, but I vowed to try. Beside her on my bed, I offered food and water, but all were denied by more gut-wrenching tears. Her whole body jerked and pulsed through every shattering sob, as if her torment was killing her from the inside out.

Not sure her heart could survive this catastrophic breakdown, my mind raced with what I could offer immediately to soothe her grief-stricken soul. Holding Fire, my eyes slammed shut as I could come up with no solutions. I was becoming alarmed she would die in my embrace. Her death would have been one I couldn't live through myself. My eyes opened when I realized, at that very moment, what Crash's self-sacrifice was all about. He understood his actions weren't his own, or at least not only for him. They were for her, and for everyone else she indirectly affected. That thought had me seeing how my own

actions weren't my own, not when they affect those around me. With Fire's tears drenching my chest, I laid there, dumbfounded by all those I had disturbed. Not only did I take human beings from their everyday lives, but I stole from those around them. How did those friends and family members react to the loss?

The answer was in my arms.

I rocked her. "I'm so sorry."

Was there an end to the ripple effect I built in others?

"Psst."

My eyes raced to my bedroom door. I jolted when I saw Crash again. He was smirking. "She needs warm water."

Suddenly overtaken with the sensation of needing to apologize to him, too, I let go of Fire and leaped out of my bed, but as I ran around the mattress, Crash disappeared. I stood in front of the bedroom door, wishing he would reappear. That is when I heard water running.

My head slowly turned toward the bathroom. No faucets or showers were on, and now all was quiet except for Fire's sobbing. When I first brought her here, all she asked for was warm water.

I ran to the tub as if my life depended on it and started filling it with hot water. I let it continue to fill while I rushed back to Fire. She was trembling, slipping into shock. Tears leaked from dead eyes as she stared at the ceiling. I was losing her. She was drifting away...

The hands and arms that had brought her so much pain now lifted her from the mattress. The legs and feet that had kicked Crash now rushed her into the bathroom. I somehow knew, if I lost her, Crash's sacrifice would have been for nothing. So, I begged, "Fire," desperate to reach her. I simply couldn't let her go—

"Let go of what?" Crash's voice violently tossed my mind into a memory. He was on my bedroom carpet, Rainbow's blood still on him. I had just pulled the nurse's dead body from his grasp, and he was hysterical. "I don't even know her name! Do you?"

Then, I remembered Mrs. Thompson in the SUV, in my lap, telling me, "And you don't even know my name."

It was as if the name was a metaphor. I didn't know their names because I didn't know them. Did I know Fire? If I did, why call her by a false name? I swallowed bile as I realized changing my victims' names prevented me from having to know them. If I did take the time to learn who they truly were, harming and selling them might not have been feasible.

I thought of Wolf and how I knew his name before I'd had him abducted. Due to his price, much research had been done. I knew of his wife and child. I knew... his name.

Doctor Bram Janssen.

Bram and I had long conversations and tender moments. I had, for the first time, taken the time to get to know a slave. Because of that, it was difficult to bring him pain.

Fire? I literally knew her before she was born. I knew where she came from and by whom; Seafoam, the woman who had a connection to me no one else would ever have. Fire and I were so intertwined; she was never just another unknown slave to me. I knew more about her than she knew about herself.

Fire had never been; it had always been... "Whitney."

Her body stilled.

At that moment, I released the notion of "Fire" into the night and welcomed Whitney into my life, once and for all. "I have hot water." I had never kissed anyone's forehead before, it was an act of affection that I lacked, but Whitney was special. My lips to her skin was a silent thank you for opening my eyes to a world that needed to come to an end.

Light green eyes, just like her mother's, gazed up at me. The magic, the message inside, was as if both women were full of forgiveness. Father had it all wrong. Seafoam wasn't a curse, nor was her daughter. They were both blessings.

As dramatically as it started, Whitney's sobbing ceased. She was drained, and she was pale, but she still found the courage to find gratitude for the

beast. "Thank you." Then she rested her sweet little head on my shoulder and melted against the murderer who had literally stolen her life and everything she treasured. "Will you ever tell me your real name?"

All air drifted from my lungs as I realized my father refused to use my real name. I had learned this trick from him because I was experiencing it. I was his victim. I was a slave, just like the girl in my arms. And, she didn't deserve to be here. None of the slaves did.

My cheek caressed her because her inner beauty was bewildering. "No, because my name will only remind you of this place."

The burst of tears she exuded next didn't frighten me. They were tears of joy. I had just told her I was setting her free.

Weak and not wanting to be alone, Whitney asked me to join her in the bath, so I carried her frail body as we sat in the water. I say frail because, now allowing myself to see the true Whitney, I saw how malnourished she had become. Her body had fed on itself in order to survive my treatment, my abuse. It would take some time for her to become strong, healthy, and vibrant again. But, at least, she would be given the chance. For now, it was only she and I in that tub. Those quiet moments were needed. With very few words, we soaked as the water cradled us both. I thought of the water that she swam in with Timothy and Link, the same water that drowned Crash. And, I prayed that Whitney would someday find her way back to that tainted water and see it clear of all the malice that had taken place there by my hands.

I would someday be a part of that prayer, more than I knew at that time. I would get the chance to personally see that water be a part of her for the rest of her life, but first, I had to destroy her, one more time.

CHAPTER TWENTY-TWO

More than One Life

Magical moments are few and far between amongst the abundance of darker ones. Unseen clouds brewed around Whitney and me as we shared a night which we would treasure yet never have again. I can't say how one tender kiss to my cheek developed into passion because it was too magical for someone like me to comprehend, but magical it was. There were no whips, no chains, and no forced acts or releases, only two lost souls finding comfort and peace in the physical touch that reached us both far beneath our skin.

Before the final storm was to erupt, Whitney had a piece of me to carry with her, to remind her of the time she brought a human trafficker to his knees. She effortlessly brought out the tiniest kindness I possessed, and she gave it the courage to grow. I held her and kissed her as if she was my last breath of fresh air—air I never wanted to exhale because then it would be forever gone.

In my arms, she slept. And, when she called out for Link, I cried. Fire had never been mine, and Whitney never would be. She would always truly belong to the young man waiting for her to come home. Wiping my tears, I chuckled, knowing Crash had been smarter than me all along. He saw the impenetrable love between Whitney and Reether and wasn't stupid enough to try to stand in its way. Kissing her forehead again, I decided I would no longer try, either. I whispered, "If I am capable of love... I love you."

I slipped from her sleeping embrace, already missing her touch. With my cellphone in hand, I went into the bathroom and shut the door. I pressed my back to the outer wall of the shower and wiped my wet face, then tapped on my phone's screen.

When Mr. Jones answered, I spoke to not be overheard. "I am not asking

for money for her return."

I heard his sharp inhale. His voice was barely audible. "She's still alive?"

Up to this point, I had refused all of his calls. It had been months since he had heard from me. "She is."

His exhale trembled over the receiver. "My son loves her."

Even though it hurt, my heart knew this was the right thing to do. I wiped the wetness from my face. "I know, and she loves him."

"Yury, will she ever be the same?"

My eyes slid shut as I rested my head against the wall holding me up. "None of us will."

"Timothy was right. She is a treasure, isn't she?"

It wasn't a question, so there was no need to answer. "I will meet you at a disclosed location if you are willing to give me the coordinates to where you buried him." Crash's body was hidden where no one would find him. I suspected it was in the woods beside the neighborhood Mr. Jones resided in but had no time to search all the untouched land. "I am not willing to leave a trail that can ever lead back to her."

Silence… "My wife. She—"

"Needs her living son to survive, which he won't, not without Whitney. I highly recommend you take this one-time offer. I will *not* be this generous the next time we talk. I don't want to let her go."

"I understand, and thank you for the offer. I accept your conditions."

"I need time to get her out safely."

"I am at your beck and call. Anything I can do to help?"

"Pick a meeting place. Not Russia. I need her far from here."

I can't be sure, but I believe a sob escaped him before he chose. "I once told her that Hawaii is a beautiful place to get your thoughts together."

That she will need. "Then we have a place."

Mr. Jones was quiet then said, "I don't know what happened to get you to this point, but you are saving more than one life with this decision."

My throat closed with overwhelming emotions, so I didn't reply, nor did I stay on the phone.

Bringing down my father and uncle's growing empire didn't seem feasible, so I wasn't even going to try. I was only going to rescue those I could. By now, there were not many slaves present because Uncle had requested deliveries be made to his new location, to get the inventory stocked for new customers. High-quality Elites were being collected to impress and steal rich costumers from Father and Uncle's past employer. It was a daring move, since we were lucky to have gotten away with it once—

I thought *That's it!* when remembering the night my mother was murdered and what was written on the warning letter attached to her skin.

My business is my business. Yours is now yours.

Get in my way again and I will steal your whores.

Father and Uncle had surpassed their original goal and were now broadening their reach further. I classified that as 'getting in the way.' I alone could not stop my father and uncle, so I would let their competitor do it for me.

My sigh echoed off the bathroom walls. Once Father and Uncle learned I had betrayed them, I was as good as dead. I gazed at my bathroom door, picturing Whitney sleeping in my bed, dreaming I was going to make things right. I gently touched the lips she had tenderly kissed, then I searched my cell for a number I had stolen years ago. I made a very deadly phone call.

"*Who the fuck is this?*" A bodyguard answered.

"*This is Yury, Макар's son and Семён's nephew.*"

There was a shuffle as the phone exchanged hands. Then the leader of the organization said, "*My nephew, speak.*"

I jolted. "*Excuse me?*" I had always wondered how my father and uncle lived through the betrayal of such deadly men. Now, I had my answer.

He started laughing. "*My brother has left out some details, I see. And now, you are my enemy.*"

Flabbergasted, I uttered, "*Yet, I thought they were all the family I had.*" I

set my shoulders back, hoping this was a sign I might live through my betrayal. *"Uncle, I wish to be your enemy no more. To show my good intentions, I call with information and an address..."*

Not only did my newfound uncle accept my offer, but he had an offer of his own; to work for him. I humbly declined and made it clear I wished to disappear, and that I would never be entering this line of business again. Since I was attempting to sabotage the one that I was currently running, my uncle claimed to believe me. He did warn, if I were ever to change my mind, he would not think twice about slicing my throat—family or not.

I quietly slipped back into my room, put on my clothes and shoes, grabbed one gun with a silencer, and a second gun. While I was gone, I needed to know Wolf could defend himself. I had one week to prepare for the permanent "closing" of the new location; therefore, I had one week to be sure all my money was in different countries, so I had places to run and a chance to vanish without ending up in a grave.

There were different bank accounts already set up in various locations with enough money to support me for the rest of my life, but sometimes cash is best when on the run, so I wanted to be prepared for every scenario.

After loading many duffle bags with clothes and an immense amount of cash, I left my room, sure to lock Whitney away until it was safe for her to travel. Moving her now would raise suspicion and get us both killed.

It was the middle of the night, and my car was loaded. I had just re-entered the house and locked the door when I heard a noise upstairs. On edge, with my guilty conscience, I hid in a dark corner to see who was coming. Imagine my surprise when I saw I wasn't the only one leaving this family behind. I held no ill feelings while watching Kirill sneak down the stairs, holding Valerie's hand. They both had bags over their shoulders and scanned their surroundings as if terrified to get caught.

He never saw me in that dark corner, and I never tried to stop him from leaving. The girl he clutched was clearly who he was picking over all of us. I

had done the same. Who was I to judge? As his car drove down the long, lonely driveway, I held my hand to the window. *"Goodbye, my friend. May you and your love be safe."*

Love…

In Wolf's room, I sat on the floor in the dark, with only the light from under the door casting a shadow on his face. I had seen him every day to feed him, shower him, and care for him, but not to love him. So, in the silence, I watched his chest rise and fall as he deeply slept. Entranced by Wolf's serenity, Crash's words hauntingly came to me. *"Have you ever listened to someone sleep? Think about it. Have you ever slowed down your world enough to take the time to appreciate someone's breath?"*

And, here I was, doing just that, and it brought me immense and unexpected peace… and pain. For on his sleeping body, there reflected his white gold leash, the constant reminder of where he was and what I had done to him.

Trying not to wake him, I slipped a gun under his mattress, and then I stood to leave.

"Don't go." The gravelly voice wasn't calling me Master to teach me a lesson. It was sincere and caring.

So, I figured it best to return the honesty. Standing beside his bed, I asked, "Am I too late?"

"I haven't seen the sun in months, and I'm on the verge of losing what little sanity I have left. But when you are near… I always feel a warmth that tells me not to let go."

I dropped to my knees. "Don't let go… Bram."

After a gasp, Wolf finally said, "That's not my name."

I grinned. "Isn't that my line?"

"Yes…" he quietly added, "and mine."

My heart began to thunder. My ears rang. I was about to be bitten by the wolf, expertly cloaked in a slave's skin. Already feeling a punch to the heart, I

slowly stood and backed away. Wolf rose from the bed in one swift but cautious movement. As he prowled forward, gun skillfully palmed, I finally understood what it was like to be the prey.

Wolf was angry. "Why did you give me this gun? Setting me up?"

I stopped moving. "No…" Lacking proper oxygen, I thought of Whitney and how I might not be able to rescue her after all. "I have to go and take down my father and uncle. If I fail, I wanted to know you had a chance to get out of here."

He snarled in my face. "And who else do you want me to try to help?"

I couldn't look in his eyes. I knew he would see how much I cared for her.

"The one I smell on you?"

Even though I had another gun in the back of my pants, I didn't reach for it. If Wolf wasn't who I thought he was, there was nothing left to fight for. "Yes."

As the barrel was pushed under my chin, I closed my eyes. Body flush with mine, except the arm holding the weapon, his mouth went to my ear. "Why?"

My mouth wanted to taste my murderer before he killed me. "Because she doesn't belong here."

He took a long inhale at my neck. "But I do?"

Hoping to feel his lips, I exposed my neck as much as I could without the gun moving. "No. You belong with me."

His teeth nipped at my chin. "Fuck you." A madness flared from his whole naked body. "Grab that gun I know you have."

Nothing to fight for… "No."

There was a pause, and then his body rubbed along mine as he moved around me. Now, he stood with my back to his chest, the barrel of the gun turning but never losing its point of entry if the trigger were to be pulled. "Why?"

I was seconds from death but so very thankful to feel his breath on the back of my neck. What a beautiful way to die. "If I kill you, I'm afraid to be so

lost I'd never be found."

The gun dug deeper as he snapped, "You don't even know who I am."

Panting, I replied, "I don't believe you."

A disturbing chuckle erupted. "A liar recognizing a liar?"

It was the slip I needed. Wolf had just admitted he was lying. "Fine. Then tell me who you are."

His fingers grazing my back had me desiring him as he untucked the shirt from the back of my pants. "The man who is about to kill you." He pulled my weapon free and reached around my waist, offering it to me. "Take it."

"No." My left hand reached around his hips and grabbed his ass, pulling him impossibly closer and not letting go. "Tell me who you are."

Wolf did not refuse my touch, and I could feel him hardening. His panting breath brushed past my ear because he was so close. "Take it." He pushed the gun against my stomach.

"Never."

"Have it your way then." His open mouth landed on my neck, his angry tongue causing chills to rivet my whole body, inside and out. After lifting the front of my shirt, he tucked the offered gun in the front of my pants. The barrel of the other shoved up harder. "Don't move." So desperate for air, my mouth couldn't even close as his free hand cupped my growing erection. "Was she good?"

My chest heaved. "She was beautiful."

"Is that what you're going to say about me when I slide inside you?"

"No. I will say you're sensational and all I want."

His hand left my penis to unbutton my shirt. "Now, who is the liar?"

"She's in love with another."

He bit the back of my neck. "I hope that hurts you."

My right hand reached around his hips to touch his ass, begging him not to stop this torture. "It does."

"Good." His hips surged forward, and then he pushed me toward the bed.

"I want to make you hurt, too."

"You have the power. Leave me and watch me die." I pulled the gun from my pants and threw it on the bed. "Now, are we going to fuck or what?"

After a slight hesitation, Wolf tossed his gun on the bed. From behind, he ripped my shirt from me then attacked my pant buckle. Before I knew it, I was naked and bending over, my hands planted on the mattress. I heard him spit then felt wet fingers slip between my cheeks, lubing me. He spit again, then I finally felt what it was like to be on the receiving end.

Wolf pressed the tip of his erection inside me while hissing, "You're so tight."

The room fell quiet. He stopped trying to enter me. When he started to back away, I spun around. "Don't you fucking stop now."

He appeared shameful. "I can't do this to you—"

I rushed him. "I want you to." He kept shaking his head, infuriating me. "Wolf, you don't understand—"

"You don't understand! I'm a—"

"I may die soon. If what you're about to say is more important than that, then say it. But, if not, then hear this man asking another man to be with him, in this moment, so that he won't die never knowing—" I swallowed. "Never knowing—" My throat tried to close down the emotions demanding release, but it was time I took control over my own destiny. "Never knowing what it is like to make love with the one he cherishes above all."

Surrender. I had no idea it was such a salve to the soul.

Warm, strong lips devoured mine. Every swipe of his tongue was a silent promise that it was safe to give myself to him. I needed that adoration to fuel me for the unknown future that I had to face, to right my every wrong. So many slaves were dead, but maybe, like Crash, they would smile down upon me if I stopped the cycle of death of the body and spirit.

Attached in so many ways, physically and emotionally, Wolf laid me down. How he could make me feel so delicate, I don't know, but he did. Maybe

he just sensed the fragile state of mind I was in and chose not to let me fall. He held me so tightly in his arms, I felt my ribs bruise. I didn't care. His strength was my salvation.

On our sides, his chest to my back, he pulled my upper thigh over his. Never had I been so exposed, so vulnerable… and willing. His thick thighs spread, opening me even more. Breathless, he told me, "Do you know how many times I've laid here, masturbating, dreaming of this moment?"

I was gasping, enthralled by his words and his body preparing to own mine. "No."

His arm under my body found my erection and started to stroke me. "Like this," he panted in my ear. "I pulled on my sensitive skin like this, thinking of you, even after I exploded on this bed." After lubing again, he positioned the tip of his dick at my entrance. "And now, here you are," he pushed in slightly, "in the flesh," my head fell to the pillow as he pushed deeper, "for me to sink into."

My hands braced against the wall next to the bed, my fingers gripping the concrete as I was filled in a way I had never experienced, all the while his rough hand was working my dick, bringing me to the edge of an orgasm. "This… This feels so—" I couldn't finish speaking. He smeared the wetness at my tip around the head of my dick while giving me time to adjust to his size. Enjoying the feel of him inside me so much more than I suspected I would, I begged him, "More."

He groaned as if he needed to know I loved how he felt, possessing me like this. His body practically curled around mine as his hips surged. "A dream. You are a dream for me." Fully seated inside me, expertly stroking me to the point of losing my mind, it was what he said next that had me feeling like falling off the highest cliff I had ever stepped on. "I'm giving you a name now. Jorien."

I have a name…

He kissed my ear before whispering, "Jorien… I love you."

An explosion erupted from my erection, my heart, and… my soul.

Wolf was running across a field of snow, his left behind footprints all red. "No,"

I moaned as I realized he was bleeding. I tried to get to him, but something was restraining me. "Nooooo." Wolf looked back at me and smiled... then he disappeared into the waiting woods. "No!"

I woke to being locked in an alarmingly firm grip, but the voice I heard had me settling immediately. "Wake up, Jorien. Wake up."

Facing Wolf, we were on our sides. The care in his eyes soothed me even more. "If I were to live through this, I would wish I could ask you to be mine."

Wolf kissed me. "Even if you die, I'm still yours."

I sighed, leaning my forehead to his chin. "I have to let her go. Let her live the life she deserves." I whispered, "But I'm not sure I will know how to let *you* go."

"Then don't. I will go with you."

My lips and heart smiled. "You do not even know where I am headed."

"It doesn't matter."

My heart picked up speed at the thought, but it wasn't realistic. "What about your wife?"

He stared at me for a while, then shook his head no.

"You don't have one, do you?"

Again, a head shake full of sorrow.

"A child?"

Another head shake, the worry in his expression thickening.

The time had come where he had to tell me what I think, deep down, I knew all along. I buried my face in his neck and held on tight. "Do I dare ask why?"

His arms around my shoulders tightened. "You already guessed it, once."

An agent. I refused to open my eyes. I wanted to stay hidden. Did this mean we were automatic enemies? Did the truth wash away the relationship we had built? "What kind?"

He whispered into my hair. "FBI."

I held on tighter, our bliss fading away. All I could do was tease. "Not a

handsome doctor? They make more money."

He chuckled, accepting my attempt at humor. "No. I'm not a big moneymaker, but I was a medic before switching fields, if that helps with the handsome part."

Blindly, my mouth found his. Wolf let me kiss him. Hard.

Once I calmed down, I asked, "Why has your team not come for you?"

Adoringly, he forced a smile. "Because I was kidnapped while off the clock." Then he gave up the ruse. "They must have been frantically searching, clueless to where I am."

"Off the clock? You *knew* we were coming?"

His leg laid over my hip as if to prevent me from running. "You were set up. My would-be owner was trying to avoid a hefty prison sentence for tax evasion. He made a deal. Told prosecutors about how he had recently been told how to buy a slave. Not that he was searching, of course." Wolf rolled his eyes, knowing the man was lying.

"Of course."

"That's how we got involved. My office thought it was a bogus lead. We wired him while he talked to some guy," he tapped me on my nose, "but you were so elusive during the conversation, we figured you were just trying to rip him off."

"My guard was up. I had asked my father if it was a set-up the night he sent me to meet the man." I pointed to my stomach between us. "It felt wrong."

His thumb ran over my lips as if he were lost in thought. "Why would God give a terrorist such gut instincts?" I winced at his comment but let it go. It was the truth. "You're brave to accept your past."

"Are you just as brave? Can you handle what I have done?"

Staring at me, he appeared pained by his answer before he even said it. "Only time will tell. I've never been out of these walls with you."

Kissing his arm, I nodded. Neither of us knew how we would be together, living outside of the walls that caged us. "How much do you know

about me?"

He sounded dumbfounded. "Nothing. You were just some ghost named Yury. Your organization has been off our radar, even after the millionaire squealed. As I said, we didn't believe you were anything other than a crook. We had no idea of the depth of this league you were in." He exhaled. "I don't know what my team knows now."

"They still haven't found you."

"Or any of your other victims here."

Yes, being out in the open together would be quite a challenge, if we were ever to get the chance. "How were you chosen to be my bait?"

"I volunteered."

My eyes widened. "Why?"

"It's a horrible crime, stealing lives. If there was a chance you were real, and we could penetrate an organization, I was game. We made up a trail, but it wasn't real. That's why, once you actually had me, I was terrified you would retaliate. I have no idea how you found some innocent little girl we made up."

I confessed, "We didn't, I but knew you would believe us after," I looked down, "after teaching you a lesson with—" I waited for him to fill in the blanks.

His eyes welled. "My FBI partner."

I nodded. He had started to call her "partner" before catching himself that night I showed him the video. "I'm sorry."

He slowly shook his head. "That is one I can't forgive. The only reason I could be near you after that was because you weren't there. I want to believe you wouldn't have—"

I softly spoke, "Then you are a fool."

Mesmerized, he stared at me. "How do you have me so twisted?"

Soberly, I exhaled. "I locked you away from everything you know." I touched his face where he needed to shave. "As much as you may believe I deserve prison time, and as much as you may be correct, I'm not going. This is something you need to know."

299

He wiped his fingers through my hair. "You behind bars—" He closed his eyes and shook his head. "Don't let them catch you."

I sounded weak but tried to reassure him, "This ghost has a plan. My best disappearing act yet."

Wolf swallowed. "Will I ever see you again?"

My throat tightened. "I do not see how, with your profession." I kissed his lips again. "Can I teach you a phone number?"

He smirked while lifting a flirty brow. "Phone sex?"

Laughter burst from me. "Wasn't what I had in mind, but sounds great." I grabbed my chest. "Will you help her? If I am killed?"

His eyes softened. "Of course, Jorian."

With that promise, I taught him the cell number of a phone I was now never going to lose. I thought maybe, just maybe, someday, he would use it, find me, and be back in my arms.

It was a beautiful dream.

CHAPTER TWENTY-THREE

Who is to fall?

If you knew the road you were traveling to reach eternal peace would have many pit stops, in gut-wrenching hellholes, would you still proceed? Would you face all the terror for the final ending? Isn't that what life is? A glorious promise at the end of an, at times, torturous life?

My future promised dark times, but I kept walking forward, no matter how many times I stumbled and fell back. And, I held two sets of hands while I did it. Yes, I yanked and dragged Wolf and Fire along my treacherous path.

Bang! Bang! *"Yury, we have a situation."*

"I'm coming." I got out of Wolf's bed and quickly got dressed. I leaned down to his bed and kissed him. "I'll be back, if I can." I placed the gun back under his mattress, then headed for the door.

"Wait." I turned just in time to see him before he slammed his body to mine.

Balance. We brought each other balance.

I could feel our roles had switched, and he was now the one who needed me to be strong for him as we fell into a deep kiss. That is why I wrapped my arms around him, to offer any shelter I could in our horrid situation.

Breathless, he pulled his mouth from mine. "I need you to know I love—"

I kissed him again because I didn't need words, not when our connection was so powerful.

Outside his room, I was confronted with a handler who seemed very

Gesturing for me to follow him, he ran. *"Whit."*

Panicked, I ran, following him. *"What? What happened to her?"*

He raced up the stairs. *"I'm so sorry! She jumped!"*

Grabbing my chest, I fell sideways into the wall. *"No."*

"Yes! Right over the railing! Blood! Everywhere!"

It felt as if my feet had suddenly turned to stone as I rushed to lift them up each step. My hands gripped the railing and half-dragged me up the rest of the stairs. I didn't want to see her beautiful little body mangled from the fall, now on the ground, her skull wide open. *"This cannot be."*

The handler tapped his remote and opened the door. *"Dressed for her delivery, I was walking her toward the stairs this morning. She ran from me and leaped over the railing."*

Wait. Dressed for delivery?

With new hope, I rushed past him.

It is shameful, I know, but when I saw Fake Whit's hair was almost as red as the blood spilling on the white marble, I sighed in relief. There was a dead body by the entrance in my home, yet I bent, resting my palms on my knees, and took deep breaths.

Another life over... because of me, and I was thankful.

I peered up at my bedroom door. *Stay strong, Whitney. Only a few more days.*

After that handler's poor 'handling' techniques, he knew he technically owed me a slave. I told him that if he took supreme care of Wolf and Fire while I was gone, his debt would be considered paid in full. I instructed him to provide food beyond the normal slave menu for each of them. Fire could bathe herself in my bathroom, but he needed to escort Wolf to the shower room when needed. I didn't mention that my male slave had a gun and the heart of the handler's boss.

Using different connections, to purposely leave trails in all different directions if someone wished to hunt me down, I used several contacts to obtain

fake identities. To be sure I had money in different countries, so I could travel
light when running from enraged family members, I traveled to each of them, set
up living arrangements, and hid cash. One identity was in the name of Jorien. It
was the one I planned on using most.

When my phone rang in France, I knew I had to answer it. *"Where are
you?"* asked my uncle.

"I have a few errands to run."

"I see." After a slight pause, he asked, *"My son?"*

"On a vacation."

"We don't vacation, understood?" He was not very sneaky, nor did he
mean to be with his underlined warning.

I was days away from taking any more orders from him, so I said, *"Kirill
wanted to fuck his whore elsewhere for a couple of days. What is the big deal?"*

The big deal would be revealed soon enough.

I flew back to Russia, but not to my home city. It was time for me to
bring justice to Seafoam, hoping it would inspire her spirit to help me save her
daughter. I went to hunt down Whitney's father. I meant what I said to Mr. Jones.
All ties to her would be severed. I was leaving no trail for anyone to find and
harm her ever again.

Years ago, after I had learned my true name, I became curious about
what else my father was hiding. That's why I searched his office one day for
information on his competitor. I didn't use it, but I found the phone number. I
also had come across a debt ledger. I saw "paid by Seafoam." I jotted down the
name of the man who had paid his debt with a woman, and I never forgot it. Deep
down, I must have known this day would come.

Seafoam's husband was still in the little town in Russia where he
ventured too far and got into trouble with gambling. To this day, I am not sure
how exactly Father inherited the unpaid debt, but I assume it was in trade
for another. Either way, the drunk sitting on the barstool had no idea he was
in danger. I sat in the corner of the rundown tavern, drinking a pint—since

the establishment had none of my usual poison, vodka—and waited for my opportunity to arise.

As Whitney's father stood and said goodbye to locals, I knew my chance had come, and I left before he did. Knowing the direction of his home, I stood in an alley and waited for him to pass. It was dark with very few streetlamps on, making it easy to hide in the many shadows. I could practically smell his consumption as he stumbled by. Intoxication had him not registering my presence behind him until we were walking past a hog farm.

Alone on the deserted dirt road, he leaned against a post of the handmade fencing. "Do I know you?" he asked in Russian.

Hogs gathered nearby, inspecting us through the railing made of well-used fallen branches nailed together. I grinned because this man was clueless his last moments had arrived. "Your wife knew me. Does that count?"

Even in the dark night, I think I witnessed him pale. Hogs snorted their noses in the dirt as he replied, "I do not have one."

"No, you do not. Not anymore." I took a step closer to him. "Did you know she was pregnant when you gave her to us?"

As soon as his jaw locked, my suspicions were concreted. He knew. And he still gave up his wife to pay a senseless debt. This was exactly why I was here. He knew there was a possibility he had a child. What if he grew a conscience and searched for her?

The man sneered, "She was not."

The smile that crossed my face was most likely menacing, but it felt good to share. "Oh, I assure you, she was, as you already know." I pulled a knife from my back pocket. "Your wife suffered throughout the whole pregnancy, then had an untimely and unmerciful death. Your daughter has led a tough life that has only gotten worse as of late, but she is strong, beautiful, and *witty*." I chuckled at my hint of her name. "Her life will improve soon." I tightened my hold on the handle. "And, there are to be no interruptions to the peace I am offering her."

Before he could register my movement, I slammed the knife into his

chest, the blade slipping between bones. The man gasped and started to fall back, but I grabbed his shoulder and told him, "That is how your wife died while giving birth to the daughter you will never know, not even after death, because she will rise into the sky and you will descend below."

He was still alive as I pulled the blade from his bleeding chest then tossed him over the fence. He even screamed as the hogs began to eat him.

I had never purposely killed anyone before. I always had it done for me. I wish I could say it felt criminal to murder this man, but that would be a lie. I stood there for a few moments, enjoying his misery, before getting lost in the night's shadows once more.

My next stop was to observe a certain officer and the company he kept. It didn't take long to find my dead cousin's wife, who was bedding the law. I wasn't an idiot, so I let him live. The same would not be true for his girlfriend. After some torture and threats, she finally handed over the birth certificate she had held over my father's head for far too long. Her throat was sliced without a trace to be followed—for her or Whitney.

Upon my return home, I was faced with a new slave in the driveway. Stepping out of my car, I wanted to go check on Whitney and Wolf but had to deal with an unscheduled delivery. She was young and crying. I asked the recruiter, "*Why is she here and not at Uncle's?*"

He shrugged. "*I got a call from your father and was redirected here.*"

A *ping* went off in my stomach, but I ignored it and took the girl inside. She was a mess because she had pissed on herself, most likely due to fear. With the way she cowered, it was clear the recruiter had not been gentle with her.

Since she needed a shower, I stopped by Wolf's room to take him, too. I simply couldn't wait to see him. After unlocking his door, I took the new slave

into his room with me and shut the door.

Wolf jumped up from the floor where he was doing push-ups. He was more than surprised to see me with a slave. "What is she doing in here? Is this... this Fire?"

The girl backed away from him. "Why are you naked?"

I pointed at her in the corner. "If you go near that door, I will kill you."

"No, he won't!" demanded Wolf.

"Yes, I will," I assured her then turned to my slave I adored. Stepping in his line of sight so he could only see me, I whispered, "This is not Fire. This girl is not even supposed to be here, but she needs a shower." I stepped as close as I could without knocking him over. In his ear, I said, "I missed you."

"She looks terrified."

I kissed his ear. "Did you hear me?"

His cheek rubbed against mine in a quick motion to appease me, then he said, "Yes, but I'm not used to this sight. Help her."

Forcing my eyes not to roll and piss Wolf off, I stepped back and asked him, "Will you join us in the shower?"

"J-Join us?" asked the slave that was getting on my nerves.

I went to explain that touching her was the last thing on my mind, that I wanted Wolf, but he stepped around me and raised his hands in a manner that portrayed he was trying to calm her. "No, neither of us will touch you. We just want you to feel more comfortable. Uh..." He glanced over his shoulder to see me standing close behind him.

I had no attachment to the girl and couldn't have cared less to know her name, so I looked at her eyes for the first time. They had specks of green, brown, and gold. Gorgeous. "Jewel. Her name is Jewel."

Wolf looked at her suspiciously. "Is that your name?"

She peered at me.

From behind Wolf, I glared at her with flared nostrils.

Jewel got the hint and nodded to Wolf.

Calmly, he said, "That is a beautiful name. Let me see if I can change the 'me being naked thing.'" He turned and faced me. "Me, being naked, is making her upset."

Again, I couldn't have cared less. Covering him wasn't going to happen because the sight of his body was too stunning, and I quietly told him, "I have mere days before my world is going to change completely. I can't screw this up by doing something I have never, ever done in the past." I begged, "I need you on your best slave behavior until this mayhem takes place and I can get you out of here."

Wolf nodded with an endearing sympathy that I appreciated. Then he faced Jewel. "Just look at my face to avoid any awkward moments."

Of course, her eyes immediately drifted down then slammed shut. "S-Sorry."

"No problem. Take a deep breath." He waited for her to follow his lead in breathing then asked, "Do you know why you're here?"

She started crying again. "That guy, the one who…" She shook her head as if lost in a memory.

Wolf's shoulders caved. "Did he hurt you?"

Jewel wiped at the snot dripping from under her red nose. "H-He forced me to… and told me this was my new life."

Wolf stepped in to hug her, but she cowered back, so he stopped and said, "I won't touch you and will do my best to help you." He thumbed at me behind him. "He will, too."

"Meh."

Wolf glared at me from over his shoulder.

This time, I did roll my eyes. "Fine." I told Jewel, "If you do not wish to be sold to someone who will rape you every day, like my handler did, then you will do everything I ask of you. You will follow my every command. Understood?"

After she nodded, Wolf gawked at me.

I huffed. "I did what you asked."

Wolf's smirk gave me hope he would be patient with me. Then he turned to me and whispered, "I've been thinking." He peeked over his shoulder to see if Jewel was listening.

When she realized she wasn't supposed to be, she closed her eyes and put her hands over her ears and started softly humming. Her vocal cords were trembling, but I appreciated her effort to give us privacy.

Wolf smiled at her, then whispered more to me, "We don't know what you look like." My brows scrunched in question. He added, "It was only a voice recording we got from our informant. We didn't even have the strip joint under surveillance. That is how much we didn't believe this guy."

I cupped his face in my palms, needing to taste his lips. After a soft kiss, I asked, "Why are you telling me this?"

He stared at my mouth. "I want to be with you."

My heart thundered. "But… how?"

Wolf swallowed. "Once I return home, I will resign, due to this experience having pushed me over the edge." He wrapped his arms around my waist, not affected when his arm grazed the gun in the back of my slacks. "Then I will find you. I'll call the number burned into my memory—"

I slammed my mouth to his. He was perfect for me, and this was a perfect strategy. If anyone recognized him in another country and saw him with me, none would be the wiser. No one would realize Bram was now living with his abductor.

His lips smiled against mine. "You like my plan so far?"

I kissed him again. "Yes. Tell me more."

"Where are the video cameras? No film can ever show that I was a part of the takedown. I must always appear to be a broken slave."

"There are cameras in each slave room, the filming rooms, at each entrance to the house, the driveway."

Wolf nodded, silencing me. "Just to be sure, no affection between us

outside this room."

After their showers, I escorted Wolf and Jewel back to their rooms, delivering Jewel first. She was naked and terrified but did as I asked. In her room, Wolf begged me, "There has to be a way to be sure no one will touch her again. Please, do this for me."

I huffed again. "Fine. Don't move." I left them in the room and walked across the hall. In the monitor room, I opened a drawer and grabbed a gold collar and leash.

A video tech sat in a chair, smirking. *"Getting ready for another delivery?"*

"Something like that."

Back in Jewel's room, I placed the gold collar and chain on her. "Remember what I said. Listen to no one but me."

She studied Wolf's platinum collar and chain before nodding and climbing into her bed, huddling in the corner with her skinny legs to her chest. I sighed when I realized she was one of the last scared slaves I would have to see. Wolf was right to have been kind to her. I told myself I should also be more patient, but I also didn't know that my new-to-me uncle had gone back on his word and had already proceeded with the takedown.

Wolf and I were leaving her room when I heard, *"Hello, Yury."* In the hallway, I jolted, wondering why Father was home and not at the new establishment. I immediately locked Jewel in her room, knowing something was amiss.

Wolf had his eyes down as Father toyed with his leash. *"His owner had inquired about this delivery."*

I had to bite back a growl and try to act unaffected. *"As you can see, he has become very obedient. I believe he will be ready in a couple more weeks."*

"We need his sale complete. There have been... challenges at our new location."

INDIA R. ADAMS

Pings were going off in my stomach like the American Fourth of July celebration with fireworks. *"What sort of challenges?"*

"The kind where money has been lost. But that is okay; we will rebuild here."

Just then, an unconscious, naked black man was being carried down the hallway by two handlers. Confused, because I had no scheduled deliveries yet was receiving my second slave for the day, I asked, *"What is this?"*

"A new slave for you to fuck. Where would you like him?"

Frustrated, I pointed to the room next to Jewel's. *"Where is Uncle?"*

"Tying up loose ends." He wiped his hands against each other as if touching Wolf had made him dirty. This was surprising because he had valued Wolf. There was something else happening, and I was in the dark, but I didn't miss him switching to English. "Speaking of loose ends, how is my curse? I hear she is far less obedient than Wolf here."

I couldn't figure out what his underlining meaning was. "You hear? You have spies now?"

He shrugged. "I prefer to call them monitors."

Feeling like everything was falling apart, I glanced up and down the hallway to figure out which of my men were rats. "She is fine. Why do you ask?"

"I hear you wish for more with her, beyond her claimed slave duties." His eyes raced to Wolf's as if to catch a reaction.

My stomach plummeted. He suspected Wolf and I meant something to each other.

When Wolf continued to stare at the floor, unaffected, Father coyly said to me, "I've been told the sex you had with her a couple of weeks ago could be heard all throughout the house. That she was screaming in pleasure."

And there it was, the twitch in Wolf's eye that Father was looking for.

It was a lie. Whitney had been screaming in misery, but Wolf had no idea of the truth.

I snarled, *"Why are you trying to undo all the trust I have built with this*

slave?"

Father got in my face. *"Because someone has betrayed us. Someone snuck out of this house the night before we were ambushed. Did you have anything to do with Kirill's betrayal?"*

The driveway video cameras. Uncle and Father had a live feed. *How could I have been so stupid!* I had assumed the only feed was at my location. *"Kirill has not betrayed you. He only wanted alone time with his whore. How many times must I explain this?"*

"They are not alone anymore."

Oh, shit. Uncle tightening up loose ends… *"You are wrong about Kirill."*

"You loading your car for your 'errands' but returning? It is the only reason you are alive, and the only reason your bitch upstairs isn't being tortured while you watch, like your cousin."

It took everything I had not to grab my nauseous stomach and close my eyes in regret. *Valerie.* I thought Kirill escaping was going to keep him out of the storm I had created. Instead, it made him look guiltier than the guilty. Now, Valerie was paying the price.

Father switched to English again. "Or, is having Fire fucked by many at once something you are interested in?"

In the corner of my eye, I saw Wolf's shoulders tighten. He was a true saint, wanting my slaves to be free—not raped and tortured to satisfy a madman's lunacy.

I snarled at Father, "I'm in charge here now, or have you already forgotten?"

He argued, "Kirill is my brother's son! He can do as he pleases!"

"If Uncle wants to make a huge mistake and lose his second son forever, so be it. Fire has been claimed! You touch her, you not only betray me but all of your employees." I gestured to the few gathering, including Adrian, who came to my side. "Wish to explain your bendable rules?"

Unexpectedly, Father smiled as if I had played right into a plan he had

all along. A wave of chills ran down my spine, leaving me achingly cold inside, while he licked his teeth as if already tasting his victory. "Speaking of rules, who is most important in our line of business?"

Not sure of his angle, I numbly replied, "The customer."

He smacked his hands together. "That's right! And, our most important customer wants a sample of our prized slave."

My stomach soured immediately. "But he's not ready for a new Master."

Dismissively, Father waved his hand through the air. "No. Of course not. Training is," it felt like daggers flew through the air as he finished with, "so important," as if he didn't believe any training was happening in the slightest. "*Progression* is so important." He gestured to the filming room down the hall. "This is why our client would like an example of what his money is getting him." His face, so patronizing, kept grinning. "Just a little sample of a cock inside Wolf's ass." When I didn't move, Father added, "Unless you have claimed him also?"

And there it was. The trap I had entered, unknowingly.

"No," I replied, trying to sound dismissive. We all knew we could only claim one slave at a time. "Besides, Wolf has been bought."

"Yes, he has. So, let's satisfy his new owner."

Now, I was swallowing down the bile that rose in my throat. The situation was going from horrendous to unbearable. I sneered, "I didn't know you were so soft and compliant with customers these days."

"Meh." Father shrugged. "I would have *you* fucked for the right dollar amount."

My eyes closed, and I shook my head, stung by his words but feeling more for my slave, my love. "*If we push this slave before his time, you will have him regressing.*" Wolf had just told me not to let him get on film connecting us. I would be hooded, but this all felt so wrong. Having sex with him was… private. I didn't want to share one glimpse of him during such a time. "Why is our customer not taking your fucking word for it?"

"What have I seen to give my word about?"

My eyes opened. "You want to watch me fuck another man?"

"Why are you being so sensitive about this? You fuck on film weekly." I internally cringed. This was information I never wanted to be shared with Wolf. Father coyly added, "It is not too late. You could always match our customer's price if you wish to exchange your claim." He indicated to Wolf. "No one would blame you. He is beyond stunning."

I stood there, blinking, because it was now clear Father knew I had feelings for Wolf and was punishing me for it by making me choose. With the best lie I could fake, I claimed, "This is absurd. I have no attachments to a slave."

"No? Wonderful news." He took a step toward the filming room. When he saw I was invisibly concreted to where I stood, he told two minions. "Go get Fire. Yury has had a change of heart. There will be an exchange. And, she is to be fucked by all who want her, then killed once and for all."

Adrian moved from my side to block their path.

Again, I saw Wolf from the corner of my eye. Against slave rules, he dared to lift his eyes to look at me. It broke a part of me inside because I knew what he was begging me to do.

In my mind, I was screaming, trapped in a rage I'd helped create by being a part of this horrid profession. I was finally paying—being punished for my wrongs—having to choose between two people I loved.

It was amazing, but at that very moment, I wondered what Crash would do if forced to choose between the two people he cherished: Whitney and Link. I didn't have to wonder long before knowing the answer. He wouldn't let Whitney get dragged into my father's psychosis, not like Valerie was presently experiencing. He would let Link, the stronger of the two, take the fall.

Someone, somewhere, had to be spared.

That person wasn't going to be my Wolf.

He was strong. He was an FBI agent for Christ's sake.

I believed he could take what I had to do.

CHAPTER TWENTY-FOUR

Ends of Sanity

For Whitney, for Wolf, I found courage in a place I never expected. I had to sacrifice my heart and ego for the sake of another. My miracle had arrived.

"No." In the hallway, I held up my hand to the minions. "My father's imagination has gotten the best of him. If you lay one finger on my claimed, I will kill you both, as I have the right to do."

They stopped and retook the place flanking Father. Adrian, the same with me.

I glared at the man who'd spawned me. "Wolf is under my care. That is it. There are no affections. I will fuck him as you wish, but it will not be filmed." There would be no proof this forced act ever took place, only in memories, maybe the last I would have of Wolf. I couldn't imagine that he would continue to want to be with me after this upcoming humiliation. "Wolf, come to me."

Naked, in more ways than one, Wolf bravely took a few steps to stand directly in front of me, shoulders proudly set back. Was he pleased with my decision, sacrificing his mental wellbeing for another? The answer was in his soul reading eyes.

And his lips…

My eyes slid shut when his mouth took possession of mine as if no one was watching. His tongue was the drug I needed to get an erection. If Father wanted proof that Wolf was becoming a fabulous lover for the client, he was about to get a show. My hands grasped under Wolf's hair to take control of the kiss. My slave was more than willing to be dominated, arousing me further with his hungry hands on my hips. His fingers gripped as if trying to speak to me of all

Whitney would be safe.

As I guided Wolf's body backward and into his room, I hoped Whitney would someday know of this sacrifice for her.

Still kissing me, Wolf unbuttoned my shirt while we headed for his bed—the place we knew so well, that was now to be invaded by prying eyes. Wolf bit my bottom lip as if understanding where my mind had drifted to. He wanted me focused only on him. I wanted this to already be over with, so I spun Wolf around and pushed his chest to the wall at the end of his bed, somewhat blocking the entrance so Father and his minions had to stay in the hallway. I unbuckled my pants and set my gun with a silencer on the mattress.

After my pants were pushed down around my hips and my erection was free, I stepped flush with Wolf's back and pushed his hair aside to kiss his neck and lick his collar—a personal dig at my father. Wolf arched, enjoying my touch as I slipped my hand between him and the wall and took hold of his hardening dick. As seductively as I could with witnesses, I demanded, "Slave, I want you to stroke yourself like this." I was sure to give a powerful tug along his length to spur his own arousal, so he was ready for the invasion I was about to get underway.

Stroking himself, Wolf started to pant as I spit into my palm. My other hand massaged his ass cheek, trying to offer kindness before fucking him in front of my father, who decided to stare at me as I slipped inside a man.

I groaned out my pleasure. Father's nostrils flared.

I smiled before becoming too entranced with Wolf. Even with four sets of eyes watching me, I was getting lost in the sensation of fucking Wolf. Loving how he was sheathing me, I grunted, my bare chest rubbing up against his muscular back. Holding his hips, I surged and pumped, already so close to coming when I heard, "You are to fuck him, too."

My eyes snapped to my father, and I growled, "Not happening."

Father acted innocent of his evil ways. "What is it now, Yury? The client has every intention of sharing his treat." He shrugged. "I merely need to see that

this is an option." His eyebrows wiggled. "I can always have Fire brought down to open your eyes to your options."

Before I could respond, Wolf pushed me out of him and spun to face me. He stared at me as he guided me backward until the back of my calves touched his bed. He guided me to sit then lie back, my feet still on the ground. Wolf followed me down. His long hair sheltered us as he whispered, "Be with me while it happens."

He meant mentally; I understood that, but I couldn't allow this. "No." On his hands and knees, his leash hanging between us, he was offering himself to whoever was to have him. "No." I was panicking. My body broke out into a sweat of dread. "No."

Father was now in Wolf's room, standing at the wall to my side. "No to your slave being fucked by another, or to trading Fire? Am I to refund the client's money and accept payment from you?"

The money wasn't the issue. Father knew I was more than capable of paying the sum. He also knew I wanted to, but that left Whitney exposed. That's when it dawned on me. This had nothing to do with our client, nor Wolf. Father wanted his curse to suffer. My claim on her was preventing him from snuffing out the past. That is why he was so willing to surrender his largest sale. At that tragic moment, I—Whitney's abductor who had murdered two men she loved—was now her only saving grace. Link, the man she wanted so desperately, wasn't the one to protect her this time.

From under Wolf, I hollered in frustration. I just yelled. I don't think I had ever done that before. My fists wished to punch someone or something.

Then I stepped into the darkness...

Staring into the most magnificent grey eyes I would ever know, I said, "Adrian, you are the one to do it." I had fucked so many slaves with him; I felt that gave me hope of surviving the sharing of one more. It would be the last. Something inside me was sure of it then, even when I had given my father's new location up to my long-lost uncle.

316

Now, it was Father who was roaring, "Goddammit! Just give her to me! Ever since she was brought here, hell has been let loose! She needs to die!"

I didn't reply. There was no need to. Wolf and I simply kept staring at each other as Adrian slowly moved behind my slave, solemnly unbuckling his pants. Grey eyes were locked to my blue ones as I reached up and began stroking his fading erection. I was thankful Adrian was moving so slowly. It gave me time to arouse the man I cherished above all others. The man who was helping me protect a girl I was indebted to. I owed her mother, too. She had been nothing but kind to me when I was forced into having sex, just as was Wolf now. Seafoam had helped me become erect so I could perform. If Wolf was going to be fucked, he was going to enjoy it.

Our eyes stayed locked as his mouth fell open, panting, and I started to expertly masturbate him. We stayed connected as I felt Adrian step between my legs. Wolf's body moved forward slightly, as did his hanging leash, telling me Adrian had entered him. My eyes threatened to fill with tears as Wolf was fucked on top of me, but this was no time for emotions. It was now time for survival as Father stood there with a gun drawn, then pointed it at Wolf's head.

Staring at the silencer, I froze. "What are you doing?"

Father's eyes full of rage, he ignored me. "Adrian, soil him." My hand left Wolf and blindly searched the mattress. "Touch that gun, son, and I will blow a bullet right through his head." I stopped. I knew Father would do it. He looked as if at the end of any sanity he might have once possessed.

I didn't even know a guard had a gun with a silencer to my head until Wolf cried out, "No! I'm doing what you want!"

I begged Wolf, "Let him shoot me. I just need this to stop."

Wolf was exasperated. "Shhh… It will be over soon."

Father said, "That is correct. Very soon. Adrian, you have twenty seconds to come inside this slave, or his death is on your conscience."

Adrian eyed the gun at my head, then took hold of Wolf's hips and closed his eyes to perform under duress. As the seconds passed, I tightened my thighs on

Adrian's, trying to clear his mind of guilt and encourage him to do this. He had to. Wolf's life depended on it.

Adrian whispered he was sorry, right before he ejaculated inside my slave. Once his grunts ended, he backed away, buttoning his pants, appearing winded and dazed, but he had saved Wolf. It was over.

Or, so I had thought.

Father never lowered the gun. With his free hand, he gestured, ordering, "Adrian, out the door and shut it."

"Why?" I tried to lift my head, but the gun *clicked* as it was cocked.

"Stop!" yelled Wolf. "He won't fight this. Please, don't kill him." Wolf stared down at me. "Please, stop fighting this." Wolf was the one experiencing this. How could I not do anything he was asking of me? The answer came when he mouthed, "I will be left alone."

If I died, Wolf's life would become hell. He would be sold.

Adrian stared at me, waiting. My jaw locked with rage, but I was powerless to act on it, so I nodded to him. Reluctantly, he left, shutting us in the cell with two minions and my crazed father.

"Now you," Father told one of his guards while gesturing to Wolf.

"*Don't do this,*" I growled.

"Speak English, so your love understands he will be fucked by four men today. You, Adrian, and my two men."

Wolf's eyes slid shut, but he didn't move. He was still willing to sacrifice.

There was no need to pretend anymore. Father was no fool and playing with my heart, so I screamed, "I will fucking kill you all!"

"Meh. At least, I will die knowing I had the man you desire soiled."

Wolf grunted, not in pleasure, as a minion slammed inside him. The only peace was that Adrian's cum was lube for the assault.

I told my father, "Your death will be gruesome, I swear it." From under Wolf, I held his wincing face, trying to offer any comfort as he was raped. "I

swear it!" Having committed countless rapes, I was bewildered as I finally understood how vile the act was, now that it was happening to Wolf. As he grunted in discomfort, I could practically hear all the pleas from past slaves for me to stop, all echoing in my head at once. I felt like Wolf was paying for my every crime. His torture was my agony. Horrendous. This helplessness was blinding. I wanted to grab my gun and start the murders immediately, but I was outnumbered, outgunned, and Wolf would be dead before I shot off one bullet. Even with the gun hidden under the mattress, we didn't stand a chance. I choked out, "I'm so sorry."

Wolf was now sweating, his arms starting to tremble. "Almost over."

It seemed to take forever before the minion finally moaned through his release. He closed his pants then pointed his gun at my head. It seemed like only seconds before the next guard slammed his dick inside Wolf.

Father laughed with this minion's aggressive thrusts. The guard rammed Wolf over and over, saying, "Damn, he is wet in here... I've never fucked a guy so pretty before." He asked Father, "Can I touch his dick?"

"No!" Fury was threatening to take over and get Wolf and me killed.

My father was delighted with the guard's suggestion. "Of course! As much as you want."

The memory of another man's arm, wrapping around my Wolf to reach his dick, would haunt me. I had to watch as his palm worked the tortured organ, while he pumped inside his ass. Wolf fought it, but eventually, he became erect. His expression showed how appalled he was to react to the violence. Shame encased me as I thought of how many orgasms I had forced throughout my years, how I had recently demanded them from Whitney while teasing her with food.

Again, Wolf was paying the price of my crimes.

His eyes welled as his arousal grew.

"Look at me."

He did.

I mouthed, "I love you."

319

Tears dripped from Wolf as he orgasmed, cum spurting against my stomach. As if slipping into shock, he kept staring at me as his attacker roared through his own climax.

Once it was over, Father sneered, "I want Fire dead. Stop protecting her."

Guns lowered, and shoes shuffled out of the room before the door slammed shut.

Wolf collapsed on top of me, his cum smearing between us as a reminder of what just happened. I wrapped my arms around him. "It's over. It's over." He gasped through tears. I kissed him all over his sweaty head. "You did it. You spared an innocent."

He sobbed. "I-I-I couldn't let them hurt her."

Tears leaked from the corner of my eyes because he had never even met her. "They won't. You did it. We will be out of here soon. I love you so fucking much."

It was true. I was sure of it. He was the one for me.

Bordering on hysterics, he clung to me. "I'm so sorry I let them do that to me. I hope you still want me."

I lifted his face from my chest so fast it probably hurt. "I think I've loved you for months, but now, even more so, because now I see how wonderful and self-sacrificing you are. Her brother, who I killed, he called her his Treasure. That is what you are for me my fucking treasure." My lips kissed his, not in a passionate way but to reassure him I was speaking the truth. Tears, sweat, and snot didn't stop me from loving him. "My fucking treasure."

After showering Wolf and watching him fall to sleep, the gun no longer under his mattress but in his hand, I locked him in the room. I had a plan to finish, despite my long-lost uncle betraying me. Wolf still insisted he didn't want to be filmed with me, so we could eventually try to be together after he resigned from the FBI. It made me adore him even more.

Outside his room, I pointed to his door and announced, "*If anyone feels*

320

like dying today, dare to touch this slave."

I didn't see Father or his minions. No one else dared, and all gave me lots of space.

Leaning against the wall next to me, his eyes to the floor, Adrian shook his head. *"I'm so sorry I had to do that. I know you care deeply for him."*

With barely enough energy to talk, I said, *"I thought I never had a friend before. Now, I know I have always had one in you."* His eyes slowly rose. I nodded. *"Thank you for trying to be gentle and for trying to keep him and me alive. Will you watch over him now for me?"*

His shoulders set back with pride. *"I will stay here all day."*

Climbing the basement steps, I was worn to the bone and yearned to see Whitney, certain her purity could settle my raw nerves. I had just sacrificed Wolf for her, yet I knew she was worth it. She was the only one who could bring me comfort besides Wolf.

In the foyer, I groaned, seeing Father waiting for me. He teased, *"How is your special slave? Well, I hope."* As I climbed the next set of stairs, I did my best to ignore him. *"I hope your Fire was worth it. My men will be leaking from Wolf's soiled ass for days."* Tuning him out, I focused on Whitney and the smile I was hoping to see when she saw me. He yelled up from the bottom floor, *"You have abandoned your family, for her. Your career, for her. Everything you have worked so hard for, for her. You are nothing but a disgrace to this family and empire. And for what? Nothing. She loves another, you imbecile!"*

Father's tone, his dominance, somehow had me starting to revert back to the scared child I once was. All the strength and courage I had discovered was evaporating in seconds. It was astonishing to understand, from the inside out, but I kept trying to be strong. I told myself he was wrong, and that every sacrifice was worth it.

Walking toward my bedroom at the top of the stairs, I thought of how, very soon, Uncle would know the truth; I was the one who ratted about their new location. I wondered how long Valerie would last during her torture, or if she was

even still alive.

Needing to conjure up more inspiration to fight my insecurities and Father's continued words from below, I focused on Whitney again and how I craved to smell her hair and hold her one last time before setting her free—

As soon as I opened the door, I saw Whitney sitting at my desk, touching my laptop screen. Or, should I say, touching who was on it: Link. And, she was saying, "I love you, too." Without my permission, she had just watched another of his blog videos and was missing him.

I. Saw. Red.

Then black. Black rage singed my ego and soul.

Wolf was painfully huddled in a bed, due to his sore body, yet this bitch was up in my room, daydreaming of her Link. All the pent-up anger I had finally rose to the surface and *unleashed* onto the poor person in my path. Due to everything that happened next becoming a blur, I don't know all that I said to her, or all that I did, but soon, I had her in the basement and was demanding two employees to take her in a room.

She was to be soiled… just like my Wolf.

I felt his sacrifice had been for nothing, and I would not allow him to go unavenged.

As the door shut her in the room with her soon rapists, and all other employees had dispersed because I demanded they go home, Adrian joined my side. I stared at the closed door, close enough to rest my forehead on it. The room Whitney was now in was across the hall from Wolf's.

Adrian was beyond concerned. "*What are you doing?*"

Wide-eyed, I was out of breath. "*I…*" I blinked. "*I…*" I exhaled. "*I do not know anymore.*"

"*You must go in there and stop this.*"

"*But Wolf—*"

"*Will feel betrayed. He will have just suffered all that for nothing.*"

My shoulders sunk. Whitney was only speaking the truth. She loved

Link, indeed. Having her soiled was beyond unreasonable and cruel. *"You are right."*

As my hand reached for the doorknob, I jolted when blood splattered across my face.

In slow motion, I watched as Adrian dropped, his body simply forgetting how to stand.

It took me a second to comprehend he had been shot in the head. Someone I had worked with, since the beginning, was now on the floor with blood pouring over everything. I had been in gunfights, but my own had always survived. Seeing my lost comrade felt as if the ground was unearthing itself. My whole world felt as if it had to realign in order to make sense. Maybe I was in shock. Maybe Wolf's violence and the violence I was casting on Whitney was finally too much. Maybe this is how it felt to actually care for someone.

Either way, I numbly reached for the door handle again, not checking to see who had just killed my friend. It was like an out of body experience. I simply had to put all aside and open the door, to once again keep Whitney from the harm that I had created. My ears no longer heard, but my eyes refused to stop working for me. They saw another bullet hole, right in front of my face. I stared at the splintered wood. Then I witnessed another hole form…

Is someone trying to kill me? But I have to open this door.

A voice I knew well entered my mind as my ears decided to let me hear again. It was a male who was in anguish. "Yury! What is happening out there?" Wolf was banging on his door. I peered over my shoulder to see that Adrian's blood had leaked under his door. "Yury! Please, answer me! Tell me you are fucking alive, goddammit!"

In a daze, I turned to face the door. As I did so, I uttered, "I'm alive," right before a bullet grazed my shoulder. I stared at a little blood forming on my jacket as I told Wolf, "I think I've been shot."

He roared from within his room, then asked, "Can you run?"

So lost and confused, I gazed at my unharmed legs. "I think so."

323

"Then, fucking run!"

"But—" I reached out to him, even though I couldn't see him. "What about you?"

The door vibrated as he kicked it. "Fucking run! Fucking run!"

I never reached for my own gun in the back of my pants. My mind was not firing on all cylinders, but it begged me to do as Wolf demanded. So, I ran down the hall, to the right, down another hallway, and up the stairs. I hit the buzzer in my pocket and rushed into the foyer. I didn't stop. Why did I end up in the kitchen? I may never know, but my mind started to clear as I found myself standing there with a butcher knife in my hand. I was gasping for air, rattled beyond comprehension, yet was starting to hear another familiar voice. This one had sparked a hatred many years ago, and as I listened to his words, that loathing became a tidal wave of murderous craze.

Prowling through the kitchen and into the massive living room, I saw Father looking out one of the many huge windows. The reflection of the snow lit off his dark suit as he held a cellphone to his ear. "*Yes, they are toying with him to keep him below until the soiling is over… Oh, he never even saw the note we gave her.*" He laughed. "*All he could see was her watching that blogger on his laptop. Such a fool.*"

At that moment, I knew I was. When I had left Whitney to hide money, we were solid and committed to our twisted fate. I wasn't sure what note Father was speaking of, but he had tricked me twice that day. Both trickeries cost me dearly. Wolf had been sodomized, and Whitney had surely started being raped by now. With guns waiting for me in the basement, I knew I had to find another way to get to her. In order to cease the violence in my world, I had to snuff out my father. My skin broke out in chills as I decided it was time for him to die, and I was going to be the one to bring his demise. My lips formed a smile as I hid, waiting for him to get off the phone, so he couldn't notify whoever was on the line. And, I knew cellphones didn't work in the basement. Unless his minions came to check on him, Father had no way of knowing I was no longer down

there.

Once off the phone, he didn't hear my stealthy approach, but he jumped in surprise as I wrapped my arm around his neck from behind. I was bigger. I was stronger. And, I held him to me as I sneered in his ear. *"You brought me into this world. Is it suiting that I am the one to take you out?"* His answer meant nothing to me. It was far too late for explanations or excuses for being the biggest piece of shit I would ever know, so I kept my arm incredibly tight, blocking his air. *"It may sound trite, but never loving me has made me your true curse, not the one being raped. Maybe that means* you *are the fool after all."* He struggled, grasping at my arm that refused to budge. *"Settle, Father. I will not kill you by strangulation. No, that would be far too kind."* I whispered, *"Which I am not, because of you."* My arm loosened enough to move my hand to the front of his throat. Once I had purchase, I stepped back just enough to give room so I could slam his back to the ground.

Stunned by the impact and fighting for his lungs to work again, I took no pity nor did I pause so he could collect himself. I put the knife in my right hand while saying, "You watched as I was forced to find my dead mother. You watched as I was forced to fuck Fire's mother. You watched as I killed an innocent slave, vomiting behind her gag. You watched as I learned my true name. You watched me witness Wolf's rape. You will watch no more." I drove the knife into his right eye, twisted, and popped out the mutilated ball. Father wailed in agony as I growled, "Never again will you witness my suffering." I slammed the knife into his left socket, twisted, and removed that damaged eye. Screaming, blindly reaching out, Father tried grabbing any part of me he could find. I ignored his every attempt to stop me from the wrath I was bestowing upon him, and lifted the knife into the air, as he had, above Seafoam's body that fateful night.

Then I slammed it into his chest, over and over… until all fight left him.

It was cold but necessary, for too many reasons to recount.

Seafoam's curse had come true. *"With the blood from my body as a sacrifice, I pledge for you to find agony in your death. Let it be by the hands of*

one of your own. Let your spawn be your downfall and your demise. And I pray that my daughter witnesses it all."

Rushing to my bedroom for more ammo and another gun, I thought of Father mentioning a note. In my room, there it was—a letter claiming to be from me, telling Whitney I was giving permission for her to watch another Link video.

Father had set me up, and Whitney took the fall.

Not sure of how much time I had before Uncle would return permanently to this home, I quickly grabbed my keys and cellphone and made a call to order a private jet to fly me, Wolf, and Whitney far from this hell on earth. While on the phone, I grabbed a necklace that had not been mine to take. I slipped Link's charm in my pocket, knowing he would be the only one to give her the strength to survive what I had just put her through.

With the false note in my pocket, and the gun and knife in hand, I raced down the basement stairs, believing I would soon be hit by silent bullets. My feet faltered when I saw the two young employees that had been with Whitney, now laughing and speaking of the good fuck they had just had.

Was it right to kill them? I had asked them to commit the crime against her.

I wanted every tie to Whitney gone. They were now a tie.

When they saw the bloody knife in one hand and a gun with a silencer in my other, they trampled each other to get into an available room. They desperately tried to shut the door, but I was already there, pushing it open. After barging in, I shot one and stabbed the other. "Whitney, I am so sorry…" I left, leaving the knife so I could retrieve my extra gun.

Now, it was time for my father's two minions.

Slowly rounding the corner, I saw them past the monitor room, laughing and talking to each other, as if they were drinking vodka at a card game. I guess there was no need for them to shoot at me any longer. Their mission had been completed.

It is so hard to put blinders back on once you begin to see clearly. In fact, my blinders no longer fit me. I was an irrevocably changed man now. And, even if there was a chance of going back to who I had been, I knew I no longer wanted to. I was moving only forward from here on out.

When they saw me, they lifted their hands into the air, still acting casual and relaxed. The one who had been harder on Wolf smiled at the guns hanging at my sides. "*Hey, no hard feelings, right? Just doing what we are told.*"

No hard feelings? Wrong. I pretended to laugh. "*It is your job, after all.*"

They walked toward me. The other minion said, "*They're just slaves, right?*"

"*Right.*" I lifted the barrels and shot them both. "*Just slaves.*" Then I stared at the bodies on the floor until a whisper pulled me from my thoughts.

"Yury?"

Trying not to look obvious, since I wasn't sure where father had hidden cameras anymore, I walked past Wolf's door, whispering, "It's me. Showtime." I hoped he understood that meant to act like a slave in front of the cameras. I exhaled relief as I heard him scuffle to his kneeling position.

Whitney's door wasn't locked. There was nothing left to do but go inside and see what was left of her mental state. Horrific didn't describe the heartbroken girl I now witnessed. She was naked, collarless, and her body had red marks from where she had been hit and pinched. Cum dripped from her little breasts, stomach, and hair. Her eyes were closed, and she was leaning against the dark grey blocks, slapping her chest, again and again, calling out for Link to help her.

Oh, how I instantly wished my blinders still fit, and I still owned the ability to freeze my heart, but neither applied. All I had was sorrow and regret to offer her, so I set the guns on the floor so they could cool off, then pulled the note from my pocket. As I touched her arms to try to explain, I was greeted with fierce hits from her tiny, angry, little fists. Whitney blindly fought, not knowing it was me, but she was not going to be raped again without a fight.

I called out, "Whitney. It's me. Stop. Stop…"

Once she opened her eyes and stopped striking me, I held up the note.

CHAPTER TWENTY-FIVE

Savoring Goodbyes

Exiting her room, Whitney gasped when she saw Adrian and the two minions' bodies on the hall floor. There was no time to explain. I had no idea when Uncle would arrive, but I was confident he would not take well to finding his brother dead. Our race for survival had just begun, so I collected my guns and rushed to Wolf's door and unlocked it. Whitney followed me inside. I spoke as if his Master once again, "Rise, I am setting you free."

As Wolf stood from the floor, more beautiful than ever, he studied Whitney. It was his first time ever seeing his competition, but there was no jealousy present. Only pity. I knew he could see what I saw; a young girl, not only soiled from forced sex but soiled in the deepest part of her soul. She was distraught, her eyes wild and her fair skin the palest of colors.

Full of despair, Wolf questioned, "Master?"

My eyes closed. Struggling to explain that her condition was entirely my fault, my eyes popped open as Whitney asked, "How much, Yury? How much were you going to get for him?"

The question seemed so off-subject that I was stunned into silence. Wolf seemed to have even more sorrow for her, as if he realized she had lost her mind and was no longer making sense.

"How! Much!" Her naked little body shook with anger that I could not comprehend. Not until I saw her examine Wolf's perfection, then her own condition, including the scars on her leg. The care difference was as evident as a bright sun and a very dark night.

The destroyed girl deserved an answer, so I told her the truth. "One-

Wolf gasped.

The young woman, who might be worth thirty-five dollars in her current condition, growled, "I'm going to smack you now." I didn't move. I deserved all the anger she held for me. I hoped that letting her strike me would make her aware of her true worth. Whitney had become priceless to me.

My cheek stung, and my heart bled.

Wolf gasped again, but it wasn't due to her hit. It was because he had just realized that I was at fault for her state, both physically and mentally. Solemnly, I nodded to him. There was no point in denying it. Then I handed him the keys from my pocket, wanting him to free the last two slaves that would ever be in my pitiful care.

I felt drained and so sorry for what I had done with my final punishment; all I could think to do was show her that being soiled didn't change how I felt for her. Father was wrong. Cum dripping down her thigh changed nothing. I loved her, unconditionally, as love should be.

I quietly repeated her words but altered them for me. "I'm going to kiss you now."

The way her mouth opened, I knew she still cared for me, too. "It will be the last."

And it was. For the last time, ever, I kissed her precious little lips, savoring this goodbye.

Returning to the hallway, I watched Wolf attempting to calm the new slave. He was naked and pissed. "Where the fuck am I?" I sighed, sad that the Master in me had already mentally named him Sky, due to his incredibly blue eyes.

Not wanting to reply, due to my lack of energy and unwillingness to be his Master, I asked Wolf, "Where is she?"

He stood at Jewel's open door. "She doesn't believe me."

Again, I felt grief for appreciating that she had already become such an obedient slave, following my rules, not listening to anyone but me. It was

disheartening because a part of me was pleased with her and wanted to reward her good behavior. It was then that I realized that I would not be leaving my Master role behind when I left this place. Being a Master was ingrained so deeply; it would always be a part of me. "Jewel. Come."

She immediately scurried from the room. "Master."

I was shocked to see her prepped for delivery. My Prepper must have been told of my collaring Jewel and done her job by getting her ready. Jewel's hair was long, full of waves, and blonde, her makeup and freshly waxed body on point. She was the perfect doll. Lost in Master mode for a few seconds, I thought about how I would have made a high profit off her.

"You claimed her?" gasped Whitney.

Like moments ago, her concern seemed out of place, but she had truly become jealous of a slave I had trained. I had been her Master for approximately ten months. She fought hard for my protection. She hated the idea of me claiming another because I had tortured her with my pretend Whitney.

While retrieving black robes from a closet near the filing room, I tried to explain Whitney's reaction to her, that I was her food source. Any other slave was a threat to her survival. I also tried to answer her other questions about Fake Whit but kept being interrupted by Wolf. "Master."

I ignored him because his tone was putting me on edge. I could hear his judgment, something I didn't want between us.

Of course, Whitney felt she was to blame when I admitted Fake Whit had committed suicide. I reacted quickly when Wolf demanded, "Catch her!" I thought Whitney was responding to the news of Fake Whit's death, but Wolf scorned me, "What did you do to her?"

With Whitney cradled in my arms, his guilt was debilitating to me, so I barked, "Leave us be!" and tried to assure Whitney that Fake Whit's death was not her fault.

Wolf continued on, claiming Whitney was in shock. My heart raced, and I only heard bits and pieces of what he was saying. "…she is in danger. Her

pupils... Not only with mental shock... Medical shock... Her lips are so dry... She is skin and bones..."

Now that I was paying attention, she looked even more fragile and weak. Had we come this far for her to die on me? "She may not have eaten well while I was gone." I started walking down the hallway to get to the stairs while telling the slaves, "Follow me. I am setting you all free."

Wolf was angry as he kept up with me. "What the hell does that mean? 'While I was gone'?"

"She had not been permitted to feed herself. It confuses them. Slaves forget to feed themselves, fearing they don't deserve it."

"Jesus... Did *you* give her food when she earned it? She is emaciated."

I turned the corner, not giving a shit who was following me. All I wanted to do was properly feed Whitney. "It was how things were done."

"Were?" asked Wolf.

I stopped at the bottom of the stairs, all slaves in tow. "Are you blind to what I am doing? For you? Look." I gestured to the anxious slaves staring at us. "Now, can you lecture me later about my poor Master techniques? We are possibly minutes away from all being shot. Help. Me. Save. Them."

Wolf's demeanor changed back to in-control FBI agent right before my eyes. "Tell me your plan."

I climbed the stairs with a barely conscious Whitney in my arms. "On my ring of keys, there is one to the bedroom at the top of the stairs. Get them into some clothes. I can't show up with naked bodies to get on this private jet I have waiting. Don't forget shoes. There is snow on the ground. Don't lose the keys. We need them for my car."

Wolf raced up the stairs with Jewel and Sky. I raced into the kitchen with Whitney. Sitting her on the island, I made sure she could stay there without falling. She kept looking around, but her eyes were not properly focusing. They were distant and lost. I tried to talk to her, but nothing was registering. "You deserve so much more than what I have offered you." I rushed to the refrigerator

and searched for food and a drink. "Crash told me about karma once. If he is right, I have a horrible life waiting for me." I grabbed fruit and orange juice. Grabbing a glass from a cabinet, I explained, "For the rest of my life, I will be helping others to make up for what I have done, not only to you but to all the others as well." When her lips refused to grip the glass I held up to them, I squeezed her cheeks to purse her mouth, then dribbled what I could from the glass through them. I waited to see her throat working to swallow the juice down.

Himself dressed, and with two dressed slaves in tow, Wolf ran into the kitchen. "Master, she is too malnourished—"

Orange juice projected from Whitney's mouth, drenching my shirt.

"—for the acid."

It was such an alien experience to care for others, but once started, it ran like wildfire. I couldn't control myself. The need to right any wrong and protect these two people became my sole focus. I handed Wolf a dish towel and positioned myself behind him.

As he gently wiped the juice vomit from Whitney's chin, I slipped one of my guns in the back of his pants. If my suspicions were correct about Uncle being on his way, I needed another expert with a gun on my side. Trying not to be obvious, I quickly grabbed his hips and gave a squeeze. It was shocking to feel clothes on him after experiencing his nudity all this time. Not knowing if we were going to survive this escape, I needed him to know I adored him, beyond words.

As I slid back to his side, he whispered over his shoulder, "I love you," then spoke normally, "Do you have a doctor available for her?"

I was terrified we were running out of time. "That would be my uncle. Not an option, since he is the one we are running from."

"Okay, I am not judging, just accessing. How long has she been with this neglect?"

I was about to answer, "As long as she has been here," but a scent I had hoped to never smell again drifted into my nostrils.

333

Sky shocked me by whispering, "Cigar smoke."

Jewel was at his side, fear her only expression.

Uncle was already here. Panic seared through me. I wasn't going to succeed in saving my loved ones if we didn't run now. There was no time for my car. I was sure that the entrance was already blocked by now, but we still had the back kitchen door. I scooped up Whitney and silently told everyone to run for the door. As soon as it was open, Russia's winter air burst into the kitchen. But something colder lingered. It was Uncle jovially calling for me from the living room where my dead father was. My eyes closed. His tone was almost playful, as if I had spurred his hunger to fight. The need for revenge eerily danced on his tongue.

Karma had come sooner than I had hoped.

Breathing in Whitney one last time, I laid my head against hers then said, "I will stay behind. I will buy you time." Her precious eyes stared up at me as if understanding this was it, our last moment in each other's presence. My throat tightened as I realized the hardest goodbye had yet to come. My eyes lifted to see Wolf, the courageous man I would have cherished spending the rest of my life with.

Underneath Whitney, he clutched my hand. His eyes screamed that he loved me and wanted to stay and help me, but that was not something I could ever allow. My arms stretched to hand him the girl who had to find her way back home. I silently begged him to take her, finish what I had started.

My ears rang as I struggled to hear all of Wolf's whispered words, but I caught, "… severe shock… prolonged exposure… do my best to keep her alive…"

These words affected Whitney, too. As if waking from her starved state, she faintly smiled at Wolf. It was mesmerizing. Then I quietly said, "Go. Save the savable," weakly pointing to the slaves he had a chance at saving.

Wolf was entranced immediately. He stared at her in awe. Maybe he was lost in the memory of his rape and recognized she was worth it.

Time stood still as the sweet angel nuzzled into my chest; she had decided to die with me. I didn't miss the gently placed kiss she pressed to my chest.

Shell-shocked, I stood there, realizing she had finally chosen me.

And I hated it.

I didn't deserve it, nor Wolf's sacrifice, as he quickly faced Jewel and Sky and told them to run. Tears filled my eyes as I lifted my shoe then shoved Wolf out the door. Not expecting it, he flew outside. As he scrambled to his feet to come back in, my foot kicked the door shut. Horror crossed Wolf's face as he realized what I was doing. His mouth formed the word, "No," as he raced for the doorknob. He was too late. From under Whitney, my hand quickly locked it.

His hand slammed against the glass. My lips quivered as I tried to smile. *I love you.*

I carried Whitney, death waiting for us in the living room, and I prayed that karma would allow Wolf to survive.

Breathless, in alarm, I pulled her close and whispered, "I want to run for my car, but we will never make it. He knows what I've done." *Be brave, Whitney.* "Grab my gun."

If there was anything to say about Whitney Summers, it was that she never gave up. Fierce, even when facing death, her trembling hand searched the back of my pants, then tucked my gun between us.

I entered the living room slowly, shocked to see my dead father propped in a chair. Uncle, casually sitting on the couch, puffed on his cigar. "My brother did not deserve to be on the floor."

He didn't mention that Father didn't deserve to be dead. Or maybe he did, and I simply couldn't hear it because my eyes were locked on Valerie, dead, in a distraught Kirill's arms. He was standing in the corner, staring at me, nothing but agony present. We looked like a mirrored image, both of us cradling the girls we loved. One soon to die. One already gone.

Valerie was naked and bloody. Her blonde hair was now red and in

disarray.

She had put up a hell of a fight. *I'm so sorry. This is all my fault.*

The only thing that pulled my attention from Kirill and Valerie was Sky and Jewel running across the backyard, with Wolf not far behind them. One of Uncle's men was already waiting with a rifle pointed out the only open window. Sky was shot first. Then Jewel, letting loose a scream.

My whole body seized, terrified to watch Wolf die. I'm not sure how I was still holding Whitney without dropping her when I saw Wolf dart for the woods behind my home. Avoiding bullets, he entered the woods, then turned and looked back at the house. Maybe it was the lights in the living room that helped him find me, but he did. His eyes met mine... Then, he disappeared.

And like that, my Wolf was gone.

All the air felt as if it was seeping from my lungs. Only the beauty in my arms gave me the strength to dare inhale again, while Uncle told his guard, "Do not kill my biggest sale ever. Go fetch him. Not a scratch. I need to recoup all I can."

As I watched, the other guard raced out the French doors and headed toward the woods, and I was grateful the FBI agent had a gun. *Please survive. Please.* So focused on Wolf, I never felt the last guard approach me from behind. Not until his knife was at my throat.

Whitney's breath caught when she saw it. Possibly due to shock and starvation, she actually reached up to remove the knife. "No." I couldn't bear her angering Uncle. I was praying she could avoid the damage Valerie had suffered.

A sense of pride rushed through my chest as Whitney, being so brave, stopped, then nuzzled to my chest, placing her finger on the gun's trigger.

"My son betrayed me," said my uncle, "trying to hide his new infatuation. Look what it cost the bitch. Yury, tell your whore to see what will become of her."

Whitney didn't budge. More pride boomed when I realized my Whitney was only going to take orders from me.

"I said, look!" screamed Uncle.

I truly had hoped Whitney hadn't seen Valerie, or the fate she might be forced to face if I were to be killed. It was the only way anyone was going to have a chance at hurting Whitney. To appease my uncle, I told her, "Fire, look."

As she dared to peek over her hunched shoulder, Kirill's legs gave out and he hit his knees, never releasing Valerie's body.

When Uncle said, "It will soon be your turn to watch your whore die, Yury," I tightened my hold on Whitney. I didn't care about the knife drawing blood as it dug into my skin, but I cared that I needed to stay alive to help Whitney. "But first, it is time to watch little Yury squirm."

There was a secret I had kept from Whitney, for fear it would repulse her. And it did.

As Uncle spoke of my having sex with Whitney's mother, she partially slid from my embrace. The blade dug deeper into my skin as I peered down, wanting to explain I had been forced to do it, but no words could bring solace to yet another horrendous detail of my life.

As much as Whitney didn't want me touching her, I couldn't release her upper body, due to the gun we had hidden. So, I held her to me, silently apologizing.

But it wasn't enough.

When Uncle explained that Whitney was still within her mother's womb as the sex took place, she pulled from me and pointed the gun at my chest.

With it clear her sanity had evaporated, the man with the blade at my neck backed away to avoid the gunfire.

Uncle laughed. He thought this was sweet revenge; one he couldn't have predicted.

Touching the scar on my lip, the one I received when refusing the sex when I was so young, I thought of Whitney's mother. *Seafoam, help her see the truth…*

My ears rang so loudly I couldn't hear when Whitney spoke, but I was

sure it was the vile thoughts she must have had about me. That is why I was stunned when the pointed gun turned toward my uncle and fired.

There was no time to process. Only react.

I spun and took the knife from the man a few feet behind me. He was staring at his boss, shocked by what had just happened. Taking advantage, I slit his throat.

Quickly turning to protect Whitney from the other gunman, I was astonished to see Kirill had already attacked, taken him down, and killed him. Whitney was dazed, staring at my dying uncle sitting on the couch. I recovered without delay and took the gun from Whitney's slack hand, then shot two more bullets into his chest. I couldn't have her living with the guilt of being like me, a murderer, so I tossed the gun and grabbed her shoulder. "I killed him. Understood? Not you."

Her stare was soft and full of kindness. "Thank you." I think she was grateful I was trying to free her conscience, but we both knew it didn't work.

Full of sorrow, I leaned my forehead to hers. "How did you learn to shoot like that?"

Her voice was gentle and eerily calm. "Crash."

My heart stuttered.

"He said he had a good teacher."

I stood up to see into her eyes. It was as if Crash was inside her. Another moment I would never forget. Had Crash been with us all along?

There would be no time to reflect on the miracle. When I heard the gun move, I looked to see it now in Kirill's possession. His eyes were dull, expressing the inner torture he could no longer live with. I stepped in front of Whitney so she would be spared the gruesome decision my cousin had made. I begged him, "Don't do this."

He had been with me all my life. It may have been a shitty one, but it was the only one I knew. Now, it was time for a different one. To live and heal through all this turmoil. I didn't want to do it without him. Even if he had

successfully run away with Valerie, at least I would have known he was on this earth, somewhere.

"Will you make sure she is buried?" was all he said. He had already resigned from this life.

I had to let him go. Swallowing so much sadness, I nodded, then choked out, "I will."

I watched, as if in slow motion, as he lifted the barrel to his temple. I refused to look away. It was only right that I see him to the end of his journey.

His eyes met mine. They had nothing left to say except goodbye.

Tears fell as I thought of the night he ran with Valerie, my hand on the glass, whispering, *Goodbye, Cousin. May I see you again.* Blowing out a shaky breath, I nodded and prepared to say goodbye again.

Kirill had been a vicious man while alive, but he exited as one who had found his heart.

His large form fell and ended next to Valerie's.

I'm not sure how long I stood there, watching blood flow from his body, but I eventually felt a little hand slip into mine. I squeezed, so thankful to have Whitney by my side. I cried, "I will miss him."

She leaned her head on my arm. She couldn't say the same. All she knew was his evil side, but she still respected my time to grieve. Eventually, she asked, "Does she have family?"

I thought of Valerie telling me of her mother and the pimp. "No."

"Was she a good person?"

I cried, thinking of the night I shared with her, how she recognized the pain in my heart I didn't know I had. "Yes. A special, lost girl." I gazed at Kirill. "And he loved her, the best way he knew how." With my free hand, I wiped at my wet face. "Whitney, I want to burn this house down."

She kissed my arm. "I will help you." She rubbed her cheek to my arm. "But, don't bury them." In shock, I gawked at her. Beautiful eyes full of mercy stared up at me. "Set them free. Don't let her body be exhumed from her grave if

339

they are ever to be found. She has clearly been through enough." Whitney cried. "It is how I would want it. My body burned, so I could finally fly away."

I pulled her to me and cried with her while rocking us both. "I'm so sorry."

She held me tight around my waist. "Me too."

With all the diesel fuel I could find in the garage, Whitney and I doused the mansion, hoping to free the many souls that had been lost there.

As I drove us away, the last time I would drive down that long, isolated driveway, Whitney stared into the side-view mirror of my car. The reflection showed my childhood home engulfed in flames.

Ironic, since it was Fire who had lit the match.

CHAPTER TWENTY-SIX

True Colors

On the private jet, I stared at my cellphone, wishing it would ring. I had searched the woods behind my home and called out for Wolf, but he was gone. I couldn't even find my uncle's guard.

Whitney was sleeping in the seat next to mine. She was curled into a ball, still in the black robe. She looked cold, so I stood and searched the compartments for a blanket. I found one under a set of earphones. After I covered her, tucking her tight to provide warmth, she softly sang words I had heard before. It was on a video of Link when he was singing in the shower.

I grabbed the set of headphones and returned to my seat.

After I placed headphones over my ears, I searched for the American song, "True Colors" by Cyndi Lauper. Pushing play, I heard a simple song with deep meaning. At different times, worlds apart, Link and Whitney had sung this song, I believe to each other.

Flying Whitney to Hawaii to meet up with Mr. Jones, the father who refused to give up, the song continued to play. I stared out the plane's window and into the night. "She's coming back to you, Link."

Standing on the tarmac, watching that girl be driven away was like flying to the moon, although all alone. The alienation was profound. I had never lived on my own or out of the only home I knew. Now, I was utterly by myself, with only one hope of having someone again. But that call didn't come. My phone was kept

charged, but Wolf had disappeared, too.

Back in Connecticut, it was time to sever another tie of Whitney's. This one was also a personal one. The coordinates took me directly to his unmarked grave. I stood there with a shovel, dreading this upheaval of earth, but I had to cover all trails leading back to the girl who deserved no more interruptions in her life.

Inside his grave, Crash had been wrapped in a beautiful blue blanket, as if a mother had swaddled her child. I paid no attention to the decomposition of his body that had taken place over the past year and carried him as if he were still whole. For he was, in my heart. My tears dripped onto the blanket as I walked through the woods. I wish I could have left him be, let him rest where his mother had placed him, but I also knew, someday, this earth would house homes, and the construction upheaving his body would bring about questions that would lead back to Mr. Thompson, the father who had never reported his son missing. Everyone Crash ever knew would be questioned. That would be many, since he sold drugs to all the kids in their town. People had seen him with Whitney and Link. What if the authorities learned of Crash's true mother? True brother?

The truth getting out would cause media attention and an endless amount of demanded answers.

No. That would disrupt Whitney's happiness. Not an option.

So, after loading Crash into a rental, I drove him back to the house he desperately ran from. I passed woods, down another long, isolated road to Harold Thompson's mansion. My plan was to bury Crash there, so if ever found, his family would be blamed, but I never expected to see his house in a roaring blaze when I arrived. I raced through the open iron gate. There were no firetrucks or Harold's employees present, but there was Harold. He was frantic, running along the outer walls, peeking in the windows, searching for something or someone.

After slamming the SUV into park, I leaped from the vehicle. "What the fuck happened?"

He saw me then roared, "Was this you?"

342

I ran toward him, yelling, "No! Is anyone inside?"

Glass shattered out of windows at the back of the house. The fire, savagely burning through the home, was as loud as Harold's cries for help. He kept running and searching every window. "Yes, but I don't know fucking where they are! The doors are blocked from the inside!"

Someone was making Harold pay. For what? I didn't know, but I needed to know who I was searching for. "Who? Who are they?"

He threw a rock through a dining room window. "My Wife!" He peaked inside but found no one. "And," he picked up another rock and threw it at me this time, "your son!"

With all I had been through, I thought nothing could shock me anymore. Oh, how I was wrong.

Lost in the mind-fuck of all ages, I stuttered, "W-What are you talking about? How?" Harold crashed his elbow through another window, frantically screaming for his wife and a boy named Kaleb. Numbly, I followed, "B-But..."

"Yury! Fucking help me! Or you will never get the chance to meet your six-year-old son!"

I stumbled while thinking about following Mrs. Thompson, all those years ago, when she took a cab to see a little boy. On that same night, she had been adamant that I would never have sex with her again. And, after I had told her to be a good mother, she had slipped into a dazed state of mind. "Oh, my God."

Harold was unraveling at a high rate. "Yes! Fucking help me!"

The Dominant in me took over. I pointed to the back of the house. "You go that way! I will go around to the front!" I raced along the side of the house and back to the front. I tried the door, but Harold was right. It was unlocked but blocked. Through the front door's foggy glass for privacy, I saw movement on the second floor. "I see someone! I see someone!" I ran to the window. It was Mrs. Thompson and a young boy at the top of the stairs, trapped by fire. She was helping the child to crawl over the railing. He had blond hair like I had as a

child. "Harold!" I screamed as I picked up a cement figurine from between the shrubbery. I threw it through the window. The oxygen seemed only to feed the fire.

When Mrs. Thompson saw me trying to enter, she screamed, "Yury! Catch him!" Ignoring my body's pleas to run away from the blazing heat, I was halfway through the window as Kaleb hung from his mother's grip. Fire was all around her. I think the heat was singeing her skin, but the brave woman held on to save her—our—son's life. Everything was on fire on the first floor except for a couple of spots on the ground leading to the front door. At the door was a 2x4 piece of wood propped to prevent entry.

Once through the window, with my arms outreached to touch my son, I ran across the foyer…

I may not be the devil, but I believe he does exist.

As fire climbed up Mrs. Thompson's legs, she howled in agony. The child reached out for me as I dove to catch him, but I was too late. He plummeted to the ground… and through it. The fire in the basement had eaten away at the floor, so it could not support the child. His screams were the worst sound I will ever hear in my whole entire life. And they were matched by his mother's as she, on fire, fell forward and over the railing, into the open pit I was sure was meant for me.

It had all happened so fast; my mind literally could not comprehend it.

Lying on the ground, I couldn't move. I simply froze in a horror I had never known, not even when I'd found my mother's mutilated body. The fire was building and falling from above, but I held still, losing all my will to live. I wanted to stay and let the house burn me, too, but I was dragged up from the floor and out the front door, Harold patting my pants that were on fire.

He was coughing. "Did you see them? I can't find them!"

I threw up… then coughed around the smoke in my lungs. Tears exploded from me as God punished me in the rawest way possible. I hadn't even met the boy but felt a loss I could not compare. "They… fell. They're gone!"

The expression of a man losing his last shred of hope and desire to live stood before me. "No! No! *Noooooooooo!*" Then he ran back toward the door he had just dragged me out of, but it was now engulfed by flames. The whole house, and the cherished lives inside, were an unfathomably gruesome loss.

The night was lit by orange flames. It was haunting. It was horrendous. It was a ghastly sight that I will never forget.

Harold and I, feeling the weight of every past crime we had committed, stood there and cried. Harold and I had been the leaders of horrific endeavors and were now paying, as we deserved. All the innocents in our lives were either dead or irrevocably altered.

Harold wailed in absolute agony, "I failed them. I failed them all."

My lungs were struggling with smoke inhalation and debilitating heartache. "We. We both did."

He *screamed* in the darkness that surrounded us, "She wanted Crash back home! Now, I can never give her that final wish!"

Divine intervention had me thinking of Whitney and what she had said about Valerie with the fire. *"That's how I would want it, so I could finally fly away."*

Snot dripped from my nose as I solemnly told Harold, "You can. I have him."

Misery can be seen by the naked eye. I have seen it. It was present on Harold's face as he thundered more screams into the dark, smoky skies. I left him to his moment of insanity because I understood he had the right to hate the world, himself, and me.

After collecting his son, I handed over his body.

Harold, with trembling arms, held Junior and cried, kissing the blue blanket smeared with dirt. "I was so bad to you. You were a good son. I should have let Marina take you and spare you from me."

As I watched Harold pay for his every sin, I prayed I was doing right by the young man he was cradling, who had been so much wiser than I.

Once the time had come to say goodbye, forever, to the human form that no longer held life, and Harold had collected himself enough to do so, he held his son's shoulders as I held his feet. With all the respect we could offer Crash, we stood in front of the fire. The heat burned our skin and hearts as we swung Crash's body, back and forth, back and forth, both not wanting to let him go, yet building momentum to do so.

And then, as we wailed out the earth-shattering pain from our souls, we released Crash into the fire so his body could rest with the only mother he truly knew.

As the house and loved ones burned, I gazed up into the sky.

Fly away, Crash... Be free, my friend.

When you have lost everything, there is nothing to be angry about. There is nothing left to fight for, nothing left to lose. Maybe that is why Harold had left everything behind, including his car, and asked for a ride to the airport. I obliged. On the way, and in between heart-wrenching tears, he explained how they hid Kaleb from me in fear of what would become of his life. There was no way I could blame him or Mrs. Thompson for the decision. I was just devastated that their efforts didn't pay off.

There were more details I should have asked about, but it didn't matter. Kaleb was gone. I had a son I would never know.

Where did Harold go? I don't know. I didn't ask. It wasn't my business. But he did say he would try and live through the horror of so much loss in his life because he said he still had a son; Link.

Somehow, I understood that reasoning. I felt I had to live, too, even with the memory of watching my son and his mother dropping to their death in an unspeakable tragedy.

I didn't leave Connecticut. I waited until Whitney returned home. I had

to see her safe and make sure she stayed that way. Unfortunately, even though Harold was unaware who burned down his home, I wasn't. I suspected my father had figured out I had a son. And, once Uncle learned of my betrayal, I believe they hired a hitman to kill him, believing I had been hiding Kaleb. Now that Father and Uncle were both dead, Whitney should be safe, but I was taking no chances. Did Father and Uncle suspect I would run with her? Was a hitman watching her? He wouldn't have found her in Hawaii, where Mr. Jones and I had her hidden away, but a hitman would definitely find her in Connecticut.

About three weeks after the death of my son, Whitney finally found her way home, and to Link. Standing in the woods, it was bittersweet to watch her walk down her boat dock, where so many fond and tragic memories had been made.

Link, sitting on his own dock across the lake, had yet to notice her. Whitney's hair was shorter now but still beautiful in its untamed way. She hadn't gained much weight back. I hoped she would learn to eat on her own again, someday.

Maybe it was her sundress blowing in the wind that finally got Link's attention, but as soon as he saw her, he slowly stood up as if not trusting his eyes. They had a short conversation, Whitney revealing she'd realized her love for him all along. Jealousy faded away when I saw how much he loved her, too, and hope filled my aching heart knowing he would give every part of himself to help her get over everything I had done to her.

Whitney had bewitched me, crawled under my skin as Americans would say, and had me caring for her survival. This was something very unfamiliar to me—to my ways—to how I had been trained—to how I had lived my first twenty-nine years of life.

I would forever be grateful.

The storm that brewed inside me, and the volatile waters I was made of, now had a chance to simmer, to calm. Like Whitney, I now had a chance of having a fresh start.

There may have been no beauty in the tragic time we shared together, but a beauty came of it. That is a truth that cannot be denied.

As Whitney and Link dove into the blue water to swim to each other, a hand slipped into my palm. Wolf leaned his head to mine. "You saved her, Jorien."

Before, when my cellphone had finally rung, I was like Link, not trusting my eyes. My hand had trembled when I brought the device to my ear, and my soul sighed when I heard Wolf's voice.

I wasn't alone anymore.

Squeezing Wolf's hand, I swallowed, overwhelmed with how good it felt to be on the right side of karma. *Karma*... Answering Wolf, I exhaled. "No... Crash saved her."

Crash made all this possible.

I kissed Wolf's head. "Now, it is up to Link to see her through."

In the center of the lake, two souls reunited...

Yes, there was a beauty... that rose from the darkness.

Beauty... that can't be denied.

EPILOGUE

Beauty Within Us All

In attempts to protect each other, Wolf and I never shared our true names with each other. If one or the other were abducted and tortured for information, neither could bring harm if we didn't know each other's legal identities. Instead, we traveled the world, gleaning to know each other outside the walls that had confined us both. It was an adjustment, to say the least. His patience with me learning not to be a Master was kind and generous. We both quickly learned I loved as fiercely as I hated, and I lacked the ability to forgive myself. So, Wolf had me working on what I could change—what I could help: Whitney.

To not blatantly interfere with her life, we kept track of her through Link's blog posts. At first, we could see the strain on his face since Whitney had returned home. There was exhaustion in his expression and upper body language, the way his shoulders drooped. But it didn't last. Eventually, a smile was present during his blogs. His shoulders set back. A proudly lifted chin.

"Why are you grinning, Jorien?" asked Wolf.

We were sitting next to each other at the dining room table in our island bungalow, each of us in front of a laptop. I explained, "The kid looks good."

"Do I need to be jealous?" teased Wolf.

He knew there would never be a reason for any jealousy. I craved no one but him. My actions showed him daily, nightly, and sometimes hourly.

I sighed as the Caribbean breeze blew in through the open windows. "She's okay." If Link was pulling through, that meant Whitney was.

His fingers stopped typing while he stared at me in awe. "I love you."

Every time I made efforts to correct one of my many wrongs, I got to

hear those words.

I swallowed, unable to offer the same words because I still did not feel worthy of his devotion. Things like this take time.

Wolf's hand cupped my cheek as he smiled at me before going back to his laptop.

Link continuously held back on his personal knowledge of the sexual servitude trade. There was much appreciation in my heart for his upspoken protection. She deserved it.

Wolf turned his laptop so I could see it. "Look. The kid has joined teams with these people." I stared at the screen to see a foundation for victims of all kinds. One of the leaders of the effort, Serenity Hamilton, was the wife of a country singer, Dereck Hamilton. The woman he sang with was Destiny. "They're into bringing about awareness and helping survivors of human trafficking."

Survivors... My stomach soured when I thought of how the number of survivors was gruesomely outweighed by the number of slaves who would never be found or rescued, or died before they could escape.

As if reading my grim thoughts, Wolf nonchalantly set his curser on the donation button then sat back in his chair, stretching his arms over his head. "Someone has been brilliant with his investments and possibly has cash to spare." *Fake yawn...*

I could feel my smirk form. I knew where my lover was headed with his not-so-subtle hint about my money.

Ignoring me staring at him, Wolf asked, "Maybe we could fly to America to see a show?"

I would fly anywhere with him. "I do not listen to country music."

After a dismissive shrug, Wolf stood then walked toward the bedroom while slowly removing his shirt, his dark, shiny hair dancing on his back. "Maybe you should start. I would do *anything* for a live country concert."

Staring at the jeans clothing the best ass in the whole world, I licked my

teeth, suddenly a fan of American music I couldn't care less for. "Meh."

One-point-five seconds later, I followed that half-naked body then ravaged my love.

The concert wasn't to start for hours, but Wolf was able to get a stadium security guard to tell us when a certain tour bus was due to arrive. So, behind the venue, in the back parking lot with empty semi-trucks that had been full of a broken-down stage, we stood on the sidewalk. If I was going to give a substantial donation, I wanted to know to whom.

Sounding somewhat impressed, Wolf quietly told me, "We are already on a radar."

"Whose?" I scanned the parking lot.

"Not sure."

When I followed Wolf's line of sight, I caught a glimpse of two large statured men who had to be at least six-foot-seven each. One was black, the other white. Both were very still and not hiding the fact that they didn't appreciate our presence. No one else was in the isolated parking lot, so, in Yury style, I lifted my chin at them, not appreciating their attempt to intimidate me or my love.

Wolf mumbled, "Jorien, knock it off."

"Fuck them."

"Do you have a gun?"

Almost pouting, I explained, "Wasn't allowed on the plane, but I'll find a way to get one."

"Well, you will have to do it in the next twenty seconds if you keep up the attitude."

"Why?"

"It's freezing out, yet neither has their jacket zipped or buttoned. Easy access."

Wolf's FBI training had him much more aware of his surroundings than I. And that was quite the feat because I lived in paranoid mode due to my long-lost uncle. "What's it to them if we are standing here, minding our own business?"

"I'm suspecting our business is theirs, also. They have bodyguard written all over them."

Before Wolf could say more, a tour bus drove into the parking lot. When the door opened, a rowdy group of eight men filed down the stairs, all either talking or laughing. A shorter blond, who looked as if he was fresh off the coast of California, was chuckling. "I'm just sayin'! She was smokin'!"

Another man, with drum sticks clutched in one hand, playfully popped him on the back of the head. "Blake, are you ever going to learn?"

"We just had lunch at Hooters! I'm still on a beautiful thigh high, my friend."

Another young man with a long beard spoke with a strong country accent. "Destiny ate so many buffalo shrimp, she may puke them all on the stage tonight."

That caused an abundance of free laughter from them all.

Crowded around their bus's door, the eight men seemed to be very close-nit and full of life. They had smiles from ear to ear and were goofing around with good-humored punches, headlocks, hair tousling, and lewd comments as if they didn't have a care in the world.

Wondering how long they had been cooped up in that bus, I noticed the two bodyguards now crossing the parking lot, but not toward us.

The young, festive men, after spotting the two men, howled, "Towers! Destiny has wings for you guys—" but quickly ended their play when the two 'Towers' barely waved in return because their focus was still locked on Wolf and I as they walked toward the end of the bus. The young men's eyes instantly raced to us. Suddenly, as if a well-trained unit, they walked to catch up with the bodyguards, never losing sight of us. Their interaction went from glee to an

impressive intensity with not one shared word.

Wolf's brows bunched in confusion. "Are you seeing this?"

"I am, but I'm not understanding what I'm seeing."

Just then, another tour bus entered the parking lot. It pulled up right behind the first one. As if the drivers were experienced with building a barrier to block out the city beyond the parking lot, they made a line. The men huddled at the closed bus door while the black man quietly said something to them. The other guard nodded then faced the door as if expecting it to open any second. It did. His stance had been some sort of queue.

As the black man started crossing the parking lot, headed for us, the white guard spoke with a man descending the bus's stairs. He appeared to be about six-foot-four and had on a cowboy hat. After listening to the guard speak, he peered over the white guard's head and observed us.

With the black bodyguard almost to Wolf and me, Wolf whispered, "Head of security."

I gave a slight head nod so he knew I heard him.

The black man lacked a smile but still approached with manners. "What can I do for you, gentlemen?"

I asked, "Are we not permitted to be here?"

His eyes were live scanners as he studied us both. Then, his politeness evaporated. "Let's try this again. Why are you waiting for these tour busses? You are clearly not here for the music."

Wolf lied, "I'm a huge fan of Destiny's. That's all."

The man smirked, but it wasn't humorous; it was annoyed. "Oh, yeah? How old are her twins?"

Wolf, most likely aware his lie was not wise, deadpanned his answer, "Ten."

The black man calmly stated, "It's time for you to go."

"Was I wrong?" asked Wolf.

"Yeah. They died at birth."

I jolted. *Kaleb...*

The man noticed my reaction, his eyes studying me again before speaking into his wrist. "That's a negative."

Believing this to be odd, I lifted a brow at Wolf. He tapped his ear to inform me the guard had a monitor.

Listening again to the monitor in his ear, the guard's eyes widened. "He is who?" His jaw fell open as he stared at me. Then his nostrils flared, his jaw now impossibly tight. "Not a good idea," he said into his wrist. The guard groaned after listening for another moment, then told us, "She claims she has something to tell you." He didn't even bother to peek over his shoulder to see his group now all moving toward us. He simply, and sternly, stated, "Keep your hands where I can see them. No phones or recordings are permitted. If you move in any threatening manner, whatsoever, we will take you to the ground and not let you up until the cops arrive." He didn't ask if we understood. I guess we didn't appear to be babbling idiots.

Someone was in the middle of the moving human circle that was approaching. The protection made it as if an endangered queen stood at the center, not the petite country-dressed woman who emerged before us. From under a worn cowgirl hat, enchanting brown eyes with speckles of red and gold peered up at Wolf and me as she stepped around her black guard. "I'm sorry they are behaving like this. It is," she pointed to me, "your presence that has them so uptight."

"Angel," growled the tall man in the cowboy hat that had been on her bus. He stood behind her in a very protective mode, his arm moving around her to rest across her chest.

If Wolf and I meant her harm, it wasn't her guards I was most concerned about.

It was him.

The question of whether or not he would lay his life down for hers needed not to be asked.

She endearingly kissed his arm yet didn't try to remove it. Cowgirl boots that looked older than the woman in her late thirties, or early forties, scuffed the ground as she studied Wolf and me. Her smile grew in some sort of amazement with what she was viewing. "Yin and yang. I didn't know it truly existed like the drawing, the symbols. I've never seen someone with so much light be near, or with, someone full of such darkness." She gestured between Wolf and me.

After blinking in dismay, Wolf and I looked at each other. He appeared as shocked as I was.

"May I touch you?"

Our stunned heads swiveled back to the little one who sounded like kind of a missionary.

"Angel," again growled the man in the hat.

She laid a palm on his bicep and gently whispered, "Shh."

His body eased right in front of us.

"So, may I?" Since she wasn't speaking to me, Wolf swallowed then nodded. He didn't move, not one bit, as she left her men behind and stepped directly in front of him. Wolf wasn't threatened into his stilled state; I think he was more enthralled by unseen magic this little being possessed.

She couldn't have been over five-feet-two. Her delicate hand reached up and touched Wolf's face. "The answer to your question," he gasped as if she had read his mind, "is no. True love is a gift. No matter where it started."

Wolf's eyes drifted shut as if she spoke the most perfect words ever whispered.

She nodded with tenderness, not letting go of his face. "It is true. His love. It is boundless when it comes to you." When his beautiful grey eyes opened, brimming with tears, her eyes welled also. "Yes, Soul Reader—"

I gasped.

"—he will follow your light."

As a tear fell from Wolf's eye, he asked, "Are you a true angel?"

Grace. This woman was full of grace as she replied, "No. I am only

355

Destiny, who simply can see the beauty within us all." Her eyes found mine as she released Wolf's face and stepped back to what seemed to be her greatest comfort. The man in the hat rewrapped his arm around her chest. As she now stared at me, her head tilted to rest on the male arm she clung to as if needing him even closer. "It is there. Believe your beauty is there, and it will continue to grow."

Staring into her eyes was almost like trying to lie to Wolf. She had his gift of reading a liar, so I couldn't tell her I believed her.

Her hand lifted as if to offer me comfort, but it then slowly found its perch on the cowboy's arm again. With a sincere apology, she told me, "I am sorry I cannot touch *you*."

I felt a renewed shame of my past encase me. I didn't need to ask why she refused to touch me. I had already been living with regret and self-doubt daily. An enlightened person would be able to read my wrongdoings by a mere glance.

"It is because of her."

Confused, I asked, "Who?"

"Your Fire."

I almost fell back a step. No one threw us to the ground as Wolf put an arm around me.

Destiny, watching Wolf comfort me, gave us an angelic smile. "She has that, too, now. He loves her... Yury."

My eyes snapped to hers.

She held up a hand. "She didn't mean for me to see her past or learn your false name. But I saw... As I just did with your love."

Wolf pulled me to his side and placed his lips at my temple, refusing to let me go with his arms or lips. We were in some sort of divine presence that couldn't be denied, and it seemed to be the evidence Wolf needed to bear my weight, physically and mentally.

Destiny continued, "That is how I knew who you were." She exhaled.

"So, it is you who I have something to say to." She held up two fingers, gesturing for permission to tell me two things.

Too dumbfounded to stop now, I accepted the ride I was presently on and nodded.

"One: she kept her promise. Your true identity is held so close to her heart, not even I could find it. Believe me, I tried. I wanted you to be arrested. Whitney is protecting you as much as you are protecting her."

As I burst into tears, Wolf cried against the side of my face, holding me fiercely. There was such a message and such a relief to know I hadn't truly broken Fire.

Destiny's kind voice echoed over our sobs. "Two: any money you want to offer is greatly appreciated and somehow seems more-so from someone who personally partook in the crime. But—" she waited until I paid close attention to her words, "start with her." She patted the man's arm securely at her chest. "My husband bought my childhood home to let me do what I chose with it. It empowered me."

Startled, I suddenly stood up straight. Wiping under my nose, I nodded eagerly. "I understand." I don't know why, I don't know how, but the idea of gifting Whitney her childhood home felt pure and wholesome. "It will be hers."

Destiny smiled. "That is wonderful." Another tour bus rolled into the parking lot, parking behind Destiny's.

I hadn't even noticed the tall white guard leave us, but he was already at the door of the new arrival. Destiny's husband told the black guard, "I want her to stay on that bus."

The guard repeated the orders into his wrist.

As soon as the door opened, a young man was on the stairs, watching us like a hawk as the guard spoke to him. There was a young woman, even smaller than Destiny, trying to peer around the man on the stairs, but he kept blocking her exit with his hips while asking the guard questions I couldn't hear. She disappeared back into the bus that had drawn shades.

Within seconds, Destiny took a sharp inhale, stared at us with entranced eyes, then chuckled while closing her eyes. The looming husband groaned while pulling his cellphone to his ear. The young man on the stairs pulled a cellphone to his ear to answer the call.

Destiny's husband growled into the phone in a fatherly manner, "You tell her to knock that off." After listening for a few seconds, he said, "She keeps saying what?" His jaw locked before he slid the phone back into his pocket.

Destiny appeared proud as she told me, "See? Yin and yang. She's never seen one either."

Bewildered, Wolf and I stood there, not daring to ask what had just happened. It was too otherworldly. Clearly witnessing a rarity, I thought back to the first time I saw Whitney dance.

Is this desire where Seafoam's curse truly began? Was this the beginning of my family's fall? Or, are all souls linked by the crime of sexual slavery destined for a much bigger picture? The answer would soon be a marvel and would reach far beyond what I could see or comprehend at the time. Maybe it is true; if you look hard enough, there is always beauty present within the ugly. That beauty may not be within your grasp, but may benefit others also in dire need. Either way, what was to come would prove an undoubting connection between myself, those I knew, and those to come...

"What if everyone could understand the bigger picture?" Destiny asked as if reading my mind. She bowed her head against her husband's arm. "What a world this could be."

To learn more about Destiny, please start with the first novel in my Forever series, Serenity.

You are born in a certain form due to your parents. Their DNA, genes, many factors make you who you are physically. Then, throughout your childhood, they have more opportunities to mold you into something else. What becomes of you after that? That is up to you. That is why I love the butterfly representation when it comes to myself. I may have faced many challenges, some gruesome, but have found a way to grow, spread wings, and take flight in my new beautiful form; happiness.

This story wasn't only about trafficking. It was also about breaking the chains that bind us. Finding the strength to not let our past control our future and dare to see the picture beyond our own circle, such as victims all around us. Keep your eyes open. Do research of the signs. Next time you're in a plane, actually see who is sitting next to you. Do they need help? If they did, what would you do?

National Human Trafficking Hotline
Call 1-888-373-7888 | Text BeFree (233733)

Thank you for this novel.
Thank you for being brave.
And thank you for wanting to make a difference.

BOOKS BY INDIA R. ADAMS

Tainted Water Series
Blue Waters
Black Waters
Red Waters
Volatile Waters
Ashen Waters

Standalone Novels
My Wolf and Me
Ivy's Poison

Haunted Roads Series
Steal Me
Scar Me
Bleed Me

A Stranger in the Woods Series
Rain
River
Mist

The Forever Series
Serenity
Destiny
Mercy
Hope

CONTACT AUTHOR

Want to get in touch with India? She loves hearing her readers thoughts!
You can email her : india@indias.productions
Or join her reader group on Facebook : India R. Adams' Flames
Check out her website for updates on all things India!
http://indias.productions
If you want to stay in the loop, make sure you sign up to her newsletter!

THANK YOUS

Writing is a passion for me. I actually get crabby when I don't write. The fact that booklovers want more of my stories—that my reach grows with every book release—and more and more fabulous people are becoming a part of my author world; I am beyond grateful and amazed. Readers, you are beautiful souls that I simply can't get enough of.

As far as my finished product, it would never be without an incredible team. Alpha reader: Snow, thank you for your bold approach and always guiding me with such character insight.

My betas: Deb, you have been one of my biggest supporters in and out of the spotlight, but this was our first beta project together. You are now stuck with me! Amy and Christine, I simply can't ever have a release without you!

My editor: Kendra, oh how I love you so. You do anything to see me through… You are the unseen force that brings my books to the next level. I treasure you far beyond the words I write. My proofreader: Annette, you are a gentle soul that I hope to always have in my author world.

Lyndsay, my Postmaster, I literally have a sense of ease in my heart knowing you are always there in the background, making sure my books are being seen. You are truly my Unicorn.

Sophie, your name is always swimming in my notifications with your fabulous posts and tags. You rock!

Bloggers: you guys are fierce! It takes a lot to read so many books, support the authors, and be sure to tell everyone you know about them. I can't say thank you enough for all the work you do!

To the best PA in the world, Cat, my Love Bug, you don't know how to fail and therefore refuse to let me do so. You not only try to organize one of

the most chaotic authors in the biz, but you give me encouragement and your friendship. There is no measure when it comes to what you mean to me.

Family, our lives have taken hard hits, adjustments, and trying times, yet you always give me the room to continue to grow and write because you know what it means to me. You are selfless and a light to always bring me warmth and the best love in the Universe.

INDIA'S SONG LIST

This book ended up being a very personal process for me. I learned, during research, a lot about my own abusers. Because of this, my song list is not long. I stayed very quiet in my mind as Yury led me through his journey. I hope my readers understand.

~India

"Way Down We Go" by KALEO

"Into the Fire" by Erin McCarley

"I'd Love to Change the World" by Jetta (Matstubs Remix)

"More Than Life" by Whitley

"My Songs Know What You Did" by Fall Out Boy

"ROADS UNTRAVLLED" by LINKIN PARK

"The Sound of Silence" by Disturbed

"Thy Will" by Hillary Scott & The Scott Family

"Uninvited" by Alanis Morissette

(This song helped me create Chapter 26. This song is for Yury to Whitney)

"Like a River Runs" a remake by Sia